THE STONE
OF MADNESS

Nick Baker

Published by Wessex OMFS Ltd 2018
www.stoneofmadness.co.uk

British Library Cataloguing-in-Publication Data
A catalogue record for this book is available from the British Library

ISBN 978-1-9999762-0-0

Typeset in 12/13pt Perpetua by Geoff Fisher

Cover art design by Franzi Haase

Printed & Bound in Great Britain by
CPI Group (UK) Ltd, Croydon CR0 4YY

With Very best Wishes

Nic Lowe

November 2018

For Nicola

Contents

Everything good is the transmutation of something evil

Friedrich Nietzsche

1

The Piotrowski Manuscript

PROFESSOR HENRY PRICE SAT in his customary armchair next to a dwindling open fire quietly contemplating. He rubbed his arm absent-mindedly, a succour to the incessant nagging pain of a childhood injury. He had tied his straight, shoulder-length hair neatly back, but his grooming could not mask the worry lines etched across his face. He felt a great sense of foreboding wash over him as he stared at the glowing embers in the grate, lost in thought.

He was exhausted following a recent trip abroad, but his sense of fatigue went beyond mere physical tiredness. He had returned to the four-storey Victorian house that he shared with his daughter, Lily, late in the afternoon, and had immediately realised something was amiss.

While the theft of a single book would not ordinarily arouse his suspicion, he found it deeply disconcerting that someone would choose a book that had always kindled his interest for reasons he had never been able to reconcile. He shook his head; he suspected the book harboured something that he must have missed. Evidently, someone else felt the same way too, and the manner in which the thief had acquired the book suggested that they had an expertise in alchemy to rival his own.

He shook his head, unsure of what it all meant. The new millennium was just over a decade away, and with the emergence of so many astonishing scientific discoveries, he sometimes wondered whether alchemy would survive at all.

No matter, he supposed. There was little else he could do that he had not done already, and if, as he suspected, the theft of this book was somehow linked to past events, he seriously wondered whether he alone and the few resources left at his disposal would be sufficient to meet the challenge.

Price did not rouse at the sound of the double doors opening behind him. His manservant, Albright, ushered a tall, dishevelled-looking man into the room, then coughed, a signal for Price to get to his feet and greet the visitor. The man looked lost, fidgeting uncomfortably behind Price's servant. He searched inside his jacket for a cloth to wipe his glasses, which had steamed up the moment he entered the room. Giving up the fruitless search, the man removed his glasses, rubbing them briefly on a sleeve before replacing them as Albright left the room.

'Ah, Isaacson, forgive me, please come in,' said Price, greeting his guest with a perfunctory handshake. 'I'm sorry, I'd completely lost track of the time.'

Price regarded the man circumspectly. Isaacson held a pivotal position in the functioning of the Council for Home Affairs, bridging the uneasy gap that existed between the Council—a select body tasked with matters pertaining to national security—and his true political masters in Whitehall. Isaacson was Cabinet Secretary to the Prime Minister and held the dubious honour of being the government's representative on the Council, charged with the task of reporting back to Downing Street on all Council business.

'Good evening, Isaacson. Please, come and sit down.'

Isaacson nodded. He looked anxious as he stood facing the founder of the Council. 'Good evening, Professor. I'm sorry for the delay. The traffic, you understand.'

'London never stops,' Price agreed.

'Yes, I'm afraid so. There was a snarl-up on the bridge on the way out of Westminster. It's taken almost an hour to cross the city.'

'Well, you're here now,' said Price calmly, doing his best to alleviate Isaacson's conspicuous agitation.

Price ushered Isaacson towards an armchair conveniently

placed next to his own. He bent over a small table and picked up a decanter sitting next to two tulip-shaped glasses. He raised the decanter in Isaacson's direction. 'Smith Woodhouse 1927. Would you care to join me?'

Isaacson nodded and took a sip before settling back in his chair. The men sat in silence, enjoying the heat radiating from the open wood fire and the soporific effect of the sweet fortified wine.

'I've relayed news of this regrettable event to the Council as you requested but I don't understand the urgency. I realise the theft of a book is alarming but is it *that* important?'

Price gave the man a rueful smile. 'Perhaps, Isaacson, perhaps. I'm still not sure of the book's significance, but how the thief acquired it is certainly worthy of our consideration.'

'Very well, Professor, perhaps you'd be kind enough to tell me what's been going on?'

'I've been away on Council business, but when I returned today, I immediately realised a book was missing from the library.'

'As I surmised from your message, Professor. Was there any sign of a break-in?'

'No, although Albright thought he heard footsteps last night coming from the passage that runs along the side of the house.'

'Did he see anything?' Isaacson asked.

Price shook his head. 'No. He went outside to investigate but the grounds were deserted. I also quizzed Lily, but she hasn't seen or heard anything out of the ordinary in all the time I've been away. Apart from Albright and the housekeeper, Lily's tutors are the only other people to have come and gone in that time.'

Isaacson took a sip of port while he waited patiently for Price to elaborate.

'The house is extremely well protected. The doors and windows have locking mechanisms well beyond all but the most knowledgeable thief or alchemist.'

'What's so special about the locks?' said Isaacson, frowning.

'They work on the same principle as standard locks but they can't be opened with simple keys. The tumblers have to be aligned utilising energy raised by alchemical means.'

Isaacson looked perplexed. 'Professor, may I politely remind you that I'm a civil servant and not a scientist. While I know better than to question you on the complex alchemical devices at your disposal, perhaps you might care to explain.'

Price sighed. He disliked dealing with politicians and civil servants, but on this occasion, he had no choice. He needed Isaacson onside if he were to garner the Council's support. 'They're simple wards, but only an adept alchemist would appreciate the complexity of such a mechanism, let alone have the recondite skill to operate them. When a hand is placed in contact with a metal plate located on the door, alchemically induced energy is conducted through the plate, generating an internal resonance in each of three parallel locks. The plugs will only rotate and release an overarching lock when the correct combination of resonances is used. The possible permutations are virtually limitless. Only Lily and I know how to turn the locks.'

A look of apprehension appeared on Isaacson's face. 'Is it possible, Professor, that one of the staff—?'

'Never,' interrupted Price. 'I've no reason to question their loyalty. They've been with me for years and I trust them implicitly.'

'But surely there must be a simple explanation.'

Price paused for a moment before offering his response. 'The only explanation is that an individual with knowledge of alchemical lore breached the doors. If the tumblers are not activated with the exact resonance frequency in each of the three locks, and in the correct order, a bolt of energy is discharged from the mechanism. The intruder bypassed a door at the back of the house, and from there, they negotiated most of the ground floor to reach the library. If Albright's timing is right, Lily was in her classroom upstairs with one of her tutors at the time. The door was open but she never heard a sound.'

'You said the locks discharge energy if they're not activated correctly.'

Price nodded. 'Don't worry, Isaacson,' he said in response to the look of alarm on Isaacson's face. 'It's just my way of protecting the house. The locking mechanisms, if breached, merely discharge a bolt of electricity that will temporarily incapacitate the intruder, while alerting those inside to their presence.'

'Is that sort of thing, er, legal?' said Isaacson.

'Whether it's legal or not is of little concern to me,' Price retorted. 'You of all people should appreciate the undesirables I've had dealings with in the past, not to mention the items at my disposal that would be of considerable interest to my enemies. I'll continue to take whatever precautions are necessary to protect my family and my belongings,' he said dismissively.

Isaacson nodded. 'Yes, of course, Professor.' He paused for a moment and scratched his nose self-consciously. 'So, I take it that whoever broke in was able to bypass these sophisticated locks of yours without raising the alarm.'

'Exactly, Isaacson. The alchemical locks are fitted on all main doors leading into the property, and there's a similar mechanism protecting the library. The thief was able to open the doors while anticipating and absorbing the insults without consequence. When the thief left, they even attempted to hide the fact that they'd tampered with the locks.'

'How did you discover the theft?'

Price gave Isaacson a wry smile. 'It would be impossible for anyone to open the locks without my knowledge. If you've learnt anything of alchemy from your association with the Council, you'll know that energy raised by alchemical means leaves a unique trace.'

'Does that mean you might know the perpetrator?'

'I'm afraid it's not that easy, but if I ever encounter the individual again, there's a good chance I'll recognise their alchemical signature. As it is, I already have my suspicions.'

'Who—?'

Price held up a hand. 'I'd rather not speculate. I intend to make further enquiries and I'll report back to the Council as soon as I know more.'

Isaacson frowned. 'And only one book was taken?' he said, sounding incredulous. 'Is it important?'

'I'm not sure, but it must be for someone to risk stealing it from here. I acquired the document from the Ambrosian Library in Milan. It's a unique manuscript, purportedly written in the early part of the sixteenth century by a Dutch alchemist, Alfons Piotrowski,' replied Price.

'What could be so important about an alchemical manuscript written over four hundred years ago?'

A flash of disapproval passed across Price's face. 'You're beginning to sound like those politicians you work with, Isaacson. While many of your colleagues consider alchemy an area no longer worthy of consideration, you of all people should know better. Have you learnt nothing from your position on the Council?' Price chided.

Isaacson nodded. 'Yes ... yes, of course, Professor,' he replied, sounding contrite.

'Alchemy in its purest sense is still a valuable area of study, despite the dwindling resources it currently affords. Alchemy remains fundamental to the purer sciences, but in many people's eyes, its association with darker, more dangerous research has tainted what was once a great tradition. For that, we must thank Pearly Black,' Price spat.

'Black died ten years ago,' stated Isaacson.

'So he did, Isaacson, yet his tainted influence still pervades the way alchemy is perceived.'

'But why this particular book? Surely you have any number of valuable items a thief would wish to acquire?' he suggested, surveying the grandeur of the artwork adorning the walls.

'I agree. Why would a thief take an obscure manuscript when they might have taken so much more? This in itself concerns me. I studied the manuscript for some considerable time after I acquired it, yet I can't help thinking that I must have missed something. What you must remember, Isaacson, is that when Piotrowski wrote this manuscript, alchemy was held in great esteem, unlike today. Don't forget, there have been many distinguished alchemists in this country's illustrious past. Take one of the greatest scientists the world has ever known, yet who primarily considered himself an alchemist.'

'I, er ...?' said Isaacson, looking nonplussed.

Price shook his head. 'I'm talking about Sir Isaac Newton,' Price snapped. 'During Newton's time, many of the greatest thinkers of the age were alchemists. These men were the forefathers of modern science.'

Isaacson raised his eyebrows. 'And what do you know of Piotrowski?' he said eventually.

'A little, but not as much as I'd like. Remember, not all alchemists were like Newton. There were those who pursued more esoteric and metaphysical aspects of the science, studying the darker arts that, to some, verged on necromancy. I believe Piotrowski was aligned to such a group.'

'What do you know of this group?'

'They were a cult known as the Esoteric Brotherhood that thrived during an age of great religious and scientific upheaval, a period that became known as the Dutch Revolt. It was an important era in the creation of the Netherlands as an independent republic.'

Isaacson smiled, looking relaxed for the first time since his arrival. 'You forget that I have a first in history. My area of expertise also happens to be the Reformation.'

Price nodded, vaguely recalling that Isaacson had been an Oxford scholar.

'You're referring to a time of perpetual turmoil when the Seventeen Provinces of the Netherlands were vying for control of the land with their mighty Spanish overlords, the Habsburgs,' Isaacson said.

'Indeed. The northern part of the Netherlands was slowly evolving into a powerful and wealthy state, largely from the thriving trade that was developing there. The dispute occurred during the Reformation when various religious groups were attempting to reform the Catholic Church in Western Europe.'

'Yes, but there were several facets to the war. It was fought, not only as a battle for independence, but also as a struggle between Calvinism, the evolving Protestant tradition of the time, and the might of the Spanish Catholic nobility. The Spanish had already declared it their duty to fight Protestantism as heresy, and

7

any expression of thought, if it didn't accord with their Catholic doctrine, was punishable by death.'

'Exactly! Piotrowski alludes to some of the darker arts studied by the Esoteric Brotherhood in his manuscript. Although the information is not specific, it was not well received. The authorities considered the Brotherhood to be a bunch of dangerous fanatics, and although the manuscript only makes veiled references to their necromancy, there's no doubt they engaged in it. It was the Brotherhood's intention to keep the contents of the book secret, yet somehow it surfaced. Not surprisingly, given the volatile circumstances of the age, it was considered blasphemous. Piotrowski mysteriously vanished soon after he'd written it, and although it was widely assumed that he was assassinated by religious zealots, this was never corroborated as he simply disappeared.'

Isaacson looked baffled. 'What makes this manuscript suddenly so important?'

Price reflected for a moment. 'I'm not sure, Isaacson. The combination of how the thief broke in and the nature of the stolen document leaves me feeling distinctly uneasy. I'm convinced that the Council should give this matter its urgent attention, which is why I propose a meeting early next week. Perhaps you'd be kind enough to organise the formalities?'

'Of course, Professor, leave it with me.'

'In the meantime, I'll do some research on Alfons Piotrowski. I should have more information for the Council when we meet.'

The men sat in silence until Isaacson eventually stirred. He rose and drained the dregs from his glass. Price ushered him towards the exit, surreptitiously pressing a button adjacent to the door as he passed.

Price opened the double doors and followed Isaacson into the hall where they were immediately joined by Albright.

'Ah, Mr Isaacson, a cab is on its way. It should be here presently,' Albright said, proffering a thick, woollen coat, which Isaacson draped around his shoulders. Moments later, the sound of a taxi's horn rang out in the distance.

'Goodnight, Professor,' Isaacson called out as he hurried across the driveway towards a vehicle that was parked beside the common, its engine idling.

Price returned to the sitting room and poured himself another drink. He retired to his chair to reflect on the events of the day. He had already decided that he would seek the assistance of Cornelius Spydre, an old friend and expert on antiquarian manuscripts. He would undoubtedly need more information before the Council gathered, and if anyone could help, it was Cornelius.

Price took a sip of port as he deliberated over the theft of the book and the unshakeable conviction that it was somehow connected with the past. He thought back to a time fifteen years earlier when he had assembled the Council to counter the rise of a mysterious sect known as the Order of Eternal Enlightenment, which had sprung up from nowhere behind a façade of benevolence. Price had battled to expose the Order for what it truly was—a murdering bunch of renegades responsible for the assassination of several leading figures of the time. The challenge posed by the Order had been met head on by the Council under Price's jurisdiction, ultimately resulting in the death of the Order's leader, Pearly Black. Ironically, Black and Price had once been students together at the Academy of Arcane and Alchemical Arts, but eventually, their friendship had degenerated into one of bitter rivalry following a run of increasingly acrimonious clashes over Black's abstruse alchemical research.

Black had gone on to found the Order as a means to pursue his inscrutable goals and had watched it flourish under his leadership. Following Black's death and the Order's demise, the Council had evolved into the country's main body responsible for national security and counter-terrorism. Over several years, the Council had built up a network of informants and an army of unidentified workers who had infiltrated or subverted many undesirable organisations with some considerable success.

If only it were still so easy, Price thought disconsolately. He shook his head, recalling the Council's many successes during its formative years. With time, internal squabbles and petty disputes had slowly undermined the principles the Council had been established to uphold, culminating in its current predicament linked to a dispute over membership. At a recent rancorous meeting, two distinct camps had evolved, vying with one another over the suitability of respective candidates to fill a vacancy. Price had tried time and again to satisfy all parties but he was becoming increasingly concerned that the Council was being destabilised from within.

And now the theft of this book at a time when the Council's stock was at its lowest ebb. He closed his eyes, his glass empty on the table next to him. Too many problems, he thought as he got up and made his way slowly from the room.

'Goodnight, Albright,' he called to his manservant who was loitering in the hall.

He climbed two flights of stairs to his bedroom feeling like a man whose problems were only just beginning.

He was eager to get to bed in the hope that sleep would provide a temporary respite from his troubles, but as he removed his jacket and unbuttoned his shirt, he was suddenly overcome by an overwhelming sense that something was amiss.

He rushed to the window under the sway of an uncontrollable urge to part the curtains and peer out. There, bathing in the dull glow of a street lamp across the road was a smartly dressed figure unmistakeably staring back at the house. The man looked up to the bedroom, perhaps drawn by a flicker of movement at the curtains. Even in the dim light, Price could see the man's sharp features and goatee beard.

The men briefly locked eyes, but the stranger, seemingly satisfied that his job was done, casually adjusted his collar and raised a scarf from his neck to wrap round his face. He turned his back on the house and swept away through masses of rotting leaves littering the path before disappearing into the impenetrable darkness shrouding the common.

2

A Subterranean Reunion

THE STREET WAS EMPTY as Josef Frankl made his way down the steep, ill-maintained track into Riddlescombe's main thoroughfare. The coastal village had flourished as a small fishing community since the sixteenth century, but its denizens were now a ragtag bunch of dubious characters making a living from smuggling and even the occasional foray into piracy. Little had changed in almost a hundred years, and Riddlescombe's uncertain reputation hung over the place like a pall of black smoke.

Nearby places had evolved into quaint seaside tourist traps drawing in visitors, and more importantly, their money. Not so Riddlescombe, a place that protected its independence with a fierce secrecy bordering on animosity towards all unwelcome intruders. It was no surprise that modernisation had bypassed Riddlescombe with many of the youngsters born to the village gone, leaving behind a community of hardened old folk who spent their time scraping together a living by fair means or foul; this and a penchant for drinking in The Serpent's Nest, the only vaguely thriving place in town.

The few remaining habitable buildings were all in varying states of disrepair, apart from a single respectably maintained structure standing alone at the end of the street. The sign swinging lazily above the door portrayed a snake with vicious blood-red fangs and maniacal yellow eyes, seemingly intent on striking out at whosoever approached.

Any sensible visitor who stumbled on the village would turn and flee at the sight of those evil-looking eyes, yet Frankl was not deterred. His eyes darted down to his wristwatch, then returned to the creaking sign that was badly in need of lubrication.

So am I, he thought, before veering off at the last moment and making his way towards the inn.

It was late afternoon, and as the December light rapidly failed, a sea mist rolled in with the tide, bringing the unmistakable tang of salt to the air while insidiously enveloping and soaking anyone who was foolish enough to be out.

A light flickered at a window, suggesting a flourishing open fire within, confirmed by a sudden rush of warm air that spilt out to greet the stranger as he opened the door. Frankl surveyed the stark interior of the pub from the threshold. The Serpent's Nest was empty apart from a handful of unsavoury looking men sitting in silence at the bar with their heads bowed over their tankards.

Frankl crossed the room and headed towards the men at the bar. 'A glass of your finest red wine,' he declared to the scruffy bartender.

'Beer,' the barman replied, eyeing the corpulent, bald man with suspicion.

Frankl immediately got the gist of what the barman was saying by the sniggers that came from the motley crew propped up at the bar. 'Very well. I'll have a pint of ale,' he replied, suppressing an urge to scowl at the men.

Frankl carried the tankard of cloudy ale back to an empty table next to the fire and sat down without a second glance. He knew the patrons were staring at him, but he ignored them in a dismissive manner and sat bathing in the warmth radiating from a spitting fire happily thriving on damp logs. He reflected on the events of the past few days and felt a glow of pride at how much he had achieved in such a short time. As he mulled this over, he was interrupted by the sound of size twelve boots pounding across the sawdust-strewn floor. Frankl turned to see a thickset man with heavily tattooed forearms built like tree trunks peering down at him in the shimmering light of the dingy bar.

'We don't be likin' no strangers in this place, particularly them that don't be introducin' 'emselves,' said the man, glowering at Frankl.

Frankl pointedly ignored the interruption and continued to look beyond the interloper, seemingly lost in thought. The man hesitated, unsure of what to do next. The man's face was unshaven and ill-kempt with long, greasy hair straddling dark brooding features, and small, wide-set eyes with widely dilated pupils. A spider's web was tattooed across his forehead that was rudely interrupted by a deeply furrowed scar, which extended to the corner of his mouth, tethering it into a permanent scowl that merely added to the malice clearly written across his face.

'My name be Razor. No one enters 'ere without my say so,' the man said.

Frankl continued to stare into the fire and took a sip of beer as if nothing untoward had happened.

'I be speakin' to you, mister,' said Razor, looking puzzled by the stranger's lack of a response. 'Strangers that wander in 'ere all alone might find 'emselves as crab bait, if they ain't too careful.'

Frankl finally looked up and met his aggressor's gaze square on. 'Please forgive my ill manners. I'm here on some personal business. I've simply stopped by for some warmth and refreshment. I'll soon be on my way,' he said, looking dismissively at the man towering above him. He turned away and stared deeply into the fire.

In an instant, Razor drew back to give himself some space and pulled a frighteningly thin stiletto from his jacket. The reflection of the fire glistened menacingly in the cold steel as Razor pointed the tip of the blade towards the stranger.

''Bout time someone taught 'e some manners, mister,' spat Razor in a deadly tone.

Frankl turned to face his assailant and exhaled a loud sigh. He did not wish to argue, knowing it was likely to be futile. He slowly rose from the chair and lifted his hands in a gesture of supplication, muttering a few inaudible words with an effect that was instantaneous. He held the flats of his palms towards the man, despite the knife that was pointing directly at his chest. He edged forwards, his hands radiating a bright unnatural light that illuminated a look of astonishment on Razor's face. The eerie glow rapidly intensified as it drew away from Frankl's hands to envelop the man, holding him helplessly in limbo like a rabbit snared in the headlights of an approaching car. The knife slipped harmlessly to the floor as Razor's hands sagged listlessly by his side.

Frankl flexed his arms, drawing Razor towards him as if pulled by invisible strings. In a sudden thrust, Frankl extended his arms as he allowed the light to wane. The invisible grip holding the man dissipated but the force generated by the motion of Frankl's arms sent Razor flying across the room. He landed with a great clatter in a dishevelled heap several feet away from Frankl and did not move. Despite the spectacle, the bar remained silent apart from the gentle moans of the semi-conscious man. The men seated at the bar continued to sup their ale and gave no indication that anything unusual had happened, although their telltale expressions failed to mask a combination of surprise tinged with fear.

'Don't rush back,' the innkeeper called out bravely after Frankl, who had turned his back on the men and was walking casually towards the exit.

Frankl left the inn without looking back. In the short time he had been indoors, nightfall had arrived in all its jet-black splendour, and with a thickening sea mist, it was difficult to see more than a few feet ahead in the poorly illuminated street.

Frankl stopped and raised his hands a few inches in front of his face. 'Beluchten,' he whispered. His hands began to emit a strange glow that gave him a phantasmal appearance in the swirling mist, yet the give-away light did not concern him. He was not expecting to meet anyone where he was heading, nor did he anticipate that one of Razor's cronies would follow him after his show of force inside the tavern.

The luminous glow eased Frankl's progress, lighting up the way as he set off for the coast. The track was muddy and treacherous, but he quickly located the infrequently trodden path he was searching for. The wind had picked up as he neared the coast, and with it, the mist was beginning to clear. The path led to a grassy headland, which ended abruptly, falling away onto a steep cliff. Frankl did not hesitate and strode boldly forwards over the brink onto a hidden track that led precipitously down. His unnatural light marked the way, but it was not easy going, and his footing repeatedly slipped, sending scree tumbling down before him.

Frankl was greatly relieved when he clambered down onto a rocky shore. After a brief pause to regain his breath, he set off towards a narrow inlet at the base of a towering cliff that marked the entrance to a cave bordered by a natural accumulation of rocks. Frankl smiled on observing the tidemark etched several feet above the cave's low entrance. Waves were beginning to crash onto the base of the cliff, causing water to pool with the flow of the incoming tide. It was no coincidence that he had chosen this time for the meeting. A full moon was due, and the spring tide to accompany it would submerge the cave's entrance in little more than a few hours' time.

Frankl scrambled through the small slit into a spacious cave. He watched in fascination as the light emanating from his hands cast strange shadows onto smooth glistening walls, perpetually moist from the constant drip of water permeating through dense overhead rock.

After several minutes of easy passage, the cave became steadily more tortuous until it finally came to an abrupt halt. Frankl craned his neck to look up, espying a narrow, vertical channel inches above his head. He pulled himself up on the natural stone handholds and squeezed his bulk the short distance through the claustrophobic passageway to emerge into a small, rounded entranceway that opened into a vast cavern. He could not comprehend how such a geological oddity could form such a distance from the sea, but he did know that the space was sufficient to accommodate the four people whom he had invited to assemble with him tonight.

He had made sure that he was an hour ahead of his guests and had timed it so that they would arrive when the tide was beginning to force its way beyond the entrance, having learnt this trick from his erstwhile leader, Pearly Black, as a tactic to disconcert his associates.

Following his arrival, Frankl allowed the light emanating from his hands to fade. He withdrew a handful of sturdy candles from his jacket, lighting them with a touch of a finger, then securing them with drops of molten wax at various points around the cavern. When he had finished, he sat down, propped himself up against a wall and waited.

The cavern's irregular shape appeared to heave in the guttering candlelight, distorting its features. Frankl closed his eyes, seduced by the flickering light. His breathing gradually steadied after the exertion of the journey, and in a short while, he fell soundly asleep.

Frankl remained motionless for almost an hour before a slight disturbance in the air forewarned him that the first of his guests had arrived, in advance of their accompanying footsteps. Shortly afterwards, two people emerged through the natural stone entranceway, one after the other. First, Abel Strange, followed by Aurelia Nightshade, both long time compatriots and former members of the Order of Eternal Enlightenment.

Abel Strange, leading academic and polymath, genius in healing, mysticism, alchemy and science, and current Chief Mentor of the Academy of Arcane and Alchemical Arts, was breathing heavily. Beads of perspiration had collected on his forehead and were steadily trickling into his eyes.

Strange gasped when he saw Frankl. 'Josef ... yes, er, of course,' he faltered. He fumbled for a handkerchief, which he managed to drop. He bent down and groped blindly around his feet in the gloomy candlelight in an attempt to regain it.

Strange's inauspicious entry was in stark contrast to the dazzling Aurelia Nightshade, who looked as exotically alluring as ever. She nodded to Frankl and proffered a hand.

'Josef, how good to see you,' Aurelia said coldly, the tone of her voice contrasting bleakly with her words.

Frankl stooped and set the bold solitary jet stone ring that dominated Aurelia's middle finger to his lips. He noted Aurelia's tightly cut, black hair and her sharp, classical features that masked a deeply disturbing undercurrent. Her make-up, a stunning combination of gold and black, exemplified Aurelia's trademark colours and matched the swirling cloak draped around her shoulders.

Frankl beamed, revealing preternaturally large teeth that reared frighteningly into view whenever his lips parted. 'As always, Aurelia, the pleasure's mine,' he replied sycophantically.

Aurelia had been Black's closest confidante before the vanquishing of the Order, and while she had shown a singular lack of purpose in pursuing Black's goals in the aftermath of his death, Frankl was optimistic that he could persuade her to play a pivotal role in his plans.

'Candles. How quaint,' pronounced Aurelia sarcastically.

Strange was looking about him. He had managed to retrieve the handkerchief and was mopping his brow. 'Yes, and an interesting choice of venue for, er, this evening's meeting,' he said uneasily.

'I'm sure you recall the places we met for Pearly's gatherings,' replied Frankl.

'I, er, remember only too well, Josef. Pearly always held important meetings in places such as this.'

'Yes,' Frankl agreed. 'The added edge of a million tons of rubble toppling down on top of us does tend to focus the mind somewhat, wouldn't you say, Abel?' he added.

Strange nodded. 'Er, yes. I recall only too well the Order's final meeting before Pearly's death.'

'Indeed,' Frankl agreed. 'The basement of a tenement block due for demolition around the time of the meeting. Pearly always believed that the Order should only make its most crucial decisions when faced with rather daunting circumstances.'

'It was more than that,' stated Strange. 'He, er, believed that it engendered a sense of unity.'

Aurelia snorted. 'Yes, but he also saw it as a test of loyalty. Being committed to Pearly was never something to toy with.'

'P-Pearly never, er, asked anything of us that he was not willing to risk of himself.'

17

'Oh, Abel, it was always inconceivable that you would not be fooled by Pearly's charm. He may have been a genius, but out of all of us, you always seemed to overlook the fact that his judgement was, at times, misguided,' said Frankl.

Strange grimaced. 'Yet P-Pearly was never, er, motivated by greed,' he said, challenging Frankl.

'And I am? You know nothing of my plans,' he replied dismissively.

'Then w-why are we here in this detestable place? And, er, why did a black pearl pitch up at the Academy for me?'

'I thought it would make you feel nostalgic, Abel. It must have piqued your interest, otherwise you'd not be here.'

'Why imitate the way Pearly always sent messages to us?'

'I never thought about it, Abel.'

'Pah!' Aurelia scoffed. 'You know as well as I do that Pearly only ever hid his most important messages in a black pearl bound by his unique alchemical talents.'

'Yes, and, er, whoever he sent the pearl to could only unlock it by uttering a keyword they shared with Pearly that, in combination with their touch, would act as a, er, catalyst to initiate the transubstantiation that would release the message hidden inside,' said Strange, emboldened by Aurelia's words.

Aurelia nodded. 'It seems, Josef, that by sending invitations bound by the same keyword we only ever shared with Pearly, you have somehow gained access to secrets I always assumed had perished with him,' she said.

Frankl smiled enigmatically, exposing rows of imbricated, stained teeth.

'You have much to explain, Josef,' said Aurelia, losing no time to find a natural enclosure in the bedrock as far away from Frankl as possible. She sat down and looked disinterestedly at her black nail varnish, steadfastly ignoring the disconcerting stare Frankl was directing at her. Strange also seemed to be in no mood for further conversation and moved quickly to join her.

The cavern remained frighteningly silent until a sudden blur of movement at the entrance signalled the arrival of a man known as

Liquid Lex. All eyes turned towards the dishevelled-looking man as he made his way into the throng. He was wearing a long khaki trench coat and combat trousers that were frayed and torn, and shabby, wet walking boots that squelched noisily with every step. A mass of hair sprawled riotously from beneath a beret that sat at such an improbable angle it defied the laws of gravitational physics.

Lex smiled boyishly, revealing a multitude of telltale crow's feet around his eyes. 'The tide's coming in,' he said, making a show of his wet boots.

Aurelia was the first to get up and greet him, and moments later, Strange and Frankl rose to join them. 'Lex!' she said, delighted.

Lex beamed back at her. 'Aurelia. It's *so* good to see you. It must be the best part of ten years,' he said, and after greeting her with a kiss on each cheek, he shook hands a little less amiably with the men.

'I'm so glad you're here, Lex,' Frankl said, despite the cool reception he had received.

As Lex moved away with Aurelia, Frankl looked appraisingly at a man who had always been a great asset to the Order but also something of an enigma. Liquid Lex was not his real name, of course, but stemmed from a childhood bereft of parents and a life forever on the wrong side of the law. He had always been known as Lex to his friends, but had acquired the nickname as a result of a penchant for using a variety of noxious fluids, mostly of his own concoction, in his role as a cat burglar, bank robber, housebreaker, safe-breaker and all the other villainous activities that occupied his time.

It had always struck Frankl as ironic that Lex considered his activities as an aesthete would his art. Lex had never thought of himself as a rogue and genuinely believed that he lived his life in an honourable way with his own set of standards that would have been considered principled in any other profession. On one occasion, when the police had leaked erroneous details of his criminal methods to the press, an incensed Lex had not hesitated in breaking into the police headquarters in the middle of the night with the sole intention of finding his file and amending it. It took him several hours to track down the records, but once located, he rewrote them to the best of his satisfaction before replacing the file and leaving without further ado.

The following day, the police commissioner was baffled to learn of a break-in, yet with no sign that anything had been taken. The mystery remained unsolved until Lex's records were subsequently pulled following a heist possibly linked to the Order. When the commissioner was presented with Lex's, by now, amended records, he finally came to understand what had happened.

Lex's previous description that described him as, 'An unprincipled lifetime offender who should be considered extremely dangerous at all times', had been crudely scrawled out, and underneath, in Lex's characteristic handwriting, replaced with the words, 'Lives for the challenge of outwitting the dunderheads who call themselves the police and are oh so corrupt and inept. Oh, and incidentally, he wouldn't hurt a flea'.

The red-faced commissioner could not live it down, and once the details of his ineptitude were published in the press, early retirement was a foregone conclusion.

Despite his shabby appearance, Lex was an affable, light-hearted man, who prided himself on having never worked a single day in his life, yet effortlessly acquiring wads of cash through unlawful means before proceeding to fritter it away on the two great loves of his life—alcohol and gambling.

None of this was lost on Black, who recruited Lex to the Order to raise funds by whatever means he saw fit, thus creating a match made in heaven. For single-handedly masterminding the Order's nefarious activities, Lex was rewarded with an almost mystical protection from the law that somehow seemed allied to working for Black, but in reality, was a consequence of the Order's illicit deposits made into the offshore bank accounts of the land's most senior custodians of the law.

'I presume this meeting's going to be brief, Josef?' Lex enquired, addressing Frankl with a disarming smile. 'It won't be long before we're trapped in here, judging by the state of the tide.'

'We're still awaiting the arrival of one final guest before we start. I suggest we all sit down quietly and wait,' Frankl declared.

The ensuing silence was only punctuated by the distant sound of the sea growing imperceptibly louder with each passing moment, but it was not long before a pale, gaunt young man appeared at the entranceway to the cavern.

The man clambered ungainly through the gap, his eyes darting uneasily from one face to another as he steadfastly sought to avoid the searching gazes that fell upon him while wringing his hands and hopping nervously from one foot to another. Like Lex, his boots were wet, a legacy of the sea that was inexorably making its way into the cave.

The man spoke methodically with a staccato rhythm without addressing anyone in particular. 'We'll soon be cut off in here at the rate the tide's coming in. Surely you're not planning to stay ...'

'You're worrying unnecessarily,' said Frankl dismissively, getting to his feet and making his way to the centre of the natural stone arena. 'Although you're right, of course, Michael. The water's heading our way and I'm sure you all saw the tidemark before entering the cave, but it won't be lost on you that the height of this chamber is well above tide level,' he said, gesturing expansively with his arms. 'The water will fill the channel but cannot reach us in here. We may have to wait some hours, but once the tide recedes, we can retrace our steps. In the meantime, we can conduct our meeting without interruption and in complete secrecy.'

'You surpass yourself, Josef,' said Aurelia with a shake of her head. 'I'm sure you could have chosen any number of suitable places for this meeting without the need for all of this grandeur. Whatever you are, Josef, you're not Pearly.'

Frankl smiled but passed no comment. He raised a finger and pointed at the newly arrived man. 'Let me introduce Michael Styx. I doubt you've had the pleasure of Michael's company before, but I'm delighted he's agreed to meet with us this evening. He's the bearer of some rather crucial information.'

A look of loathing passed across the young man's face and he shuffled uneasily under Frankl's scrutiny.

'Let's just hope it's worth it,' spat Aurelia. 'Reaching your venue is one thing, Josef, but I for one would rather not have to swim from here. Incidentally, am I alone in supposing there'll be enough oxygen for us in here once the tide cuts us off?'

Frankl was unfazed. 'I don't know, Aurelia. You should have your answer in a few hours. I was going to add, "if you're prepared to wait", but it looks as if the water's already upon us,' he said, nodding in the direction of the entranceway that was now occluded with water. 'Maybe Abel could do some calculations with that prodigious brain of his and tell us whether we're going to suffocate.'

'Er, quite so,' said Strange, turning his head slowly from one individual to another as if considering the problem while sitting at his desk at the Academy. In the dim candlelight, he looked like a fish out of water, the thick round lenses of his spectacles magnifying bulbous eyes that appeared far too large for his small face and wiry frame. He removed his handkerchief to wipe his glasses, more from habit than need, as he contemplated the challenge Frankl had set for him.

It was some minutes before Strange finally spoke. 'Based on the dimensions of the cavern, I've, er, estimated the amount of oxygen that is available to us, assuming a normal composition of air, of course. I've made, er, a few assumptions relating to each individual's size, allowing an approximation of their basal metabolic rate, and extrapolating from this, their oxygen consumption.'

'What are your conclusions?' asked Frankl, sounding as if he hardly cared for the answer even before Strange had voiced it.

'I believe we have a maximum of three hours before the oxygen runs out,' Strange said matter-of-factly.

Strange's words were met with a stunned silence as the audience absorbed the implications of the prediction until Frankl calmly declared, 'It'll be high tide shortly. In a couple of hours, the tide will recede and allow air back into the cavern. Let's just hope your calculations are accurate, Abel. Now, I suggest we begin. Once we're done, we can all sit quietly and not expend any more energy than is necessary.'

'Get on with it then,' said Aurelia.

'Very well, Aurelia, although a little more courtesy would not go amiss,' replied Frankl.

'By now, most of you will have realised that this meeting relates to the Order, despite its abrupt end with the unfortunate demise of our former great leader, Pearly Black, almost ten years ago—'

'Oh, come now, Josef, we all know what happened. What is this, a history lesson?' interrupted Aurelia.

'Not quite, Aurelia. You forget that not all of us were part of the Order,' retorted Frankl, inclining his head in the direction of Styx. 'I suspect our friend, Michael, here, was still in shorts when Pearly was in his prime. I think it's only appropriate to provide him with some background, don't you?

'Now, Michael, have you ever heard of the Order of Eternal Enlightenment?'

A slight shake of his head was the only sign that Styx gave to suggest he had heard the question before Frankl continued.

'When Pearly first assembled the Order, it was an ultra-secretive organisation made up of little more than those of us gathered here tonight,' he began, noting the uneasy exchange of glances between Aurelia and Lex. 'Inevitably, as word of the Order's activities spread, support developed in areas that we had not foreseen. We were fortunate that Pearly had the ear of many influential people, particularly Dionysus Bing, the editor of *The Morning Comet*.'

'Er, yes,' said Strange. 'With Bing in Pearly's pocket, it was easy for the press to romanticise the Order's activities, even if, er, Pearly's ultimate goals were closed to us.'

'Perhaps, but our faith in him always ensured that we would follow him in whatever direction he saw fit,' said Lex.

'Or accept the consequences if we did not,' sneered Aurelia.

'We all knew about his obscure alchemical research, and we did whatever he asked of us to achieve his aims,' said Frankl, ignoring Aurelia's slur. 'For this, he needed money,' he added, looking at Lex.

'Yes, and with small time criminal activities perpetrated in

23

many and varied ways, the Order began to grow,' Lex responded. 'Pearly's random killing of an adversary or an innocent bystander was lost by subtle manipulations of the media. Equally, acts of kindness purportedly carried out by the Order were cynically orchestrated and publicised. Little by little, the name of Pearly Black became synonymous with good.

'As his popularity grew, he began to exert influence in the highest echelons of the land, allowing the Order to subtly undermine the undisturbed balance of power the country had enjoyed for so long.'

'Until Price and his beloved Council began to flex their muscles and it all started to go wrong,' said Frankl bitterly. He paused and looked at the group as if sizing them up through eyes lost beneath pendulous folds of flesh that hung from his brow.

'To the majority of you,' Frankl continued, 'it should be evident that the reason you were invited here this evening is because of your previous involvement with the Order. The fact that all three of you are here,' he said, looking at Abel, Aurelia and Lex in turn, 'tells me that you were intrigued enough by the means in which you were contacted to learn more.'

Frankl smiled, revealing teeth that made him look like a bulldog. 'The black pearl was more than just a means of communication. It kindled your interest in a possible re-emergence of the Order. After a break of some years, your willingness to meet here confirms that.'

Aurelia showed no emotion while a smile flickered across Lex's lips.

Strange looked even more unnerved than when he had first arrived. When he spoke, his voice quavered unnaturally, betraying a great sense of unease. 'How ... how possibly could we have not responded? The black pearl was Pearly's method of contacting us. Well ... that is until now ...' he said as he reached for his handkerchief once more and mopped his brow. 'I just thought that Pearly ...' he began before his voice suddenly trailed off.

'You thought what?' demanded Frankl. 'That Pearly had sent the message himself? For such an analytical mind, Abel, you sometimes reach devastatingly ridiculous conclusions. Let me tell you why you all came: the black pearl stirred something in you and reminded you of your responsibilities.'

Aurelia gave a hollow laugh. 'Don't be ridiculous, Josef. Who are you to speak of responsibilities?'

Frankl held up a hand. 'Don't be so judgmental, Aurelia. Just hear me out and perhaps you'll show a little more decorum than your demeanour implies.'

Aurelia shrugged her shoulders. 'Get on with it then, although it's not as if there's anywhere else for us to go,' she added sarcastically.

Frankl glared at her. 'With Pearly's death, the Order was finished. Those who had pledged their allegiance to the Order crawled back into the woodwork, only concerned for themselves. It was as if support for the Order had never existed, leaving a handful of Pearly's loyal advocates isolated and alone, doing all they could to avoid the recriminations that followed.

'That was many years ago, but for those of us here tonight, the Order has never been forgotten. I, for one, have worked tirelessly these past years, trying to unravel Pearly's plans. Now, my friends, the time approaches. At last, I have something tangible to bring back all that was lost ...'

With these words, Frankl reached inside his coat to reveal an old, beautifully inscribed book that, just a few days earlier, had been gathering dust in the library of the Order's greatest adversary, Henry Price.

3

The Stone Statue

LILY CRAWLED FROM BED after a fitful night's sleep. She had dreamt of being in her classroom conjugating Latin verbs under the doleful scrutiny of her tutor when she heard a noise downstairs. Much to her tutor's astonishment, she leapt from her chair and shot from the room to investigate. She tiptoed into the hall, but as she searched for the source of the sound, she was grabbed from behind. She thrashed out in her desperation to escape, but a slight teenage girl was no match for the powerful arms squeezing the air from her lungs. Despite her attempts to scream, no sound escaped from her mouth, and as her terror mounted, she awoke with a jolt, drenched in a cold sweat and a pounding in her chest that took a considerable time to slacken. She spent the next few hours staring into the impenetrable corners of the bedroom imagining all manner of unspeakable thoughts before finally slipping back into a restless sleep.

When she awoke, a further wave of apprehension washed over her. Following her father's return, he had barely spoken to her before informing her that the house had been burgled. Despite her shock, he told her little else, and although she repeatedly quizzed him, he brushed over the details as if they were unimportant. It was no surprise that the thought of an intruder filled her with terror, particularly as her father had been away at the time, and this, combined with the elaborate measures he had taken to protect the house only compounded her sense of unease.

She got up and drew back the curtains, wiping away the condensation that had formed on the window. She leant forwards and peered across the road towards the common. The grass was coated with a heavy frost and a low mist lingered over the rooftops, despite the early morning sunshine. The sight caused Lily to recall the childhood walks she had shared with her mother, Saskia, on mornings such as this, strolling hand in hand across the common to the river. They had stood side by side, captivated by the sunlight sparkling on the water's surface while the labourers toiled on the construction of a new bridge, losing all track of time as they marvelled at the ingenuity of the engineers and the daring of the workers as the structure took shape.

Lily smiled to herself before the happy thought was blotted out by the memory of her mother's death. She was six years old when her mother died, and ever since, the completed bridge had become a reminder of the all too brief time they had shared together before she had been brutally snatched away.

Now, standing on tiptoe looking out of the window into the dispersing mist, she could just make out the zenith of the bridge rising above the trees in the distance. Whenever she felt unhappy, she would look towards the bridge from the house or walk down to the river, enjoying the tangible connection this forged with her mother. With her lesson looming, she would not have time to visit the river, but the distant view of the bridge had gone some way towards settling her unease.

Lily quickly dressed but stopped to gaze at her reflection in the mirror. She subconsciously ran her fingers through her hair in an attempt to bring some order to the unruly curls that tumbled to her shoulders. Despite her poor night's sleep, she was amazed to see that she still looked fresh. She spent a moment squinting at her large, inquisitive blue eyes and the dark ringlets that fell about her oval face, characteristics that were a direct acquisition from her mother.

Lily was not hungry and decided that breakfast could wait. On a whim, she collapsed back onto her bed and picked up the book that she had left on the bedside table after reading late into the night. She was studying the art of transubstantiation—the alchemical transformation of one form of matter into another— and stared at the pages, but soon found her mind drifting back to more troubling thoughts.

When her father had commenced her alchemical education, it had all been so exciting, but gradually, as her studies intensified, the burden of learning had slowly taken its toll. She always looked forward to her father's lessons because of the great excitement they engendered, but the problem lay with her tutors—the formal and boring Victor Mirkstone for Latin, history, philosophy and theology, and the enigmatic and unpredictable Anatoly Volkiev for sciences, mathematics and engineering.

Despite Lily's respect for her father, she frequently pressed him on the need for her tutors, invariably leading to discussions about her education that ended in a difference of opinion. She knew she was strong-minded, but so was her father, and their arguments inevitably ended in deadlock leaving her feeling dejected and frustrated.

Lily could still remember the keen excitement she had experienced following her first lesson with her father soon after her mother's death. Her introduction to the alchemical arts had begun with the simplest of techniques but she had shown an extraordinary aptitude for the ancient lore he taught her. Her education rapidly advanced into deeper realms of the alchemical arts, and the more obscure the topic, the more eager her desire for learning. She often wondered why her father had not chosen to send her away for her education, and she was surprised to discover that the dwindling number of alchemical institutions no longer taught much of what she was studying with him. She also suspected that the events surrounding her mother's death also had something to do with the decision and it was inevitable that he would not want her to leave in the aftermath of such tragic circumstances.

Lily picked up the book that had slipped into her lap; *Transubstantiation: An Alchemical and Philosophical Treatise* by Isambard Meekins. The book was an adjunct to her father's lessons

28

and began with the rather mundane origins of the subject. Her lessons had recently moved onto the practical applications of transubstantiation, a topic she was finding increasingly fascinating. She had already learnt how to change the properties of substances at a molecular level and she had graduated onto the transformation of various compounds into others. She had even started reading the final chapters of the book ahead of her lessons, which delved into even more complex and esoteric transformations, but after studying the small text for several minutes, Lily found she could no longer concentrate, and returned the book to the bedside table.

Casting further thoughts of study aside, she went downstairs and headed for the kitchen. The housekeeper, Mrs Brimstork, was nowhere to be seen, but she had left some porridge warming on the range. Lily helped herself to a bowl and filled it from the pot before adding a generous helping of honey. She sat down at the table and soon felt the reinvigorating effect of the stodgy mass of oats. She poured herself a mug of coffee from the cafetière and took in the dark liquid's aroma as it drifted up to her nose, stimulating her even before her first sip.

The clock on the wall read a quarter to nine; still fifteen minutes before she was due to meet her father. Although she was often late for her tutors' lessons, she would never allow this to happen with him. She quickly downed her drink and deposited the empty bowl and cup in the sink before leaving for the attic. If her father were not already seated at his desk, she would wait for him to join her there.

Although the house was spacious, the attic had been converted some years previously into her father's personal study and somewhere to teach Lily without fear of interruption. The result was a room perched on the top floor with plenty of space to accommodate two people, and although the pitch of the roof was low, the room never felt cramped because of three large dormer windows that gave it a light and airy feel. At one end, a small door led onto a north-facing balcony giving spectacular views of the river, and when it was warm, they would often sit there for lessons while admiring the bridge they associated with Saskia.

Lily never failed to feel amazed whenever she entered the study. The room was home to all sorts of peculiar-looking devices and implements including crucibles, telescopes, astrolabes, theodolites, flasks, retorts, gears, levers, fractionating columns, condensers, sprockets, springs, callipers, presses and even a small furnace. A large oak table sat in the middle of the room with an odd assortment of her father's gadgets strewn across its surface, and even now, Lily still had no idea how many of them functioned. She had lost count of the times she had asked him to discuss his contraptions with her, but all he would say was that her education had not reached the appropriate juncture.

The object that fascinated her most was an instrument her father referred to as the Historoscope. It was a beautifully ornate, metallic cylinder made of an alloy she did not recognise, and it always stood in the centre of the desk. Almost a metre in length, it sat on a stand, intricately decorated with a multitude of surface patterns that reminded her of a child's kaleidoscope with a small eyepiece at one end and a flat cylindrical screen at the other. Lily had repeatedly questioned him regarding its function, but as usual, he told her little. She knew it acted as a means to store memories and she had even seen him use it, but like so many of his other instruments, she had no idea how it worked.

Her father was already sitting at the desk when she entered the room. He did not stir and was concentrating on a statue of a small creature perched on the tabletop in front of him. As she approached, she noticed that he looked tired and haggard, and suspected that he, too, had slept badly. Her eyes were drawn to his shoulder-length hair, and noted with a start, how it was beginning to grey at the temples. He usually wore his hair neatly tied up to keep it from his eyes, but this morning, it hung loosely about his shoulders. He eventually looked up and smiled, his careworn expression dissipating with the arrival of his daughter.

'Morning Lily, sleep well?' he said brightly, getting up and putting an arm around her shoulder.

Lily smiled. 'Not really. I'm still feeling a bit anxious if I'm honest.'

Price returned her smile. 'The break-in, I presume? I know I haven't told you much, but that's only because I don't know that much myself,' he replied as he ushered her into a chair next to his own. 'Now, what were we discussing at the end of our last lesson? Ah yes, transubstantiation,' he added, changing the subject before Lily had a chance to reply.

He picked up the statue, glancing at the figure cursorily, before handing it to Lily. 'What do you make of this?'

Lily took the figure and weighed it in her hands; it felt considerably lighter than it looked. 'Well, it's a lifelike effigy of a squirrel. The way it's standing on its hind legs and the hackles on its back suggest it was startled by something.'

Price was watching Lily intently as she scrutinised the object. 'I'd like you to explore the object with your mind as if you're about to attempt a conversion.'

She nodded, immediately understanding what her father was asking of her. She had learnt that transubstantiation, in alchemical terms, was the transformation of one type of substance into another. The early alchemists had toiled for centuries in their laboratories to transform common metals into gold or silver, but now, rather than crucibles and furnaces, it was the power of the mind that was the key to modern alchemical success.

Her lessons on the topic had started with learning to picture a substance at its most basic atomic level before harnessing the intense mental exertion that was necessary to transubstantiate one simple atom into another. With considerable patience and laborious practice, she had learnt to scrutinise complex molecular structures and attempt increasingly difficult transmutations.

In time, Lily learnt to appreciate both the structure and form of matter by exploring it with her mind. At first, this required a tangible connection to the substance, but as she became more adept, she achieved success by reaching out with her mind. Now, with practice, she could explore and manipulate form at will, rearranging internal structure, sometimes in dramatic fashion.

Lily considered the statue and began to explore it exactly how her father had instructed, shutting out all other thoughts and closing her eyes to visualise the microscopic detail of the structure with her mind. Some minutes later, when she was satisfied with what she had done, she handed the statue back to him and said, 'Mm, that's strange. It's made almost entirely of quartz. That wasn't what I was expecting.'

'Quartz?'

'Sorry, I should have said silicon dioxide.'

'Ah, yes. The most common of all minerals and the basis of certain types of igneous rock.'

Lily frowned. 'It's odd, though, because the statue isn't uniform and contains voids and cavities. I wouldn't normally expect to find flaws in a piece of rock derived primarily from magma.'

'Well done, Lily. You're right. Can you formulate any conclusions based on your analysis?' Price asked, looking curiously at her.

Lily shook her head, having no idea where her father's line of thought was leading.

Price returned the statue to the desk. He stared intently at the figure before raising his palm above the statue's head. Without warning, a spark of blinding light flew from his hand, cleaving the statue neatly into two equal pieces that clattered apart onto the tabletop.

Lily gasped once the smoke from the discharge had dissipated, immediately realising that the statue was not uniform, just as she had predicted. She picked up one of the halves and felt her stomach lurch as she looked at the figure. What she saw made her recall the first time she had opened one of her father's anatomical manuscripts, *De Humani Corporis Fabrica* by Andreas Vesalius. The plates of the anatomical dissections she had always derived so much pleasure from were replicated in the same detail on the inside of the statue.

Price was studying her face intently when she looked up. 'What do you think?' he whispered.

Lily looked confused. 'I don't understand, unless ...' she began, furrowing her brow.

'Go on,' he prompted.

'Unless this really is a squirrel that has somehow been transformed into stone ... mummified even.'

'You're almost there,' said Price proudly. 'The squirrel, I'm afraid, was very much alive until recently. Albright found it at the bottom of the garden this morning. He stumbled on it by chance and brought it back to the house for my inspection. This squirrel has been petrified, Lily. I believe that our recent intruder was disturbed as he left, and instinctively reacted by casting a spell.'

'But that means whoever broke in was an alchemist,' she gasped in response to the unnerving news.

'Exactly,' replied Price. 'As you are all too well aware, this kind of transformation, outside of these four walls, is rarely encountered these days. The few alchemists practising the art of transubstantiation are well known to me, yet this recent burglary has none of the hallmarks of my allies. No, I'm afraid that this event somehow marks the beginning of a new threat, which leaves me feeling decidedly uneasy.'

'What will you do?' enquired Lily.

'The key to this affair is the book that was taken. The intruder knew exactly what they were after, and that's where I intend to start. I've arranged to see Cornelius later this morning.'

Lily smiled despite feeling a sudden pang of guilt. Cornelius was a lifelong friend of her father's, and inevitably, he had become a surrogate uncle to her. 'Give him my love and tell him I'll be over to see him soon. I haven't visited in ages,' she said, silently chiding herself for neglecting him.

Price nodded then settled back in his chair. He picked up a battered book that fell open to reveal beautiful handwritten script inscribed on creased vellum.

'What's that?' said Lily, jumping up to look over his shoulder. The book was written in Latin, but despite her studies, she could not immediately decipher the words.

Price looked at her and smiled as their eyes met. 'Perhaps you should pay more attention to your other lessons, young lady,' he said in jest.

'Mm. Maybe you're right,' Lily replied grudgingly.

'Now. I have a lot to do this morning. Perhaps we should continue your lesson tomorrow, but before you go, there's one more thing I'd like to discuss.'

'Of course.'

'There's an area of alchemical lore you've not yet met. Have you come across the term "psychic defence" during any of your reading?'

Lily pondered for a moment. 'No, I don't think so.'

'I thought not. It's an area of study that's been neglected in recent years. It's well beyond the expertise of even the most accomplished alchemist. I've purposely avoided the subject up until now.'

'Why the sudden change?'

'I believe you're ready, Lily, it's as simple as that. Your practical abilities have matured beyond my wildest expectations. The study of alchemical lore is one thing, but the ability to put it into practice is another. Theory can be taught to almost anyone with the intellectual capabilities to understand, but turning that knowledge into a defined physical effect seems to be beyond even the most capable students these days. Alas, it was not always so.'

'Why?'

'That's a question I cannot answer, I'm afraid. The simple truth is, I don't know. Many years ago when our greatest alchemical institution, the Academy of Arcane and Alchemical Arts, was at its height, students acquired these skills with consummate ease. Sadly, the institution has been in decline for many years, even going back to my time as a fellow there.

'The Academy may be the last bastion of alchemical learning, but its deterioration has been accompanied by an inextricable link with the students' abilities to acquire the practical skills with which we aim to equip them. There appears to be no obvious explanation for this, but it makes your progress all the more remarkable.'

Lily felt a glow of pride. Praise from her father was a rare commodity indeed, and she was more familiar with the frequent criticism he handed out for her failure to appreciate aspects of her education, particularly on the subjects taught by her tutors.

'What do you mean by psychic defence?'

Price rubbed the bridge of his nose contemplatively. 'You've already mastered many of the skills that are necessary to internalise and assimilate information through simple analysis as you've just so ably demonstrated. The next step is to recognise and convert the energy residing within you, and then absorb, channel and ultimately exteriorise that power.'

'Are you going to start teaching me this now?' Lily said, struggling to contain her excitement.

Price smiled. 'The time's right, Lily. While I've directed most of your lessons towards the analysis and realignment of matter, the new skills I aim to teach you are more offensive in nature. Remember, though, you should utilise these skills for your protection rather than harness them as a destructive power.'

Lily was astonished. 'I don't believe it! You've always steered me away from anything that's dangerous.'

'For very good reasons, Lily, but before you get ahead of yourself, you must learn to recognise danger before it arises in order to protect yourself—the realm of alchemy known as psychic defence.'

'I'm not sure I understand,' replied Lily.

'Let me explain. Ana's been teaching you the basics of neurophysiology and psychology. You're aware that the brain can assimilate vast quantities of data at any given time. This information enters the nervous system via the senses, although much of it never reaches conscious level and is ignored by the higher centres of the brain.'

'I don't suppose it could be any other way otherwise a flood of unnecessary data would overwhelm our thoughts.'

'Exactly, but that doesn't mean to say that this subconscious information is irrelevant. I intend to teach you ways to monitor what's going on around you, yet without interfering with everything else that's going through your mind at the same time. This concept underpins the rationale behind what you will soon come to understand as your psychic defence mechanisms.'

'I'm not sure I understand.'

'Okay, let me give you an example. You've heard the term "the smell of fear", I take it?'

'I have, but it's always seemed a ludicrous expression to me. Who can smell fear?'

'Well, animals can for a start. Chemical factors known as pheromones are released by one organism and trigger a subconscious response in another. Human behaviour can similarly be influenced in this manner. If you master these signals and combine them with the ability to read non-verbal cues, it will put you at a significant advantage against any adversary.'

'Mm, yes, I see.'

'The flicker of a facial muscle or a particular body posture or movement can belie many human emotions but may be missed by the casual observer. If you learn to read these expressions, you can tell when someone is fearful, or angry, or even reckless; when they're lying or telling the truth; or whether they're a threat or trustworthy.'

'So that I can decide on the best course of action to take.'

'Exactly! A movement or gesture made by someone you'd not normally notice may give you an edge when you're challenged and may even save your life. You've almost certainly already experienced this before.'

'What do you mean?' she asked, perplexed.

'Have you ever had the feeling that you were being watched but couldn't quite explain it?' enquired Price.

Lily thought for a moment. 'I suppose so.'

'Yes, and although you may not have realised it at the time, that sneaking suspicion may have been there for a reason.'

'Go on.'

'I mean, quite simply, that your subconscious senses may have picked up a subtle change in the environment that you hadn't noticed. It's possible that your senses were alerting you to a threat; this is the basis of psychic defence. You learn to accept and interpret all manner of sensory information at a level just below consciousness, thus allowing you to perceive changes in the environment that may signal danger.'

'Putting me at an advantage in dealing with the situation,' said Lily, looking at her father eagerly. 'I've wanted you to teach me stuff like this for ages.'

Price held up the flats of his palms. 'Don't be in such a rush,' he counselled. 'I can see where your thoughts are leading, but first, we'll begin by channelling your mind to read the environment for your protection. Only when you've mastered this, will we start to explore how to unleash the destructive powers you harbour inside you.'

Lily was overawed. She had witnessed the raw power that her father had occasionally been called upon to use. The sight of such prodigious energy had both frightened and excited her, and she had always assumed that she would not begin studying the topic until she was much older than her current sixteen years.

'How can I learn about psychic defence?' she asked eagerly.

Price smiled. 'Well, it just so happens that I have something for you,' he said, brandishing the book that was still residing in his hands. 'It's an old book that ably covers the topic; study it well, Lily, for there's much in here you'll find rewarding.'

Lily accepted the book with great anticipation and inspected the bland cover. The title was inscribed in Latin, which she quickly translated. '*The Inner Strength of the Mind* by Arturo Casiraghi. Thank you,' she said, cradling the book as if it were a long-lost friend.

'You should make some time to get started on this before our next lesson. Off you go and I'll catch up with you later.'

As she turned to leave, her father called out, 'Just one more thing, Lily. The stolen manuscript; I'll discuss it with you as soon as I've found out more. And Lily, don't mention it to anyone else, will you?'

Lily nodded, beaming from ear to ear as she headed down the stairs.

4

The *Comet* and the *Star*

HERMES BING SURVEYED THE world from the fortieth floor of the eponymous Bing Tower, not only the zenith of his empire but also his personal residence. The building, a structure constructed almost entirely of steel and glass, dominated the London skyline, not only as an architectural landmark but also as a navigational beacon for those searching for direction in the city six hundred feet below. Daylight had long since waned, but a lurid neon light depicting a comet and stars flashed mercilessly from the top of the skyscraper, illuminating the glass-dominated room.

Bing reached out across the large bespoke walnut desk and raised a glass that had lain undisturbed for some time. He swilled the slivovitz and watched the liquor settle in droplets on the side of the glass before draining it in a single slug. The plum brandy bit hard as it hit the back of his throat before burning all the way down to his stomach. He settled back in the chair and waited for the calming effect of the alcohol to take hold.

The day, as usual, had been long and hard. It was only now in the early hours that Bing could feel himself relax. He had not eaten, and it was not long before his eyelids began to droop. He reclined the chair, and in minutes, he lay fast asleep, his chest gently rising and falling in harmony with the flashing sigmoid-shaped spray of light sitting below a constellation of stars that was the logo Bing had commissioned to sit on top of the building as a reminder to the city below of the most successful newspaper empire it had ever known.

Bing woke some hours later with a start, his dream rudely interrupted by an extraneous tapping noise impinging on his consciousness. His eyes parted with difficulty as he cursed himself for forgetting to remove his contact lenses. Despite the pain, he prised his eyelids apart and was met by the sight of a bird perched precariously on a ledge outside repeatedly picking up a shell with its beak and smashing it against the sill. When the bird finally managed to shatter the chitinous casing, it stopped and inclined its head, staring at Bing with a piercing yellow eye before flying off, the soft contents of the shell dangling uncertainly from its beak.

Bing briefly wondered why the blackbird had ventured so high, but the thought passed. In the short moments since awakening, the dream had dissipated leaving a sense of frustration as he tried, and failed, to recall the vision. His mouth was dry, and his head hurt—a familiar sensation given the amount he habitually drank. He cast aside the irritation, reassured by a subliminal yet strangely calming hum that resonated throughout the building's core emanating from the constant working of the presses many floors below.

The first run of *The Morning Comet* had been dispatched before midnight and attention had now turned to *The Evening Star*. The workforce below never ceased in their activity, and thanks to Bing, the production of the papers was a self-sustaining process. Every employee was exquisitely aware of the role they played, no matter how small, in the editorial process. The sum of these parts made for a seamless transition from the instant the news broke to when the papers hit the stalls. From the reporters on the ground to the multitude of clerks, runners, journalists, photographers, columnists, copy editors, graphic artists, crossword compilers, secretaries, proofreaders, typesetters, cartoonists, commentators, printers, engineers, down to the most junior of tea-boys, the newspapers flourished. Each part of the journalistic process was streamlined and fed through a series of increasingly senior editors up to Bing, whose role as editor-in-chief was still as active as ever.

When he had taken over the business following the death of his father, Dionysus, just under ten years earlier, the newspapers were at their lowest ebb. Bing's editorial style soon changed all that and the papers blossomed while his rivals floundered, basing his success on the principle of ruthless investigative journalism, and for him, anything that increased the papers' circulation was fair game. An insistence on truth, only as Bing saw it, and an enigmatic style tempered this goal, leading to strange quirks in publishing at times when they were least expected.

Following the Prime Minister's re-election for a second term in office with an increased majority, Bing led with an article on the plight of rare alpine plant species threatened with extinction because of a change in the microclimate. Hardly big news, but when questioned, he asserted that, because the result of the election was never in doubt, what was the point of reporting it? It was widely assumed to be editorial suicide, but as Bing predicted, circulation of the newspapers rose by half a million copies. On occasions when he deemed the news to be too boring, he would lead with obscure, cryptic stories or eye-catching headlines that bore no resemblance to the stories residing below them. Whatever he did, the public seemed to love it, and the burgeoning Bing empire went from strength to strength. The editor of Bing's great tabloid rival, Montague Fielding, was the only person to counter his fame, taking every opportunity to disparage and ridicule him in *The Daily Sting*, but no matter what, Bing's popularity with the masses continued apace.

He rose from the chair and poured himself a coffee from the percolator on the desk. The pot had not been replenished since the previous evening, but the cold Yemeni coffee tasted thick and bitter, just as he liked it. The coffee had an instant effect, revitalising and invigorating him as he prepared for the daily meeting with the sub-editors of the *Star* to discuss the content of the day's edition before it hit the presses in time for its early afternoon circulation.

Bing had just enough time to wash and change before breakfast in the boardroom on the floor below. He entered the bedroom and shook his head in dismay at that sight of the undisturbed bed following his all too brief sleep in the chair. He suddenly felt a pang of hunger and realised he had not eaten since lunchtime the previous day.

He subconsciously flexed then extended his neck, which cracked unpleasantly as he tried to soothe a lingering stiffness. Crossing the threshold to the bathroom, he caught a glimpse of his reflection in the mirror. He was almost fifty years of age, and it was beginning to show, a combination of unhealthy living and inadequate sleep. He still retained some of his youthful looks, but the lines on his face and the folds of skin below his jaw were creeping inexorably into view. His fair hair was matted and untidy, yet his short upturned nose overlying the thin, pink vermilion of his lips displayed an exactitude that never seemed to change. The combination of these features and his intense trance-inducing eyes belied his hard living and still held an attractiveness that, with his extrovert and expansive personality, had the ability to charm and captivate all who knew him.

He quickly showered and changed in preparation for the vagaries of the forthcoming day. As he entered the office, his watch emitted a loud beep, a reminder of the imminent meeting. He crossed the hexagonal-shaped room to a glass cylindrical shaft forming a central core of the building containing a lift authorised for his use and a select few alone. He placed his palm on the jet-black panel adjacent to the doors and waited. A red light above the panel flickered before turning green, confirming the security check had been completed, and the lift was on its way up. As he waited, he closed his eyes, clearing his thoughts in preparation for the meeting.

An annoying buzzing noise suddenly interrupted the all too short-lived solitude. He shook his head as if to orientate himself before finally realising the significance of the sound. He returned to the desk and lifted the telephone receiver in one languid motion.

'Mr Bing, I have a call for you.' It was the voice of Cassiopeia, his personal assistant.

Bing felt mildly annoyed at the interruption. 'It's customary to tell me who's on the line, Cassie,' he replied, rather curtly.

'Oh, and how many times have I told you not to chew gum?' he added irritably.

'Sorry, sir, but Mr Bing, I'm afraid the caller wasn't prepared to give his name. I can't say I recognise the voice, but he did call via your personal number and gave the correct security code. I told him that you wouldn't talk to him without a name, but he was most insistent that I put him through. He says he has some information that will interest you.'

Bing was interested. Only a handful of people had access to his personal line, and all were known to him. It was odd that the caller had not given a name, but this only served to heighten his intrigue. 'Okay, Cassie, put him on.'

He heard a click on the line as his secretary transferred the call.

'Ah, Mr Bing, so good of you to take the time to speak with me.' The voice was thin and quiet, but the man spoke with a clipped accent that was vaguely familiar.

Bing spoke quickly, almost too eagerly. 'Who is this? What do you have for me?'

The caller paused before replying, 'Mr Bing, I'd prefer not to introduce myself at this juncture. Perhaps when you've heard what I have to say, you'll understand my motives.' After a further brief pause, the caller went on. 'You have an interest in the Council and its machinations?'

'If you read the papers, you'll know full well that I'm no friend of the Council.'

The caller chuckled. 'It's fairly obvious that you attempt to undermine the Council whenever the opportunity arises in your newspapers.'

'You consider it funny, do you? You may think it's all right having the composition and methods of this country's principal body responsible for national security closed to scrutiny, but it's not all right with me,' Bing retorted, making no effort to hide his seething antagonism towards the Council.

'Naturally making the Council an easy target for your newspapers,' the man replied glibly. 'So what exactly is your beef with the Council, Mr Bing?'

'The Council is a clandestine organisation that the masses are not party to. It holds a position of power that's an insult to democracy,' Bing said, churning out the usual stance of the *Comet* while not yet understanding the caller's motives. Deep down he knew that it was not the Council's policies that bothered him, but his own glaring omission from its membership.

'Oh, come now, Mr Bing. Who are you to talk to me of democracy? I would hardly call some of your newspapers' methods egalitarian.'

Bing sighed. 'Look, cut to the chase. What's this all about?'

'Very well, Mr Bing. Have it your way. First, let me tell you why you hate the Council so.'

'If you must.'

'As a man of inordinate wealth and power, you consider yourself the ideal candidate for the Council's ranks, but it seems that they do not agree. No matter how hard you canvass your influential political allies, your inclusion has been systematically overlooked, continually gnawing at you like a boil that can't be lanced.'

'Poppycock!' Bing roared, unsure whether his anger stemmed from hearing the truth or that the stranger had voiced it. 'Apart from Price as the damned leader, the Council's membership is shrouded in mystery. The Council is a self-selected group handpicked from the higher echelons of the land, no less.'

'Are you really telling me that if the Council approached you, you wouldn't be interested?' the caller replied.

'Look. I don't know who you are or how on earth you managed to access this line. Just tell me what this is all about,' replied Bing.

'Ah yes, I'd heard how quickly you become irritated,' said the caller with an edge of contempt that was not lost on Bing. 'I shall get to the point, I would not wish to annoy you any further,' the caller continued dryly. 'I can tell you, Mr Bing, that you are on the verge of being selected for the Council—'

'What! Are you certain?' interjected Bing.

'Your name has been put forward as a candidate that will culminate in a vote at the next meeting. You won't be aware of this, but the voting operates by secret ballot on a blackball system.'

'Is there anything I can do to … er … facilitate the process?' said Bing eagerly.

'That is for you to decide, Mr Bing, but let me tell you this: Henry Price is planning to vote against you. You may have the opportunity to influence his decision over the next few days if you so wish.'

Bing heard a faint click on the line, signifying the conversation was over. As Bing replaced the receiver, his mind was flooded with disparate emotions. He was irritated that the caller had breached his security and that he had also been caught unprepared, yet he was equally exhilarated by the information the caller had volunteered.

He immediately picked up the phone again. 'Cassie, call security and get Valentine up here right away. Cancel the rest of my appointments. I'm going to be busy.'

'But, Mr Bing, what about your schedule? You were supposed to be at a staff meeting ten minutes ago,' exclaimed his secretary, sounding exasperated.

'Yours is not to reason, Cassie,' he said dismissively. 'Tell them downstairs they're running the show today. Oh, and Cassie, send up some fresh coffee, will you?'

Bing sat down and surveyed the early morning skyline. He wondered why anyone would want to divulge information about his possible election to the Council. It was clear that the caller wanted to help by the very nature of their conversation, but he was going to have to think this through very carefully before he acted. With time short, he needed to know when the Council was due to meet.

With just enough time to make a further call before Valentine arrived, Bing picked up the phone and dialled a number he had committed to memory long ago. The call was answered promptly on the second ring.

'Nicolas? It's Hermes here; I wonder if you'd mind sparing me a few moments of your time?'

5

The Nautilus Shell

L ILY WENT STRAIGHT TO her bedroom after leaving her father in his study. She had time to kill before her afternoon lessons with her tutor, Anatoly Volkiev, and without thinking, she sat down on the bed and began flicking through the book her father had just given her. She briefly studied the text but soon realised that any attempt at study would be useless. She was still preoccupied with the petrification spell the intruder had cast. She knew that such an act required a profound knowledge of the very subject she had recently been studying, and although she had already mastered some simple transubstantiation spells, she marvelled how someone could turn a living creature into stone.

Lily thought about the skills she had already mastered but quickly realised that they had always involved transmuting one relatively uniform material into another, no different from the metals that the alchemists-of-old had craved to transform. She could not comprehend how a living animal composed of such varied and complex structures could so quickly be rendered into stone. She suspected that even her father would be hard pressed to master such a spell, despite easily being the most powerful alchemist she had ever known.

Ever since she had been told about the theft, Lily had not been able to settle. How could someone break into the house so effortlessly when it was so well protected? And how could someone walk off with a book that was located such a short distance away from where she took her lessons before nonchalantly casting such a complicated spell? She did not wish to think about it, yet her mind kept returning to these troubling thoughts.

Lily closed the book and deposited it on the bedside table. She looked around the room, taking comfort from her belongings on show, ranging from numerous books neatly arranged by subject on the wall shelves in front of her, to the surfaces of worktops, cabinets and drawers covered with a multitude of her favourite objects that she had collected over the years. As she scanned the room, her eyes settled on a sizeable collection of seashells stacked together in a glass bowl on the windowsill. She was especially fond of the shells of varying shapes and sizes and of the vague memories they stirred in her. She recalled walking along the beach as a child with her mother foraging for the varied wonders washed up on the tide. She rose and selected one particularly evocative item hidden amidst the vast number of cockle, razor, whelk, limpet and periwinkle shells piled high in the bowl. She smiled as she remembered the gentle sparring she had enjoyed with her mother as they vied to find the most unusual specimens. The shell she had singled out was a Snakehead cowrie, the only one of its kind they had ever found. She remembered how envious she had been when her mother had picked it up, desperately wishing she had been the one to find it. As they huddled together on the windswept beach, they both realised they had never seen anything like it. Following her return home, Lily went straight to her books to identify it, and even now she could still remember the thrill of proudly announcing to her mother, not only the shell's common name, but more grandly, its Latin name, *Cypraea Caputserpentis*, a name she could still remember to this day. Quite how a seashell of the Pacific had turned up on a Norfolk beach was something she had never been able to fathom, and the mystery only added to her appreciation of a shell that was more common to the beaches of Hawaii than Hunstanton.

Lily placed the cowrie back into the bowl and turned her attention to a single, much larger shell that stood in pride of place at its side. It was a nautilus, and much like the squirrel, it had been expertly cleaved in half to reveal its beautiful internal shape. She picked it up, recalling a recent lesson with Volkiev when he had requested that she bring the shell with her. She had considered this rather odd at the time as she had been expecting a maths lesson. Until that moment, she had always considered mathematics to be a bit of a chore, but this lesson was entirely different and had opened up a whole new world to her.

Volkiev began the lesson by talking about 'Fibonacci numbers', which seemed somewhat irrelevant to the nautilus that she had taken along with her. Staring blankly through the window, the sound of Volkiev's voice now suddenly came flooding back to her.

'Now, Lily, if you add one and zero, the sum, of course, is one. If you continue the sequence and add the last two numbers together, one plus one, you get two. If you continue this stream, you'll get the following numbers ...' Volkiev said as he picked up a pencil and paper and wrote down the sequence: 1, 1, 2, 3, 5, 8, 13, 21, 34, 55, and 89.

'The Fibonacci sequence continues forever, adding the last two numbers together to find the next,' he continued, rapidly adding a further series of numbers to the list: 144, 233, 377, 610 and 987. 'There's a complicated mathematical formula that allows you to calculate every Fibonacci number based on its order in the sequence. You'll need to learn the equation eventually, but it can wait.'

'But how does this relate to the nautilus shell?' she asked, proffering the shell and looking quizzically at Volkiev.

'What you may find surprising, Lily, is that Fibonacci numbers regularly appear in nature. If you take the ratio of two successive Fibonacci numbers, they approximate to the same number, 1.618, the so-called golden ratio. Now, look at the shell.'

Lily inspected the internal structure of the nautilus. She had always appreciated the beauty of the spiral curve of the shell and the inner chambers that were sequentially added as the animal grew, but she could not understand it in relation to Volkiev's discursive.

'Here,' Volkiev continued, pointing to the shell. 'Imagine drawing a line from the centre in any direction. Next, find two places where the line crosses the shell so that the spiral has gone round just once between these two points. The outer point will be 1.618 times as far from the centre as the adjacent inner point, which tells us that the shell has grown by a factor of the golden ratio in one turn. The curve of the shell is a logarithmic spiral. Look, I'll demonstrate it for you.'

Volkiev picked up the pencil and paper and began to draw. 'See here, Lily, I've drawn two squares of the same size, side by side. If we now draw a third square on top of the other two, it's size is double that of the others. You can continue adding squares, in a clockwise direction, corresponding to the longest side of the rectangular shape,' he said, adding to the drawing as he spoke. 'As you can see, the next square has a relative size of three ... then five ... and then eight. Do you see what's happening?'

'Fibonacci numbers!'

'That's right. If we draw a quarter of a circle in each square, then link it to a similar quarter circle in the next square, and so on, we get this ...'

Volkiev drew the circles as he had described and created a spiral within the squares that reproduced the shape of the nautilus shell. 'This is not unique to the nautilus shell. Such spirals are seen in the shells of snails as well as seashells and in the arrangement of seeds in flowering plants, too.'

'A simple mathematical sequence reproduced in nature. How can that be?' enquired Lily, intrigued.

Volkiev smiled at her. 'That, Lily, is not a question I can even begin to categorise. Some would argue that your question is mathematical; others would assert that it's biological. I would suggest that the question is neither of these but is more likely a philosophical or even theological problem.'

'What do you mean?'

'Perhaps it's a question that only God himself can answer,' said Volkiev mischievously. 'Whatever your thoughts, it's a beautiful conundrum that I'll leave with you. Before I do, you may also like to ponder how frequently Fibonacci numbers and the golden ratio crop up in nature.'

Volkiev produced a picture of a cornflower from the desk and handed it to Lily. 'You can see that the petals form spirals curving to the left and right. Look at the edge of the picture. See if you can count those spiralling to the right as you go outwards.'

Lily studied the photograph while her tutor waited for her to answer. 'I make it 55,' she said eventually.

'Excellent! If you look a little further towards the centre, there are 34 spirals. If you count the spirals curving left and right, the pairs of numbers follow one another in the Fibonacci series.'

Lily shook her head in disbelief. 'That's amazing!'

'Yes. There are many other instances like this in nature. The same numbers keep cropping up time and time again. Take the magnificent sunflower, for example, with 89 and 55 spirals at its edge.'

'How can it be?'

'Precisely! There's much more, though, Lily. Just look carefully at the leaf arrangements or spirals in many plants and vegetables and you'll discover that the number of petals is a Fibonacci number. There are 5 on a buttercup, 8 on a delphinium, 13 on some daisies, and 21 on an aster. The list goes on with 34, 55, and even 89 petals on other flowers. And what of the lily, Lily?' A smile briefly twitched at the corners of Volkiev's mouth following the eloquence of his pun. 'Three petals, which even links you to the Fibonacci sequence!'

Lily replaced the nautilus shell on the windowsill as the memory of the lesson waned. She had often gone back to the shell since then, and each time she had looked at it with great wonder. She had deliberated many times over this peculiar phenomenon since the lesson with Volkiev but she still remained intrigued and a little confused.

She was about to move away from the window when she was distracted by a high-pitched whirring coming from above her head. She looked up and saw a moth frantically fluttering along the architrave. The insect intermittently stopped before resuming its futile attempts to escape through the closed window, and in its moments of immobility, Lily could see its unusual red and black markings that she identified as a cinnabar moth.

For reasons that were unclear to her, she suddenly thought of the petrified squirrel and her earlier meeting with her father. Before she realised what she was doing, she reached out to the moth with her mind, intuitively examining its structure. Maybe it was the analytical way her mind had been working, thinking about Fibonacci numbers, but she now saw the moth with a clarity that she had never experienced before. Rather than a complex amalgamation of internal organs, she saw beyond the moth's macroscopical form. Her mind delved beyond mere structure until she perceived the functioning of each individual cell. Deeper still, her mind continued to probe, appreciating the beauty and form of the individual molecules and their composite atoms. All of this was happening in an instant, yet she was still able to rationalise all that she saw. In a moment of great lucidity, she understood the moth for what it truly was—a hugely complex organic structure comprising of a staggeringly small number of building blocks made up of carbon, oxygen, hydrogen and nitrogen. In that moment, she understood what she had to do.

She began by taking these basic elements and manipulating them into lots, no different than if she had been sorting dominoes by number. She seized the parts she had distilled and began the rearrangement, recollecting the conversation with her father and her assessment of the petrified squirrel.

Then, in the way that he had taught her, Lily summoned an innate power originating deep inside her and simultaneously allowed her mind to open. With a sudden outpouring of energy, she transformed the organic building blocks of the moth into the same silicon dioxide she had recognised in the squirrel.

What had begun with seeing the moth at the window and the meticulous examination of a new world was slowly transformed into an exquisite experience. She could still not quite grasp what was happening and felt as if she were on a long journey. In reality, the whole process lasted no more than a few seconds. As the event unfolded, a startling crash interrupted the trance in which she had found herself. She stared transfixed as, what had recently been an animate creature, plummeted from the air like the stone it had become, shattering into countless pieces on the windowsill in front of her.

Lily gasped with the realisation of what she had just achieved. She reached out to touch the debris lying in front of her and instantly recoiled, feeling heat radiating from the stone, yet intuitively understanding that this resulted from the release of energy accompanying a chemical reaction.

Lily's mind was lost amidst a multitude of contrasting thoughts as she stepped back from the window and sat down on the bed. She tried to rationalise what she had just achieved considering the enormity of what she had always thought to be out of her reach. She was amazed that she had been able to perform the task subliminally in an entirely different manner from all the other transformations she had previously undertaken. If she could apply what she had just learnt in a slightly different way, maybe she could achieve something even more spectacular?

In a sudden rush of expectation, Lily stretched out her hands and studied her palms. During her examination of the moth, she had felt as if she had actually been inside it. She thought briefly and speculated whether she could apply the same principle to herself, beginning with her physiological functions. She visualised her blood vessels and sensed the innumerable red blood cells streaming within them. She perceived the vegetative functions of her internal organs working below any appreciation of her consciousness. Next, she probed even deeper, sensing the mechanisms behind the function of her cells just as she had done with the insect, while she simultaneously concentrated on her hands outstretched in front of her. She stared quizzically as she slowly began to draw her fingertips together until they were almost touching, while sensing her body crammed full of ionised particles and electrons. Then she recalled what she had learnt from Volkiev. Electrical activity was no more than the movement of electrons in a circuit. He had also taught her that electricity was a component of many normal physiological functions. What if she could take control of these phenomena and bring them together?

Slowly but surely, Lily felt a tingling in the ends of her fingers that grew into something more unpleasant. As the pain intensified, she began to feel queasy. She tried to focus her mind as she had done minutes before but she wondered whether she would have to abandon the experiment as the pain became too great.

Her fingers were now unbearably hot, causing a sweat to break out on her brow, but just as she was about to give up, she once again felt the twist of power surging somewhere deep inside her, taking her by surprise as if she had no control over what she was doing.

She looked down at her fingers, and with an air of detachment, she saw a shock of flickering blue light running from one hand to the other. As she witnessed this, the pain eased, and with it, her confidence soared. Ever so slowly, she pulled her fingers apart, but rather than the current diminish, she felt it intensify. Now she was in complete control and could manipulate the force at will. With a sudden jerk, she pulled her fingers apart, and looking straight ahead, she allowed her eyes to converge on the bowl of shells. She could sense the danger, but the exhilaration of what she was doing was too much to be denied. In complete abandonment, she sent a searing bolt of energy hurtling towards the glass. The bowl shattered in a cacophonous tumult, sending shards of glass careering across the room in a lethal cloud of shrapnel.

It was over in an instant, and when Lily surveyed the debris strewn across the floor, she realised how lucky she had been not to injure herself. A fine layer of glass had settled on the carpet amidst innumerable shells scattered haphazardly around the room.

She craned her neck and listened for the sound of Albright's footsteps on the stairs. After what seemed like an age, she sighed in relief. It would take an age for her to clear away the mess, she reflected ruefully, particularly as she would have to sift through the remnants of the bowl to pick up the surviving shells.

As she knelt down, she knew that it would take some time to

rationalise what she had just achieved, but for now, all she felt was a strange combination of exhilaration and confusion. These emotions would pass, of course, but for the time being, what had happened was something she would rather not share with anyone else, not even her father.

6

The Historoscope

HENRY PRICE SAT MOTIONLESS at his study desk, deep in thought. He scratched reflexively at the unsightly scar on his forearm and cursed; it always seemed to itch when he was preoccupied and now was no exception.

It was not often that he had time for contemplation, but he desperately needed to bring some order to his thoughts. Even before the break-in, he had been aware of an ill-defined change in the natural balance and had felt an inexplicable sense of unease for some weeks. The theft of the manuscript had only confirmed his fears that the equilibrium the country had enjoyed following the death of Pearly Black was about to be disturbed. What concerned him most, however, was the absence of any reliable intelligence regarding the threat. He wondered whether the Chief of Internal Security, Nicolas Fox, had come up with anything following Isaacson's brief, but so far, he had heard nothing. Internal Security was an amalgamation of several unclassified departments that had previously been part of Military Intelligence, making Fox pivotal to the effective running of the Council. Fox's jurisdiction and power were virtually limitless with matters pertaining to national security, but when Price had quizzed him at a recent Council meeting, he had offered little to suggest a change in the status quo.

It was with great frustration that Price sat at his desk dwelling on how the thief had procured the book. He was all too well aware that the number of gifted alchemists had dwindled during his lifetime, but this was hardly surprising. The arcane arts that had been such an important part of his upbringing had gradually fallen into disrepute, and this had only been compounded by Black's meddling.

Price had been educated at the last bastion of ancient lore, the Academy of Arcane and Alchemical Arts, but this once famous institute had become no more than a decaying tribute to a disappearing field. His old student friend and associate on the Council, Abel Strange, was the Chief Mentor of the Academy, or the 'Four A's' as it was colloquially dubbed by its former pupils. Despite Strange's attempts to maintain the Academy's once pre-eminent standing, its influence was slowly diminishing through a lack of interest, and more importantly, investment.

The few respected individuals still actively practising alchemy were well known to Price, but the thought that the burglary could be linked with a friend or acquaintance was not something he could countenance. There had always been those who had used their skills in the pursuit of darker aspects of alchemical lore, but they were either dead or had vanished. Sadly, the hope of rounding up the Order's ringleaders after Black's death had never materialised, and despite the Council's vigilance, Black's allies had managed to go to ground so successfully in the aftermath of his demise that any trail to locate them had long since turned cold.

Price could not help thinking that the recent theft was, in some way, linked to the Order of Eternal Enlightenment, but how and in whose guise, he just could not guess. The rise of the Order had been meteoric, carried on a swell of misconception by the charisma of their leader. What was so astonishing when all of the facts were laid bare was that so little was known about the group, including its infrastructure, or more importantly, its members. Rumour and hearsay had pointed the finger of suspicion in the direction of some prominent figures around the time, but any link had quickly dissipated after Black's death. It was most frustrating that he had never discovered the Order's true motives, and although his confederates on the Council largely assumed that Black had been driven by a quest for power, Price remained unconvinced, always suspicious of a more abstruse goal.

Price got up and crossed to a small mirror hidden under the eaves. He stooped to survey his reflection and was dismayed to see dark rings gathered around his eyes like storm clouds. He ran his fingers through his unkempt shock of hair in a futile attempt to bring it under control. He had not shaved, and the grey flecks scattered throughout the stubble on his chin only accentuated the dishevelled appearance that stared back at him from the mirror.

Price briefly contemplated tidying himself up before leaving to visit his long-time friend, Cornelius Spydre, but then thought better of it. Spydre kept an antiquarian bookshop in the city and was a wealth of information on any subject to do with old and rare books, and was just the person to enlist under the circumstances. Price had sent him a message regarding the stolen book, and with it, some notes he had made when he had first acquired it. He was convinced that if anyone could help, it was Cornelius, and he wondered speculatively whether the notes would enable his friend to discover something he had missed.

Price returned to the desk and sat down. He lifted the Historoscope from its stand to while away some time before departing for the city, passing the instrument pensively from one hand to the other as if deciding what to do with it next. The Historoscope was undoubtedly his favourite invention, and although it was a valuable tool, Price was often just as happy to look at the beautiful designs filigreed in silver and gold braid in a multitude of shapes and sizes on its surface. The intricate network of metals on the instrument's housing flowed in an attractive design, creating patterns within patterns that changed perspective in varying lights.

While he was scrutinising the instrument, the sun appeared from behind a bank of thick clouds and cascaded through the skylight above the desk, catching the instrument in a swathe of light. The reflections cast by the instrument's iridescent surface were scattered around the room and threw off dancing lights that flitted across the walls as if a swarm of fireflies had been released into the room, flying haphazardly in all directions. Price looked on entranced as he followed the shimmering lights, but then, the sun disappeared and the moment was lost.

Price sighed after the all too brief distraction and returned his attention to the instrument. He had assembled the Historoscope many years before as a means of storing thoughts and memories derived from the minds of friends, allies and even enemies, to create a coherent and permanent record of past events. It was an ingenious device that he had conceived by fusing scientific methodology with obscure alchemical learning, but the instrument had only become a reality following his collusion with Saskia Schalk, his late lamented lover and Lily's mother.

The instrument worked in conjunction with a transparent flexible cap made of a gel formed via a laborious alchemical process. Thousands of minute electrodes were scattered about the cap, which on close inspection could be seen as tiny black dots standing proud of the opaque matrix. When applied to the scalp, the electrodes picked up small changes in electrical activity emanating from deep within the skull. Price had designed the contraption so that whenever a memory was recalled, the unique electrical pattern corresponding with neuronal and synaptic brainwave activity was picked up and fed into the instrument by the external metallic circuitry. The core of the Historoscope was manufactured from the manipulation of electrum and copper in a smelting process derived from an old alchemical technique, giving rise to a unique metal alloy that, in essence, acted as a central processing unit, receiving data from the cap and collating it into a visual representation of the memory. A single thought or memory created a simplistic image that could be visualised through the eyepiece, but even Price had been surprised to discover that the greater the number of individuals recalling a particular event, the more sophisticated the resultant image.

Over the years, Price had built up a comprehensive database of memories, creating a stored archive of past events that had proved invaluable in the Council's crusade against the Order. Viewing past scenes even allowed Price to discover subtleties relating to events that he had missed at the time. He was well aware of what a valuable tool the instrument could be but also knew that it was not infallible. Past events may have been misinterpreted or not recalled clearly enough, and it was quite possible that some memories were festooned with embellishments, others with deficiencies, and some, no doubt, stored as downright lies. Nonetheless, the greater the number of memories corroborating a particular event meant that rogue or unreliable sources were much more likely to be excluded. What he found frustrating, however, was that the most valuable information often only came from one or two unreliable sources. Even so, he had still managed to build up a coherent, chronological representation of the near-distant past that he anticipated would be of value in countering any future threat.

Using the Historoscope required a great deal of concentration, and with this in mind, Price cleared his thoughts. He picked up the cap and slipped it onto his head. He redoubled his attention as he placed the instrument to his eye. The screen was blank, but after a brief interlude, a mist of swirling lights appeared on the screen that slowly coalesced into a recognisable image. It was not long before he identified the outline of three teenage boys sitting on a wall in front of an imposing Gothic building with pointed arches and vaults set amidst tall, bell towers. It was his old alma mater, the Academy of Arcane and Alchemical Arts. The backdrop blurred as the scene converged upon the boys who appeared to be in their late teens and were dressed in drab, rather formal robes that seemed inappropriate given the glaring sun that was beating down. The boys' discussion was becoming more and more animated until one of the trio jumped up from the wall, seemingly having lost his cool. He raised a hand and pointed fixedly at one of the other boys still sitting on the wall in a gesture that was undoubtedly hostile. When he prodded a finger forcibly against the boy's chest, it seemed as if the boy would, at any minute, lose his balance and topple over the wall onto the beautifully manicured lawn six feet below him.

Price recognised himself as the boy sitting on the wall under duress. He shook his head, reflecting ruefully how he had aged in the past twenty years.

He stared intently through the eyepiece at his aggressor. The angry young man had long, wavy, dark hair that fell in curls onto the lapels of his gown and soft, boyish features that persisted despite the sprouting shadow of a moustache. His face radiated an angelic charm that contrasted starkly with his actions. His bright blue eyes shone fiercely, and despite a brief flash hinting at incipient violence, the boy's expression quickly flitted back to its earlier benign disposition.

'Henry, my dear fellow, I don't believe we should be quarrelling like this on such a beautiful day,' said the boy in a soft, vaguely melodic manner.

Although Price knew the instrument was generating impulses through the cap and creating the impression of the boy's voice inside his head, it seemed as if he was back there on that very day, listening to the words of Pearly Black.

At that moment, the third boy, who had been watching the exchanges with growing concern, jumped to his feet and positioned himself resolutely between the pair. He absent-mindedly pushed his spectacles onto the bridge of his nose before laying hands on the boys' shoulders, smiling at them in turn before addressing Price. 'Pearly's right, this is no time for arguing, especially over a ... er, girl,' he said.

Once again Price was taken aback by the realism of the images and the sound of Abel Strange's voice as the interjector. He marvelled at the scene playing out before him when he saw his own lips move in response to his fellow student. 'I didn't raise the issue as you well know, Abel. I can't help it if Pearly's jealous of the time I've been spending with Saskia.'

At these words, Black visibly tensed as if readying himself for action.

'I've tried to reassure him that we've been studying together and nothing else,' Price continued, pointedly ignoring Black. 'I'll repeat this one last time. Saskia and I have been pursuing an area of mutual interest and nothing more,' he said in a vaguely threatening manner.

'If that's the case then why not tell me what you're so interested in?' enquired Black.

While listening and watching through the Historoscope, Price detected an undercurrent of resentment that betrayed the calm expression on Black's face, despite his recollection of the event being somewhat different from the scene he was witnessing. He briefly reflected on Strange's interpretation of what had happened and assumed that his friend's memory must have been stronger and subtly different from his own in several ways.

Price watched transfixed as his doppelgänger jumped down from the wall, set himself in front of Black and said, 'Saskia wants to keep our work to ourselves. I aim to honour her trust and I'm not prepared to discuss it with anyone else, and that includes you, Pearly. I suggest that, if you wish to know more, you should take this conversation up with her.'

Price turned his back on the boys and made his way towards the building, not stopping to look back as he disappeared through a high, pointed archway.

Strange looked uneasily at Black, unsure of how he was about to react. 'I'm, er, sure that Henry is telling the truth, Pearly. I don't believe he's purposely misleading you.'

A flash of anger passed across Black's face, but just as quickly disappeared. 'Don't be so naive, Abel. You always take things at face value. Maybe that's why people take advantage of you,' he said in a manner that was not unkind. 'Perhaps I, too, am at fault. My mind's different from yours. I tend to search for motives that aren't always there. Somehow, though, I don't trust Henry in this; I believe he's hiding something. I'll speak to Saskia about it again, but, so far, she's been reluctant to talk to me about their meetings.'

The conversation seemed to be over, and moments later, the scene faded, leaving a blank void on the Historoscope's screen.

Price returned the instrument to its stand. As he removed the cap, his eyes turned reflexively towards a silver-framed photograph that held pride of place on the desk. He took the picture-frame in his hands and looked intently at the photograph, seeing a younger version of himself standing in the background with his arms draped around the shoulders of an alluring young woman with long, curly black hair. She was smiling intently with a radiance that illuminated her attractive features and implied that the photograph had been taken at a time of great happiness. Cradled in her arms was a baby girl, no more than a few months old. The woman was looking down at the child, who seemed to be gazing back into her eyes.

Price continued to stare at the picture that showed him standing behind Saskia and Lily, but it was not long before a film of tears obscured his view of the two people he loved most. He wiped his eyes with a handkerchief just in time to prevent the tears from spilling onto his cheeks. With a sigh, he placed the frame back into its space amidst the clutter on his desk. He sat for a while reminiscing about the happiest period in his life before he shook himself down and got up from the chair.

This is no time for melancholia, he told himself. He looked briefly at the clock suspended on the wall with its long pendulum swinging silently below it before striding purposefully from the room, determined to bring some respectability to his appearance before his meeting with Spydre.

7

THE STONE OF MADNESS

Number 34, Curiosity Street

A N HOUR LATER, PRICE was walking briskly along the northern
embankment of the Thames. The sky was a dramatic shade
of gunmetal. The clouds were low and foreboding with dampness
in the air, hinting at impending rain. He stopped and looked across
the river. A chill easterly wind was gusting across the water causing
it to roll and boil. Water traffic was sporadic apart from the
occasional barge toiling upriver against the current. Price briefly
contemplated heading down the adjacent gangway to take the
vessel stationed there, but thought better of it. The water taxi
would save time, but he was in no hurry. Despite the buffeting icy
wind, he was enjoying the fresh air and the sense of purification
that went with it, cleansing him of the uneasy thoughts that
lingered following the scenes he had viewed on the Historoscope.

Price watched a solitary gull perched on a buoy looking for easy
pickings in the middle of the fast-flowing river. The large bird
hesitated before pushing off into the air. He heard it call with a
lone, harsh cry before it headed towards him, then wheel away
and glide on the breeze before disappearing into the ever-
increasing gloom on the opposite bank.

Price turned away and crossed the road into a secluded side
street, which opened onto a tree-lined square. A crowd was
gathered there, milling around several market stalls with brightly
coloured awnings billowing in the freshening breeze. He wondered
what was attracting their attention and set off towards the throng.

He edged into a small space between two stalls to peer over the shoulder of an onlooker and was intrigued to see a man with a long, grey beard solemnly dealing cards to a group of men gathered around a trestle table covered in worn baize. The men were examining their cards while the onlookers encouraged them to bet far more than they could afford, judging by their unkempt looks and shabby attire. The dealer asked each player whether they wished to keep their card or exchange it with the person next to them. Then, after some fearsome betting, the cards were turned face-up, and the person with the card bearing the highest value took the winnings. Price was amazed at the stakes involved in what was, after all, a simple game of chance. The game was engrossing for all that and he found himself drawn into the spectacle because of the sheer intensity of the play.

Despite trying to fathom out the various denominations of the cards, he struggled to work out how the winning card was determined, even after watching several hands trying to puzzle it out. The cards were beautifully hand-painted with intricate artwork depicting fantastical creatures of obscure and bizarre forms. Eventually, Price began to identify a pattern to the play, but he was still bemused by the hierarchy of cards grouped into four suits of air, fire, water and earth.

A card portraying a terrifying sea serpent named Yofune-Nushi won the first hand, but in the next game, when the same card appeared again, it lost to a rather odd-looking bird called the Ouzelum, which seemed to be flying backwards. Every now and again a great shout went up as money exchanged hands. Judging by their careworn expressions, Price suspected that the men had been playing for some time, but even in the brief period since his arrival, he could sense the game building into a feverish climax.

As he watched, he sensed a movement a dozen paces behind him. To the casual observer, it was the innocuous act of a market browser, but to Price, it was a sign that someone was watching him. He recalled his recent conversation with Lily concerning psychic defence and felt a thrill of excitement course through his body. In the space of a few seconds, a leisurely stroll had turned into something menacing, although what threat he was facing, he could only guess.

He continued to watch the game with feigned nonchalance. The man with the grey beard was dealing another hand of cards, and while he expertly flicked the cards across the table, Price took the opportunity to study the onlooker loitering behind him in the shadowy reflection of the dealer's glasses. The man was hanging back, aimlessly examining the cheap goods laid out before him, and did not appear intent on coming closer. Price relaxed a little; perhaps the man was merely tailing him. He made up his mind to find out and pulled away from the game.

In the time since Price had arrived at the market, it had started to drizzle. He elbowed his way through the throng and crossed the square. He passed a row of deserted stalls and left by a narrow street diagonally opposite to his entry point. He listened intently for the sound of pursuit but all he heard was the echo of his own steps on the cobbled paving stones. As he turned a corner, he veered off into the recessed doorway of a terraced house and waited. In the silence that followed, he briefly wondered whether he had been mistaken, but while he was debating whether to emerge and continue his journey, he heard footsteps, irregular and circumspect, and not the sound of a straggler heading home to escape the rain.

He waited until the pursuer was almost upon him before he sprang from the alcove, bringing him face to face with a small, shabbily dressed man, whose expression showed, first surprise, and then fear. The look on the man's face was both an admission of guilt and an indication that he had recognised Price. As the man turned to flee, Price, anticipating the move, threw out a hand and grabbed him by the sleeve of his tattered jacket.

Price stared into the man's eyes and spoke calmly. 'Make no attempt to escape, and I won't hurt you. I know you followed me into the market. What do you want?'

The man lowered his head under Price's intense gaze and looked down at the wet pavement. 'I ... I wasn't following you, sir,' he replied nervously.

The man was poor at hiding the lie and Price noted the telltale signs etched on his face: the brief dilation of his pupils, beads of sweat on his brow and the rapid pulsation of an artery at his temple.

As he studied the man, Price suddenly realised that, not only was he lying, there was something else. In a sudden blur, the man reached into his jacket, and with surprising agility, brandished a pistol, which he lifted uncertainly and pointed towards him.

Price did not flinch but smiled casually at the man, fuming with himself at having misread the signs. 'Don't be foolish. You cannot hurt me,' he said in a voice that was calm and resolute. He reached out calmly with a free hand and gestured to the man to hand over the weapon.

The man laughed nervously, and from the whites of his knuckles, Price could tell that he was squeezing the trigger.

'Back off, and I won't fire this thing,' the man called out, his voice wavering with uncertainty in tandem with the gun shaking in his hand.

Price readied himself. In an instant, he unfurled a hand as if merely casting something in the man's direction. The sudden movement startled the man, and as he backed off, the gun discharged, sending out a loud report at precisely the moment the gun flew from his hands.

The weapon spun through the air and fell into the gutter. The man looked blankly at Price assuming that the weapon's recoil had kicked it from his hands. As he waited for the inevitable fall of his target, he was shocked to see Price still standing there, staring impassively back at him in a calm and assuring manner.

The man looked crestfallen, unable to comprehend what had happened.

'You've just witnessed power that is well beyond you, my friend. Had I so chosen, I could have struck you dead where you stand, but luckily for you, rather than use my abilities in such a nihilistic fashion, I created a shield.'

The man shook his head, awestruck. 'How?'

'I'm only going to tell you so that you know *exactly* what you're up against. Do you understand?'

The man nodded mutely.

'Very well. The instant I knew you were about to shoot, I sent a pulse of electromagnetic energy flying from my hand like an invisible barrier. It rushed towards you like a wave, deflecting both the bullet and your weapon harmlessly away. Now, I expect complete co-operation. Do I make myself clear?'

The man nodded again.

'I assume you also appreciate that lying is pointless. Tell me the truth, and you may yet walk away from here unharmed. Now, firstly, what's your name?'

The man met Price's gaze then hesitated as if he was weighing something up before he began to speak as quickly as he could get his words out. 'My name's Joseph McCall. I was informed that you'd be travelling this way and that I was to wait for you down by the river. I—'

'Who are you working for?'

'I received a phone call yesterday from a man I've done jobs for in the past. I was put in touch with him some months ago ... and before you ask, we've never met. He knows I'm suitably qualified to undertake jobs of a certain, er ... sensitive nature. He pays me for doing simple tasks ... nothing dangerous, usually,' said McCall.

'Tell me then. What precisely were your instructions for today?'

'I was told to track you. I knew you'd be travelling alone. I followed you to the market, although I don't understand how you spotted me. You never once looked back. Were you warned about me?'

'I'm asking the questions,' said Price with a wry smile. 'But no, for your information, I was not. As you've already witnessed, I have skills well beyond your comprehension. Now, what else were you meant to do?'

'I was to follow you and report back on your destination. I was also instructed to find out the purpose of your visit.'

'How do you make contact with this mysterious employer of yours?'

'I'm sent a number to call. It's never the same. I leave a message, and the man rings me back.'

'And you have no idea who you're supplying this information to?' demanded Price incredulously.

'All I know is that he pays well,' replied McCall.

Price thought for a moment. There was not much more he could glean from questioning this man, but he still might be of use. 'Joseph, listen carefully. Do as I say, and you may yet avoid getting into trouble with either your contact or, more importantly, me. I want you to make the phone call as normal and say that I managed to give you the slip. I also want you to write down the number you're meant to call,' said Price, withdrawing a pencil and a small scrap of paper from his pocket.

McCall took the paper and quickly wrote down a number.

'I can assure you that I'll not call this number. I've friends in high places that can trace it without anyone knowing. I don't suppose your employer will be overly pleased that you failed in your task, but you may yet be able to work for him again if he's not too displeased.'

Price examined the number that McCall had scrawled on the paper before he returned it to a pocket. 'I suggest you go back in the direction you came,' he instructed, pointing towards the marketplace. 'I presume you're not foolish enough to follow me again?'

McCall shook his head and turned quickly on his heels without glancing back. Price watched until the man had disappeared before he set off briskly in the opposite direction.

*

Fifteen minutes later, Price arrived in a quiet part of the East End, satisfied that he had not been followed. The drizzle had become more persistent, but the narrow road was so tightly packed with tall, old buildings, it was surprisingly dry, despite the rain. As he looked up to survey the deepening gloom, he noted a placard on the adjacent wall; Curiosity Street, it read. It was some time since he had last visited here, but the street remained unchanged and as familiar as it had been then with shops of varying kinds interspersed with residential properties sporting regal doors. The street was quiet apart from the occasional browser moving lazily from window to window, enjoying the solitude and unhurried luxury of examining the wares on display.

Price bustled along the street until he reached an inauspicious shop, highlighted by a fading sign above the door that lay askew. It was written quite plainly and read, No. 34, Antiquarian Books – Bought and Sold. His eyes darted to the opulent sign overhanging the impressive shop next door, which was exhibiting exquisite jewellery of obvious expense in its window. He smiled to himself at the stark contrast with Spydre's shop where the glass panes were caked with grime, making it impossible to read the words displayed in the old manuscripts open on stands. He shook his head; he suspected that no one ever gave the shop a second glance.

Price gave the door a hefty shove and entered a dimly lit vestibule that was even less hospitable than the shop's exterior. He stumbled on a step as he passed below a low arch that took him into a small room crowded with books of all shapes and sizes, irregularly arranged from floor to ceiling that left no part of the walls uncovered. The room was damp and cool, and a musty smell permeated his nostrils causing him to cough and splutter. It was difficult to see beyond an arm's length, but his eyes slowly adjusted to the light emanating from a lamp on a small reading desk surrounded by towering bookshelves. Price listened for signs of life as he approached the desk. A large book lay open amongst a haphazard array of writing implements and manuscripts, precariously balanced on the table's edge. He picked up a magnifying glass next to the book and studied the beautifully illustrated anatomical plates of reptiles and lizards on show, marvelling at the skill that had gone into creating the detailed artwork.

Price sat down and waited patiently on a rickety wooden chair, closing his eyes as if in meditation. He sat in silence without moving, but eventually, he stirred when he heard a dull, muffled sound behind him and felt a faint movement of air across the back of his neck. He turned in time to see a bookcase swinging silently towards him, revealing a communicating corridor leading further back into the shop. The floor sloped upwards from an equally haphazard room to the rear, and Price glimpsed further shelves and stacks of books behind a stooped figure brandishing a book in his leading hand while dragging a chair awkwardly through the entrance with the other.

The man shuffled into the room but did not acknowledge Price, his concentration seemingly engaged on walking without stumbling. He pulled the chair erratically up to the desk, and set the book down on the table with a trembling hand. The fine tremor did not stop as he sat down and he took some time to compose himself before he looked into the face of the visitor sitting opposite. Their eyes met, and at last, Spydre seemed to focus on his surroundings, extending a gnarled hand in Price's direction.

Price started at how much his friend had aged since their last meeting before reciprocating Spydre's gesture, closing his grip gently around the man's deformed digits in a manner full of warmth. 'My dear Cornelius, it's been too long. It's *so* good to see you.'

Spydre gave a lop-sided grin, which made him look grotesque in the dim light. His face was heavily lined on one side, yet oddly free of creases on the other. His white, leonine hair, ruthlessly irregular and thinning on top, revealed an alabaster skin stretched like parchment across his scalp. 'It, too, is good to see you, my friend,' he replied in his habitual precise and formal manner.

When Spydre spoke, the effect of a recent palsy was plain for Price to see with the movement on one side of his face only serving to accentuate the paralysis of the muscles on the other.

'And how is Lily?' said Spydre eagerly. 'Is she well?'

Price placed his hand softly on top of the flexed hand of his friend and smiled. 'Yes, she is, Cornelius, but you know how it is with teenage girls. She's growing up quickly, and though she's only just beginning to realise it, she has talents that surpass even my expectations. Her mother was unique in her abilities, as you well know, but Lily has an aptitude for learning that outweighs any that I've encountered in one so young.'

69

He paused to examine Spydre's features and noted the deep hollows above his cheekbones that had been absent at their last meeting. A drab pullover, darned at the elbows, hung loosely about the man's skeletal frame.

'She'd like to come and see you. She feels guilty that it's been so long.'

'And so she should,' Spydre replied, his eyes sparkling with amusement.

'But what news of you, Cornelius?' enquired Price with some trepidation.

Spydre hesitated before he replied. 'Well, as you can see, I barely manage with my gammy leg and this useless arm,' he said, holding up a withered limb with his other hand, 'but I still have my books for company. Who could ask for more? I do not want for much, and it is always nice to receive the occasional visitor.'

Price was not sure whether he detected a hint of reproach in his friend's voice, and realised with some embarrassment that it had been several months since his own last visit.

The two men sat in silence before Spydre took up the conversation. 'I received your message, was it yesterday, or the day before? I do find it difficult to remember these things, Henry. I believe a book was stolen from you, and I suspect from the way your note was written that it was rather important. Am I right?'

'Yes, Cornelius, I've a rather pressing need of your help, but who better to come to than the most learned man that still lives!'

'You flatter me, Henry, but you should have said, "the most learned man that barely lives"!' replied Spydre, accompanying his words with a hollow laugh. 'I find it intriguing that there was only one item stolen from your magnificent collection of books. What do you know of Piotrowski?'

'Very little, in truth. I wrote the notes you received some years ago while I was in Italy researching early alchemical practices. Piotrowski was part of an obscure group of alchemists known as the Esoteric Brotherhood. They were based around Amsterdam during the sixteenth century, and it was rumoured that they were involved in areas of occult hermetical practice. Piotrowski's manuscript is the only written record linked to the Esoteric Brotherhood known to have survived into the modern era, and so it was naturally of interest to me, although I'm afraid I found it all rather disappointing. Despite the speculation that Piotrowski had been carrying out research into obscure alchemical lore, his writing did little to substantiate this. The book contains many veiled references to recondite alchemy, but little to back it up in practice. Not long after Piotrowski completed his work, he disappeared amidst rumours that he was dispatched by religious zealots. Whether this is true or not, I don't know.'

'So if you do not hold Piotrowski's work in any great esteem, why are you so concerned?'

Price smiled ruefully at his old friend. 'That's where I was rather hoping you could help me out, Cornelius. I had a similar discussion with the Cabinet Secretary some days ago. He was not impressed by my ambiguity.'

'Why?'

'This manuscript baffles me, I can't deny it. I can't stress how difficult it should be for someone to gain entry to my house, yet whoever accomplished it did so effortlessly. Not only that, but they also cast a petrification charm with equal apparent ease. Such ability is seldom encountered these days. Whoever wanted Piotrowski's work is not someone to be trifled with.'

'I see. Well, it just so happens that I may have something for you. Before I start, Henry, please forgive me. Would you like some refreshment?'

Price shook his head, eager to hear what his friend had to say.

'Come now, Henry, I am sure you would like to enjoy a glass with me. There, just next to your right hand,' said Spydre, pointing awkwardly with his deformed hand at the large book he had arrived with.

Price leaned over to lift the surprisingly heavy book. He set it down in front of Spydre, scattering several pencils and pieces of chalk in the process. Spydre opened the book to reveal, not the spine or pages as Price had been expecting, but a hollow interior containing a green bottle and two whisky tumblers.

Spydre took out the liquor bottle and proffered it to his guest. 'Lagavulin. A 16-year-old single malt, ideal for many occasions, but particularly a discourse between old friends. Did you know that this fine whisky comes from one of the oldest distilleries in Scotland, made from the crystal-clear waters of the Solum lochs in Islay?' he said, removing the glasses but struggling to find a space for them on the cluttered table.

Price poured a generous measure into each glass. 'A fine choice, indeed. Your good health, Cornelius,' he said, lifting a glass and gently tapping that of his friend's. He inhaled the strong peaty aroma and took a sip that produced a familiar burning sensation on the back of his throat.

'*Slainte Mhath*, as they say in the Glens,' Spydre replied, quaffing the whisky in a single gulp before proffering his empty glass in Price's direction with a subtle nod of his head at the bottle. He waited patiently for Price to refill the glass before he began. 'You may be interested to hear that your version of Piotrowski's manuscript was incomplete or, at least, there is another copy that contains additional information to your own. Firstly, though, I would like to begin with some background,' said Spydre.

'Another copy? But—'

Spydre held up a hand. 'All in good time, my friend.'

Price shuffled uneasily in his chair, eager to get to the crux of the matter, but he knew from experience that a little forbearance now would reap its rewards later.

Spydre took another drink but this time somewhat circumspectly. He stared for some minutes in the dim light at the patterns left by the alcohol on the inside of the glass, gently swilling the flame coloured liquid around and around before returning the glass to his lips and draining the contents. This time, he did not ask for a refill. He remained silent for some moments before lifting his badly clawed hand and setting it softly down with the other. 'Before we discuss Piotrowski, I would like to begin some years before his birth. I believe it is relevant to the tale I have to tell,' he said, evidently enjoying himself.

Spydre settled back in the chair as if he expected to be there for some time. 'You are familiar with the term Hermetic Philosophy,' he said matter-of-factly, 'or, as I prefer to call it, Hermeticism.'

Price smiled indulgently, encouraging Spydre to continue.

'Hermeticism began as a set of philosophical and religious beliefs that are believed to have originated as a fusion of ancient Greek and Egyptian teachings. It is said to contain secret wisdom based upon the writings of Hermes Trismegistus, a name coined by Greek neo-Platonists for the Egyptian god, Thoth, who was said to be a great teacher of religion, magic and alchemy.

'The teachings of Hermes Trismegistus were popular until the fifth century when they fell out of favour and largely disappeared from Western culture until they were rediscovered in Byzantine texts in Italy during the Renaissance. In the late fifteenth century, at the beginning of the Medici political dynasty, a philosopher by the name of Marsilo Ficino translated a collection of Greek texts known as the Corpus Hermeticum from Latin, heralding the reintroduction of Hermeticism into European thinking. The text makes reference to the Emerald Tablet of Hermes Trismegistus and the three parts of wisdom of the whole universe. This triad of alchemy, astrology and theurgy forms the basis of the name Hermes Trismegistus, or Hermes the thrice greatest, and represents the areas in which his knowledge was said to be unrivalled.'

'Cornelius, I hate to disappoint you, but you're merely regurgitating what is taught to students at the Academy during their formative years. Where exactly is all this leading?' enquired Price, trying not to sound too exasperated.

'Come now, Henry, why not pander to the foibles of an old man? I am merely setting the scene. I will ignore your impatience.'

Spydre reached over for the, by now, half-empty whisky bottle and refilled his glass. He did not, however, take a drink, but merely set the glass down in front of him before he continued.

'The reintroduction of Hermeticism into European culture at this time gave rise to many groups, each with remarkably divergent philosophies. The basis of Hermeticism taught that there was only one God, but also subscribed to the existence of other beings such as angels and demons, masters and elementals. The three parts of the wisdom of the whole universe led to various schools of thought, and not surprisingly, some markedly distinct groups emerged, the majority of whom studied various aspects of alchemy and astrology.

'However, it was the third area, theurgy, in which research and learning moved in decidedly different directions. Theurgy was subdivided, at its simplest level, into two types of magic that were poles apart.'

'Yes,' Price agreed. 'Divine magic, a branch of alchemy that was reliant on alliances between virtuous spirits such as angels and gods, and Goëtia, or black magic, which referred to the evocation of evil spirits or demons.'

'Indeed. Not surprisingly, Hermeticism was fervently opposed by the Church, and it was not long before it became part of the occult underworld as secretive brotherhoods and cults.'

Price nodded. 'Yes, they were dangerous times, there's no doubt about it. It was the association between alchemy in its purest sense and the darker arts that fell foul of the Church. The study of alchemy became shrouded in mystery and was often undertaken in secret. Individuals practising what we'd now consider valuable areas of alchemical research were considered blasphemous. For this reason, a ragtag mixture of cults and brotherhoods arose, giving rise to disparate groups, some of whom pursued valid areas of science, while others became embroiled in darker aspects of the occult.'

'Precisely,' agreed Spydre, 'and it was just such a group—the Esoteric Brotherhood—that arose towards the end of the fifteenth century, and ultimately attracted the likes of one Alfons Piotrowski.'

'What do you know of Esotericism, Cornelius?'

'That is not such an easy question to answer, as well you know, Henry,' replied Spydre, his attempt at a sardonic grin distorting his misshapen features.

'Esotericism per se was not a single tradition, but an

amalgamation of various ideals and beliefs that first became manifest during the Renaissance. Ask any number of intellectuals to define it, and you will receive many different interpretations. To some, the word is synonymous with the occult, while, to others, it is associated with the secret teachings of the arcane. In religious circles, Esotericism came to be associated with the understanding of religious principles through experiment rather than dogma. For some, it is one and the same as Hermeticism, but for me, it represents a fusion of many concepts. I believe it evolved from an occult philosophy of the Renaissance and diverged into areas as varied as Alchemy, Paracelsianism, Rosicrucianism, Kabbalah, Theosophy, and more latterly, various occultist sects of the nineteenth and twentieth century.'

'And what about the Esoteric Brotherhood itself?' Price asked.

'Ah, now that is a question to which you know as much, or perhaps, I suspect, as little, as I do.'

'Yes,' agreed Price. 'Not much is known of the Brotherhood, I'm afraid, but there's one name that stands out. Piotrowski's manuscript makes reference to certain members, but the majority of the names are insignificant. Hieronymus Bosch is still considered one of the greatest Dutch artists ever to have lived. Examples of his work hang in some of the most famous galleries throughout the world, yet what is not generally known is that he was also one of the founder members of the Esoteric Brotherhood.'

Spydre nodded sagely. 'As I learnt from your notes. What else do you know?'

'Bosch was born in 's-Hertogenbosch in 1451 and spent most of his life there. He was a prolific painter known for his enigmatic panels illustrating complex religious subjects containing fantastic, often demonic, imagery with references to astrology, folklore, witchcraft and alchemy, in addition to the theme of the Antichrist. Piotrowski makes reference to Bosch in his manuscript and alludes to hidden meanings and secret messages hidden in his work. Art historians have consistently debated the nature of Bosch's work, but his association with a brotherhood of hermetical cultists is largely unknown. For this reason, Bosch's work is widely interpreted as a labyrinth of late medieval Christian iconography with a preoccupation for the human propensity to commit sin in defiance of God, as well as with God's eternal damnation of lost souls in hell as a fateful consequence of human folly.'

'And if I understand you correctly, Henry, what you are suggesting is that if we re-examine Bosch's work in light of his link with Hermeticism, it is possible that there may be alternative interpretations of his works.'

'Precisely! It may be that information fundamental to the Esoteric Brotherhood was hidden in Bosch's work as a means of relaying information to the brethren without incurring the wrath of outsiders, especially the Church. What better way of encoding information to other occultists than hidden in art supposedly purporting to tackle big religious themes of the time. Ingenious, I'd say.'

'You may be right. It is definitely worth researching. Give me some time and I will see what I can come up with,' Spydre said excitedly. 'After all, it is not as if I will be going anywhere,' he added, surveying the book-filled room and giving Price another skewed grin.

Price smiled sympathetically and said, 'You mentioned earlier that the stolen manuscript was incomplete.'

Spydre nodded. 'Remember the notes that you sent me? You highlighted an inscription written in Latin at the start of the book.'

'I remember,' said Price.

'The inscription intrigues me,' continued Spydre. 'As you may recall, written inside the front cover are the words "cave ab homine unus libri", which translate to "beware the man of one book".'

'At first, I thought this was merely a straightforward proverb— albeit one I had never heard before—indicating a man who is not wise, but the deeper I delved into the book, the more I began to wonder. It is possible that the phrase is not so much a statement but more a warning. Eventually, I came round to the possibility that Piotrowski was hinting at the existence of a second copy of the manuscript.'

'Go on, Cornelius,' Price urged.

'I took the liberty of contacting an old friend of mine, Markus De Wolff. He is the curator of the Bibliotheca Philosophica Hermetica in Amsterdam. It is a small, privately funded library that contains many books of great scientific and artistic value and houses the single biggest collection of books in the world pertaining to the Hermetic tradition. I was surprised to learn that Markus knew of the book. He told me that only two copies were ever written, and amazingly, a copy is held there. I proceeded to quiz him a little more assiduously and discovered that the book residing with him is somewhat different from your own.'

Price raised his eyebrows but passed no comment.

'In the notes you sent me, and correct me if I am wrong, Henry, you state that the text is one hundred and eighty pages long.'

'If that's what I wrote then I've no reason to doubt it,' replied Price.

'Good. Now, I hope you do not mind, but I took the liberty of discussing your notes with Markus. What is interesting is that the book held in Amsterdam is longer by a single page, raising a very important question: why should the only two copies of this book be different?' Spydre took a sip of scotch and smacked his lips. 'The book clearly interested you at some stage, judging by the extensive notes you made. Why *exactly* is that?'

'It was a long time ago, and it reawakens some memories that, in some ways, I'd rather leave undisturbed. Nonetheless, I fear I no longer have a choice in the matter.

'I acquired the book some years ago. It was at a time when the Order of Eternal Enlightenment was gaining popularity and followers at will, but I knew Pearly Black and his motives all too well. I set up the Council to counter the threat but gaining evidence to prove Black's true motives was difficult. I set out to learn all I could of the Order, which took me on a trail that eventually led back to the Esoteric Brotherhood.'

'Which clearly demonstrates a link between the Order and Piotrowski's manuscript. How very interesting!' said Spydre, evidently enjoying the conversation. 'What did you find out?'

77

'The Esoteric Brotherhood began as a sect of individuals interested in only the darker aspects of Hermeticism. They gradually evolved into an underground brotherhood of occultists who, it was rumoured, made a startling alchemical discovery. This secret was made accessible to only the highest disciples of the group, although there is no record of what happened to their knowledge. Men of great stature were associated with the Brotherhood for the hundred years or so that it flourished. Eventually, and for whatever reason, the group dwindled and apparently disappeared. That is not to say, of course, that the Brotherhood ceased to exist. The Freemasons and Rosicrucians had similar origins to the Brotherhood, and although their ideals may differ from the time of their inception, they still thrive today in one form or another.'

'And the link you found between the Order and the Brotherhood?'

'During the time Black was at the Academy, he became embroiled with the Hermetic Order of the Golden Dawn. The Golden Dawn originated in the nineteenth century and were involved in occult theurgical practice, and while they shared the same ideology as Black, it didn't take him long to fall out with them. Soon after he left, the Order first appeared, and you're well aware of what happened next.'

Spydre nodded but did not interrupt.

'I began by trying to learn more of the Golden Dawn. They are said to have descended from Rosicrucianism, a Hermetic movement with origins in the fifteenth century. There are rumours that the Brotherhood and Rosicrucianism were closely allied, and it wouldn't be difficult to imagine a link between the Golden Dawn and the Brotherhood. The beliefs of the Golden Dawn are based on ritual and spiritual alchemy, an affinity they also share with the Brotherhood, which may explain why Black aligned himself with the Golden Dawn. My greatest concern was that Black somehow managed to gain access to the Brotherhood's secret, which is why I sought out Piotrowski's manuscript. Now, with its theft, my fears have returned.'

Spydre nodded uneasily. 'I see. It would appear that the manuscript residing in Amsterdam might be of use to us. I am sure Markus would allow us access. It may help to understand why the book was stolen and whether the difference between the two copies is relevant. If you are happy to wait a little longer, I will speak with Markus now.'

Price smiled affably, nodding his head in assent. He was in no hurry to leave while he was enjoying the calming effect of the scotch and the intriguing conversation with his friend. Spydre smiled back as best he could before slowly rising from the chair and shuffling towards the opening in the bookcase.

It was almost fifteen minutes before Spydre returned. Following his brief excursion to the shop's rear, his breathing was laboured, and his face glistened with sweat.

'I fear we may need to … move a little quicker than … perhaps I had anticipated,' Spydre said between great heaving breaths.

'What is it?' said Price.

'Markus would be more than happy … to allow us to scrutinise his copy,' Spydre said as he slumped back into the chair then paused for a moment to regain his breath. 'He wondered why I was so interested in this particular work, and so I explained to him about the theft.'

'What!'

'Do not worry, my friend. I can assure you that Markus is trustworthy,' said Spydre.

'Very well, Cornelius, but what's the problem?'

'Markus was intrigued that we should be so interested in Piotrowski's manuscript as his own copy received the attention of a particular individual some years ago. The library was even offered a considerable sum of money for the book, which I am pleased to say was declined.'

'Don't keep me in suspense, Cornelius. Who was the mystery buyer?' demanded Price.

Spydre paused for a moment then exclaimed, 'Pearly Black!'

Price gasped. He had not been expecting this news and suddenly felt a great wave of anxiety wash over him. He sat for some minutes staring vacantly ahead, lost in thought, before he eventually stirred. 'You're right, Cornelius, this changes everything. It's the incontrovertible evidence linking the manuscript with the Order,' he said, rubbing his chin pensively. 'At least I know what to do next. I shall to go to Amsterdam to see the manuscript for myself.'

'I think that is a very sensible decision, Henry, as I fear there is more. Markus also informed me that there is a short paragraph of additional text on the final page that is written in code. I am worried that this code might be hiding the Brotherhood's secret.'

Price looked aghast. 'But if that's the case, then surely whoever was searching for the Brotherhood's secret would have taken the copy from Amsterdam.'

'Perhaps,' said Spydre circumspectly, 'but I suspect we may be missing something here. The Bibliotheca Hermetica Philosophica has held their copy of Piotrowski's manuscript for many years, and during this time, it has been subject to the most fearsome scrutiny from some of the finest Dutch mathematicians and cryptologists, yet all their attempts to decipher it have failed. Why should that be, I ask myself?'

'No idea,' replied Price. 'Perhaps they just weren't up to it.'

'You do not honestly believe that, do you, Henry?'

'I must admit it seems unlikely.'

'Let me suggest an alternative explanation. Perhaps both copies have to be held together to decipher the code. This would explain why your copy has never yielded anything of use and why attempts to decipher the code have ended in failure. Remember the Latin proverb at the start of the book. As I surmised earlier, Piotrowski was indicating that one book alone is useless. I have heard of codes that require a keyword to decipher them. Perhaps that is the purpose of your copy, Henry. Was there anything about the book that was unusual in any way?'

'Not that I recall, but if your theory is correct, then an attempt will be made to acquire the other book.'

'Quite so,' replied Spydre steadfastly. 'We must do everything in our power to prevent it from falling into the same hands that took your own. I will contact Markus immediately to warn him, and if you let me know when you are planning to travel, I will make the necessary arrangements at the other end.'

'Thank you, Cornelius. The Council meeting is scheduled for Wednesday. I'll leave as soon as it's over. Perhaps you'd be kind enough to inform Markus?'

Spydre nodded. 'Of course. Leave it with me.'

'I'll be in touch,' said Price, getting up and leaning forwards to shake hands with Spydre, who remained seated.

Price turned and made his way out of the shop into the damp evening air. The street outside was deserted, but as he trudged home, he was overcome by a great sense of unease and a multitude of thoughts that swirled aimlessly inside his head.

8

The Vigenère Cipher

THE WALLS OF THE natural cavern were damp with condensation. Small droplets of water trickled silently down the slick stone surface and collected in small pools in the concave irregularities of the floor. In one place, the water had formed a tiny rivulet that weaved like a silver thread towards the sump in the centre of the cave, then fell with a steady drip into the brine that had risen with the tide.

Josef Frankl held the manuscript aloft while carefully studying the expressions of those surrounding him. No one stirred or passed comment, waiting for him to continue, but he, too, remained silent. The light thrown by the candles set irregularly around the cavern's floor had dulled imperceptibly in the time since their arrival.

'It would help if you told us *exactly* what you have there, Josef,' said Aurelia eventually. 'It's far too dark in here to see. What is it?' she added impatiently.

'This manuscript, my friends, was languishing in the library of an old friend of ours just a few days ago,' Frankl replied calmly.

His former confederates from the days of the Order squinted at him blankly while Styx looked away, disinterested.

'Henry Price!' exclaimed Frankl, spitting out the name with disgust. 'He has held this book for some years, but it was formerly the property of a group of alchemists known as the Esoteric Brotherhood. It was hand-written by one of their brethren, Alfons

Piotrowski, and passed down to only the most privileged of their secret society,' he continued grandiosely.

'Ah, I see I've struck a chord with you, Abel,' he said, noting the look of recognition that flashed across Strange's face.

Strange fidgeted uneasily under Frankl's intense gaze. 'Er … yes,' he replied hesitantly.

Frankl nodded his encouragement. 'Tell us what you know of it, Abel.'

'Er, well … some of you may have already heard of the, er, Esoteric Brotherhood. They were a group of alchemists that existed over five hundred years ago; Pearly was obsessed with them because of a potent secret they had supposedly discovered. This secret was so intrinsically dangerous, it was as much to be feared as it was revered, and only the most influential of the group were ever allowed access to it. The Brotherhood were determined that it should never fall into the wrong hands. They guarded it jealously, but what happened to the Brotherhood or their secret is a mystery because they vanished over a hundred years after they first appeared.'

'Did Pearly ever discover their secret, Abel?' said Lex.

'As far as I'm, er, aware, he never learnt the truth, but he was so preoccupied with Piotrowski's manuscript, he managed to track down a copy residing in a library in Amsterdam. He spent a considerable time studying it and was so convinced of its importance that he even attempted to purchase it.'

Lex frowned. 'What happened?'

'They wouldn't sell it to him, deeming the book far too valuable despite the considerable sum he offered them.'

'Quite so, Abel, quite so,' agreed Frankl with a nod of his head and a flash of large, irregular teeth.

'Well, well, Josef, it seems that by acquiring this book, you've managed something that was beyond even Pearly,' said Aurelia. 'Tell me, does it reveal this mystical secret you refer to? The suspense is killing me,' she added scornfully.

'Your mockery does not become you, Aurelia. I find it hard to believe that recovering an item Pearly so coveted does not kindle your curiosity.'

'Maybe it does, but I can't help wondering what you aim to achieve with this book. When Pearly died, our aspirations died with him, which is why I've never shared your preoccupation with the Order's resurrection.'

'An interesting philosophy, but perhaps you should wait until you learn the secret of the Esoteric Brotherhood before being so judgmental,' replied Frankl.

'All right, Josef, go ahead. Tell us this secret.'

'I hate to disappoint you, but at this present moment ... I have nothing to reveal,' Frankl said melodramatically. He stared intently at Aurelia through beetle-black eyes and allowed a smile to flicker across his lips, enjoying the sudden anticlimax.

'I should have guessed! You bring us here on the pretext of some earth-shattering discovery only to tell us you know nothing. What's in this manuscript, anyway?' Aurelia demanded, spitting the words out with contempt.

'Ah, Aurelia, you haven't changed. You always were so quick to jump to conclusions. I've learnt much from this manuscript, and it's only a matter of time before I unravel the Brotherhood's secret. I've been following the trail Pearly left for me for many years now, and it's only recently that I've discovered what he truly expected of me.'

'And what *exactly* is that?' demanded Aurelia.

'The answer lies in this book,' he said, holding the manuscript aloft once more. 'It also explains why Michael is here tonight,' he added, extending a squat finger in the direction of the man who was sitting quietly at his side.

Styx squirmed uneasily under the group's attention, bowing his head and fixing his gaze firmly on the limestone floor.

'Michael, why don't you tell us something about yourself, or would you prefer that I do so on your behalf?' said Frankl.

Styx refused to look up but nodded imperceptibly.

'Very well. Please forgive Michael's reticence. You forget what an imposing audience you are. In any case, it's probably better that I do the introductions; I'm not sure Michael would do himself justice.'

The young man looked up uncomfortably, not relishing the attention. He had remained anonymous since his arrival and clearly preferred it that way. His eyes shifted furtively from one face to another. He wrung his hands ceaselessly, unable to keep still under the intense scrutiny directed his way, but when his gaze landed on Frankl, there was no mistaking the expression that immediately turned from misery to loathing.

'Michael has kindly agreed to talk to us on the subject of cryptography—'

'How exciting,' interjected Aurelia sarcastically. 'A lecture by this geek while we slowly suffocate. I do commend you, Josef.'

Frankl shot her a withering look. 'Aurelia, please show some decorum. Michael is one of the youngest people ever to have worked for Internal Security. He graduated with a first-class honours degree in mathematics from Oxford at the age of fifteen and obtained a doctorate barely two years later, which, correct me if I'm wrong, Michael, was on the subject of ciphers. His work has led to many unprecedented revelations from texts that were previously considered indecipherable. Not surprisingly, he was recruited by that detestable man, Nicolas Fox.'

'Very impressive, but what exactly is an employee of, er, Internal Security doing in our midst? It's bad enough that you bring us to this place,' said Strange, registering his distaste with a brief survey of the cavern walls. 'Not only that, but you also introduce us to someone who's working for one of our, er, greatest adversaries.'

'I've said it before, Abel, you worry too much,' said Frankl with a dismissive flick of a hand. 'Rest assured, I have no intention of jeopardising my plans. Michael came here of his own free will. He is no threat to us. Isn't that so, Michael?' he added with a grotesque smile, challenging the young man to say otherwise.

Styx got up and finally began to speak of his own accord. 'I'm here b-because of h-him,' he said, pointing a finger accusingly at Frankl. Styx hopped uneasily from one foot to another and appeared to be shivering, whether in fear or as a result of the cold, it was not clear. He addressed the cavern floor, unable to meet the eyes that were fixed on him, and spoke hesitantly with a tremor that he could not mask. 'It's t-true that I came here of my own v-volition and I will not betray you to my organisation. *He* approached me some days ago to d-decipher a document,' he said, uttering the words through clenched teeth while looking disdainfully at Frankl. 'I was left with no alternative but to come.'

'Thank you for your kind words,' said Frankl sarcastically. 'Michael's here to explain about a short piece of code Piotrowski used in his manuscript and how we can go about deciphering it. It is, after all, what I believe to be the key to the Brotherhood's secret.'

'What do you know of this secret?' said Lex, showing a little more interest than Aurelia, who was nonchalantly inspecting her fingernails next to him.

'Thank you, Lex. I was just about to come on to that,' replied Frankl. 'I always knew that Pearly coveted this manuscript but it was only when working through his prodigious notes that I began to realise why. Much has been said in the past about *lapis philosophorum*—'

'The living stone!' called out Strange in astonishment.

'Quite so, Abel, thank you,' continued Frankl undeterred. 'The living stone has existed, whether in truth or as a myth, for far longer than is generally accepted.

'In the early days, alchemists sought to transmute base metals into gold, a concept that originated twelve hundred years ago with the Islamic alchemist, Jabir ibn Hayyan. He believed that every substance was comprised of four basic qualities—fire, earth, water and air—and that every known metal was a combination of these four principles. He conjectured that the transmutation of one metal into another could be achieved by the rearrangement of these fundamental elements—'

'Which, as we know,' interrupted Strange excitedly, 'is how modern-day alchemists undertake internal rearrangements.'

'Thank you again, Abel,' said Frankl, casting a glare in his direction. 'Perhaps you'd do me the courtesy of allowing me to finish?'

Strange nodded and dropped his head. His face coloured at the rebuke, but his embarrassment was not easily discerned in the crepuscular light.

'Now, where was I?' said Frankl, more to himself than his audience. 'Ah, yes, with our friend, Jabir.

'He considered that the rearrangement of these four qualities required an additional substance, which he named "al-iksir", which is, of course, the Arabic word for the English "elixir". Jabir's elixir was purportedly a dark red powder, which he called Carmot, made from a mythical stone. This, my friends, was alchemy's first encounter with the living stone.'

'Do tell,' said Aurelia unenthusiastically.

Frankl gave a slight shake of his head but continued unwaveringly. 'This stone was the much sought-after substance that allowed the transmutation of base metals into gold. With time, the stone became associated with dangerous metaphysical alchemy and was thought to be the key to the fundamental secrets of the universe; not only transforming base metal into gold, but also the resurrection of life!'

A gasp went up inside the natural stone auditorium, and while Frankl scanned the audience for the source of the sound, they all stared back at him, waiting for him to continue.

'Are you, er, all right, Josef?' enquired Strange suddenly. 'You're breathing has become rather, er, rapid and the candles have dulled to a glimmer.' Strange frowned before a look of enlightenment appeared on his face. 'Ah, yes. I suspect these are signs of oxygen depletion,' he concluded, gazing uncertainly at the others.

'I'm fine, Abel,' Frankl retorted, shaking his head dismissively. 'Now, Please, let me continue,' he added, briefly composing himself before he went on with his narrative.

'I learnt from Pearly's research that the Esoteric Brotherhood inherently believed the living stone to be allied to an elixir of life,' he said, displaying a fierce passion that burned in his eyes. 'Whether they had truly discovered this secret for themselves, Pearly never found out, but it led him to make certain preparations in the event of his death.'

'What do you mean by "certain preparations", Josef?' demanded Aurelia.

'I'm not at liberty to reveal this to you at the moment, Aurelia, I'm afraid. I have Price's copy of Piotrowski's manuscript, but we must also recover the only other copy before I can fully answer your question.'

'But—'

'I have said all I can, Aurelia,' Frankl cut in. 'For the time being, you'll have to make do with what Michael knows of the Piotrowski manuscript.'

'I suppose there's little point in arguing,' said Aurelia, throwing Frankl a look that threatened to shake the bedrock in which they were incarcerated.

'Now, Michael, perhaps you'd be kind enough to explain what you know of the code,' said Frankl.

Styx stood up and squinted into the gloom. With his audience invisible, he raised his hunched shoulders and began to speak with more confidence than he had previously displayed. 'As you've already heard, there are two manuscripts written in Piotrowski's hand. I've managed to analyse these copies based on the recently stolen manuscript and Black's notes, and it is evident that there are subtle differences between the two. The manuscript held in Amsterdam contains a short passage of text that, at first glance, appears unintelligible, but it's pretty obvious to anyone worth their salt that it's encrypted. It's been examined by the country's foremost cryptologists, but despite intense scrutiny, it's never been successfully deciphered. With just one copy, that doesn't surprise me.'

'Do you have any idea what's hidden in the code?' said Aurelia, suddenly showing some interest.

'Firstly, it's a cipher and not a code. The distinction is important as I'll explain later. As to what the cipher is hiding, well, presumably it has something to do with this ludicrous secret that was mentioned earlier,' said Styx dismissively. 'Before you ask, it is not for me to speculate on the text; that is for you. I'm here to decrypt the cipher and nothing more. I believe that Piotrowski wrote two copies of the manuscript with the specific purpose of hiding a secret for as long as the books were separated. Individually, the manuscripts are useless; together, we'll have all we need to decipher the text.'

'What do you know of this cipher, er, Michael?' Strange asked.

'I believe it is a polyalphabetic substitution cipher first described by Blaise De Vigenère from the court of Henry III of France in the sixteenth century.'

'Oh, please spare us the history lesson. Just get on with it,' said Aurelia.

The flush that spread across Styx's cheeks was evident despite the murky light, and when he replied, there was a shakiness to his voice. 'As … as you w-wish. It's not … so … er … s-simple to explain to someone who's not familiar with this sort of cipher. I'll try to be brief … please bear with me,' he said, trying to regain his composure.

'Perhaps you'd be so kind as to begin with an explanation of the difference between a cipher and a code,' said Frankl, placing a reassuring hand on Styx's shoulder.

Styx recoiled as if he had been touched by a leper. 'A cipher implies that one letter substitutes for another, whereas a code may be a letter or symbol substituting for a word, phrase or even an entire message. A polyalphabetic substitution cipher works on the principle that the encrypted text is linked to a keyword or phrase that's only known to the writer and, of course, the decipherer. What makes the cipher so difficult to crack is the keyword or phrase can be any combination of letters. Not surprisingly, the longer the keyword, the harder it is to break the cipher. This particular cipher was so effective that it remained virtually unbreakable for three hundred years after it was first described. Even now, without knowing the keyword, it can be a tough cipher to crack.'

'How can you be so sure about the, er, exact type of cipher?' enquired Strange.

'A good question,' replied Styx, beginning to warm to the task. 'I've carried out a provisional analysis of the enciphered text and

I can conclude that it's a substitution cipher with all the hallmarks of Vigenère.'

'So how does this fit with Piotrowski?' continued Strange, eager to hear more from this pale, strange young man.

'Ah, I was just coming on to that,' replied Styx, his uneasy, gaunt expression barely evident in the shadowy candlelight. 'I suspect that the moment Piotrowski completed the manuscript, the two copies were separated and have been kept apart ever since. The copy that we have here, I believe, contains the keyword that will enable me to decipher whatever is hidden in the cipher.'

'But surely if we have the copy containing the keyword, then we're already in a position to decipher the code … cipher … whatever you want to call it. You've already told us Pearly made a copy of the cipher when he visited Amsterdam. What are we waiting for?' said Aurelia, sounding exasperated that no one else had already grasped the fact.

'A good point, but I'm afraid finding the keyword is not as simple as you might assume. I've already made a superficial evaluation of the manuscript, and there's nothing in the text to point to the keyword. You've already heard of the differences that exist between the two copies. I believe that only by comparing them will I be able to determine the keyword.'

'Oh, and please don't spare the detail,' said Aurelia, yawning theatrically.

Styx was no longer fazed by Aurelia's predictable interruption and continued unabated. 'The process of encryption begins with a table of alphabets in the form of a square measuring 26 by 26 for each letter of the alphabet. The alphabet is written in its customary order from A to Z in a row across the top, and a second alphabet is written out in a column perpendicular to the first, leaving a blank square containing 676 spaces.

'On the first line, the alphabet is again written out in its usual order, but on the line below, there is a shift of one, two, three, or however many letters the author chooses. In this way, the alphabet is written out but moved to the right by the number of units corresponding to the shift selected—a technique known as a Caesar shift. It was named after Julius Caesar who used this method to communicate with his generals.

'This process is continued on each line until the tabula recta, or Vigenère table, is complete. It's a little too dark in here to see as clearly as I would wish, but I've written one out for you to inspect,' said Styx, withdrawing a piece of paper covered in small, neat hand-writing, which he passed to Strange. 'The example, here, shows a Caesar shift of one letter on each line.'

Strange scrutinised the creased paper inquisitively, holding it inches from the concave lenses perched on the end of his nose. He studied it for a few moments, but perhaps because of his poor sight in the failing light or because he was already familiar with the cipher, he wasted no time before handing it to Aurelia. The note spent even less time with her, and without a glimpse, she passed it on to Lex, who began to read with interest.

'Now that I assume you all understand how to construct a Vigenère table, you'll see that it's relatively straightforward to convert the plaintext into a cipher,' said Styx. 'Again, I've got an example for you here,' he added, proffering a second piece of paper.

'If you look at this example, you'll see that I've used the name of the village we passed through on our way here as the plaintext, and my surname as the keyword. It is a simple example, but it should illustrate the point.'

Strange accepted the paper and began to read.

Plaintext:	RIDDLESCOMBE
Keyword:	STYXSTYXSTYX
Ciphertext:	JBVADXQZGFZB

Styx waited for them all to inspect the note before he continued. 'Take the first letter of the plaintext and that of the keyword, and you have the letters R and S. If you scrutinise the table, the combination of these letters produces the first letter of the ciphertext, which in this case is the letter J. If this process is

91

repeated in the same manner for each pair of letters, then the ciphertext begins to take shape.'

'All very fascinating,' said Aurelia, 'but I'm rather surprised by your assertion that this cipher is hard to break. It appears to me that it's little more than a simple substitution cipher.'

'A perceptive point, but if you don't have access to both the ciphertext and keyword, the cipher is *extremely* difficult to crack, particularly if the keyword is long. It may be possible to break the cipher without the keyword by using frequency analysis, but that can be a most laborious task taking months, if not years, to fulfil. It's much simpler with the keyword—'

'Assuming we *find* the keyword,' interjected Frankl, 'which might be difficult without the other book. For the sake of argument, though, how does frequency analysis work?'

'Simple mathematics,' replied Styx. 'We know that letters such as *e* and words such as *the* appear regularly in the English language. This creates an inherent weakness in the cipher and allows patterns to develop in the ciphertext that can be exploited by a suitably gifted mathematician. The key to breaking the cipher is to determine the length of the keyword. Once that's done, the ciphertext can be broken down into strings of letters consistent with the length of the keyword, thus allowing the ciphertext to be dealt with as separate, but relatively simple, substitution ciphers.'

'How can the length of the keyword be determined without knowing the keyword?' enquired Strange.

'That's also an interesting question,' continued Styx confidently, finally appearing at ease while being questioned on a subject that was the only major interest in his life. 'I'm afraid, however, that without a major dissertation on the subject of cryptology, it's almost impossible to explain.

'Suffice to say, it's possible to determine the length of the keyword by undertaking a mathematical analysis of the strings of letters in the ciphertext and looking for repetition. By measuring and factoring the distance between repetitions, it's feasible to work out various possibilities for the length of the keyword. If the whole process is repeated for different repetitions, eventually, only one number will appear in all of the lists, which is likely to represent the actual length of the keyword. Is that clear?'

No one replied, but the bemused expressions on the faces of the audience were only masked by the increasing darkness as the candlelight dwindled.

'Once the length of the keyword is known,' continued Styx, 'the ciphertext can be broken down into separate strings consistent with individual parts of the keyword. Each string can be treated as a simple substitution cipher. As I mentioned earlier, this becomes a relatively straightforward exercise for the cryptologist to break.'

Frankl stood up and smiled. 'Thank you, Michael. Your explanation has given us all an essential understanding of the problem. To put it quite simply, it could take forever to crack the cipher without the keyword, and that, of course, is where you come in, Lex.'

'Yes. All we need now is the other book,' Lex said casually, trying to conceal his excitement, but as he was speaking, a candle guttered and died, sending a plume of smoke spiralling into the unfathomable recess above his head.

It was now almost impossible to make out the faces of those scattered about the cavern, but as Frankl looked down, he whispered to himself, 'Cyanosis!'

The cavernous space amplified and echoed the single word so that no one could mistake what he had said.

'Cyanosis?' said Lex inanely. 'What are you talking about?'

'My fingernails have turned blue!' Frankl replied, still staring intently at his hands.

'Cyanosis is a, er, medical term,' Strange explained, 'that relates to the condition known as hypoxia.'

'Would someone please speak in plain terms?' said Styx, who was becoming increasingly agitated.

'That's a fine request coming from you, Mr Cryptologist,' said Aurelia in a sudden fit of pique, still reeling from Styx's recent exposition.

'Now's not the time for bickering. Please, just be quiet for a moment,' said Frankl.

'An interesting philosophy coming from you, Josef,' said Aurelia, unable to contain herself.

'Silence!' called out Frankl. 'Now listen. For those of you who don't know, hypoxia refers to the condition that arises from a lack of oxygen. Its onset is insidious and leads to confusion and irritability, something that's been in clear evidence during these past few minutes. I fear the oxygen is running low, just as Abel predicted. There's nothing more for us to do than to sit quietly and hope that the tide recedes before we all succumb.'

Having spoken, Frankl sat down on the cool, stone floor, and flexed his amorphous legs so that they came to rest against his chest. He clasped his fat fingers around his knees and tucked his head into the void between his thighs, giving a clear indication that the time for conversation was over.

An eerie silence descended upon the cavern as they all followed Frankl's lead. It was not long before the remaining candles gradually dimmed as a prelude to their final demise, leaving the cavern in a darkness that was absolute.

In the ensuing silence, Frankl closed his eyes and cleared his mind. What he was about to attempt required a combination of great mental fortitude and absolute silence. It had always been possible for the most talented alchemists to communicate silently by tapping into subtle changes in the ether that occur in response to the nanoscopic quanta of electrical activity the brain produces with mental exertion. Frankl had utilised this technique for many years, enjoying considerable success by silently colluding with Pearly while in the company of others. Like most things, however, this was never enough for Frankl, and by poring over ancient alchemical texts in search of forgotten lore, he slowly acquired the ability to hack into people's minds and read their thoughts.

Armed with the knowledge of what he was about to do, now was the perfect opportunity to utilise this skill. He cleared his mind of all extraneous thoughts until his mind was an empty void. Then, he cast his mind about him in the perfect silence of the secluded cavern to search, probe and ultimately distil the thoughts circulating around him.

*

Lex did not move. He was not threatened by the precarious situation he suddenly found himself in, having been in far worse plights in the past. An occupational hazard, he mused. As a professional criminal, he had masterminded many successful ventures in his insalubrious past, but even with the meticulous preparation he always employed in the pursuit of his misdemeanours, he remained wise enough to realise that even the most scrupulously laid plans could be overtaken by unforeseen circumstances.

To his friends, Lex had always displayed an easy-going manner, but his carefree exterior hid a sharp mind with an eye for detail that often went unnoticed. From the moment he had entered the cavern, he had keenly observed every aspect of their predicament, assimilating and analysing almost at a subconscious level.

Now, with a complete loss of sensory input, he was able to recall and regurgitate this information. He did not intend to sit idly by and wait for events to overtake him, and in his mind's eye, he had already pictured where each of his co-conspirators was positioned. The lack of sound following Frankl's words told him that no one had moved, and the voluminous cavern that echoed and amplified every noise was unlikely to stretch his keen sense of hearing. No one could move without him knowing, and while everyone else was focusing on the threat of impending suffocation, he was intent on making sure that he was ready to act the instant circumstances changed.

While Styx had been droning on about ciphers, Lex had been staring at the water in the sump. He had watched the water slowly rise, level off, and then recede with the ebbing tide. Thus, it would not be long before the water fell below the uppermost limit of the cave, allowing air to rush in and replenish the dwindling oxygen.

He sat back, relaxed, and carried on with the silent vigil, maintaining his concentration just in case the situation suddenly changed.

*

Aurelia was not thinking about imminent suffocation. No. She was far too angry for that. She had objected to almost everything that had happened from the moment they arrived, particularly when she discovered that Frankl was pulling the strings. She could not deny that the black pearl had sparked her curiosity, and it had made her wonder whether it was the signal to finally end the misery she had endured following Pearly's death.

After the Order had fallen, it was easy for Pearly's faceless supporters to slip back into their previous lives without fear of recrimination, but Aurelia was not so fortunate. At the outset, as news of the Order spread, she had inevitably been at Pearly's side, revelling in the publicity that followed wherever he went. When Pearly died, his true exploits were revealed, and she was branded a common criminal. It was all right for Lex, who had always lived his life that way, and even Abel had somehow managed to continue his life as if nothing had happened, maintaining a relationship with Price and retaining his position at the Academy despite his known fraternisation with the Order.

Alas, the same could not be said of her. She had never managed to shake off her bitterness at how events had transpired. She was hunted mercilessly in the aftermath of Pearly's death, and it had taken all of her cunning to avoid capture on numerous occasions. It had also engendered a gnawing resentment for the many years she had been forced to live as a fugitive, forever fearful that she would be recognised and hunted down. She deserved better and longed for the time when she had been admired for her beauty, enjoying the notoriety from her association with Pearly and the decadence that inexorably went with it.

She reflected on how circumstances had forced her into obscurity and isolation. Sitting here now, she also realised that much of her anger stemmed from the resentment she felt for Frankl. It galled her to think that he was responsible for this meeting, and it was no surprise she had been antagonistic towards his suggestions, but as she pondered all he had revealed, she began to wonder whether there might be something to this manuscript after all. She had never been party to Pearly's darkest secrets, and although this had not bothered her at the time, it made her wonder what he had been up to in the months before his death. As she contemplated this, she gradually came round to the idea that, perhaps, for the time being, she would go along with Frankl's plans.

*

Abel Strange sat impassively while cogitating the prospect of impending suffocation. Something did not add up, and he intended to get to the bottom of it in his usual analytical manner. He began by recalling his first observations of the cavern after his arrival and recalled that a typical sea cave was formed by the repetitive action of the sea acting at the interface between dissimilar rock types in a cliff face. The entrance to the cave was a small fissure opening into a much wider vestibule, and the penetrating force of the waves he had witnessed on the way in could easily account for the distance the cave extended into the bedrock, but it did not explain why the cave suddenly turned upwards through a smaller channel that led to a vast enclosure. The more he thought about it, the more he wondered whether an inherent fault could extend all the way back from the cliff face to account for the formation of the vaulted cavern. If that were true, then it seemed plausible that the cave not only communicated with the outside via the entrance, but also through a fault somewhere high above his head; if so, then oxygen should be seeping in by that route.

This revelation led to something else that was bothering him, and as he mulled it over, he realised why. The candlelight had gradually dwindled to nothing, yet if there was insufficient oxygen for the candles to burn, then how could he still be considering the problem so lucidly? These two processes were mutually exclusive, because, after all, his brain needed oxygen just like the candles. The only solution was that Frankl had orchestrated the whole charade, but why would he go to such elaborate lengths to fool them? He sat back mulling this over and waited patiently to find out.

*

Michael Styx was feeling increasingly uncomfortable due to the oppressive atmosphere and the all-enveloping darkness. Frankl had coerced him into coming here, and his resentment towards him was rising in direct correlation with his agitation.

He asked himself how he had come to be trapped in this god-forsaken place with these criminals before ruefully reflecting on the circumstances that had led him to this, the lowest point in his life.

It had all started so well working for Internal Security, hand-picked to do a job that he would gladly have done for nothing. At first, he could not believe his luck, but when the bills to pay for his ailing mother's medical care started to pile up, the situation spiralled rapidly out of control. He recalled his increasing desperation and his struggle to stay afloat, borrowing more and more money from the bank. Eventually, when the bank called in the debt, he foolishly approached a disreputable moneylender, who accepted him with relish. The interest alone was crippling, and it was not long before he was unable to meet the ever-increasing repayments. When the threats began, he finally realised the gravity of his predicament.

With the appearance of Josef Frankl, it seemed as if his prayers had been answered. A chance meeting in a bar, or so it appeared at the time, was a prelude to Frankl surreptitiously wheedling his way into his affairs, gaining his confidence by revealing interests that miraculously mirrored his own. It was only a matter of time before he was completely entranced, and after a night spent drinking far too much wine, it seemed the perfect opportunity to unburden some of his problems onto his new-found friend. Naturally, it only seemed reasonable to accept Frankl's generous offer of financial help in return for a simple favour, which was little more than deciphering a simple piece of text, after all.

He felt sure that his troubles were over, but when a chance message passed across his desk at work, he instantly recognised a description of the recently stolen manuscript as the very same item Frankl had shown to him. At first, he refused to believe that Frankl could be implicated in such a crime, but after confronting him in the vain hope that there had been a misunderstanding, he would never forget the look of disdain on his face when Frankl said, 'What did you expect, you fool?'

From that moment on, he knew he had been duped, and he was well aware of what would happen if his employers learnt of how he had been compromised. There was no choice but to co-operate, and he had reluctantly agreed to make the journey to Riddlescombe. After arriving at the cave, he immediately realised just how much trouble he was in.

As time dragged interminably, he began to feel like a rat trapped in a cage. All he wanted was to get away, and now, with the oxygen running out, he could feel his throat closing up. He wondered whether anyone else had already suffocated, and briefly thought of calling out. As he felt his terror rising, he realised he had to escape.

*

Josef Frankl smiled to himself as he allowed his mind to recede from those around him. It was working out just as he had planned, even down to piquing Aurelia's interest. Now, with the atmosphere more stifling than ever, it merely added to the credence that the air was running out. It would not be long before the ebbing tide allowed them to escape, but there was still one outstanding problem. He could sense the meeting building into an overwhelming climax, which only added to his exhilaration. The grand finale was fast approaching, and all he had to do was to wait for Fox's poor, young lackey to act.

Almost on cue, Styx leapt to his feet. In his rising panic, he realised he no longer had a choice—stay put and suffocate or take a chance and swim. As he lurched blindly towards the exit, his trousers snagged on a jagged piece of rock. He toppled over, striking his head on the cavern floor with a sickening thud. He staggered to his feet, blood trickling into his eyes, but as he fought to keep his balance, the sound of a voice he had grown to despise rang out behind him.

'Going somewhere, Michael?' boomed Frankl, his words echoing menacingly around the cavern. 'Tut, tut. Surely you'd prefer to sit it out with us here?' he added, pointing ominously at Styx.

Styx looked confused. 'I—' he began before his words were cut short by a coruscation of blinding white light and an ear-splitting thunderclap.

Frankl felt a surge of ecstasy, revelling in the power that erupted from his fingertips. The bolt crashed into Styx like a tsunami, tossing him like a rag doll into the air, such that he was dead before he struck the ground.

Paradoxically, there was neither flame nor heat following the blast, but when the darkness returned, the murderous cataclysm remained etched on his retina until the macabre image slowly faded.

'Josef, I, er, think you should, er, at least allow us the consideration of some candlelight,' said Strange finally, his voice unable to mask a slight tremor of fear.

Frankl extended a finger, and one by one, the candles reignited, illuminating the cavern in defiance of the darkness they had endured for so long.

Frankl got up and walked leisurely towards the inert figure lying adjacent to the exit. 'Well, that solves one problem,' he said coldly, rolling over the lifeless form with a judicious boot. 'Styx was always going to be a threat. I couldn't allow him to leave here alive. The information he has divulged will suffice our needs. All we need now is the manuscript. What say you, Lex?'

Lex did not immediately reply. He looked startled by what he had just witnessed. 'You stage-managed the whole charade, didn't you? I may be used to stealing things, Josef, but murder? Never.'

'Rest assured, Lex. No one will ever know. Once again, we are all in this together ... just like the old days. So, Lex. The book?' said Frankl.

Lex shivered involuntarily before composing himself. 'One thing, Josef. What about Price? Surely the theft of this book will warn him that something's afoot?'

'Perhaps ... and yet ... perhaps not,' replied Frankl contemplatively. 'True, gaining access to his house is beyond mere ordinary mortals, but don't forget, I'm not the only one who could have carried out the theft. The manuscript was lying dormant in Price's library for many years, and if he couldn't work out its significance when it was sitting under his nose, I don't suppose he will now.'

'I wish I shared your confidence,' replied Lex with an imperceptible shake of his head, 'but look, we're no longer trapped!' he said excitedly, jumping to his feet and pointing towards the exit.

Aurelia got up and joined him to peer into the void. 'You're right, Lex. I for one don't intend to spend any more time than I have to in the company of a corpse. There's much to discuss, but now is neither the time nor the place,' she said, and with that she clambered into the tunnel and disappeared from view.

Frankl smiled. 'It seems Aurelia has just given her tacit approval to my plan or at least as close as it gets. Price is sharp, but even if he does realise the significance of the theft, I don't suppose he'll suspect we're planning a raid elsewhere. Even so, there's no time to lose. I take it you're with me, Lex?'

Lex returned Frankl's disturbing grimace with his own natural smile. 'Despite your duplicity, I'm surprised you have to ask. I'll be on my way as soon as I've made the necessary preparations. Leave it with me, you'll have your book,' he said, and with that, he turned on his heels and followed Aurelia into the tunnel.

The cavern was silent for some moments, but when Strange spoke, the hesitant manner in his voice was gone. 'Was that really necessary, Josef?' he said, staring intently at Frankl through the thick lenses perched on the end of his nose.

'Was what necessary?' retorted Frankl with feigned nonchalance.

'You know exactly what I mean,' Strange replied, keeping his eyes fixed on Frankl.

'Oh, come now, Abel, I've never had you down as a sentimentalist before. You of all people should realise the importance of tying up loose ends. Styx has given us everything we need. We could never leave him free to return to Internal Security. Surely you understand what's at stake?'

'I'm not sure I do, but more importantly, do you?'

'Trust me, Abel, I've no doubt that what I'm planning will be worth our while. Just you wait and see. Come on, it's about time we made our way out of here. I don't think Michael Styx will be greatly missed, and in any case, the crabs will cover our tracks,' he said impassively.

Abel Strange did not reply as he made ready to leave. The expression on his face had barely changed, and although he had not voiced it, it was still blatantly obvious that trust was not something he was prepared to share with the man he followed from the cave.

9

THE STONE OF MADNESS

Perca Fluviatilis

L ILY'S LESSONS WERE OVER for the day. She had spent the previous two hours debating the philosophical aspects of modern alchemical practice with her tutor, Victor Mirkstone. She realised that her father's influence lay behind the discussion as it related to a topic she had recently been studying with him, and although the argument was challenging, the debate failed to hold her attention. Eventually, Lily lost interest, which was quite apparent to her tutor, who became irritated at her chaotic and ill-conceived reasoning. When they reached yet another impasse, Mirkstone suddenly announced that he was terminating the lesson early, and while Lily was delighted at this turn of events, she knew that the news would filter back to her father, fuelling yet another discussion about her attitude towards her studies.

She dispelled these thoughts and considered what she would do with the unexpected free time that had suddenly materialised. She briefly thought about going back to her room to continue her studies there, but quickly dismissed it. She knew her father was out and would not be back for some time.

In a flash of inspiration, she decided to go and see the boys. Her sombre mood dissipated in an instant, giving way to the thrill of visiting her friends. She had not told her father about Aedh and Seoc, knowing full well that he would not approve. It was her secret, and now, having made up her mind, there was no time to lose. She shot from the classroom, making a quick detour to her bedroom to change into some warmer clothes, despite the watery sunshine that was cascading through the window.

Lily felt a flutter in her stomach as she crept downstairs. She had no desire to be caught and could only imagine the inquisition that would follow if she were spotted on the way out. Fortunately, Albright was nowhere to be seen, and with Mrs Brimstork busy working her culinary magic in the kitchen, she would not be missed. She picked up a thick coat that was hanging in the hall and tiptoed into the kitchen, sneaking behind the cook's back as she was pounding dough.

She left by the back door and crossed the lawn. She pushed apart the undergrowth at the bottom of the garden to reveal an old bay tree that hid a rusty gate. She lifted the hinge and put her weight behind the metal bars. The gate groaned in protest before yielding under Lily's force, sending her toppling unceremoniously through the gap onto an overgrown path that led down to an old railway embankment.

She set off at great speed and did not hesitate at the verge, skidding down the icy path that was still swathed deeply in shadow. She crossed the rotting sleepers that were scattered haphazardly about the old track and scampered up the other side. The path was much clearer here and opened onto a grassy knoll, which she bounded up as fast as she could. She paused at the summit and surveyed the land that lay ahead. In the distance, she could just make out the canal lying beyond yet another copse. Her route looked impassable from where she was standing, but Lily knew better. As she set off, she recalled the first time she had made this trip some months earlier energised by feelings of excitement and wanderlust. She had utilised the singular skills her father had taught her to bypass a set of railings barring the way, and the divergent gap between the upright struts remained to this day, a testament to the alchemical abilities she had used to transform the rigid metal barrier into ductile rods that could be bent apart with ease.

She squeezed through the gap with some difficulty because of her bulky coat then forged ahead through a dense thicket of beech trees sportingly hanging onto curly brown leaves. Eventually, the vegetation cleared to reveal an old canal basin. The place exuded neglect judging by the crumbling concrete overgrown with moss and algae surrounding the still, dank water, but her eyes were drawn to a brightly coloured green and white canal boat moored there. Despite the boat's exuberant exterior, it was badly in need of maintenance. The paint was peeling in places, exposing longitudinal planks of the boat's wooden hull that was crudely sealed with oakum tar-soaked rope. One item, however, did not need repair: a brightly painted wooden plate neatly engraved with bold letters highlighting the craft's name. Na Cruacha Dubha. Lily smiled to herself. She inherently liked the odd combination of Gaelic words even if she still had no idea how to pronounce them.

As she surveyed the scene, she recalled when she had first stumbled upon the clearing on a bright, sun-filled day, almost toppling over two boys seated on the towpath playing marbles. The surprise on their faces was merely a prelude to their hospitality, and they welcomed Lily into their game without a second thought. The boys' pleasure at the easy pickings on offer playing against an outsider—and a girl at that—soon turned to disbelief as the first game took shape. After accepting the boys' monetary challenge, Lily proceeded to strip their pockets of the few remaining coins they had ventured to wager with her. The loss was even harder for the boys to take, as this was a game of their invention with its own quirky rules, and a game at which they had always assumed they would be masters.

The game began with each competitor choosing six marbles, strategically placed inside a sizeable circle drawn out on the towpath. Each player started with five standard, glass-coloured marbles, and one 'fobber', the boys' term for a large, highly polished, stainless steel marble. Each player took turns in trying to displace an opponent's marbles from the arena via a deft flick of the thumb, but absolutely no movement of the arm. Under certain conditions, various actions were allowed, such as 'blocking' or 'fanning', terms the boys used to describe specific foot manoeuvres to protect the marbles or distract an opponent. The key to winning was to knock the opponent's fobber from the circle, but this was never as easy as it sounded. Wise manoeuvring of the fobber was essential to achieve victory while tactical and judicious positioning of the smaller marbles often dictated the result of the contest.

After Lily had won the first game with consummate ease, the boys wrote it off as beginner's luck, but they became more circumspect after the second match when she won again. It was only after the third game when the boys colluded to ensure her downfall that some parity was restored.

Within that first hour, friendships were firmly established, cemented by the thrill of the game and the laughter that accompanied the ferocious intensity of the play. The trio hardly spoke while they battled, but after the final contest, the boys invited Lily back to the boat for some refreshment and to reflect on where the games had been won or lost. Once inside the snug cabin, introductions were finally made over a boiling kettle and the preparation of a strangely pungent tea from a collection of dried leaves and herbs the boys had gathered on their travels.

Sitting in the small galley around a table flanked by wooden benches, Lily drank the brew in silence, reinvigorating her in a fashion that took her rather by surprise.

Eventually, the older boy broke the silence, smiling coyly at Lily but steadfastly refusing to meet her gaze. 'My name's Aedh, and this is Seoc,' he said in a soft, almost melodic, voice that suited his fresh, youthful face.

Lily smiled back. She had not had the opportunity to study the boys while engrossed in the game, but now, as they drank their tea, she looked at them afresh. She guessed that Seoc was the same age as her, and Aedh maybe two or three years older. The boys looked alike, and Lily had no difficulty in concluding that they were brothers. Aedh was a head taller than Seoc, with rusty brown hair that fell in tangled knots to his shoulders. His soft, round hazel eyes complemented the colour of his hair, and the only blemish on his face was the freckles scattered haphazardly across the bridge of his nose. He spoke in a soft lilting accent hinting at Irish origins. Once in a while, Lily picked up the odd word or phrase spoken with a slightly different dialect, suggesting he had not lived in his native land for some time, yet Aedh's general demeanour somehow reassured her that he was someone she could inherently trust.

Seoc was sitting close to Aedh with a similarly contented expression on his face. His features were a little smaller and rounded than his brother, and his hair was a deeper red, but his eyes and the freckles across his nose were the same. He smiled at Lily, expectantly awaiting her reply.

'I'm Lily,' she said as she sipped the refreshing liquid and felt a glow of warmth wash over her. 'I didn't expect to find anyone here. I was out exploring when I found this place. I never knew there was a canal down here. Is anyone else with you?' she blurted out.

'No, it's just me and Seoc,' Aedh replied, looking up from his mug and gazing a little more confidently at Lily.

Lily was relieved to see that the calm expressions on the boys' faces had not changed despite her presumption.

'We've been here for a few weeks now,' Aedh continued.

'It's great for hunting,' Seoc said, at last finding his voice, leaning forwards on the bench to get a better view of Lily. 'We've caught a few rabbits,' he added proudly.

Lily smiled back at the boys. 'I'm impressed. Do you live here, then?'

'Sort of. We're travellers,' Aedh said. 'We move around from place to place, making a living wherever we can,' he added quickly in response to the puzzled expression that flashed across Lily's face.

'We don't steal, though,' Seoc said fixedly, determined that Lily would not get the wrong impression.

'I'm sure you don't,' Lily replied. 'I take it you're not from around here then?'

'What makes you say that?' Aedh replied defensively.

Lily responded with a reassuring smile. 'I couldn't help notice your boat's name. It's Gaelic, isn't it?'

'That's right,' Seoc said, beaming with pride. 'I bet you don't know what it means, though.'

Seoc emitted a great whoop of delight when Lily shook her head. 'Na Cruacha Dubha is a range of mountains in the south-west of Ireland,' he informed her, grinning mischievously. 'Some people call them MacGillycuddy's Reeks, but we prefer the Gaelic name, don't we, Aedh? It literally means the Black Stacks. Aedh and I were born in the shadows of Carrauntoohil, the tallest mountain in all of Ireland.'

Lily smiled again at the boys. 'It sounds wonderful.'

'Aye, it is that,' Seoc said. 'We'll go back there one day, won't we, Aedh?'

'I'm sure we will, little brother, I'm sure we will,' Aedh replied wistfully.

'Never stay in the same place for long, that's us. I suppose we'll be here for a while, but when we've got enough money to buy some more diesel, we'll move on,' Aedh continued.

Lily made no comment. She felt jealous that these two boys enjoyed far more freedom than she had ever been granted by her father.

As Lily regarded the boat, the memory of that first meeting gradually receded. Since then, she had slipped away to see the boys whenever she could. She had enjoyed many hours in their company, and whether they went out exploring or just sat around chatting, it never seemed to matter.

Whenever Lily set off to visit the boys, she was always worried that they might have just left without any prior warning. This afternoon was no different, and when she burst into the clearing, she felt a surge of excitement to see the boat still moored there. There was no one to be seen, but the telltale plume of smoke drifting from the boat's chimney suggested the boys were around.

She approached the wooden-hulled narrowboat from the towpath, knowing that the boys would not be wasting good fuel to keep the cabin warm unless they were inside. She clambered over the side and knocked on the stern door.

Almost immediately, the muffled sound of movement came from inside, and moments later, the double doors opened to reveal Seoc's beaming face. 'Quick, come in, I've got something to show you,' he said, almost as if he had been expecting her.

Lily stooped to follow Seoc inside. Aedh was seated at the

cramped galley table crouched over a long piece of cane with a reel attached at one end. He appeared to be threading some line through a row of evenly-spaced metal eyelets that were attached to the pole.

'It's a fishing rod!' Lily shrieked in amazement, recognising the centre-pin reel that she had gifted the boys a few weeks earlier. She had found it in the garden shed in an old wooden box full of knick-knacks and implements, and was convinced that they would find it useful.

Aedh barely looked up at the sound of Lily's arrival. 'Hello, Lily,' he called out happily, staring intently at the fishing line gripped tightly between a thumb and forefinger. Suddenly, before he realised what was happening, Seoc had grabbed the rod and proffered it to Lily.

'Watch out! You nearly took my eye out,' Lily yelled, laughing.

'Oops. Sorry,' Seoc said, grinning back at her. 'Look. We managed to make the rod from the trunk of an ash that came down in the storm last week. We've been searching for the right piece of wood ever since you gave us the reel.'

'It's fantastic,' Lily said, studying the rod and marvelling at the ingenuity and skill that had gone into its construction. Quite how they had managed to split and plane a raw piece of wood into a fishing rod, she had no idea. The boys had used strong twine to attach regularly spaced, decreasingly sized metal loops to the rod, and had finished it off with several coats of varnish to give it a dazzling sheen.

'All we need now is a float and hook and some weights. Then we're ready,' said Seoc, brandishing a float in Lily's direction, which the boys had fashioned from a piece of cork that they had streamlined into a tapered bobbin painted with bright red and yellow stripes to ensure maximum visibility when in the water.

Lily watched as Seoc pinched several small metal weights onto the line below the float before tying a delicate home-made fishing hook to the end of the line.

'We call this a Grinner knot,' said Seoc, beaming broadly while deftly securing the knot. 'It's a type of blood knot. It'll have to be a hefty old fish that manages to throw the hook!'

'You'll never catch anything today. It's far too cold,' said Lily sceptically.

'Just you wait and see,' replied Aedh. 'You've never seen us fish. Supper will be in the pan before you know it.'

Seoc picked up a small tin that was perched on top of the table, together with an old, rusty landing net, while Aedh followed with the rest of the tackle.

'Come on, Lily. Keep up,' Seoc called to her over his shoulder as they bustled out of the boat and onto the towpath. The boys marched ahead until they reached a spot that was so heavily overgrown, it was almost impossible to see the water.

'Watch out. These brambles will give you a nasty old scratch if you're not careful,' Seoc warned as the boys carefully pushed their way through to the waterside.

Seoc prised the lid from the metal container but managed not to spill the contents. 'Nice and lively,' he said, thrusting a mass of wriggling worms under Lily's nose.

'Yeuch!' Lily screamed, recoiling in disgust.

Seoc laughed. 'We've been keeping them warm since I dug them up this morning. See those old stumps over there,' he continued, pointing in the direction of the opposite bank where two pieces of wood were projecting from the water below an overhanging bush. 'We've been tossing some worms over there all week. It's an ideal spot to catch my favourite fish—*Perca fluviatilis.*'

Lily furrowed her brow.

'It's the Latin name for perch.'

'I know,' replied Lily. 'It's just that I wasn't expecting a Latin scholar.'

'Da used to teach us things like that,' he replied sombrely, looking affronted at Lily's comment. 'Knew tons of things about nature, he did.'

'He must have done,' Lily replied in an attempt to appease Seoc. 'All right then, let's see if you can catch some fish,' she added, still sounding dubious.

Aedh took up the rod first. Freeing some line from the old but perfectly serviceable reel, he cast the line out towards the wooden posts. Lily had to stifle a laugh when the float soared into the overhanging bush, and as Aedh tried to retrieve the line, the hook snagged on the intertwined branches. With a judicious tug, Aedh managed to free the tackle without breaking the line. With the second cast, the float flew to exactly the right spot. The boys settled down as quietly as they could, dangling their feet over the edge of the canal. As they stared intently across the water, Seoc selected a few smaller worms from the tin and expertly scattered them around the float. The boys sat back and waited, and despite a conspicuous lack of activity on the water's surface, their concentration never wavered.

Eventually, Lily began to get impatient, but each time she tried to speak or even gesture to the boys, they merely threw her disapproving glares.

After almost twenty minutes of inactivity, the float took a slight deflection, sending a ripple across the still surface of the water. Nothing further happened, but Aedh was ready, his hand hovering expectantly a few inches above the rod.

Then, without warning, the float plunged below the water's surface. Almost immediately, Aedh struck hard, causing the rod tip to arch. 'I've got one!' he cried in excitement, fighting to keep the rod upright as the fish darted first this way and then that in an attempt to throw the hook.

Seoc was stationed behind his brother, jumping up and down in excitement. 'Quick, look out for those snags!' he shouted, pointing desperately towards a mass of weeds near the opposite bank where the fish was heading.

Aedh lifted the rod as high as he dared, his muscles straining manfully in an attempt to turn the fish without snapping the line.

'Phew! I thought he was a goner,' Seoc called out when the fish suddenly veered away from danger. Time and again the fish shot off in all directions, desperately fighting for freedom. The battle continued, but as the fish slowly tired, Lily marvelled at Aedh's angling skills; fishing was an art he had evidently mastered through years of practice.

Soon after, Aedh steered the fish into the landing net expectantly held by his brother at the water's edge.

Lifting the fish gently from the net, Aedh slipped the hook from its mouth and held it proudly up for Lily to see. 'It *is* a perch!' he said, beaming broadly at Lily.

'It's a good size, too,' said Lily, looking in wonder at the striking vertical brown stripes on the fish's green back.

Seoc took his turn to hold the fish and demonstrate its impressive dorsal fin and sharp spines. 'You have to watch out for these. They'll give you a nasty cut if you're not too careful!'

Seoc returned the fish to Aedh, who turned his back on them, and with a well-placed blow to its head, he expertly dispatched the fish with a priest he had secreted in his pocket.

Seoc was desperately keen to show Lily that he was also no slouch with the rod. He quickly cast the line, and it was not long before another perch had found its way into the net, much to the boy's delight. By now, the weak winter sun had fallen below the trees, and its meagre warmth dissipated, leaving the three friends feeling chilly, despite the excitement of the last hour.

'Come on. We better be getting back,' said Aedh.

They quickly packed up and returned to the boat just as it was getting dark.

'Would you care to join us for supper?' Aedh said to Lily once they were safely inside.

'Fresh fish and potatoes are on the menu,' Seoc said. 'I'll show you how to gut and prepare the fish if you like.'

Lily briefly thought about heading home. She did not want to be out when her father returned, but she did not know where he had gone, and with a flash of defiance, she decided that if he could come and go as he pleased, then so could she. The excitement of the fishing and the cosy atmosphere inside the cabin with her friends was too much to refuse, and with a smile, she replied, 'I wouldn't miss it for the world.'

10

Death and the Miser

HENRY PRICE SAT BATHING in the warmth of a small, sparsely populated café tucked away on a narrow side street close to the old city docks. He had arrived well ahead of schedule for a meeting brokered by Cornelius Spydre and was killing time before setting off for a run-down area of deserted warehouses that sprawled down to the river in a decaying tribute to the once great trading heart of the conurbation.

The coffee sitting in front of him was dark and a little too bitter for his liking. The remnants of the acrid liquid lay cold and vanquished at the bottom of the cup. The coffee was an attempt at self-reinvigoration, yet so far, the caffeine had failed to alleviate the fatigue and melancholia that had afflicted him for the past few days. He swept back a strand of straight, shoulder-length hair that had strayed across his face and scanned the pages of the newspaper laid out before him. He looked up from a copy of the *Comet* he had picked up from a corner street news vendor and reflected on the call from his old friend that had led to the appointment. Spydre had made some enquiries following their recent discussion and had come up with the name of an art scholar who was an expert on Hieronymus Bosch. Price was sceptical about the meeting, but it was still better than treading water ahead of the Council meeting that had already delayed his plans to visit Amsterdam by several days.

He glanced at an article unrelated to its bold banner headline, but when it failed to hold his attention, his thoughts drifted back to a topic that had troubled him for as long as he could recall: the path his life had taken following the death of his beloved Saskia. At the time, he had craved for revenge, yet with the concurrent death of Pearly Black, his only remaining choice was to track down Black's allies. Not surprisingly, his lack of success in finding them had done little to lift his dark brooding, and if it had not been for Lily, he would never have had the strength to carry on.

After Saskia's death, Lily had been the main impetus in his life, and while he was delighted at the way she had matured, he sometimes wondered why he was so intent in pushing her into areas of study that had dominated his own early years. Her aptitude for learning was extraordinary, and although he would never admit it, she was far further advanced in alchemical lore, particularly in a practical sense, than he had been at a similar age.

Lily had recently demonstrated her potential to a level that had shocked him, and while the burgeoning in her abilities was quite remarkable, it also troubled him in a way he had never anticipated. He sometimes wondered whether the knowledge he was teaching her was too much or even too dangerous for her, and despite her undoubted alchemical talent, she also lacked application in areas of her education she considered irrelevant, and this, of course, was the reason behind their increasingly acrimonious clashes.

Price took another sip of coffee. He returned the cup to its saucer, grimacing at the bitter taste the thick, dark fluid left in his mouth. He vowed to stop thinking about Lily and turned his attention to an experiment he had performed earlier in the day.

One of his many talents as an alchemist derived from an age-old principle of the discipline—the ability to manipulate metals. Alchemical science had evolved over many hundreds of years following attempts to transmute base metals into gold, subsequently effecting many miraculous discoveries that, inconceivably to him, were regarded as dangerous meddling by the mainstream scientific community.

The occasional witnessing of an awe-inspiring spectacle had only compounded this sense of mistrust, giving rise to the widespread belief that alchemy was little more than a form of witchcraft. It was no surprise that alchemy had fallen into disrepute, resulting in a rapid diminishing in the numbers of those studying the arcane arts with even fewer institutions left to teach them. Price had no desire to see the discipline die out altogether and this had convinced him that alchemy's fortunes could only be resurrected by blending it with contemporary scientific research; his current alchemical research was a case in point.

He had always held a fascination for the sub-molecular properties of metals and he had spent many hours in the basement laboratory of his home theorising and testing the practicalities of varied hypotheses. For some time now, his thoughts had been occupied by the properties of electrons in metals and how alchemical lore could harness their oddly incongruent behaviour. At a fundamental level, electrons were the infinitesimally small, negatively charged particles that whizzed around the atomic nucleus in a cloud of ethereal nothingness. Movement of electrons in response to a potential difference was responsible for the inherent conductivity of metals, and through painstaking study, and to some extent, trial and error, he had discovered that it was possible to make electrons move, not as they habitually did in an electrical current, but in a rhythmical motion on a metal's surface.

He had been experimenting with a variety of silver alloys and had recognised that by setting the electrons resonating, he could produce a dramatic reduction in the metal's light-scattering properties. Spurred on by this, he had fashioned a complex metamaterial with unique circular geometry demonstrating variable electromagnetic properties across its surface that made it interact with light in a precise way. Objects were only visible to the naked eye because of the way they reflected light, and miraculously, the material he had fabricated made light flow around it, thus rendering what lay beyond it invisible.

While recalling these thoughts, Price absent-mindedly removed a small square of a peculiar, shimmering foil from his pocket. He looked down at the material nestling in the palm of his hand, and without thinking, he draped it over the redundant coffee cup still perched on the table in front of him.

He looked up to make sure that no one was watching him and noted the waitress leaning on her elbows, aimlessly filing her nails at the serving hatch. She appeared engrossed in her thoughts and uninterested in this strange-looking man who provided little respite from the boredom of her mundane job.

Price returned his attention to the iridescent material that, unlike a metal foil, could adapt itself to the shape of an object. He reached out and touched the material. He smiled as the coffee cup shimmered, then faded, and finally disappeared from view. Although he knew that the cup was still there, he felt a great sense of satisfaction when all that remained visible was a coffee stain on the gingham tablecloth adjacent to where the cup had been standing.

'Top-up, sir?' the waitress said pleasantly, proffering a percolator full of fresh coffee.

Price started, having been staring trance-like at the spot where the cup had been visible. 'Er, I ...' he began, flustered.

When the girl went to pour some of the foul-tasting brew, she took a sudden step back when it dawned on her that the cup was no longer there.

Before Price realised what he was doing, he had slipped the material from the cup with a sleight of hand that would have done credit to the cardsharp he had passed on his way to the docks.

The waitress blinked in amazement, evidently at a loss to make sense of what she had just witnessed. She backed away to the safety of the counter without taking her eyes from the cup that had somehow miraculously reappeared in front of this mysterious man.

Price could see the waitress eyeing him suspiciously from the safety of her stool, making him realise it was time to go. He deposited more than enough money on the table to settle the bill and left without a second glance at the girl.

As he slipped from the café, he returned the material to his jacket pocket. It had taken many years of toil in the subterranean vault of his home to get the blend of metals right, crafting the alloy by painstakingly mixing and melding silver, vanadium and neodymium in crucibles until he had the right quantities of each.

Many times he had removed the cooling metal from the furnace and beat the malleable mixture into a foil with the sweat and toil of his own hands on the anvil next to the cooling water bath, until eventually, he had finally succeeded in constructing a material he had always known was possible.

He hoped he had not frightened the waitress, but he could not resist a smile as he headed for the river, thankful that the melancholia that had plagued him for the past few days had temporarily lifted.

Price made for the Old Wharf Road, a long, straight thoroughfare separated from the river by warehouses and depots that had once served the thriving inland docks before they had fallen into disrepair. The trade that had once flourished here had gradually been supplanted by more accessible ports to the south. The river traffic, once so plentiful, had dwindled to the occasional small vessel making the arduous journey upriver for obscure, or more likely, illegal activities.

The road was empty and the surrounding dilapidated buildings lay deserted, but this was not a place to wander alone, particularly at night. Price was well aware of the gangs that had taken refuge in these buildings, using them as a base for their nefarious, and often, drug-fuelled activities.

Price made his way circumspectly towards a large warehouse that was still reputedly importing to the location. Spydre's concise directions were most impressive. As the instructions predicted, the building sported the sign, Praego Da Largos & Sons – Importers of Fine Wines, est. 1792.

He turned into a narrow street at the far end of the building and set off towards the river along a cobbled street bounded by the towering walls of the depot on one side and a row of neglected garages and lock-ups on the other. The place was strangely quiet apart from the resonating sound of his own clipped heels, but just as he was beginning to relax, he sensed movement. He whirled round to confront any would-be assailant, but with a combination of relief and repulsion, he saw a brown rat scurrying from under the grate of a manhole cover. Price watched in amazement as the

117

brazen rodent passed within a few inches of his black leather shoes before squeezing under the rotten wooden door of a garage. He waited to regain his composure and allow the hammering in his chest to recede before heading off towards his destination.

Further along the alley, he caught the sound of labour ringing out from a garage a few doors down. As he approached a set of peeling doors propped open on bricks, his eyes were drawn to a young man sitting on a stool amidst myriad nuts and bolts, gaskets, pistons, cylinders, gears, valves, rods and shafts surrounding the skeleton of what appeared to be a motorbike. The man had dark cropped hair and a bushy black beard. He looked up as Price walked past and threw him a friendly smile before returning his attention to the contraption. His calloused hands were thick with grease, and as Price paused to watch him work, he noted with approval how dexterously the man manipulated the pieces in his reassembly of the machine. The man's skill was evident from the fleeting moment Price had witnessed him work, and after he had passed the garage, he could not resist turning round to look back and admire the craftsmanship on display. The man, however, was no longer at his stool and had disappeared from view.

After a final check of Spydre's instructions, Price was pleasantly surprised to discover that he had arrived at his destination. The imposing glossy black double doors seemed oddly out of place with the rest of the neighbourhood, although there was no doubting he was at the right place. He squinted at the small brass plaque next to the door engraved with the words, 'Le Cart', which he knew to be the name of the business. Despite racking his brain, he could not recall the meaning of the words from his limited French vocabulary. Just below the plaque was a bell, which he pressed. He waited patiently and was beginning to wonder whether anyone was in when an intercom next to the door crackled into life.

'Hello?' said a soft, female voice.

'Hello. My name's Henry Price. I believe you were expecting me?'

The woman did not reply but a short buzz followed by a sharp click indicated the door's locking mechanism had released. Price turned the chrome handle and noted with approval the weight of the hardwood doors, bearing in mind the insalubrious reputation of the neighbourhood.

He entered a sparse hallway leading directly to a set of stairs. When no one came down to greet him, he made his way upstairs. The climb was steep, but the effort was worth it. He gaped in wonder as he entered the vast space that opened out in front of him, bathing in dazzling light that streamed in through two impressive glass skylights.

There was no sign of the girl, and as he waited patiently for her to appear, he looked around at the numerous tripods carrying frames of various shapes and sizes hidden beneath white muslin drapes.

'Hello,' he called out again while lifting the nearest drape to peer at the canvas. The painting was only partially complete, but Price vaguely recognised the bold depiction of a large tree trunk in a channelled glade. The painting was sketched in graphite, but shades of green and brown had been added here and there to make up a meticulous portrayal of the trunk that dominated the foreground.

He stood gazing at the half-finished painting, feeling baffled by the emotions it stirred inside him. He quickly released the drape when he heard footsteps on the wooden steps leading down from a galleried landing behind him. He turned round to see a woman wiping her hands on a filthy rag covered in paint, and as their eyes met, she smiled, causing his stomach to lurch. He was immediately startled by her eyes, which radiated an inner calm. Her face was most beguiling, and as he looked at her, he realised that she was scrutinising him with the same curious manner that he supposed he was directing at her.

The sunlight cascaded in through the skylight, enhancing her dark brown, shoulder-length hair that shone with a high lustre. The draw of her emerald eyes was irresistible, and as he stared in wonder, a sense of guilt spread through him as his thoughts turned to Saskia. He crossed the studio to greet her at the foot of the stairs while attempting to banish the memory of his former lover.

'Professor Price, welcome. I'm Natacha Lec,' she said, extending a hand.

Price shook her hand warmly. 'Please, call me Henry,' he said self-consciously.

'And you must call me Natacha,' she replied. She ushered him towards the large glass windows fronting the studio and into a comfortable leather sofa that looked across the street to the warehouse.

The glass was meticulously designed, Price noted, to maximise the light pouring through the sloping skylights, and also to provide an extensive view of the river to the north and a broad expanse of skyline to the south. The resplendent sunshine flooded through the glass, and he could feel its radiated heat as he sat down on the sofa bordered by two lush coconut palms happily flourishing in the room's temperate climate.

Natacha sat down beside him. 'I think you know my father, Sir Robert.'

The connection suddenly dawned on him. Spydre had been deliberately evasive when Price had quizzed him about the meeting. All he would reveal was that the girl was an expert on Reformation art, and apart from her name and the directions, he had offered little else. He recalled that Spydre had been a contemporary of Sir Robert Lec and they had studied together at Oxford. His old friend's evasiveness disturbed him, and he wondered whether there was anything else Spydre had kept from him at their last meeting.

Brushing aside these thoughts, Price nodded his assent. 'Indeed, I know him well. We've worked together for many years.'

Natacha returned the nod, suggesting she already knew this. 'My father called me yesterday. He asked if I'd be happy for you to pick my brains. He said he had no idea what it was all about, although I'm not sure I believed him,' she replied, accompanying her words with an enigmatic smile. 'I was intrigued, however, when he told me who'd requested the meeting.'

Price returned the smile. 'You honour me. I appreciate your time. You're clearly very busy with your work.'

'Busy by necessity, I'm afraid. Despite the location, I struggle with the rent, not to mention the costs I incurred when renovating the place.'

'It's most impressive,' he remarked, looking once more in astonishment around the room.

'Yes,' Natacha said proudly. 'The light is, of course, paramount. Of the numerous sites I visited when I was searching for a studio, this was by far and away the best. The glass was specially manufactured. It filters out all the unwanted lower frequencies of the spectrum, the reds and yellows, and allows only the higher frequencies, the blues and greens, to pass. Speak to any artist and they'll tell you the nature of the light goes a long way towards the quality of their work.'

'Have you always worked in the city?'

'Like many artists, I spent some time living by the sea. The light is of a much purer quality there; a combination of the deep blue of the sea and our beautiful skies.'

Price nodded. 'What brought you back?'

'Quite simply, I missed the city. I love the hustle and the bustle, the people, the crowds, the sheer intensity of it all, you know. When I returned, I decided to bring the light with me,' she said, gesturing in the direction of the vast overhead windows.

'What are you working on at the moment?' he asked, entranced by her obvious pride and enthusiasm.

'I'm afraid I have to work on several projects at any one time. The canvas you were studying is one of them.'

Price felt himself colouring; she must have spotted him peering under the drapes when she came down the stairs.

'It's a reproduction,' she continued, oblivious to his discomfort. 'Many of the commissions I receive are for such requests. My primary interest lies in conceptual art, but unfortunately, I have to pay the bills. I've gained a reputation for replicating the styles of renowned artists. As a result, I receive commissions to duplicate many famous old masters. I could make a fortune as a forger … if I chose to,' she said with a wry smile.

'I thought the sketch was familiar, although I still can't place it.'

'It's Constable's *Study of the Trunk of an Elm Tree*. It's one of my favourites. It has a complexity that belies its apparent simplicity. The painting can be appreciated on many levels, the least of which is the unadorned beauty of the tree itself. It's easy to reproduce a treasure that's like an old friend to me.'

'I'd be interested to see it when it's finished,' he said, hoping she would not mind the presumption.

'It won't take long. I'd expect to complete something like this in a matter of weeks. I was working on it just before you called. Please forgive the delay when you rang, I was upstairs cleaning the oil from my hands.'

Price frowned, wondering how she had known of his imminent arrival.

Natacha smiled in response to his puzzled expression. 'Luc rang to warn me that you were coming. He works in the garage a few doors down. Perhaps you saw him on your way past?'

Price nodded, recalling the sudden disappearance of the young man after he had passed the garage.

'This area has an undesirable reputation, you know. Luc's a friend. He keeps a lookout for strangers.'

'That must be reassuring.'

'It is,' she replied, throwing him another captivating smile.

'What makes you so happy?' asked Price, unable to help himself from commenting on the perpetual radiant expression that seemed to grace Natacha's features. Despite feeling embarrassed for a second presumption, he suddenly realised the uplifting effect she was already having on his sombre mood.

'Karma.'

'Karma?' Price repeated, sounding taken aback.

'Yes. I fervently believe in a universal justice and do my best to live my life accordingly. Through the positive energy of my karma, I believe I'll reap my rewards now, or perhaps sometime in the future.'

'Yes, I understand,' he replied, nodding his head pensively. 'There's something else that interests me, Natacha. Why is your company called Le Cart? My French is not so good.'

Natacha laughed unreservedly, making Price wonder whether

he had said something stupid.

Natacha put her hand on his knee reassuringly. 'No. Don't worry, I'm not laughing at you. When I first moved here, it was part of my grand scheme for the business. I intended to have an imposing plaque with the company's name outside. I met Luc soon after I moved in, and we became friends. He arranged for a local engraver to make the plaque for me as a house-warming present. Unfortunately, handwriting is not one of Luc's strongest attributes, and the engraver struggled to interpret what he'd written. I intended to have a simple name for the business and wanted to use my surname. The plaque was never meant to say "Le Cart", but "Lec Art" instead!' she said, enunciating the words carefully.

It was Price's turn to laugh, despite feeling a pang of jealousy at the thought of Luc buying a gift for Natacha, and he wondered how he could feel this way when he had only been in her company for such a short time.

'Anyway, I've grown attached to the sign and so I chose to keep it. It makes for good conversation, don't you think?'

Price nodded. As they sat in silence, he enjoyed the relaxed atmosphere that was more like a re-acquaintance between old friends.

'I assume you didn't come here for a commission. What can I help you with?' she said finally.

'I need some information.'

Natacha sat forwards looking intrigued. 'What do you want to know?' she said eagerly.

'I'm interested in Hieronymus Bosch, and perhaps more importantly, his association with a cabal known as the Esoteric Brotherhood. Can you help?'

Natacha's smile returned almost immediately. 'It depends on how much you already know. It's fair to say I know more than most on the subject. I graduated as an art historian, but my principal interest is Renaissance art. As part of my studies, I undertook a thesis on Bosch's life and works. What specifically is it that you're after?'

'Whatever you can tell me. I've been the recent victim of a theft. Without boring you with the details, the name of the

123

Esoteric Brotherhood surfaced. I believe that Bosch was associated with the Brotherhood, and I'd like to know why,' he said, having no immediate desire to reveal his exact motives until he knew what Natacha had to offer.

'I can sense your reluctance, but given your association with my father, it's my duty to help,' she said light-heartedly. 'Sitting comfortably?' she added with a sarcastic grin, 'or would you prefer some refreshment before I start?'

Price shook his head, feeling a creeping sense of expectation at what she was about to say.

'I think I should start with some background. There have been many misinterpretations of Bosch's work.'

'In what way?'

'The so-called experts either did not delve deeply enough or chose to ignore some of the most fundamental issues of the age when scrutinising his art.'

Price detected a hint of admonition in her voice but did not interrupt.

'Hieronymus Bosch was not his real name. He was born Jheronimus van Aken in 1450. The name means "from Aachen", which tells us that his family originated from Aachen and not 's-Hertogenbosch, where Jheronimus was born. He became known by the name Bosch when he began to sign his work with that name. It's a derivative of the name of his birthplace, you see.

'During Bosch's lifetime 's-Hertogenbosch was a prosperous, provincial town, situated to the south of what is now the Netherlands, close to the Belgian border. His father and grandfather were both painters in the same town. His family had links to other Dutch and German artists before this and it's no surprise that Hieronymus had an inherent talent as an artist.'

Natacha paused for a few moments and cleared her throat. 'Before I go on, I need to digress somewhat. An understanding of the politics of the region during Bosch's lifetime may help to explain just how far he was prepared to go to ensure that certain aspects of his life remained secret.'

Price wondered where the conversation was leading but did

not interrupt.

'Bear with me. It'll all become clear as I explain,' she said, getting up from the sofa. 'It's always so warm beneath the glass. Would you mind if I opened the skylight?'

'Of course not,' replied Price, watching her intently as she crossed the room to collect a long pole.

Natacha returned to the sofa and deftly inserted the pole's hooked end into the latch of the skylight, and with several quick twists, she opened the window by a few inches.

Price could feel a gentle breeze almost immediately. Natacha sat down next to him and he was momentarily distracted by a subtle scent hinting at an exotic Oriental spice he could not place.

'Most of what is now the Netherlands and Belgium was, for the first time, united by the Duke of Burgundy, Philip the Good, in 1433, just seventeen years before the birth of Bosch. This became known as the Burgundian Union, the unification of what had been, up until then, a group of independent territories. This was the first step towards the formation of the Dutch nation. Amsterdam was already flourishing and had become the primary trading port in Europe for grain brought in by ship from the Baltic. Antwerp, similarly, became a thriving port and generated great wealth from its cloth trade. It was a period of great prosperity and growth for the region, and this was only enhanced by the establishment of the Union as a form of limited central government represented by an assembly of nobles, clergy, and towns of the region, such as 's-Hertogenbosch. Under Burgundian rule, trade, industry and culture flourished, and it was no coincidence that many famous artists, including Bosch, appeared around this time.'

Price nodded, recalling the conversation with Isaacson on the day he had returned to discover the manuscript gone.

''s-Hertogenbosch was predominantly a Catholic town, but this was a time of great religious unrest that ultimately culminated in the Reformation. The appearance of Protestant groups, particularly Anabaptists and Calvinists, merely added to the turbulence that would predominate in the region for over a century. In 1506, due to a combination of inheritance and

125

conquest, the Burgundian Union fell under the control of Charles V. Charles was born and raised in Ghent and understood the politics of the region. This became particularly relevant when he succeeded his grandfather as King of Spain and leader of the Habsburg Empire.'

'Which explains how the Seventeen Provinces of the Low Countries became part of the Spanish Empire,' added Price.

'Yes, but matters took a turn for the worse when Charles abdicated in 1555 because of disillusionment at his failure to maintain the unity of the Church. Charles had shown great tolerance and understanding, even allowing the Seventeen Provinces significant autonomy during his reign, but this faltered under the leadership of his son, Phillip II.'

'Why was that?'

'Phillip was born in Spain, and considered himself, first and foremost, a Spaniard. He knew little of the Dutch region and didn't speak the language or understand the people's mentality. In 1568, a decree originating with the Inquisition and signed by Philip condemned the entire population of the Netherlands to death as heretics. Not surprisingly, the Seventeen Provinces revolted against their Spanish rulers, culminating in the Eighty Years' War, a struggle that led to the birth of the Dutch nation.

'Despite the ensuing upheaval, the newly-formed Dutch nation experienced unrivalled success in an era that ultimately became known as the Golden Age. The Dutch provinces became the most important trading centres in Northern Europe as the newly-formed nation flourished both economically and culturally.'

'All very interesting,' said Price, 'and of course, vitally important when considering that the Esoteric Brotherhood was throwing out its tendrils at the time.'

'Yes, undoubtedly,' agreed Natacha. 'And now let me return to Hieronymus Bosch.'

He nodded. 'Mm. I'm intrigued to find out how this all ties together.'

'Bosch, on account of his prestige as an artist, became a prominent figure in 's-Hertogenbosch. It didn't take him long to gain a reputation as a prolific painter that extended well beyond the borders of the thriving town.'

'What of his art?' enquired Price.

'Ah, yes, his art,' replied Natacha, looking animated. 'This is where it all starts to get interesting. Have you ever seen any of Bosch's work at first hand?'

Price shook his head. 'I've only seen reproductions and prints, I'm afraid. Why do you ask?'

'Because I believe it's almost impossible to do justice to the immensity of his talent without visualising his work. Unfortunately, a lot of it now resides in the museums of Spain. Philip II was an admirer and acquired much of Bosch's work for his personal collection, which tells us that the Catholic Church revered Bosch's work. Had they been aware of his clandestine association with the Brotherhood then perhaps they would never have made the assumptions they did about his work.'

'What assumptions were these?'

'During Bosch's lifetime, 's-Hertogenbosch was a conservative, thriving, and predominantly Catholic community not yet touched by the burgeoning storm of the Reformation. Bosch's fame spread far and wide, and he was already receiving commissions from abroad.

'The Bosch family had deep-rooted Catholic associations, and understandably, if the young Hieronymus had done anything to undermine this, it would have had huge ramifications for them all. Bosch did everything in his power to keep his association with the Esoteric Brotherhood secret.'

'What do you know of the group?'

'Not much, I'm afraid. I suspect you already know more than I do, being an alchemist of such repute, but I'll tell you what I can.'

Price nodded. 'Please continue. You've already been most informative.'

'It was imperative that Bosch's association with a group of alchemists, and one with some fairly obscure beliefs at that, remained deeply buried, lest he was exposed as a heretic. What better way than to continue with the Catholic traditions of the family? Not surprisingly, this is what he did. He lived his life, to all intents and purposes, as a prominent Catholic artist. He was responsible for designing a stained-glass window for the town church, and joined the Brotherhood of Our Lady, an illustrious local group of influential Catholics, merely to reinforce his position as a God-fearing Catholic. This façade of respectability reduced the risk for Bosch when he became part of a network of like-minded people who shared his preoccupation with the dark arts.'

'When did Bosch's link with the Brotherhood first appear?'

'That's what's so interesting. While Bosch was alive, he managed to keep his association with the Brotherhood secret. Even when he died, the truth never surfaced for many years.

'Remember, when the Brotherhood was in its infancy, it was during a period of great religious instability and intolerance. Any connection with the Brotherhood would have meant almost certain death at the hands of the Inquisition. Existence of the Brotherhood did not emerge for some time after Bosch's death and coincided with the appearance of the Piotrowski manuscript.'

'You know of the manuscript?' enquired Price incredulously.

'A little, although I've never seen it. I learnt of it as part of my thesis. The document mentions Bosch's name and is the only reference linking him with the Brotherhood. Other than that, it contains little else of relevance, I believe. What do you know of it?'

'One of only two copies ever written was recently stolen from my library. The manuscript purportedly contains a great secret that the Brotherhood wished to keep to themselves. Piotrowski went missing soon after he'd completed writing it, but whether his disappearance is related to the riddle, I don't know. The only other copy of the book resides in Amsterdam. I'm planning to go there in a couple of days to see it for myself. I'm optimistic this will help to unravel the mystery, but until then, I'm afraid we'll just have to wait and see.'

'How can something that was written over four hundred years ago still be so important?'

'I'm not sure, Natacha, but I just hope this secret is not as dangerous as I fear.'

'Do you have any idea what it could be?'

Price shook his head. 'Not exactly,' he replied noncommittally. 'It's some time since I read Piotrowski's manuscript. All I've got to go on are some notes I made at the time.'

'And?'

'Piotrowski made no attempt to hide Bosch's involvement with the Brotherhood or all the other names he listed as original members of the inner circle, for that matter. This implies that the manuscript was only ever meant to be seen by the most privileged members of the Brotherhood. It would have been both dangerous and foolhardy in the extreme to expose those names, bearing in mind what you've already said.'

'What does the book say about Bosch?'

'The manuscript makes reference to his artwork. Although it's not explicit, it implies that cryptic messages or symbols were hidden in his paintings. It's hard to imagine that these messages were directly related to the Brotherhood's secret. Maybe it was a way of disseminating information to other members of the cult. I was hoping you might be able to help me with this.'

'Maybe I can,' said Natacha thoughtfully, 'but this particular topic is fraught with difficulty.'

'Why?'

'Bosch was years ahead of his time as an artist. His paintings incorporated obscure and peculiar imagery that was undoubtedly symbolic in nature. Interpretation of his work depends upon a deep understanding of the man, not to mention the times in which he lived. Many art experts have misinterpreted his work because of the assumptions they made about his life.'

'Go on.'

'The history books are unequivocal in the description of Bosch as a staunch Catholic of unquestionable standing. He lived his entire life in 's-Hertogenbosch, married a local woman, and joined an influential Catholic organisation that contained a small number of only the most respected citizens. If this is what the history books tell us, is it any surprise that his art has always been scrutinised with this in mind?' she said without stopping to draw breath. 'It's for this reason that the same interpretations of Bosch's work crop up time and time again.'

'In what way?'

'His paintings are generally accepted as depicting the human frailty for moral weakness and sin against God. They contain all sorts of fantastical images of demons, inhuman beings, animals and bizarre machinery, pointing to a preoccupation with the evil of man. This, of course, is based on the assumption that Bosch was a God-fearing Catholic, but as we know, he also had interests with the Brotherhood. This puts us at an advantage when trying to interpret his work. Despite all of this, it's still a matter of opinion. All I can do is expound on my theories.'

'I'd be interested to hear them.'

Natacha fidgeted on the sofa to make herself more comfortable before she continued. 'Interpretation of Bosch's work sees him as a pessimist and moralist with no confidence in the inherent goodness of man. The themes of his work are invariably religious and use symbols to represent temptation leading to the eventual ensnarement of man in earthly sin and evil. If you peel away the superficial layers in his work, you begin to see a man who was not so much a religious freak, but more a tormented man obsessed with the occult.'

'Hmm. Interesting. Can you give me any examples?'

'You only have to look at one of his most famous works, *The Garden of Earthly Delights*. It's a painting that sees Bosch at his most deprecating concerning the nature of man. It's a beautiful piece of art in the form of a triptych that can be read as a progression, beginning with the creation of man by God, followed by a fall into temptation and mortal sin, and finally culminating with eternal damnation in hell. Here, let me show it to you.'

Natacha got up from the sofa and crossed to a small wooden chest tucked away in a corner of the room. She swung the lid open and withdrew a leather-bound portfolio that she carried back and handed over to Price as she sat down. She leant over and rifled through the document, revealing a string of reproductions of

Bosch's work. She stopped at the page she was searching for.

'This painting resides in the Museo del Prado in Madrid. It's made up of three panels that, when closed, shows the earth floating in the firmament,' she said, pointing to the print.

'What's interesting is that the earth is depicted with storm clouds gathering and this portends to what follows,' she continued while opening both sides of the print to reveal the hidden reproduction inside.

'The triptych is made up of three panels. On the left, here,' she said, pointing, 'is Bosch's depiction of the creation showing Adam and Eve with God in the Garden of Eden. The central panel that dominates the work illustrates the descent of man into sin as he enjoys the fruits of the earth. Finally, on the right, Bosch has illustrated man's rewards for his sin with a frightening portrayal of hell. If you look closely, Bosch depicts the seven deadly sins being committed in various guises followed by the nightmarish torment that awaits.'

'A frightening vision,' said Price.

'Yes, and these themes repeatedly appear throughout his work.'

'I'm not sure it's necessary to show you all of them, but other paintings such as *The Haywain*, *The Ship of Fools* and *The Seven Deadly Sins and the Four Last Things* all demonstrate Bosch's obsession with the fate awaiting man for his sins.'

'This interests me.'

'How so?' she said, flashing Price a quizzical look.

'The Esoteric Brotherhood was a small group that evolved from their collective desire to pursue the darker aspects of alchemy. One of their central tenets relates to death, or perhaps more importantly, the prolongation of life. Bosch's work screams out to me that he was a man terrified of death, rather than a puritanical religious maniac preaching to the masses that they would be punished for their sins. Don't you see how it fits? On the one hand, Bosch's work was revered for its strong moral and religious themes, but on the other, it reveals Bosch as a man with an obsessive preoccupation with the fate that awaits him as an individual. To what measures would he be prepared to go to avoid this fate for himself, I wonder?'

'Yes, I see,' agreed Natacha 'This only serves to reinforce my misgivings surrounding some of the more frequently accepted interpretations of his work. You mentioned earlier that the manuscript suggests his artwork contained cryptic messages. I've studied Bosch for many years, and I've often wondered whether it's possible to interpret his work in other ways. There are at least two of his paintings that spring to mind if you scrutinise them in light of his fixation with death.'

Price looked eagerly at the pages while Natacha thumbed through the portfolio that was still lying open on his lap. When she found what she was looking for, she held it up for him to inspect. 'Tell me what you see.'

Price studied the image. 'It shows an emaciated man lying on his deathbed. There is an angel next to the bed tending him and a ghastly skeletal figure holding an arrow hovering behind the door. I assume that this is Bosch's representation of impending death. There are demons scattered around the room, and in the foreground, there's another man, who is either dropping or taking something from a wooden chest, although I'm not sure of the significance of these figures, not to mention some of the other implements in the room.'

'Excellent,' she said, sounding impressed. 'You've just described a painting by Bosch entitled *Death and the Miser*. The general interpretation of this work is that it depicts a wealthy man who has hoarded gold throughout his life and is lying in bed awaiting imminent death. We can deduce this from the figure in the foreground representing the miser counting out gold at some earlier time in his life. The moment of truth is nearby as death loiters in the background, just as you suggest, but a battle is raging in the man's mind. Behind him an angel is resting a hand on his shoulder and is pointing to a crucifix imploring the man to accept God's will, but just in front of him, a demon holds out a bag of gold to remind him of his worldly goods.'

'Do you have an alternative interpretation?'

'I've often wondered about this painting, and in light of your revelation concerning the Brotherhood's obsession with death, I just wonder ...'

'What is it?' he enquired excitedly.

'Perhaps what we're looking at is Bosch's depiction of his own impending doom; maybe the man in bed is Bosch himself. Think about it. He was a wealthy man. What this painting may be expressing is Bosch's deeply held fear as his own fateful moment approaches.'

'Okay, I go along with that. I guess this provides us with a link to the Brotherhood and their obsession with eternal life. Is there anything else?'

'Yes, there's more to it. I believe the angel depicted behind the dying man is waiting for something. See how one of the angel's hands rests on the dying man's shoulder while he looks at the crucifix in the window pleading for forbearance. Perhaps the angel is waiting for the miser's death, and at the very moment it occurs, the angel is expected to perform a task.'

'What kind of task?'

'Perhaps that's something you could help me with,' she replied ambivalently. 'What can you tell me of the living stone?'

The question took Price by surprise. He paused for a few moments, studying her carefully. All he saw was the same serene expression she had worn from the moment they had met. Natacha had already shown a great willingness to answer his questions, and his subliminal abilities had detected nothing but trustworthiness in this girl. No. This was no time to question her motives, and after weighing things up, he followed his intuition.

'The living stone means many different things,' Price began tentatively.

'Indulge me,' she said.

For the first time, Price noted a hint of sarcasm in her voice. 'I don't intend to be obtuse. It's just that the stone is referred to throughout the ages, and in some respects, what the stone meant at the time of the Brotherhood is undoubtedly different from the metaphorical concepts it has come to represent today.'

'I'm not sure I understand.'

'The notion of the living stone originated with Arabic alchemists in the eighth century. They believed one metal could be transformed into another, mediated by the use of a mythical dry powder that became known as the living stone. Not surprisingly, as the legend of the stone spread, it became associated with the transmutation of readily available, cheap metals into the rarest and most expensive of them all, gold. As alchemy spread to Europe, the search for the stone flourished, and the concept continued to grow.

'Alchemists began to believe that the living stone could not only help with their transmutations but also amplify the user's knowledge. They thought almost anything was possible, including the ability to cure illness, prolong life, and bring about spiritual revitalisation by allowing the transcendence from a lower state of imperfection to a higher state of enlightenment.'

'I see,' said Natacha. 'But has the stone as a physical entity ever seen the light of day?'

'An astute question that, I'm afraid, is not so easily answered. If you look back at alchemical study through the ages, much of the research was aimed at the creation of this mythical substance. While transmutation is now a fundamental reality, it has nothing to do with the living stone. Instead, modern transmutation has resulted from a fusion between our understanding of quantum mechanics and our knowledge of the arcane arts. That doesn't mean to say that the quest for the stone ever ceased. For hundreds of years, the stone became inextricably linked with the concept of eternal life.'

'Do you think the living stone really exists?'

Price smiled. 'You don't ask much, do you? Let me do my best to answer. Ever since its fabled existence was first rumoured, many alchemists have described the methods they used to create the stone. Some of these alchemists were undoubtedly charlatans while others were misguided, but what is consistent, is the inability of anyone who followed them to recreate their work.'

'Can you give me an example?'

'Indeed. There is a mysterious book written by a twelfth-century alchemist by the name of Artesius. A deep understanding

134

of recondite alchemical lore and a knowledge of Latin is an absolute must to make any sense of his work. With patience, it's possible to recreate the exact conditions, from the preparation of the catalyst and solvent, the so-called "secret fire", through to the extraction of a metallic vapour of vulgar mercury made from antimony and iron, under which Artesius is said to have made the stone. Artesius' manuscript is but one of many found in libraries throughout the world giving unequivocal directions to create the stone. Unfortunately, Artesius' methods, and all those like it, have never withstood the critical evaluation of the many great scientists and alchemists who have attempted to recreate what they described.

'I have no doubt that, even now, there are those who continue the search for the stone. Who's to say whether it already exists in some guise or another. Imagine the power such an artefact would bring to whoever controlled it,' said Price. He shivered involuntarily, and for reasons he was unable to reconcile, he found his thoughts straying to Pearly Black, and although the man had been dead for over ten years, the vision left Price with a considerable feeling of unease.

'I'm sorry to ask this, but it is important. Do you have any idea what form the stone might actually take?' Natacha pressed.

Price pushed the unpleasant thought of Black aside and focused on Natacha's question. 'All I can do is speculate.'

'Please do.'

'There's another name for the living stone.'

'Go on,' Natacha prompted, sounding intrigued.

'Some alchemists refer to it as the soul body. This is particularly relevant if we consider the stone in the context of an artefact aimed at the prolongation of life. The name conveys the impression that some form of physical body is needed to act as a carrier of an individual's essence or psyche. If such a vessel were to exist, then it could, indeed, be the key to immortality, although I still have no idea what form it would take.

'What is it?' Price asked in response to a look of enlightenment that had appeared on Natacha's face.

'A few minutes ago, you asked me what I thought the angel

was waiting for in Bosch's painting. I think I may have the answer!' Natacha replied excitedly.

Price looked stunned. 'Don't keep me in suspense!'

'I think we should examine one of Bosch's other paintings first,' she replied enigmatically.

'What do you mean?'

'Well, if we take the two paintings together, I think it may reveal what Bosch was trying to convey to the Brotherhood. There's another of his paintings I've often wondered about, and following on from what you've just said, I believe we may be on to something.'

Natacha withdrew another print from the portfolio and held it up for Price.

Price gasped. It was a work that he was not familiar with but the effect was instantaneous. The painting depicted a man seated at a table surrounded by a surgeon, a priest and a nun. The surgeon, blade in hand, was operating on the man's head while the others looked on. The icy sense of unease he had experienced earlier returned with a vengeance. He stared at the image, unable to break his gaze as if mesmerised by a snake charmer.

'Are you all right?' Natacha enquired.

The sound of Natacha's voice pulled him back. When he turned to look at her, it took some moments for his eyes to focus. 'Yes, yes, I'm all right. It was not what I was expecting,' he replied eventually. 'What's the name of this painting?'

'It's called *The Extraction of the Stone of Madness*. It was completed at a time when Bosch had already forged links with the Brotherhood.'

'Are you implying that this painting is one of the works Piotrowski alludes to in his manuscript?'

'Precisely!' said Natacha triumphantly. 'If you look at it, I believe it all fits.'

Price nodded. He had already begun to draw his own conclusions but was curious to see if Natacha's views concurred with his own. He waited expectantly for her to continue.

'The painting shows the surgeon removing a stone from the

man's head. Odd as it may sound, this was a relatively common operation during Bosch's lifetime as a cure for madness. The insane, or even those with limited intelligence, were thought to have a stone lodged deep in the brain causing a blockage, thus accounting for their symptoms. Surgery was not a well-respected profession at the time, but many subjects were still willing or coerced into putting themselves forward for the grisly procedure that was supposedly necessary to relieve the blockage. This is the widely held interpretation of this work, but, in truth, the painting doesn't illustrate a stone being removed from the man's head, but a tulip. It's thought to be a reference to the term "tulip head", which is the Dutch term for madness.'

'That's interesting, but perhaps here the tulip is acting as a symbol for something else. The Esoteric Brotherhood had an insignia, like most secret cults. It enabled individuals who were not known to one another to identify themselves. We know from Piotrowski's manuscript that members of the cult wore a signet ring, and the emblem on the ring was none other than ...'

'A tulip!' cried Natacha triumphantly.

'Exactly,' Price agreed.

'So it would seem that the tulip used in this painting is a symbol made in reference to the Brotherhood, rather than as an indication of insanity.'

'It would certainly seem so.'

'The inference being that the Brotherhood was somehow involved in a surgical process to remove an artefact from inside the head. If we examine this in conjunction with the first painting, it suggests that this procedure was undertaken at around the time of death, assuming our interpretation of Bosch's work is correct,' concluded Natacha.

Price felt his blood run cold.

'Are you all right? You suddenly look so pale,' Natacha said, reaching out to touch his arm.

Price reflexively withdrew his arm in response to a searing pain that arose from the scar he always kept hidden.

'What is it?' continued Natacha, sounding concerned.

'I'm sorry,' he replied eventually. 'I've suddenly come over a little queasy. Could I have a glass of water, please?'

'Of course.' Natacha shot up from the sofa and disappeared through a door at the back of the studio. She returned moments later with a glass of iced water.

Price took a sip and smiled. 'That's better, thank you. Please forgive me, I must make my apologies. I hadn't realised how long I'd been here,' he said, withdrawing a fob watch from his waistcoat pocket and flicking open the cover to inspect the face.

Natacha looked taken aback by Price's sudden decision to leave but passed no comment despite having been so deeply engrossed in conversation with him only moments earlier.

Price got up and extended a hand, which she accepted. 'I'm grateful for your help today. The meeting has been extremely productive. Please forgive my hasty departure.'

Natacha smiled, quelling the inner turmoil Price had been experiencing.

'Just one more thing,' Price said. 'Could I request that you keep this conversation to yourself? I'd prefer it if you don't discuss it with anyone else, er, even your father.'

'Of course. It won't go any further than these four walls, but in return, perhaps you'd also grant me a wish?'

Price regarded her quizzically.

'I'd be interested to hear how you get on in Amsterdam.'

'Of course,' he replied, feeling an inner glow of warmth at the request. 'I'll be in touch. Thank you once again for your time, Natacha,' he added as he made his way towards the exit.

Natacha followed him down the stairwell and opened the door. They briefly looked at one another, and after an exchange of goodbyes, Price turned his back on her and stepped outside into a bitter northerly wind that was gusting across the river.

He retraced his steps along the street and when he passed the garage, he saw the man Natacha had referred to as Luc fiddling with a gadget that he was holding a few inches from the end of his nose.

The man appeared not to notice Price, but as he walked past,

Luc looked up and smiled. 'There are typically two mistakes that are made when traversing the road to truth: not setting out, and not reaching the end. You have already departed along that road, my friend. There can be no turning back,' he called out.

Price stopped and looked at the man in bewilderment. He made as if to speak, but Luc lifted a hand to forestall him. 'I sense your urgency, although I know nothing of the troubles that follow you as plainly as a storm. Be true, my friend,' he said. Without another word, he arose from the stool and disappeared through a door at the back of the garage, taking the gadget with him.

As Price set off for home, his head was spinning like a gyroscope. He reflected on how his problems had intensified as the day had gone on, culminating in Natacha's chilling revelation. It had caused a memory to resurface that he had kept buried for many years. The chill wind urged him on, and with the mechanic's words ringing in his ears, he realised how profound they were. From the moment the manuscript had been stolen, he had indeed set off on a path, and it was one from which there was no turning back.

11

The Humpback of Notre Dame

HERMES BING WAS IN a bad mood. That in itself was no surprise as his disposition was apt to fluctuate like the vagaries of the stock market he had recently disparaged in a *Comet* editorial. Bing's newspaper had had the temerity to describe the City as a gambling den of iniquity frequented by affluent wide boys who had been too stupid at school to achieve any notable success, ending up where they were on the basis of who they knew rather than what they knew. Not surprisingly, this assessment had not gone down well in the financial quarter, but for Bing, this was no problem. His views were lauded by the masses who bought his newspapers in ever increasing numbers and, to Bing, this was all that really mattered.

Today, however, and Bing's bad mood was only ever going to get worse; it always did when the coffee was late. His outbursts appeared far too often for the staff of the *Star* whom he met each morning before the paper went to press in time for its early afternoon distribution. These meetings were fraught with difficulties at the best of times, although the beleaguered staff came to realise that Bing's fits of rage were neither personal nor likely to last beyond the first cup of strong coffee to pass his lips, although no ordinary coffee would do.

Cassiopeia, his secretary, had already managed to deliver a coffee to him almost the moment he opened his eyes, which was good. What was not so good was that Bing preferred his coffee made from beans grown on a single plantation situated on the sloping terraces of the mountains overlooking Sana'a, the capital city of Yemen. Wonderful place, wonderful coffee, but for him, nothing else would do. The fact that his usual supply had not arrived when the courier making the delivery was involved in a fatal motorcycle accident, and had scattered the cargo far and wide, was irrelevant. Neither was Bing interested to learn that a further shipment was being airlifted at that very moment and would arrive later in the day. By then it would be too late, and his black mood far too dark to contemplate.

These circumstances were only compounded when John Valentine, the newspaper's Chief of Security, rang in to request an impromptu meeting. Ever since Bing had received a recent mysterious phone call, he had done his utmost to find out who had been behind the call and what best to do with the information the caller had ventured. After Valentine had met with limited success in tracing the call, Bing had shifted his attention elsewhere. The caller had suggested that Bing was under consideration for election to the Council, but their leader, Henry Price, was planning to block the move. Bing barely had time to deliberate before he decided that being a member of the revered, and somewhat secretive, Council was definitely in his best interests. So, should he try and make Price change his mind and vote in his favour? Or somehow ensure that Price fail to make the meeting? With these options in mind, he had tasked Valentine with finding out what Price was up to.

After the application of some gentle persuasion in all the right places—bribery was never considered unseemly for an institution like Bing's media conglomerate—Valentine made the intriguing discovery that Price had been the subject of a recent burglary. Despite the authorities' best attempts to cover up news of the theft, the scoop was published in the *Comet* the following day, but to Bing's dismay, the article provided little more than sketchy information at best.

Bing prided himself on his empire's prolific database of criminals, delinquents, thieves, pickpockets, cardsharps, tricksters, fences, snitches, moles and grasses, or anyone, for that matter, who could be relied upon to perform wrongdoing of any kind. After all, as Bing was often quoted as saying, 'Where else would you expect to find the reputable information upon which we base our publications?'

Despite turning over many stones in all sorts of dubious places, little else surfaced, apart from the revelation that the only item taken was an archaic book penned by a man with the ridiculous name of Piotrowski. Bing knew something odd was going on simply by the cover-up. He also anticipated that if he could get to the bottom of the burglary, then it would give him a bargaining tool that he could use to manipulate Price. He had immediately dispatched Valentine to keep watch on Price and to track him at every turn, but thus far, the ploy had yielded disappointingly little.

Despite the awful coffee, Bing's mood lifted the moment Cassie called to inform him that Valentine was on the way up. He scrutinised the day's itinerary while waiting for Valentine to arrive with what he hoped was some new or potentially useful information. His mood, however, plummeted to yet unheralded depths the moment Valentine vacated the elevator with a hangdog expression etched on his face that was enough to make Bing weep.

As a ruthless journalist, he had learnt to read a face within a fraction of a second, and it was clear that Valentine was no poker player from the anxiety-laden creases adorning his brow and the dilated pupils betraying his fear. A symmetrical, rhythmical pulse beating at his temples merely corroborated the incipient rise in the man's blood pressure, telltale signs of someone about to go into a meeting that was destined to go badly.

'What is it?' barked Bing in a voice that was harsh and threatening.

'I'm sorry to disturb you, Mr Bing,' Valentine said as he edged across the broad expanse of floor space towards his employer.

'Cut out the flimflam. Just tell me the news,' Bing snapped.

'S-sorry, I ... I ...' Valentine stammered.

Bing glared, waiting for him to continue.

'You remember, boss, we were trying to keep track of Price?'

Bing did not reply but drummed his fingers impatiently on the table. The sound resonated sharply around the room.

'I'm, er, afraid we managed to lose him.'

'What do you mean by "lose him"?' spat Bing. '*Lose* as in mislaid or *lose* as in failed to keep up with? No, don't even bother to answer that,' he continued without coming up for air. 'Who did you have tailing Price and how could this person be so incompetent? It's not as if it was a difficult task, after all, now was it?'

'The man we use is generally very reliable,' replied Valentine, wringing his hands nervously.

'*We*! Don't you mean *you*? And *generally* isn't good enough!' barked Bing.

'I know, boss, but McCall's got an excellent track record. He's never failed me before.'

'Well, you'd better get him back on the case before we miss out on some valuable information.'

'That's what's so odd,' replied Valentine. 'I said the same to him, but he just came back with some poorly disguised excuse and declined point-blank to have anything further to do with Price.'

'Hmm. We all know how dangerous Price can be. I'd wager Price has somehow got to him; remind me, what's this man's name?'

'McCall.'

'Then I suggest you find McCall and question him a little more diligently. I expect you to get to the bottom of what actually happened. All is not yet lost. Perhaps we can turn this to our advantage after all.'

'Of course, Mr Bing,' replied Valentine.

'Get out of here and get on with it,' Bing ordered, surveying the dramatic early morning skyline while patently ignoring his loitering employee.

Valentine turned quickly on his heels and headed for the elevator. He gave an audible sigh of relief as he placed a palm on the touch pad next to the lift and waited for the green light to confirm that the elevator was on its way.

'Not long till your retirement now, John,' Bing called out unexpectedly.

Valentine did not reply, nor did his boss expect him to; it was a statement based on fact, and was a simple, but ill-disguised threat aimed at reminding Valentine of the consequences of yet more failure with his comfortable retirement away from the bustle and turmoil of the city teetering on a knife-edge.

The elevator doors opened, and Valentine moved quickly into the car.

Bing afforded himself the satisfaction of a hollow smile. There was a time and a place to be ruthless, or at least give a good impression of it, and he was never one to shirk his responsibilities. The stakes were too high, and he could ill-afford to lose this opportunity; after all, it was unlikely to repeat itself again in the future. He inherently liked Valentine and had worked with him for many years. It pained him to threaten him in this way, but Bing was too experienced not to realise what motivated men like John Valentine. It would be all too easy for him to sit back and await the comfort his pension would bring. What better way to ensure his commitment by a gentle, yet none too subtle, reminder of the consequences of failure?

The intercom suddenly crackled into life.

'Mr Bing?'

'What is it, Cassie?'

'Your meeting with the——'

'Yes, yes, I know. When's the damned coffee going to arrive?'

'It should be here by two this afternoon, Mr Bing.'

'Well, just make sure it does. Oh, and in the meantime, I want you to get all the past copies of our newspapers, not to mention any supplements or periodicals, containing references to either Henry Price or his precious Council. Is that clear?'

'Yes, of course. I'll get on to it right away, sir.'

'Just make sure you do. I expect everything to be in my office, including the coffee, by five to two,' said Bing, pressing a prominent red button on top of the intercom, bringing the conversation to an abrupt end.

Bing fidgeted uncomfortably in his chair. Too much caffeine provoked a headache in most, but for him, it was the opposite. He wondered whether substituting his craving for caffeine with a small dose of nicotine would help to relieve the pounding at his temples. He crossed the room and opened the double doors leading to a terrace that jutted improbably from the side of the building. The cool morning breeze was refreshing, but as he leaned over the balcony and surveyed the city many hundreds of feet below, he thought better of the cigarette. With his physician's recent words still ringing in his ears, he would just have to wait for the coffee.

The rest of the morning turned into a series of interminable meetings that became progressively worse as the day went on. By the time Bing returned to the office, casually casting aside his false beard and Rabbi's hat on the leather sofa adjacent to the elevator, he had long since lost his patience.

It had started badly at the pre-press meeting of the *Star*, although he knew it was not the staff's fault that there was no noteworthy news with which to festoon the paper's front pages.

'Good journalists make their own news,' Bing had boomed, but deep down he knew that, from time to time, days like this were destined to happen.

The meeting had dragged on for two hours longer than scheduled, and this, of course, had made Bing late, and increasingly vexed, for the subsequent meetings listed in his diary.

His staff were scouring the world press in desperation for a story the *Star* could lead with, and as the deadline edged ever closer, Bing finally agreed on a bizarre tale that even he found amusing, despite the depressing way the day was progressing.

One of the sub-editors had unearthed a story in a local edition of *Le Parisien* about a stray whale stranded in the Seine. Bing immediately saw that, with the right lead, the story could be a runner. Following some quick thinking, the headline writers came up with the somewhat quirky, and almost certainly factually incorrect, headline of, 'The Humpback of Notre Dame'. The fact that the whale was of the Minke variety and was nowhere near Notre Dame when it was found proved irrelevant, and with time running short, Bing agreed to run with the story.

The whale had somehow found its way up the Seine, and

despite all good intentions to repatriate the beast, it had died and been washed up in the middle of Paris. French bureaucracy determined that the whale's remains should linger on the riverbank until someone in authority decided what to do with them next.

It was only when Professor Devereux, proprietor of the Musée d'Histoire Naturelle, came forward and offered to take the whale for 'scientific purposes' that the outcome was agreed. Unfortunately, by the time the museum made arrangements to salvage some seven tons of dead whale, the residents were already beginning to complain about the stench. When three tall cranes and twenty museum workers lifted the carcass onto a suitably large truck, the vehicle only managed to trundle a few hundred yards before the whale exploded onto a crowd of bewildered onlookers.

When asked for his comments by a *Star* reporter, Professor Devereux responded with an off-the-cuff statement that was incorporated into the article as quick as a wink.

> *'Ze poor beast should never 'ave been left zere for so long. I'm afraid ze authorities are never very good when something 'appens zat is not in zeir rulebooks. Ze delay to move ze whale caused a 'uge build-up of gases inside ze animal's stomach as it decomposed. Unfortunately, Jacques, one of my men, lit up a Disque Bleu after ze gargantuan effort to get ze mammal onto ze truck. Jacques is, 'ow do you say? one short of a full pod of peas, and tossed ze butt in the direction of ze beast's waterspout.*
>
> *"Ow was he to know zis would ignite ze sulphurous gases emanating from ze beast's guts? Fortunately, Jacques was left with no more zan a set of singed eyelashes. I'm afraid ze onlookers were not so lucky and were splattered by a combination of blood and decaying guts. Et Voilà! It was an 'orrible sight.'*

Bing was delighted when some further probing by a wily old hack revealed the Professor to be the real villain of the piece. Following the whale's explosive demise, Devereux was left with the delicate task of explaining to the dog food company he was surreptitiously dealing with that the 'horse meat' consignment he had agreed to sell for a fee of several thousand Francs would no longer be coming their way. It was hardly a surprise that Bing exposed the facts exclusively in the *Star*.

Bing left the meeting with a sense of satisfaction at the ingenuity of his staff, but this was not enough to raise his spirits now that he was running late. He called Cassie to cancel a meeting with a disgruntled cartoonist then set off for a lunchtime rendezvous with his old friend and rival, Montague Fielding, the owner of *The Daily Sting*.

The *Sting* was the only coherent competitor to the supremacy of Bing's newspapers, and despite the intense rivalry between the editors and their insistence on disparaging one another in their respective publications at every opportunity, in private, they remained firm friends. For the sake of the daily battle fought to bolster their newspapers' ratings, it remained imperative that the men were seen to be adversaries in every conceivable matter. In public, if one man said, 'black', the other would say, 'white', it was as simple as that, but between them, they agreed on too many things they cared to admit. They both knew that it would have an unfavourable effect on their respective media empires if the truth of their friendship ever came out, and for this reason, their meetings were only ever held in secret.

It was Bing's turn to visit Fielding, but, fortunately, this required little more than a thirty-second stroll. The newspaper empires faced one another across the street like two behemoths wrestling in a perpetual struggle for supremacy, much the same as the feigned antagonism that existed between the media moguls that owned them. It went unsaid that whenever the men held a meeting, they travelled incognito, resulting in increasingly outrageous disguises, culminating in Fielding's recent appearance dressed in the attire of a Zulu tribal chief, complete with shield and spear.

After the profligacy of his friend at their last meeting, Bing's dress, on this occasion, was rather understated. When he slipped into the *Sting's* headquarters through a locked side door to which he had received the access code via a cryptic message sent to his secretary earlier in the day, he did so in the attire of a rabbi, resplendent in black dress and hat, and complete with a false beard.

The quick trip across the divide, however, was not without incident. When a woman clutching a babe in arms leapt out in front of the bogus scholar, eager to quiz him on his interpretation of a passage in the Torah, the interview was cut short when the child grabbed Bing's shockingly white beard only for it to come off in the tot's hands. Quite who was the most surprised during the brief intercourse that followed, it was hard to tell, but in the ensuing commotion, Bing slipped apologetically away without further ado.

Lunch was a relatively quiet affair, dining in Fielding's office on seared calf's pancreas served on a bed of Beluga caviar washed down with a bottle of fine French claret, a 1945 Château Mouton Rothschild. The discourse was somewhat stale, largely as a result of Bing's caffeine deficiency and Fielding's discomfort from a severe attack of gout afflicting the big toe of his left foot, and it was with great relief to both parties when their luncheon was prematurely terminated by the arrival of Fielding's personal physician to tender to the aforementioned big toe. The doctor was particularly displeased to see the remains of the gout-inducing meal Fielding had just partaken of and insisted he immediately retire to elevate the inflamed digit.

So it was that Bing, on his return to the summit of Bing Tower, smiled unassumingly at what awaited him in the office, having cast off the remnants of his disguise on the brown buckskin sofa next to the elevator. For most wealthy men, it was a stunningly attractive woman or a priceless piece of art, but for Bing, it was the combination of the aroma wafting towards him and the sight of a cafetière sitting on the desk. He did not need to be told that the coffee had arrived; he simply took in the bittersweet smell and rejoiced in his fortitude at not having indulged in that earlier cigarette.

He crossed to the desk with a heightening expectation that was almost too much to bear. He poured the coffee adroitly and lifted the cup to his lips, staring all the while at the dark, thick liquid shimmering enticingly in the cup. Before allowing himself a sip, he inhaled deeply, savouring the roasted flavours of leather and tobacco. He closed his eyes and imagined himself standing in the invigorating air of the mountains overlooking Sana'a on the Arabian Peninsula. Was it the imagined rarity of the atmosphere or the heady expectation of an end to his caffeine deficiency that set his head spinning? Bing did not know, and not wishing to dwell on it, he tipped back the cup in one fluid motion, swallowing the liquid with carefree abandon in a single gulp. The familiar tannic edge and dried fruit flavour combined with a hint of cinnamon spiciness flooded his senses. He flopped back into the chair almost overwhelmed.

It took barely a few minutes for the caffeine buzz to reinvigorate his body, sparking a re-emergence of the dynamism that was Bing's trademark. He focused on the pile of newspapers and magazines neatly stacked on the desk in front of him and recalled the reason for his earlier request. He leant forwards and leafed through the back-issues left for him by some poor clerk who had undoubtedly spent the morning systematically trawling through the archives deep down in the bowels of the building. He scanned the papers, discarding one after another until his piercingly blue eyes settled on an article that interested him. It was an edition of the *Comet* that led with a report on the Council in the years following the death of Pearly Black, which immediately caused his thoughts to return to that time.

In the fallout of Black's demise, Dionysus Bing was ousted from his role as editor-in-chief of the media conglomerate by the board of directors, undoubtedly for his unflinching support of the discredited Black. Rather foolishly, the same set of men subsequently instated Hermes in his father's place, only to discover that their own positions quickly became untenable for a variety of obscure reasons.

The generally held belief that the directors had sold off their stakes in the business for outrageous financial gain was nothing more than a smokescreen. Instead, each of them was compromised in scandalous situations making their stock-selling a necessity.

Otherwise, Bing secretly assured them that whatever they held most dear—whether their marriage, business or political aspirations—would be left in ruins. The name for it was undoubtedly blackmail, but according to Hermes, he preferred to describe it as gentle persuasion.

In this way, Hermes ensured that he would never have to suffer the same indignity as his father, which, in part, went some way to explaining his unflinching resentment of the Council, whom he blamed for his father's demise. His logic ran thus: Price was responsible for the inception of the Council, which in turn resulted in the downfall of Black, which in turn led to his father's ruin.

Unsurprisingly, it did not take long for the newly appointed Bing junior to vent his spleen on those he blamed for his father's fall from grace, and when Dionysus died shortly after his son's succession, this only served to exacerbate Hermes' fury even further.

Bing suddenly stopped and scratched his head. If he hated the Council so much, then where did his eagerness stem from to align himself with an organisation that he so clearly despised?

'That's obvious,' he muttered to himself with a chuckle, knowing full well that, despite his intense chagrin at being persistently passed over, what better way to frustrate Price than to become a permanent thorn in his side from within?

Bing dismissed these thoughts and turned his attention to the article. He scanned the opening paragraph and grinned at a typical *Comet* diatribe questioning the Council's raison d'être. Unfortunately, the public were neither interested nor cared, judging by the effect on the paper's circulation, but, at his insistence, these Bing-inspired rants resurfaced from time to time, usually under a different guise or in an alternative forum.

Bing discarded the paper; it was irrelevant in the context of what he was looking for, but it made him reflect on Price's role in the origins of the Council.

Price had always been insistent that Black and his cronies were a major threat to the nation's security. This concept was laughable in the minds of many people, including his father, and reflected the popularity Black had enjoyed with the public at the time. It seemed hard to imagine, therefore, how Price was able to assemble a self-selected, autonomous body with the power to exert such an influence over the highest offices of the land.

Maybe Price was party to information that was not common knowledge, but whatever the reason, the truth had never come out. After Black's death, the speed with which his supporters disappeared suggested that they were neither willing nor able to continue whatever it was he had started.

Bing shook his head. There was still so much he did not know, he thought dejectedly. He sighed and picked up the newspaper lying on top of the pile, still unsure of what he was actually looking for. He scanned the drab, unpromising front page of *The Evening Star*, a publication that, in general, followed a quirkier and more light-hearted approach to news than the *Comet*.

Some years previously, the *Star*, in a publishing coup, included a free monthly periodical with the paper on the first Friday of each month. The glossy colour magazine proved extremely popular and led to an enormous boost in sales, curiously benefiting all of Bing's publications in equal measure. As a gauge of the venture's success, the sales ploy was immediately copied by the *Sting*, and while this also proved inspirational for Bing's rival publication, he continually enjoyed reminding Fielding of where the idea had originated.

As Bing thumbed through the broadsheet, a magazine slipped out and landed on his lap. He looked down and was startled to see the face of Henry Price staring back at him from a picture plastered across the glossy front cover. His pulse quickened, and in eager anticipation, he dropped the *Star*, scattering its pages at his feet. He studied the photograph that showed Price standing on a short flight of stone steps in front of an ancient, yet attractive building he immediately recognised as the Academy of Arcane and Alchemical Arts. He sneered at what he perceived to be the imperious, self-centred expression on Price's face. Price was dressed in a college gown with his hair tied neatly back, staring impassively into the depths of the camera. It appeared to be an old graduation photo, and below it, a bold caption proclaimed, 'The Death of Alchemy?'

Bing thumbed through the journal and found the relevant article, noting the date as some three years earlier. Settling back in the chair, he began to read.

Alchemy means many things to many people and is said to have sundry diverse origins and influences throughout the ages. The word alchemy *is derived from the Arabic* al-kimia, *for* divine chemistry *or* black earth, *meaning the art of transformation, although it is widely believed that alchemy influenced other prominent civilizations well before its advent as a science in the Islamic world. Many alchemical publications have failed to survive into the modern era, being lost, destroyed or hidden from the eyes of those who neither care nor wish to understand the regal science as it is referred to by its devotees. It is clear, however, from writings still accessible that alchemy was a flourishing and revered subject well before the birth of Jesus Christ.*

Alchemy is understood to originate with the great Egyptian king, reputed to have lived around 1900 BC, whom the Greeks referred to as Hermes Trismegistus. Hermes was the author of the fabled Tabula Smaragdina, an ancient text written on green stone and which later became known as The Emerald Tablet, the most famous of ancient hermetical writings. Hermetica became the title for literature attributed to Hermes and contained secret wisdom that was the foundation of alchemy in Europe during the Middle Ages. Unfortunately, the Tablet did not survive in its original form and suffered the indignity of many incomplete translations, which may, in part, have contributed to the mystical aura associated with writing said to reveal the secret of alchemy to those who chose to search deeply enough.

After the birth of Christ, Chinese civilisation makes reference to the influence of alchemy on its culture. The first Taoist pope, Chang Tao-Ling, devoted his life to the study of alchemy and meditation and was reputed to have received a mystical treatise allowing him to distil the Grand Elixir of Immortality, the precursor of what later alchemists labelled the living stone.

Alchemy was widely practised in Greek, Roman and early Indian cultures, but it was the Islamic world that laid the foundation for the future birth of the science in the West. One of the great alchemists of the eighth century, Jabir ibn Hayyan, made enormous contributions to European interpretation of the ancient alchemical arts. Jabir, or Geber as he became known in the West, was a skilled chemist as well as a mystical devotee of alchemy. Advances under his guidance include the techniques of distillation and the mixing of various reagents. He also discovered new elements including the metals, sodium and potassium. The ability to distil led to the isolation of new acids, including aqua regia, a mixture of nitric and hydrochloric acid, a liquid able to dissolve the noblest of metals, including gold, sparking off the belief that the internal rearrangement or transmutation of one metal into another would one day be possible.

Thus began the quest for the living stone, a mystical alchemical panacea, which, amongst other things, would allow the transformation of gold from base metals. Unfortunately for Western alchemy, the writing attributed to Geber proved impossible to interpret. His annotated notes, written in an indecipherable and crude form of symbolism, failed to yield the secrets they were believed to hide. It is hardly surprising that the frustration emanating from the inability to penetrate the darkest secrets of Islamic alchemy gave rise to the Anglo-Saxon word gibberish, *derived directly from the name of Geber himself!*

Bing returned the magazine to the desk and rubbed his eyes wearily. He could not remember previously reading the article and was dubious whether it would reveal anything he did not already know about Price. So far the article had failed to capture his imagination, but he presumed that the first few paragraphs were merely an entrée to something a little more stimulating, or so at least he hoped.

He picked up the magazine once again, and rather absent-mindedly, scanned the article for the author's name. He found what he was looking for—Zoë Tsing—a distinctive name, he mused, but despite dredging through his memory, rather to his surprise, he could not recall hearing the name before. Bing assumed that this woman, whoever she was, was not on his staff, for he prided himself on his ability to remember the names of all of his employees, down to the most menial task worker in the depths of Bing Tower. He wondered whether she was a freelance journalist and made a mental note to find out.

He savoured a final gulp of coffee languishing at the bottom of his cup and returned his attention to the magazine.

Alchemy was introduced to the European mainland when the Moors invaded Spain in the twelfth century, bringing their mystical and alchemical beliefs with them from Islam. From Spain, the Hermetic word spread throughout Europe, and within a few generations, alchemical teaching had been assimilated into other cultural, religious and scientific beliefs of the age.

Albertus Magnus, Thomas Aquinas, Artephius and Arnold de Villeneuve were responsible for the development of alchemy during the Middle Ages as a valid and integrated subject intertwined with other areas of scientific, religious and philosophical thinking. The greatest of all alchemists during this period was the Englishman, Roger Bacon, who did more than any other man to establish alchemy as a respected science.

Bacon joined the Franciscan order and graduated from Oxford before moving to Paris, where he studied mathematics and medicine. Bacon was one of the first true polymaths of his age with knowledge of astronomy, optics, languages and philosophy, in addition to the subjects he had studied during his formative years. He elevated alchemy's standing as a science and brought it to the attention of all forward thinkers of the time. He is also attributed with the revelation that the living stone could be used as a means to prolong life just as his illustrious Islamic and Chinese predecessors had revealed to their respective cultures many hundreds of years before him.

Despite major contributions to science, including alterations to the Julian calendar through the study of astronomy, the production of convex lenses leading to the manufacture of spectacles and the theory behind telescopes, Bacon was eventually imprisoned for his knowledge. The Church countered his prowess as a great sage by citing magical arts and witchcraft as the base for some of his most significant discoveries. Bacon was forced to denounce much of his work to effect his release, thus allowing him to continue his studies, albeit now in secrecy.

The story of Bacon's life serves as an example of what was to follow during the Renaissance. Alchemy developed as a means of universal understanding, but this tenet gradually became blurred by the superstition that thrived during the great religious and political upheaval of the time. For this reason, Hermeticism became an occult (as in hidden) practice, mainly because of the fear of persecution, imprisonment or possibly even worse, leading to the creation of secret cults and cabals operating as small, clandestine organisations made up of self-selected groups of 'the trusted few'. New recruits or initiates were carefully observed before a gradual introduction to the arcane arts and beliefs of the group through a process of ritual and mystical teachings that became known as the rite of initiation. Thus began a long and arduous inner journey for the neophyte starting with enlightenment and illumination before acceptance into the innermost circle of the sect. Not surprisingly, texts surviving from this era were written utilising cryptic alchemical symbols and diagrams, with layer upon layer of secret, hidden and allegorical meanings. The few documents that survived into the modern era have proved notoriously difficult to decode, and many futile attempts have been made to reveal the true nature of their meaning.

Many secret organisations with alchemical associations arose during the Renaissance, and for this reason, alchemy became associated with occult practice, and in particular, dark ritual and magical arts. These initiate orders were established to propagate secret teachings, with the earliest, and perhaps greatest, example being the Rosicrucian Order.

Bing sighed; he had developed a desperate feeling that the article was about to degenerate into an exposition of conspiracy theories, which was hardly a surprise as his newspapers were full of them.

Despite the coffee, his eyes were slowly beginning to droop as his concentration waned. When his eyes briefly closed, he forced them open with some difficulty, knowing that, otherwise, he would be asleep in seconds. He peered into the depths of the mug lying awkwardly on his lap and noted with interest the concentric rings of coffee stains evenly spaced on the inner wall like the rungs of an improbably circular ladder that led down to a slurry of dark residue. He picked up the cafetière, refilled his cup and thumbed through the remaining pages. He looked at his watch and was relieved to note that there was still an hour to go before his next appointment. With a flourish, he picked up the article and began to read from where he had left off.

The existence of the Rosicrucian Order was shrouded in secrecy until two anonymously written manifestos were released within a short period of one another at the beginning of the seventeenth century. The manifestos, Fama Fraternitatis *and* Confessio Fraternitatis, *describe the life of Christian Rosencreutz and his founding of the Order. Rosencreutz was born in Germany in 1378, and at the age of five, was sent into cloisters with a Jesuit Order. Following classical training in Greek and Latin, Rosencreutz left for the Holy Land to extend his education. He travelled to Damascus, and under the instruction of Islamic occult masters, he learnt to speak Arabic while being initiated as an adept in medicine, mathematics, alchemy and magic.*

After three years, Rosencreutz sailed, first to Egypt, and then to Fez, where he gained instruction with learned Arabian magicians, philosophers and alchemists. He spent a further period with Spanish Kabbalists on his return journey before finally returning to his homeland, where he established a secret group with three brothers from his former cloisters.

The brothers erected a building, the Sancti Spiritus, and once the men had recruited a further four initiates, the Rosicrucian Order was founded. The men agreed that the Order should remain secret for a hundred years, during which time they would travel the world in search of enlightenment. They agreed to meet every year at the Sancti Spiritus, and in the event of their death, each man was to select a worthy successor as a replacement.

The Rosicrucian Order remained secret until the publication in the seventeenth century of the first two manifestos, and finally a third, The Chymical Wedding of Christian Rosencreutz, which describes the practical nature of secret alchemical learning discovered by the Order.

The publication of the manifestos declaring the existence of a secret brotherhood caused a wave of excitement to spread across Europe and led to a resurgence in alchemy, magic and Kabbalah. Despite the manifestos, the Rosicrucian Order remained a secret society free to continue with its ideals in science, philosophy and freedom of conscience in splendid isolation.

The emergence of the Rosicrucian Order was followed by a period in which many other secret societies sprang up with their own rites and initiations, all centred on various aspects of mysticism and the occult. These groups flourished and became the precursors to Freemasonry in the early eighteenth century. A handful of these secret societies still exist today, most notably the Hermetic Order of the Golden Dawn, which is said to be a direct descendant of Freemasonry and Rosicrucianism.

It is also no surprise that secret cabals and sects were established before the publication of the manifestos, bearing in mind that Rosencreutz had formed the Rosicrucian Order at the beginning of the fifteenth century. One such group known to have operated during this period was the Esoteric Brotherhood, a cult originating in Northern Europe.

The Brotherhood was an ultra-secretive group, small in number, with interests in darker aspects of alchemical lore. Acceptance of recruits into the group only occurred after an appropriate period of initiation and enlightenment, which was said to take many years. Rumours abound that, in distinction to the Brotherhood's original objectives, the sect endured with the solitary aim of protecting humanity from a terrible secret allegedly discovered by one of their initiates. The rumoured existence of this secret has long been the source of considerable speculation, raising the possibility that the Brotherhood successfully unravelled the enigma of the living stone. This conjecture does not explain the dichotomy that, on the one hand, saw the Brotherhood preserving their greatest discovery, and yet on the other, keeping it hidden for fear of the danger it could unleash on all of mankind.

It is no surprise that many conundrums persist from the ancient alchemical age when considering the secrecy surrounding the alchemical cults and their cryptic texts rumoured to exist, yet having failed to materialise, in the modern era. Whether this knowledge is lost or merely hidden is unknown with alchemical texts accessible to us today open to misinterpretation, sparking rumours about lost or forgotten secrets of a bygone age. Whether the Brotherhood's great secret or any other alchemical mysteries of the past will ever see the light of day again is unclear. What is also uncertain is how these ancient secrets tie in with modern alchemy.

The number of contemporary alchemists has dwindled in recent years despite the assurance of those still practising the art that it thrives and grows in our midst. Unfortunately, nothing could be further from the truth. Despite the great alchemical traditions and discoveries of the past, it is modern scientific technology that has superseded the older, established arts. The few alchemists who still retain the respect of the scientific community argue that their remarkable skills make them capable of unique feats never to be replicated by modern science despite the unnecessary burden of the time it takes to learn these skills in our technologically-driven era. The apprentice acquiring the master's skill has been replaced by teaching methods in modern sciences that are accessible to all and considerably less labour intensive than the archaic mode of learning that is integral to alchemy. One only has to approach the last bastion of alchemical learning, the Academy of Arcane and Alchemical Arts, to appreciate the decline in its former supremacy. A once great institution and centre of learning, the building is now a neglected and crumbling edifice, home to a handful of misguided students still willing to spend many years of their lives in pursuit of obsolete knowledge.

The task of revitalising interest in alchemy and other esoteric arts is the responsibility of Abel Strange, Chief Mentor of the Academy. Strange is reputedly one of the leading thinkers of our age, a man of prodigious talent and knowledge, but also sadly lacking in charisma. It is no coincidence that the Academy's stock has fallen to its lowest ebb under his tutelage, and it is evident that the knowledge and learning taught there is not what it once was in the long and renowned history of the institution. Sadly, rumours of obscure occult practice and eldritch lore being taught to students have done much to damage the once great reputation of the Academy. The added burden of a failure to move with the times has resulted in an institution that is beset by dwindling numbers and crippled by financial crisis.

Strange's stance has always been consistent as exemplified by his oft-quoted, yet predictable response, 'Ability in the practical aspects of alchemy is an innate gift and not something easily taught or acquired. It is my duty to protect the Academy's time-honoured standards'.

For this reason, Strange has always insisted that the Academy maintains strict admission criteria, yet in the current economic and political climate, this strategy must be considered foolhardy in a world where only the strongest survive. It is reasonable to assume that, if current trends continue, the once thriving Academy of Arcane and Alchemical Arts is on a headfirst collision with financial ruin and disaster.

Were circumstances always thus? The answer is, of course, no. It is only seven years since the untimely death of one of the most talented pupils to emerge from the Academy, the much-loved and irreplaceable Pearly Black.

Black was renowned, not only as a prodigious talent in alchemical circles, but also as a creator of educational opportunities through his charitable work in sponsoring less fortunate members of society. Black was the founder of the Order of Eternal Enlightenment, a secret society that began as an inner circle of his closest confederates along the lines of the Hermetic Order of the Golden Dawn, a group he had briefly flirted with before the advent of his own cabal.

Membership of the Order was cloaked in secrecy, but there is strong evidence that Black surrounded himself with his most trusted allies from the time he spent at the Academy. The objectives of the Order were obscure, although the practical, rather than spiritual, aspects of alchemy were amongst its central tenets based on Black's predilection for this area of lore. The Order was responsible for the promotion of alchemy as a respected science at a time when its credibility was already starting to wane. Additionally, charitable work undertaken by the Order in deprived areas of the community has been well publicised in the past and was integral to the overwhelming support foisted on Black that propelled him, reluctantly at first, into the public eye. Although Black's original aim was to keep the Order's activities hidden, once the press learnt of the charitable nature of its work, Black was swamped in a deluge of media attention.

Black's natural charm and accessibility made him a perfect target for the media, and it was not long before he achieved great fame and public adoration for his work. Black's opinion was consistently sought on scientific and current affairs, much to the chagrin of leading political figures of the time. He also began to socialise in the most exclusive places, rubbing shoulders with celebrities and prominent figures alike.

Unfortunately, not everyone shared in the adoration of Black. Not long after news of the Order surfaced, a figure arose determined to oppose Black's popularity. Rather surprisingly, it was a fellow scholar from Black's days at the Academy, Professor Henry Price, who emerged as his greatest critic.

Price was a solitary voice who utilised every opportunity to express hostility and antagonism towards the Order. It was undoubtedly a great disappointment to Black that a former friend and colleague from the Academy should see fit to oppose him on, what was, distinctly nebulous grounds. Nonetheless, Price became obsessed with the downfall of his rival based on the Order being an elitist and secretive organisation hiding behind its charitable contributions as a smokescreen to its true purposes. Ironic, you may consider, bearing in mind the nature of the, soon to be established,

Council. There was little support for Price's notion in the public domain, but he somehow managed to garner backing for his objectives from those who saw Black as a threat to their own political aspirations.

It was at around this time that the Council first appeared, tacitly as an advisory body to the Government on matters pertaining to national security, yet as so eruditely raised by Dionysus Bing in an editorial of this veritable publication, who could argue with the notion that the Council's advice was already available to the highest offices of government from other, well-established and more reliable, sources?

It was clear from the outset that the Council's objectives were to control, halt and ultimately discredit the Order because of its perceived threat to the political stability of the time. Is it any coincidence that, following Black's demise, the Council became an impotent and functionless body with few notable achievements to its name?

If one is to scrutinise Price's real motives for his opposition to Black, then perhaps an entirely different picture begins to emerge. During their time together at the Academy, Price and Black were rivals in almost every aspect of their lives. By far and away the most talented students of their generation, they excelled in their chosen fields of study, and it was not long before their prodigious abilities easily outweighed the academics supposedly there to teach them. Not surprisingly, tensions arose as the men vied for supremacy in what became a very personal battle of wills. At the time, this was considered to be healthy sparring between two intellectual heavyweights attempting to outdo each other in the furtherance of their careers, but, eventually, this personal rivalry spilled over into a bitter contest with ultimately fatal consequences.

Matters only became worse with the arrival of Saskia Schalk as a novice at the Academy at a time when Black and Price were already well established there. Schalk inadvertently became the catalyst that exacerbated the burgeoning feud between the men. Dark, beautiful, mysterious and intelligent, Schalk captivated all of those whose good fortune it was to meet her. In the close confines of the Academy where apprentices spent their time learning and socialising together, it was inevitable that Black and Price would be mesmerised by Schalk's charm.

Not surprisingly, Schalk was flattered by the attention the men showered upon her, although she claimed that she desperately avoided embroiling herself in the squabbles that inevitably intensified with her appearance. Schalk was drawn to Black's effusive and charismatic nature, and they began to spend more and more time in one another's company. It was around this time that Schalk also discovered an area of mutual scientific interest with the withdrawn and brooding Price, culminating in long hours spent together in the laboratory.

When Black graduated, he left the Academy with Schalk in tow, inevitably escalating the tension that already existed between the men. Price, dour and aloof, returned to his solitary existence as an isolated and embittered man, his alchemical experimentation his only solace.

We now know that Black had already established the secretive Order towards the end of his time at the Academy. Little was known of the recruits or the nature of the Order's activities, and perhaps it would have remained that way but for a young and enthusiastic investigative journalist working on behalf of this illustrious institution.

Clandestine organisations always make for good press, and with the whiff of a scoop, Dionysus Bing used his common sense and foresight to send an up and coming reporter on an undercover assignment tasked with infiltrating one of the secret societies mentioned earlier, the Hermetic Order of the Golden Dawn. With the aim of exposing the true nature and ideals of the organisation, the name of a former member emerged, and with it, the rumoured existence of an even more exclusive secret society.

Due to a combination of smart covert work and good fortune, the name of a small private bank with associations to the newly-formed Order of Eternal Enlightenment was discovered, and a young and inexperienced clerk subsequently compromised, resulting in the exposure of the Order, and with it, the charitable nature of its work.

Articles published, first in the Star, *and subsequently in the* Comet, *led to Pearly Black's meteoric rise to fame, setting him firmly on a collision course with his erstwhile adversary, Henry Price.*

It is easy to understand the circumstances that precipitated this feud, but Price's antagonism rose to yet unheralded heights when Black, his fame at its zenith, jettisoned Schalk as his constant companion only to replace her with yet another alluring beauty, Aurelia Nightshade. Schalk instantly fell off the radar, reappearing some time later at the side of the self-appointed leader of the Council, Henry Price. It was almost inevitable that this train of events, set in motion some years earlier, would culminate in a catastrophic showdown that resulted in the tragic deaths of both Saskia Schalk and Pearly Black.

The consequences of that night where events unfolded in an obscure refrigeration plant in a run-down area of the city have had numerous ramifications ever since, some foreseen, others less so. There is no doubt, however, that this event coincided with the starting point of a steady decline in the science of alchemy. It is still unclear where all of this will end, but it is hard to argue against those who believe that the events of that night were the precursor to the death of alchemy. With Pearly Black gone and the Academy of Arcane and Alchemical Arts on an ever-downward spiral, who could argue with this almost inevitable truth?

Bing relaxed; the coffee had finally calmed the frayed nerves that had been troubling him all day. He also sensed a feeling of accomplishment at having persevered with the article penned by Zoë Tsing. Reading it had caused many memories to come flooding back as the events leading to the fateful showdown between Pearly Black and Henry Price were laid bare. His recollection of the circumstances surrounding Black's death remained hazy, yet it was most enlightening to re-evaluate what he could remember of the history between these two greatest of rivals.

A smile had gradually appeared on Bing's face as he read, and had grown considerably larger with the realisation of the power he wielded as head of the country's foremost media conglomerate. The article was a case in point; no matter who had written it, he detected the unmistakable influence of his father hidden behind the words. Dionysus had shown unflinching support for the Order and had done much to propel Black to the fame he had desperately tried to avoid. His father had turned a blind eye to some of the less palatable, and lesser-known, truths associated with the Order, and in particular, its insalubrious association with the criminal underworld. The reality was that Black had acquired his wealth without any discernible, and legal, source of income. During Dionysus' editorial reign, these facts were consistently overlooked in articles about Black and his cronies, and it was hard to dispute the ineluctable fact that his father was, in short, partly responsible for Black's rise to power.

The article, however, also posed a conundrum. There was no doubt it had been written during his own tenure as editor, but it troubled him greatly that he could neither recollect ever having read it before nor the journalist who had written it.

While Bing still held Price responsible for the events surrounding his father's death, the article was undeniably a misrepresentation of the facts. Nonetheless, he was glad to have read it because it had given him a better idea of what to do next. The key to the problem was undeniably Saskia Schalk, for here was the answer to the rivalry that existed between Price and Black. If only he could find out more.

There were also other less pressing issues he wished to see answered. Firstly, who was the girl Zoe Tsing? And was she the journalist responsible for the coup of lifting the lid on the Order? Unanswered questions for sure, but Bing smiled smugly to himself; if anyone was capable of finding the answers, it was undoubtedly him.

12

The Spindlewick Street Siege

HENRY PRICE WAS IN a contemplative mood as he sat behind the large, cluttered desk awaiting Lily's arrival. He had slept poorly as a result of the disturbing meeting with Natacha the previous day, and the state of turmoil troubling his thoughts mirrored the haphazard overburdening of his desk. His mind kept regurgitating the conversation with Natacha with the consequence that switching off from it was nigh on impossible. She had concluded that the Esoteric Brotherhood was involved in a surgical process conducted around the time of death, although whether this was related to the Brotherhood's well-protected secret he could only speculate. Nonetheless, it had caused a memory to surface that he would rather have left buried.

Price's gaze subconsciously drifted towards the Historoscope lying amidst the chaos of the desk. He briefly toyed with picking it up, but the sound of footsteps coming up the stairs interrupted his deliberation. Lily appeared at the door and peered inquisitively at him through bright, blue eyes. A smile briefly flickered at the corners of her mouth suggesting she was pleased to see him, but just as quickly faded.

'Where've you been? I've not seen you in ages,' Lily said defiantly.

Price smiled in a vain attempt to appease the will of this young girl who continually challenged him. He was well aware that, due to his obsession with recent events, he had not given her the time she deserved.

He regarded her sheepishly. 'Please, come in and sit down. Let me explain,' he said, getting up to greet her. He ushered her towards a chair next to his own with a gently placed hand on her shoulder.

The frosty expression on Lily's face remained, but she did not shy away from his touch. Once seated, she sat impassively waiting for him to speak.

'Lily, look, I'm sorry. I know I've been neglecting you. It's just that I've been preoccupied with the break-in,' he said while watching her carefully for any sign of a reaction, but her expression remained unflinching. He hesitated, finding it difficult to gauge her mood, and unsure how best to proceed. After a brief hiatus, he came to a decision. 'I've got to go to Amsterdam tomorrow after the Council meeting. I'll be back in a few days. I promise I'll make it up to you then.'

'You can make it up to me now if you like,' she said, flashing him a mischievous grin.

'How?'

'Take me to Amsterdam with you!' she said excitedly.

Price did not reply, causing Lily's enthusiasm to melt away. She glared at him with an expression he had seen on Saskia's face many times before. It saddened him to disappoint her like this, but he had faced a similar scenario once before and he would not make the same mistake again.

'I'm sorry, Lily. It could be dangerous. I'm not prepared to expose you to that kind of risk.'

'I don't suppose there's any point in arguing,' Lily stated. 'No, I thought not,' she added in response to her father's curt shake of his head. 'Well, perhaps you could tell me what this is all about?'

'Very well,' Price said, allowing a thin smile to appear on his lips. 'It's the least I can do, after all.'

'Go on.'

'I've made some enquiries about the stolen book and it appears that my initial fears were justified. You remember our conversations about the Order of Eternal Enlightenment ...'

'I thought that was all over.'

'So did I, but perhaps I was wrong. I have reason to believe that Pearly Black's associates may be planning something. I don't have any concrete evidence to back this up, but I know that Black was interested in Piotrowski's book.'

'Do you know who was responsible for the theft?'

'It's too early to speculate, although I have my suspicions. Perhaps I'll know more after my trip.'

'Why do you have to go to Amsterdam?'

'A good question. Much to my surprise, I've recently learnt that a second copy of Piotrowski's book resides in a library there. It appears that whoever holds both copies may also hold the key to a secret that was hidden many hundreds of years ago, suggesting that whoever stole the book may similarly covet the other one. Perhaps you now understand why the trip could be hazardous. You do, don't you, Lily?'

'Well, as a matter of fact, I don't,' replied Lily defiantly. 'You keep telling me how well my studies are progressing and how far advanced I am. Maybe now's the time to give me a chance to show you what I can do.'

'That's precisely why I don't want you with me. I doubt you have any idea how much I respect your talents, but it would be extremely foolhardy for us both to go. It'll be hard enough for me to look out for myself, but if I have to worry about you as well, it could put us both in danger. No, Lily, you must remain here. I fear your time will come sooner than you anticipate.'

'What do you mean by that?' she snapped.

Price shrugged his shoulders. 'Time will tell,' he said ambivalently.

'Very well, if that's the way you're going to behave, perhaps it's time for me to do a little digging of my own,' said Lily, getting up and striding purposefully towards the door. She turned and looked back at her father. 'I've got to get to my lessons. Will I see you before you go?' she enquired sharply.

'Of course. Perhaps we could eat together this evening?'

Lily nodded cursorily. She turned quickly on her heels and disappeared down the stairs.

Price sighed. He knew Lily was headstrong but she would calm down. He would counsel her later not to do anything rash while he was away.

He frequently dwelt on his relationship with Lily, but no matter how hard he tried to do the right thing, it always seemed to end in disagreement or, in Lily's case, disgruntlement. How he wished Saskia was still here. She had always intuitively known how to deal with Lily, but, unfortunately, the same could not be said of him. It was at times like this that he felt most isolated and alone, he reflected ruefully.

He got up to stretch his legs and made his way to a door that opened onto a small balcony, stooping to avoid the wooden beams abutting the steeply sloping roof. He went outside into the cool, early morning air, rising to his full height as he passed through the door. He was wearing a khaki quilted jerkin over a thick, plain white cotton shirt, but it was insufficient to ward him from the chill wind blowing directly from the north. As he surveyed the river in the distance, he pushed aside the troubling conversation with Lily.

The surface of the water was choppy and his eyes were drawn towards a small boat struggling upstream against the tide. The traffic moving in the opposite direction made the boat appear as if it were standing still, but looking beyond it, he could just make out its progress against the backdrop of the buildings on the far bank of the river. After the boat had disappeared from view, he went inside and returned to the desk. As he sat down, his gaze settled once more on the Historoscope. He lifted the instrument from its stand and passed the surprisingly light gadget from one hand to the other while marvelling at the intricate lattice of silver and gold metalwork on its surface that resembled the delicate veins of a leaf.

As he returned the instrument to the desk, he suddenly thought of the surgical process purportedly carried out by the Brotherhood that Natacha had referred to at their meeting. It had jogged his memory of the events that had culminated in Black's death. Understandably, he had done everything he could to suppress the memory of that fateful evening, but with the Council meeting imminent, it was not something he could ignore any longer. The Council's support was paramount should his suspicions prove correct, and he was determined to have every fact at his disposal to corroborate his fears of a re-emergence of the Order.

Price lifted the gel cap from the desk and felt a flutter in his chest; anticipation that he was about to revive a memory best left buried, he supposed. With great trepidation, he slipped the cap onto his head, ensuring the protruding electrodes were in contact with his scalp. He closed his eyes and began to concentrate, banishing all extraneous thoughts as he turned his attention to the events of that evening. He picked up the Historoscope and drew the viewfinder to his eye. The curtain of murky blackness soon gave way to pinpricks of light flashing intermittently across the instrument's small internal screen. When he blinked, an image of countless bright dots had burnt into his retina like a galaxy of stars cast against a midnight sky. Colour gradually intermingled with the tiny white spots, fusing into a blurred but coherent image.

His temples throbbed from the mental exertion of the effort as an uncanny image appeared on the screen displaying him sitting in a high-backed leather chair in the familiar surroundings of the sitting room downstairs. He stared apprehensively at his doppelgänger and was shocked to see his young appearance. The grey that dominated his temples was strikingly absent and his face was free of the lines that stared back at him from the mirror on a daily basis. He took a deep breath and began to watch.

*

Price sat next to an open fire diligently reading, the sound of crackling logs burning in the basket next to him. His face was furrowed in concentration, illuminated by the radiance of the reflected light. He suddenly looked up, startled by a loud spit as a small ember shot from the fire and landed harmlessly in the grate. He stared at the glowing fragment until it faded with the ebbing of its heat.

He returned his attention to the document and remained engrossed in his reading until he was disturbed by the sound of the handle turning in the double oak doors. A tall, elegant young woman, instantly recognisable as Saskia, entered the room and headed towards him. She had shoulder-length, wavy dark hair framing brightly burning blue eyes that made her look strikingly similar to Lily. She crossed the room and placed a hand affectionately on his shoulder while peering down to see what he was reading.

Price looked up and smiled. 'Lily asleep?' he whispered.

'Soundly. I read to her, but as usual, she was fast asleep before I'd finished. What are you up to?' she asked casually.

'Nothing much. I've been looking at some notes I made a while ago about a book that, I must admit, has always baffled me. I'm afraid I'm none the wiser. Anyway,' he said, dropping the notebook nonchalantly onto the Persian rug at his feet, 'there are much more important things to do now,' he said, standing up and putting his arms around her waist.

Saskia laughed and playfully pushed him away. 'Look, why don't we eat out tonight? Mrs Brimstork can keep an eye on Lily. It's such a beautiful evening. We can go down to Nico's.'

Price smiled. Nico's was a cosy Italian restaurant down by the river that was not too far to walk. It also happened to be Saskia's favourite eating place. He knew how much she enjoyed dining out under the awning, feasting on her favourite dish—a most delicious seafood linguine—in the lee of the adjacent bridge that spanned the brightly illuminated river.

'There'll be a frost tonight. It may be quite chilly,' he warned, knowing how much she enjoyed eating al fresco.

'Yes, but just think how wonderful the stars will be. Come on, it'll only take a few minutes to get ready. We can wrap up warm and I'm sure they'll light the chiminea for us.'

'How could I refuse!'

Saskia pulled him from the chair and propelled him playfully through the door.

'*You* can tell Mrs Brimstork we won't be eating in tonight,' he declared as they spilt into the hall in a rush of excitement. 'I don't think I could bear one of her withering looks. After all, it *was* your idea.'

'Coward!' she replied, and with a playful look of admonishment, she turned towards the kitchen where she knew Mrs Brimstork would still be working at this late hour.

Saskia had barely crossed the hall when there was an urgent knock at the front door. She froze and cast Price a quizzical look, but he merely shrugged. 'You'd better answer it,' she said. 'Albright's out for the evening.'

Price turned on his heels and crossed the hall. He placed the flat of his palm on a bronze plate next to the jamb and waited for the familiar clicks as the locks released from their tumblers. He opened the inner door and entered the portico before checking a small viewing port to see who was there. An anxious looking Nicolas Fox, head of Internal Security, was waiting outside, hopping impatiently from one foot to another.

Price opened the outer door and invited the man inside. Fox was dressed in a formal, expensively cut, dark grey suit with a navy blue club tie, regaled with an insignia displaying two anchors above a skull and crossbones, which Price did not recognise.

'Please, come in,' said Price, ushering Fox through the vestibule into the hall where Saskia was waiting. She craned her neck over his shoulder to get a better view of the unwelcome guest.

'Henry, please forgive me for disturbing you at such an inhospitable hour, but I'm here to brief you regarding a recent development. I thought it would be best if we spoke in person,' said Fox. He was a tall, gaunt man with an urgent demeanour that betrayed his eagerness to enter the house.

Price introduced Fox to Saskia, and as they shook hands, he heard her give an almost imperceptible sigh. Like her, he suspected that their plans for the evening were almost certainly ruined. Price took the overcoat Fox was carrying and laid it casually over the banister at the bottom of the stairs before leading him into the room he and Saskia had excitedly vacated minutes earlier. He ushered Fox into a chair and picked up the notebook that was still lying open on the rug, surreptitiously slipping it into a pocket. He sat down on the sofa opposite, and moments later, Saskia joined him there, having followed the men silently into the room.

Fox glanced uneasily at Saskia. He appeared as if he was about to say something but then hesitated. After composing himself, he tried again. 'The matter is of the utmost importance. Council business, Henry. I ... er ... would prefer to speak alone,' he said, squirming uncomfortably in the chair under Saskia's unflinching gaze.

'I think I'll be the judge of that, Nicolas,' replied Price sternly. 'Is there a problem?' he continued. 'Your sudden arrival suggests that this is urgent.'

Fox glanced briefly again at Saskia. 'It concerns Pearly Black,' he said in an almost conspiratorial whisper. 'I wouldn't wish to upset your ... er ... Miss Schalk,' he added uncomfortably.

'I don't need to speak for Saskia, but I can assure you that anything said regarding Black will not bother her nor will it go beyond the confines of these four walls. On that, you have my assurance, Nicolas. Now, please continue,' Price replied, slipping his hand onto Saskia's thigh in a gesture of support.

Fox sat silently for some moments as if weighing things up. Beads of sweat had appeared on his forehead, possibly from the warmth of the room after the chill air outside or perhaps an expression of his growing anxiety. His small, beady black eyes shifted involuntarily from side to side, drawing attention away from his large, aquiline nose. He was not an attractive man, but his features somehow suggested a hidden strength, reflecting his position as Chief of Internal Security.

Eventually, after his initial indecision, Fox began to speak. 'Very well, but you must be prepared to accept the consequences of what I have to say, and I can assure you, Henry, there will be consequences.'

Price nodded, unfazed by the threatening undercurrent in Fox's words.

Fox kept his gaze firmly trained on Price as he settled into his chair and began to relate the train of events that had led to his unannounced visit. 'I'm here to brief you about a stand-off that's developed over the last few hours. It all started some weeks ago when we learnt about a possible break-in. There was nothing particularly unusual in the intelligence that was picked up, but it was brought to my attention when a link with the Order emerged. We've recently stepped up our monitoring of the Order after a recent spate of murders and criminal misdemeanours that we're convinced are linked to the group. Our efforts have been hampered by the overwhelming support the Order seems to enjoy with the public, not to mention the unheralded adoration for Black himself, courtesy of the downright lies that seem so prevalent in the media these days.'

'And this has hindered your investigation?' said Saskia, demonstrating her determination not to be excluded from the conversation.

A brief flicker of annoyance appeared on Fox's face. 'The intelligence we rely upon to subvert the interests of the criminal fraternity often arises from disgruntled or jealous ex-employees with a grudge or an old score to settle. When you consider how the public has been taken in by Black, it's hardly surprising that we've not had much success where the Order's concerned. There's been such a surge in support for him recently I wouldn't be surprised to see him happily ensconced as the next Prime Minister if the public have their way, particularly when the polls tell us that the current regime is ailing so badly. We, of course, know differently, but, unfortunately, no one's come forward with anything to link the Order with the illegal activities we know they're involved in; that is, until a few weeks ago when we received a tip-off regarding a burglary. For once, the information came from a reliable source.'

Price tilted his head quizzically, but Fox merely shook his head. 'I'm sorry, Henry, but I'm not prepared to divulge the name of the informant. I can assure you it's of little importance. All I can tell you is that we refer to him as Viper at The Firm. We have to protect our sources, you understand?'

'Very well,' replied Price guardedly. 'What's been going on?'

'It all began at The Gibbet, a seedy inn in the East End. It's the sort of place favoured by all kinds of thieves and ruffians. Those whose misfortune it is to stumble upon the place would be well advised to turn and leave the moment they walk through the door, if they have any sense, that is.

'Viper just so happened to be there when he rather fortuitously overheard a conversation between a couple of undesirables who frequent the place. The men were deep in conversation in a dimly lit corner and failed to notice that someone was lurking in their vicinity. They were talking about the theft of a consignment of metal from the docks six months ago. It was a rather low-key affair, being neither audacious in its planning nor risky in its execution, and didn't attract our attention at the time bearing in mind the nature of goods that were stolen. What was odd, though, was that the gang ignored some of the more valuable items and only took a stock of silver and nickel. Why they chose those particular metals and nothing else, we've no idea,' said Fox, causing Price and Saskia to exchange nervous glances.

'There was nothing suspicious about the theft at the time,' Fox said. 'It appeared to be a routine case; that is until forensics came up with a name from the evidence we found at the scene.'

'Go on,' said Price urgently.

'The man was none other than Liquid Lex, lifelong felon and associate of Black. Liquid Lex is, of course, merely a nickname for a man who hides behind many guises and aliases. As to his original name, who knows? His real identity has long remained hidden, clouded in the mists of time. He's gone under various names for the sake of the many and varied crimes he's committed against mankind, but this is the name we know him by.'

'Yes, and it stems from the trademark methods he uses for his misdemeanours,' said Saskia.

The observation raised a look of astonishment on Fox's face, and an awkward silence ensued as he waited for Saskia to enlarge on her comment.

Saskia suddenly looked self-conscious, her pale complexion pinking slightly. She smiled, almost as if she was embarrassed by her interjection, but she cleared her throat softly before continuing. 'I met Lex on several occasions. It was after I'd left the Academy when I was working with Pearly,' she said, colouring more visibly now. 'Lex used to visit Pearly regularly. I was sometimes party to their conversations, although they never talked about anything illegal, of course,' she added quickly.

'He was introduced to me as Lex Larcombe, but I always had my suspicions. Pearly called him Lex, but some referred to him by other names. It wasn't difficult to deduce his true identity. After all, Liquid Lex's reputation seems to be the source of a perverse kind of hero worship in certain quarters. He's a charismatic character, and it's easy to be captivated by his humour and enthusiasm, not to mention his rather distinctive appearance; all hair and combat fatigues, you see. It was Pearly's association with men like Lex that began to raise my suspicions well before the Order's activities began in earnest.'

'I assume the details of this are known to you, Henry?' asked Fox.

Saskia glared at him indignantly.

'Of course,' Price snapped, exuding annoyance. 'I can assure you Saskia passed on everything she learnt of Black to me, which, if you recall, was relayed to the Council. I wasn't aware your memory was so poor, Nicolas,' Price added sarcastically.

'Perhaps I should continue with my account,' said Fox, ignoring the rebuke.

Price nodded. 'Go on.'

'It was most unlike Lex to make such a mistake. He's a man whose reputation for exactitude exceeds those of a similar disreputable inclination, but on this occasion, we found a small piece of cloth attached to a barbed-wire fence surrounding the foundry.

'Forensics found a scrap of hair on the fabric and they were able to match it with Lex from our records. We've no idea why he was involved in such a low-key theft, but perhaps you could enlighten me regarding the significance of the metals that were taken?' suggested Fox suddenly.

Price and Saskia glanced at one another again, and despite their exchange of looks, no words passed between them. Price got up and ambled over to the window. He pulled back the curtains and looked outside disinterestedly. 'What makes you think we know anything about what was stolen?' he replied, looking casually up at the impenetrable wall of a starless sky.

'I know you both have a particular interest in metals, that's all.'

Price raised an eyebrow. 'There could be any number of reasons why someone would take this combination of metals. There's nothing that immediately springs to mind, but I'll give it some thought. Now, please continue if you will, Nicolas.'

'As you wish,' said Fox, sounding suspicious. 'Viper was still listening in on the conversation when one of the men got up to go to the bar. The man had been drinking heavily, judging by the way he staggered to his feet. He lurched across the room and knocked over some chairs in the process. Viper saw his opportunity and jumped to his feet as if he was about to leave. The men collided in the middle of the bar, and they ended up in a tangle on the floor.

'Fortunately for us, Viper is one of the most accomplished pickpockets of his generation. As the men tumbled to the ground, Viper was able to procure a piece of paper from the man's pocket. The dullard was too stupid to realise he'd been on the receiving end of a theft but reacted as you'd expect for a man of limited intellect by hitting out. Viper's reflexes were far too quick, though. He sprang to his feet and disappeared through the crowded bar before the man had any notion of what had happened.

'Viper subsequently passed the piece of paper to his contact at The Firm. There was an address on the note, and because of Lex's connection with the theft the men had been talking about, I thought we ought to take it seriously.'

'What did it say?' interjected Price, striding across the room and sitting down beside Saskia.

'Here, see for yourself,' replied Fox, reaching inside his jacket and withdrawing a grubby, creased piece of paper, which he unfolded and handed over.

Price studied the note. 'I presume this has something to do with the stand-off you referred to earlier?' he enquired, handing it to Saskia.

'Yes. Spindlewick Street is in a rundown area of the East End. It houses a few small factories and businesses. The address refers to a chemical manufacturing plant. Are you familiar with it?'

Price shook his head.

'We had no idea of the significance of the information Viper procured for us but I decided that we should post a watch on the address. That was weeks ago now, and believe it or not, I was on the verge of withdrawing our surveillance. We're extremely short-staffed, as well you know, Henry, and I can ill-afford to waste vital manpower on dead end tasks.'

'I presume your luck changed,' said Price humourlessly.

'Indeed. I received a call at my club this evening from one of our more reliable operatives, a man by the name of Twelftree. He was on watch and was alerted by a sound coming from the factory roof just before seven o'clock this evening, not long after the place had closed for the day.

'Since the surveillance began, we've been renting a bedsit on the opposite side of the street; it affords good views of the factory but, unfortunately, not the roof. Twelftree clambered up through a skylight to see if he could get a better view.'

'What did he see?' asked Price.

'It was dark and the visibility was poor but Twelftree was patient. Eventually, he heard the same noise again. It sounded like someone was drilling, and soon after, there was a loud report and a brief, but very bright, flare. He got a fleeting view of three men on their knees staring down at the factory roof. The flash of light only lasted a few seconds, but it was enough for him to recognise one of the men. It was Pearly Black!'

'Is he certain?' demanded Price.

'He assures me he's not mistaken, although we have no idea what Black's doing there. Twelftree waited, and not long after, he heard the sound of a door being prised open. He could barely make out what the men were up to but he was in a precarious position. He didn't want Black to find out he was being spied on, and so he hid in the lee of a chimney. From there, he watched the men disappear into the building through a trapdoor in the roof.'

'I presume you know what goes on in this chemical plant?' asked Price, intrigued.

'We've done our homework, Henry. The business goes by the name of CoolFlow Incorporated. It manufactures chemicals with applications in the antifreeze, refrigeration and air conditioning markets. It appears to be nothing out of the ordinary and it's baffling why Black would sully his reputation on such a small scale operation.'

'I agree,' said Price. 'We all know of his links with crime but he's always managed to avoid proof of any direct involvement. It's difficult to see why he'd put himself at risk like this. He has any number of men at his disposal to carry out his jobs for him. Do you know who's in there with him?'

'No, I'm afraid not. Twelftree only had a brief view before the men entered the building. I think he was so taken aback to see Black, he didn't get a chance to look at the other two.'

'Has anything happened since?' asked Saskia.

'No. Twelftree contacted me straight away. I mobilised all of my available men and went straight there. I've been there ever since; until now, that is.'

Price looked involuntarily at his watch; it read half past nine. 'So Black's been inside the factory for the best part of three hours. And you say there's been no movement?'

'We've seen neither sight nor sound of the men since they went in.'

'How do you know they won't reappear at any moment?' said Price.

'I don't think they intend to come out quite yet, Henry. Black knows we're on to him. We managed to get a tap on the factory's phone line and we intercepted a call not long after they went in. It wasn't easy to hear, and we only managed to catch snippets of the conversation, but it was undoubtedly Black. He knew we'd spotted him and that our men were already swarming all over the place.'

'Do you know who he called?' asked Saskia urgently.

'No. The wire was hastily arranged and we couldn't trace it. The call was made to a local number and we know he spoke to a woman.'

'Aurelia Nightshade?' suggested Saskia.

'Likely,' replied Fox. 'We know from the call that Black doesn't intend to leave until he's found what he went in for, whatever that is. It seems he's quite prepared to sit it out. Black ended the conversation by saying he was waiting for something, although he didn't clarify what.'

'Do you think the Order will send reinforcements?' said Price.

'No,' replied Fox emphatically. 'Black made it quite clear that he wants to sort this out for himself.'

Price eyed Fox pensively but Saskia nodded her head implying she had picked up on something the men had missed.

'As usual, Black seems to have contacts in all quarters, including Internal Security,' said Price.

Fox's face reddened. 'Are you suggesting my organisation is compromised?'

Price smiled placatingly. 'It wasn't meant as a slight on your department, Nicolas. It's just that the Order's tendrils seem to spread far and wide. It wouldn't be the first time they'd learnt of our movements the moment you gave the order. Just be thankful they weren't aware of your surveillance.'

Fox nodded. 'As usual, Henry, you're right,' he said, his colour fading. 'At least we've got them where we want them. They're cornered.'

'I wouldn't be so confident, Nicolas. I know how short-handed you are, and I'm not sure your manpower is sufficient where Black's concerned. Let's just hope you're not underestimating him.'

Fox nodded. 'Again you're right.'

'Have you any idea what you're going to do?' enquired Saskia, addressing Fox. 'I presume *we* are somehow part of your plans,' she said, enunciating her words clearly so there was no mistaking her intent.

'Your assessment is correct. We need to make sure Black doesn't slip from our grasp like he's done before. That's why I've need of your skills, Henry,' Fox replied, ignoring the implication in Saskia's words.

Price was lost in thought but stirred at the mention of his name. 'Hmm. As I see it, we've got to think of a way to draw Black out. He can't stay in there forever.'

'That's true,' said Fox. 'But it's a question of how we manage the situation without putting anyone's life at risk.'

'I believe I know of a way to lure Pearly out,' said Saskia suddenly.

The men looked at her in astonishment.

'And just exactly what do you propose?' said Fox sceptically.

'It's all to do with whatever Pearly's waiting for. If I've interpreted the situation correctly, I think he's waiting for you, Henry. Pearly's a complex man ruled by his ego. You'll know if you've studied anything from his past that Pearly believes he has no equal. His arrogance is, to some extent, founded on fact. Pearly is hyper-intelligent and is unchallenged in many areas, particularly where his alchemical skills are concerned. He's charismatic, and those who follow him do so unflinchingly. It's no surprise you've never been able to get anywhere near him or his organisation. You know that if he wants to escape, there's a good chance he will. There's only one person who can stand in his way, and for some reason, Pearly's decided he's ready to accept that challenge once and for all.'

'What makes you deduce all of this?' demanded Fox, unable to hide the resentment from his words.

'Pearly has always drawn great strength from his rivalry with Henry. In fact, he uses it as a spur to enhance his sense of self-importance. With all of his achievements since he left the Academy, he's convinced that his supremacy over Henry is absolute. He believes this unflinchingly, but it still rankles that his greatest rival is considered by many as his equal in alchemical and, more recently, political circles. This knowledge is like a festering canker that gnaws at him and undermines his will.'

'You seem incredibly knowledgeable about a man whom you supposedly have had nothing to do with these past years,' interjected Fox. 'If what you say is true, then why has Black never publicly challenged Henry before?'

'A question I, too, have asked myself many times before,' she replied with a wry smile. 'It's true that I've had no contact with Pearly for quite some time, but I understand him well enough to predict how he might react under certain circumstances.

'Pearly's had an agenda over recent years that's been inextricably linked with the Order's rise. I've no doubt that he's avoided a confrontation with Henry for the very reason that it would interfere with his ultimate plan for the Order, whatever that is. What he has in mind has been the subject of all of our consideration, but in some way, it's shaped Pearly's decision to avoid Henry, up until now, that is. Why he should suddenly change his mind, I've no idea. It's not like Pearly to make a hasty, or possibly, irrational decision, after all.'

'All very interesting, but how does this influence what we should do next?' said Fox.

'Pearly always knew that one day he would have to face his old adversary,' she said, looking at Price, who had remained uncharacteristically silent throughout Saskia's deliberations.

'I see,' said Fox circumspectly, also looking at Price.

Price stirred and said despondently, 'Yes, I suppose you're right. It was always destined to be.'

'But perhaps not as soon as tonight. I'm sure Pearly always had this in mind, but at a time and place that was right for him,' said Saskia. 'For whatever reason, circumstances have changed. I suspect Pearly understands the error he's made by embroiling himself in whatever he wants to steal from this factory.'

'Yes, but Black's not stupid,' said Price. 'Before they went in, he would've weighed up the risks and decided they were worth it. I don't suppose he planned on getting himself hemmed in like this, though.'

'I agree,' said Saskia. 'He'll have anticipated that you'd be briefed about his predicament and you'll be instrumental in what we decide to do next. He must also realise that, by getting trapped like this, he's placed the whole future of the Order in jeopardy. Imagine what will happen if we catch Pearly red-handed. The publicity will sully the Order's reputation, and its popularity will plummet overnight.'

'Making Black a desperate man,' Price observed.

Saskia nodded. 'Absolutely, and I believe the only person he's willing to negotiate with is you. The reason you've seen nothing of him since the situation developed is because he's waiting. He knows that you'll come,' she said emphatically.

Price nodded. 'Hmm. I think you're right.'

'So why should we play into Black's hands?' queried Fox.

'I don't think we've any choice,' Price said with a look of grim determination. 'Saskia, you must wait here … for Lily's sake,' he added apologetically.

Saskia got up with Price. 'I'm sorry, Henry. I'm coming with you and there's nothing you can say that will sway my decision.'

*

Price returned the Historoscope to its stand and reclined back in his chair. He rubbed his eyes absent-mindedly and looked up, squinting at the light flooding in through the overhead window. The trepidation he had felt earlier remained. The scene he had just witnessed was merely a prelude to the devastating events that were about to follow, and all it had done was to cause his long-suppressed feelings of guilt to resurface. If only he had persuaded Saskia not to go with him.

Against his better judgement, he had reluctantly allowed her to accompany him after she had convinced him that her presence would unsettle Black and draw him out from the safety of his bolt-hole. She had also reasoned that, once face to face, a diplomatic solution was more likely if she were present.

Price recalled the moment they had arrived at Spindlewick Street. They had entered the building appropriated by Internal Security through a back door, and after some careful reconnaissance, they had climbed onto the roof and crossed the divide to the factory on a makeshift ladder.

Why did I let her go with me? Price asked himself for the umpteenth time. He shook his head disconsolately. He knew he could not stop now and picked up the Historoscope, placing the lens to his eye and returning to the events of ten years ago.

*

Price was standing stock-still on the flat roof of a tall building, his long hair gently fluttering in a silent breeze. Saskia was standing a few paces behind him, her features partially obscured by the shadow of a tall chimney bathing in the dull glow of a cloud-obscured moon. A tall aluminium exhaust flue rose from the side of the building, unmistakably marked with a snowflake logo and the name of the company, CoolFlow Inc.

Price stood calmly appraising the situation. 'This rooftop will give us the best chance of drawing Black out if he wants to negotiate. Fox has his men stationed on the adjacent rooftops. They should be able to keep Black firmly trained in their sights if he appears.'

Saskia approached him and pointed towards the opposite corner of the flat roof. 'It looks like there's a recess over there,' she said, her breath condensing in the sub-zero temperature as she spoke. 'I think that must be where they got in.'

Price did not reply. He turned his head slowly to scan the rooftop as if he were surveying a battlefield, memorising every nook and cranny for future reference. His eyes finally focused on Saskia before he nodded. 'Come on, let's take a look.'

They crossed to the point that Saskia had identified and stooped down to examine a square metal door inset into the otherwise featureless roof. A small, circular hole had been cut in the centre of the door and there was a charred lock at the side.

Price ran a fingertip across the lock before holding it up to his face. 'Hmm. You're right. This *is* where they got in. They must have drilled through the metal and detonated a small explosive to break the lock. It explains the flare Twelftree saw and also these deposits,' he said, holding up a blackened finger covered with an acrid residue. 'I assume whoever broke in passed some kind of instrument through the hole to lever the door open.'

'It sounds like Liquid Lex must be inside with Pearly. This has his name written all over it,' said Saskia rationally.

Price nodded. He knelt down and thrust his fingertips into the narrow gap between the casing and the recessed metal door, but no matter how hard he tried, he could not prise it open. After a few moments straining, Price stood up. 'I can't budge it. I suspect the door's barred on the inside. We'll need to find another way to open it. Any suggestions?'

Saskia shook her head.

'Then I'll just have to employ alternative tactics. I don't doubt that Black already knows we're here. Maybe it's time we let him know what he's up against. What do you think?'

'What do you have in mind?' asked Saskia.

'I'm going to create a bit of a commotion. Come on, watch this …' said Price. He closed his eyes and laid the palms of his hands on the cold surface of the metal door. Slowly but surely, a low hum emanated from the door that built into a resounding wall of sound that gradually became intolerable, and while Price remained motionless, calmly concentrating on what he was doing, Saskia took a step back shielding her ears.

Suddenly, with an ear-splitting paroxysm, the door exploded, sending Price toppling backwards amidst a cloud of smoke and flying shrapnel. Saskia rushed to his aid, but as the fumes dissipated, he sat up as if nothing had happened.

'Are you all right?' Saskia yelled.

He smiled. 'Of course! What did you expect?'

'You were right about causing a commotion. It was a bit more than that, though. What on earth did you do?'

Price gave a hollow laugh. 'Does mechanical resonance mean anything to you?' he said, picking himself up off the floor.

Saskia glared at him. 'Of course it does but I don't see how that helps.'

'I thought *you* were the expert on metals. Maybe we've just enough time for a physics lesson.'

'I didn't ask for a lesson. I just want to know how you destroyed a door that's almost three inches thick,' she said, looking down at a lethal shard of metal that had come to rest inches from her feet.

'Very well. I don't intend to go into the building just yet. We'll wait and see if it draws anyone out.'

Price straightened himself up and stood with his back to the gaping crater he had created in the rooftop. He brushed some debris off his jacket and extended his neck reflexively after jarring it in the impact. 'Mechanical resonance occurs when an object absorbs increasing amounts of energy with a frequency that matches its own natural resonance.'

'Yes, I'm aware of that, but I still don't see how it could cause such devastation.'

'Have you ever heard it said that soldiers are told to break step when they cross a bridge?'

Saskia nodded.

'Yes, well, it follows an incident when cavalry troops were marching in cadence across a bridge. It just so happened that their rhythm exactly matched the frequency of the bridge's own natural resonance. Although the bridge only absorbed a small amount of cumulative energy with each step, it led to a slow increase in the amplitude of the bridge's oscillation. Eventually, enough energy was added to cause the bridge to break up.'

'Incredible, really.'

'Yes, and a similar phenomenon occurs when the wind's natural resonance causes a poorly constructed bridge to vibrate. Have you ever heard of the Tacoma Narrows Bridge?'

Saskia shook her head.

'It was a suspension bridge built in the States in the 1930's. Unfortunately, not long after the bridge opened, people noticed it wobbling even in a gentle breeze. It wasn't long before the locals renamed it Galloping Gertie. There was an inherent design fault in the structural aerodynamics of the bridge. It had only been open for four months when severe winds set up a mechanical resonance that caused the bridge to rock so violently it broke up.'

A look of enlightenment appeared on Saskia's face. 'And you applied a similar physical phenomenon to the metal door?'

'Precisely!'

'You're a genius! Any object, whether solid, liquid or gas, has its own inherent resonance, and you added your own energy to match it.'

Price nodded. 'Exactly. All atoms resonate, it's in their very nature. The internal structure of a metal is uniform, and that's what makes it susceptible. It would be extremely difficult to apply this process to a multi-composite structure, but a metal's inherent regularity gives rise to its tremendous strength. Ironically, though, this is also its Achilles heel.'

'In what way?'

'You've witnessed me harmonise my mind with the internal structure of matter, and by applying alchemical lore in this way, I've been able to internally reconfigure matter, but I've long theorised that this technique could be applied in other ways, and this is an example.'

'What exactly did you do?'

'I focused on the inherent mechanical resonance of the door, and once I'd calculated its resonance frequency, I flooded the metal with more and more energy until it was completely overwhelmed. Eventually, the door split apart.'

Price looked excitedly at Saskia expecting to see the exhilaration he was feeling mirrored in her own face. Instead, he was shocked to see an expression of pure horror. The colour had leached from her cheeks leaving a pale, waxy sheen that was ghost-like and translucent. She was staring behind him with her eyes fixed elsewhere. Her lips had fallen apart as if she wanted to say something but her voice would not respond. He shivered from the sensation, but did not immediately turn round, despite instinctively knowing that someone was standing behind him.

'Very impressive, Henry. Were you expecting a round of

applause?' said another voice, delivered in a mocking tone that Price immediately recognised.

Price had been half-expecting to hear this voice from the moment he arrived, but even now, the sound hit him like a sledgehammer. He turned round in a calm and collected manner that was at complete odds with the churning sensation in his stomach. He looked into the face of a man he had not seen for several years and noted that his appearance had not changed. His bright blue eyes were burning fiercely, fixed on Price with a combination of suspicion and hatred. The remnants of a smile lingered at the corners of his mouth below a thick, black triangular moustache that curled menacingly down at its ends.

'Pearly! Not exactly the best of circumstances in which to meet,' Price began conversationally, doing his best to mask his inner turmoil.

'And just exactly what were you expecting?' replied Black with a mocking sneer. 'A formal invitation, was it? Perhaps that's why you've brought the lovely Saskia with you, or perhaps you didn't feel safe enough to come alone?'

'Your insincerity does not become you,' said Saskia softly. 'You weren't always like this, Pearly.'

'Save your words,' Black snapped. 'I've not come to discuss the niceties of my behaviour. You'd be well advised to stay silent unless you have something worthwhile to say, which I would doubt.'

'What do you mean by that?' demanded Saskia.

Black turned to look at her. 'Do you remember why I allowed you to come with me when I left the Academy? Let me remind you lest you've forgotten. You had the knowledge to aid me, but as I neared my goal, you were superfluous to my needs. You *do* know all of this, of course, but … well, now this is a surprise …' he said suddenly, pointing a finger at Price. 'It seems you've never had this conversation with him, judging by his expression,' he said, enjoying the moment.

'Don't deceive yourself, Pearly. There are no secrets between us,' Price replied.

Black sneered. 'How touching! If only I could believe you. Your loyalty is admirable, Henry, but don't you try and fool me. I trust my eyes. Now, let's not waste time. What are you here for?'

'What am *I* here for?' said Price, shaking his head in disbelief. 'Don't be naive, Pearly. You may have gained much ground these past months with all the adoration of a misguided public, but you don't fool me. I understand the reasons for your scheming and your need to dominate.'

Black shook his head and smiled sardonically. 'You know, Henry, I've always found it such an enigma that you and I were born on the very same day, yet we should end up being so completely different.'

'What difference does that make? Don't tell me that you've been practising astromancy to go with all your other crazy ideas,' said Price humourlessly.

'You think you're so smart, don't you, Price? What do you know of me?' spat Black, his temper rising. 'You have the temerity to stand in front of me and accuse *me* of the will to dominate. Look at yourself before you cast your accusations, driven as you are by your misguided jealousy. You've never been able to compete with me and you just can't take it. You're only fooling yourself with your pathetic Council. How did you manage to persuade all those other fools to believe all the petty half-truths you made up about the Order? Let me tell you so that you clearly understand: you know nothing of my plans or what I aim to achieve; even you'd be impressed if you did.'

'As deluded as ever I see, Pearly. Well, go on then, impress me,' goaded Price.

'You can't fool me, Price. Now's not the time for this conversation, but you'll see,' Black said, displaying a crazed-looking grin. 'I can assure you, though, I've not been wasting my time on building pathetic contraptions like you. They're puny in comparison with my theurgical research. I'm almost there now. Just a few last pieces, and I shall have the ultimate prize,' he said, looking to the sky as if in supplication to an unseen god.

'I hate to bring you down to planet earth,' said Price

sarcastically, 'but how do you plan to extricate yourself from your present circumstances?'

Black shrugged his shoulders.

'Perhaps I should remind you that we've got you surrounded. When news of this gets out, your oh-so-carefully built reputation will be in ruins,' Price said, accompanying his words with a self-satisfied smirk.

'I'm glad you brought that up. As it happens, I have a message for your superior. I assumed you'd come to collect it,' replied Black smugly.

The smile on Price's face vanished as Black reached into his jacket and pulled out a small object that was masked by his clutched fist. Seconds later a muffled crack echoed in the distance while Price stood impotently by, paralysed by the knowledge that nothing would ever be the same again.

*

The screen inside the Historoscope turned blank. Price wondered whether the machine had malfunctioned, but when it started to thrum and vibrate in his hands, he knew it was still working. Once again, the screen lit up, but this time, as the scene on the rooftop took shape, the view had shifted perspective while foreign thoughts coalesced inside his head, repressing the amalgamation of his own memories and those of Nicolas Fox.

*

Magnus Law was closely observing the distant figures from his vantage point on the rooftop across the street from the factory. He was aware of the dark, brooding figure of Henry Price through his leadership of the Council and his dealings with his own boss, Nicolas Fox. He knew little of the woman Price had arrived with, but she was irrelevant. Of the three, it was Pearly Black who interested him most—successful, charismatic, famous—attributes he could only ever aspire to.

Watching Black only heightened his great sense of bitterness that stemmed from a miserable upbringing followed by years of disappointment and failure. He recalled his early years as a time of isolation and neglect, living with parents who did not care for him, brought up by a procession of nannies who came and went with monotonous regularity. At school, he failed to integrate, watching his classmates with envy as they formed friendships that never came naturally to him. Inevitably, he became increasingly lonely, and although his bright intelligence shone fiercely in class, this only served to alienate him further from his peers.

University was no different, forever on the fringe of the carefree students that surrounded him. After graduating with a first in physics, he was approached by Internal Security, an organisation he had only ever heard of spoken in whispers. He was told that he would make the perfect recruit because of his innate intelligence and solitary existence, and not surprisingly, he jumped at the chance.

Earmarked for rapid promotion, he had at last found a surrogate family to which he truly belonged, but after a brief interlude of happiness, an inability to teamwork under duress resulted in his progress repeatedly being overlooked for less experienced recruits, engendering a festering resentment that grew each time he was passed over.

These were the same old thoughts passing through his head as he sat on the cold rooftop watching his target through the telescopic viewfinder of an MQ-4 assault rifle—a weapon used by Internal Security for its reliability and accuracy. His orders were explicit: he was to keep Black trained in his sights at all times and only fire on receipt of the requisite order that would arrive via the earpiece nestling in the conchal bowl of his right ear.

Magnus could sense his anger rising. The unfairness of it all galled him to the core; he was an overlooked nobody, a bit-part player, watching people who really counted. He felt the weight of the rifle in his arms, and with it, a sudden surge of power arising from the injustices of his life.

All of a sudden, a burst of static erupted in his earpiece at precisely the moment Black reached inside his jacket. Was that an order he had just received over the airwaves? And was that a weapon Black had pulled from his pocket? It was all over in an instant; Magnus squeezed the trigger and let the bullet fly.

His heart was pounding as he waited for Black to fall, but once the burst of light that flashed in the night vision scope of his rifle dissipated, he frowned. Something was wrong. The bullet should have ripped Black apart, yet he remained standing in exactly the same spot seemingly untouched.

Magnus' mind turned over at a frantic rate. Black could never have survived a shot of that magnitude, and he was positive that he had not missed his target. It was unthinkable that Black had been wearing body armour bearing in mind that he had only come to rob a refrigeration plant. No. He could not possibly have foreseen being cornered like this. There had to be another explanation, and as he racked his brains for an answer, he recalled all he had learnt through diligent study during his induction into the ranks of Internal Security. A seasoned operative had instructed him about the inexplicable acts the likes of Black could perform, ranging from the transmutation of matter to the awe-inspiring manipulation of energy, and his training had prepared him to deal with any such eventuality.

He knew that an accomplished alchemist could monitor the environment and detect a change in the surrounding equilibrium, and thinking about it now, a bullet travelling at over 900 feet per second would be about as apparent to Black as a tsunami rushing towards him across a flat, calm sea. Forewarned by this knowledge, all Black would need was a fraction of a second to invoke an electromagnetic field to protect himself, thus explaining the flash Magnus had observed in lieu of Black's demise.

The impact had been like a coruscation of fireworks, hissing and fizzing inches in front of Black's body, but as the bullet decelerated and gave up its energy, like a phoenix from the ashes, it rebounded, picking up momentum and veering off in search of another, unsuspecting victim.

Serendipity, fate, chance—call it what you will—the bullet

pitched and yawed into the woman standing in front of Black with all the force of a charging bull elephant, but for her, there was no protection. The incredulity on her face merely confirmed that she had no idea what had hit her. She staggered, and then, for the briefest of moments, she stood upright before toppling backwards, dead even before she struck the rooftop.

Magnus watched in slack-jawed terror. He felt the rifle tumble from his hands and clatter onto the rooftop. Like an automaton, he rose, turned and started to run.

*

As the thoughts of the panic-stricken man dissipated, the Historoscope's screen flickered and briefly turned blank before it flashed back into life, returning the perspective to the factory rooftop at precisely the moment Price had been viewing it earlier.

*

Price watched with mounting terror as Black pulled something from his pocket. Moments later, the sound of a distant report preceded a flash of blinding light that cast Black in an impenetrable shadow like the corona around an eclipsed heavenly body. The beatific radiance dispersed in an instant, but the muted crack that followed was the only sound as Saskia fell to the ground, immobile and lifeless.

Price launched himself towards his fallen angel, staggering to his knees beside her crumpled form. With mounting panic, he placed his hands on her forehead and forced his mind deep inside her own, frantically searching for signs of life.

The small entry wound in Saskia's chest was no indication of the huge cavity of devastation that lay within and from which Price knew there could be no recovery. He withdrew his presence and scrambled to his feet. He stared at the blurred image of Black, barely registering the look of shock on his enemy's face obscured behind a thin veil of his own tears.

'You bastard,' Price snarled. 'Why?'

Black held up a hand. 'It wasn't me! It was an acci—' he began, pointing into the distance.

Price was no longer listening and was already on the move. 'QUIET!' he yelled, throwing himself at Black, yearning for the need to tear him apart and assuage the hatred that poured forth from him like magma from a volcano.

Black visibly tensed, but before he could steady himself, Price was on him, punching and tearing like a wild animal. Price drove him back and knocked him from his feet. He pinned him to the ground, yet paradoxically, he felt Black relax. As blow followed blow, a thunderous pulse of energy erupted from Black's hands, sending Price flying through the air. He crashed into a knee-high parapet guarding the roof, gasping for air, all wind forced from his lungs. Flames licked around his clothes, releasing plumes of dirty grey smoke that rose hungrily into the sky while the smell of singed flesh pervaded the air, nauseous and repulsive.

Price hauled himself up amidst a cloud of smoke rising from the charred remnants of his clothes. A livid scorch mark was visible on his chest where his shirt had melted away, yet despite the damage he had sustained, he still summoned a terrible power of his own, materialising in his hand as if he had plucked it straight from the core of a nuclear reactor. He took aim and launched the bolt of seething energy as Black backed towards the shelter of a broad chimney. The flaming missile sliced through the air, leaving a trail of golden vapour lagging in its wake, but just when the collision seemed inevitable, Black vanished, allowing the raging hellfire to pass harmlessly by, ploughing into the chimney and dissipating in a shower of fiery reds and yellows.

In the blink of an eye, Black re-materialised mere feet away from where he had last been visible. He smiled malevolently at Price, who had fallen to his knees, all energy spent following his fruitless attack. Black raised his arms in triumph. As he savoured the moment, a low rumbling as of thunder arose behind him, building into a terrifying roar. The chimney disintegrated into a raging torrent, engulfing all that stood in its path. The victorious look on Black's face morphed, first into shock, and finally fear, as the avalanche of bricks propelled him over the parapet. He spun head over heels into a free fall amidst a mass of tumbling masonry and dust, and before he could react, he crashed into the ground with a sickening thud. After a reflexive gasp, his lifeless form came to rest on a sea of rubble four storeys below.

Price felt the weight of a hand on his shoulder as he sat with his head bowed, cradling the motionless form of Saskia. He looked up to see the face of Nicolas Fox staring down at him and wiped away the tears streaking his face. He regarded Fox dully before bowing his head once more.

'Henry ... I need to know what happened. Where's Black?' said Fox uncertainly.

Price did not look up, sweeping away a strand of hair matted with blood. He pointed in the vague direction of the shattered chimney. 'Gone ... over the edge,' he muttered.

Fox approached the parapet and peered over. Streaks of light were visible in the sky to the east, but in the lee of the factory wall, it was impossible to see the ground with any certainty.

'Into the building!' Fox yelled at the group of men who had appeared behind him. 'Black's gang won't have the stomach for a fight now. Quick! Flush them out.'

Fifteen minutes later, the men re-emerged on to the rooftop, and from the looks on their faces, it was obvious that things had not gone well.

'What happened?' Fox barked.

The senior officer shuffled forwards. 'Well ... er ...' Richard Lynx faltered, looking beyond his boss.

Price stepped out of the shadows. 'What's going on?' he said in a voice that was flat and emotionless.

'We couldn't find Black's men,' replied Lynx nervously, looking at Price rather than his superior. 'They escaped through an exit out the back. We found one of our men lying unconscious there.'

Fox appeared oddly out of place still dressed in his formal clothes, but nothing could hide the ferocious look that appeared on his haggard face. 'What?' he snarled.

'Surely you had more than one officer guarding the exit, Nicolas?' said Price.

Fox shook his head.

'There's something else,' said Lynx. 'We found Black's body. I think you should come and see.'

The men followed Lynx in silence through the shattered doorway, utilising a makeshift stepladder that was propped up against the frame. They traipsed down the decrepit stairwell in single file, following Lynx to the ground floor where he shepherded them into a cavernous room filled with an assortment of odd-looking machinery. The men were assailed by blasts of icy air as they pursued Lynx through the factory to a door that opened onto wasteland. The door was swinging lazily on its hinges, and the lock lay ruined on the floor. They exited onto a sheltered walkway and Lynx directed them towards a man sitting propped up against the wall, his head slumped unnaturally on his shoulders.

'He hasn't moved since we found him. He's still breathing, though,' said Lynx.

Price bent over and placed a hand on the unconscious man's forehead. He closed his eyes in concentration, but just as quickly looked up and addressed the expectant men. 'He'll be all right. He's been sedated. He should come round soon enough.'

Price began a meticulous search of the vicinity, and almost immediately, stooped down to retrieve a small object lying at the feet of the comatose guard. 'Someone must have fired this from the window up there,' he said, holding aloft a feathered dart and pointing it in the direction of a narrow opening in the wall above his head. 'You'll need to submit it for forensic examination,' he added, carefully handing the dart to Fox. 'I think you'll find traces of whatever was used to drug this man. Now, where's Black's body?'

Lynx led the band of men through a dense patch of vegetation that opened onto a small clearing adjacent to the steeply rising factory wall. In the early morning sun, there was no hiding the broken form of a man lying amidst a pile of shattered masonry.

'Nothing's been disturbed; this is how we found it,' said Lynx as Price bent over the motionless shape.

'My God,' Price muttered. He shivered involuntarily as he scrutinised the body lying face down amongst the rubble. He peeled back a shock of matted hair to inspect the man's face, yet there was no mistaking Pearly Black, despite the bruised and bloated features. Price turned his attention to a livid wound that extended vertically down from the scalp onto the back of the neck. The incision had been crudely made and passed deeply through flesh and muscle. The tissue had been prised apart to leave a gaping hole that glistened shockingly in the early morning light.

'What the blazes has been going on here?' said Fox, peering uncertainly over Price's shoulder. 'Is ... is that something you did to him up there?' he added hesitantly, looking reflexively towards the rooftop.

Price shook his head. 'No. I've no idea what caused this. Whatever the reason, it happened after the fall. Look,' he continued, pointing to the margins of the wound. 'There's no sign of any blood. This cut was made once Black was dead. I suggest we don't disturb the body. Nicolas, could you arrange for a pathologist to examine the corpse here at the scene?'

Fox looked nonplussed. 'Surely you must have some idea ...?'

Price raised a hand. 'I wouldn't wish to speculate, Nicolas. Now please, do as I say.'

*

Price returned the Historoscope to its stand. He heaved a sigh of relief and slumped back in the chair. He was tired after reliving the grisly scene and was suffering from the same sense of loss almost as palpably as he had on that night. Try as he might, he could not shake the desperation that lay like a heavy hand across his heart. He knew there had been no choice in revisiting the events of that evening, yet despite the distress it had caused him, it had raised some crucial questions.

He had been so wrapped up with the loss of Saskia, he had not dwelt on the mutilation that had been served on Black's body after his death. After Natacha's revelations, he now wondered whether the events of that night held even greater significance than he had suspected at the time.

As he sat pondering this, he recalled the pathologist's arrival soon after Fox had put out the call. The doctor had spent some time examining the body at the scene before the corpse had been taken to a local mortuary for further evaluation. Once the pathologist had completed the task, the body was refrigerated in preparation for transfer to the headquarters of Internal Security the following morning for a more detailed post-mortem.

Bizarrely, and much to Fox's embarrassment, Black's body was stolen later that night. There were no clues to the motive, but Price had always assumed it was linked to the Order, although quite what they would want with the body was another matter.

Price lent forwards and unearthed a sheet of paper lodged beneath a book on the desk. He recalled with relief that the pathologist had had the foresight to conduct a meticulous examination of the body and sampling of the wound before it was stolen. The paper was the written report of Dr Philip Cantonus MD MRCPath, the country's pre-eminent forensic pathologist of the time. Price scanned the pages until he found what he was looking for.

A 12" linear incision is present in the midline of the posterior aspect of the neck extending from the superior occipital protuberance to the spine of the sixth cervical vertebra. The margins of the wound suggest that the incision was made through a pre-existing scar. The incision extends through skin and subcutaneous tissue to the level of the postvertebral fascia and muscles. The muscles have been split longitudinally to expose the inferior aspect of the occipital bone, the posterior arch of the atlas and the laminae of the upper cervical vertebrae. The posterior arch of the atlas and the spinous processes and laminae of the axis have been removed to expose the spinal cord and medulla oblongata in the region of the foramen magnum.

The first and second cervical vertebrae have been stabilised with an atlanto-axial arthrodesis using a laminar screw system. There is evidence of new bone formation at the smooth bony margins of the ostectomy suggesting that the surgical procedure was conducted some time, possibly years, before death.

There is a well-formed soft tissue cavity measuring 1.5" in diameter at the site where bone has been removed adjacent to the exposed Dura Mater of the cervical spinal cord. The smooth appearance of the cavity's lining suggests that a foreign body was in intimate contact with the exposed covering of the spinal cord and medulla. The appearance also indicates that there was no time for healing, implying that the object was removed immediately after death. There is insufficient information to allow speculation on the exact nature or function of the object, but given the lack of an inflammatory reaction, it is likely that it was small and smooth, and made of an inert, biocompatible substance.

Microscopic examination of the cavity lining shows a mass of proliferating neuronal tissue arising from the cervical spinal cord. The nerve cell axons pass out of the cord and end abruptly at the site where the object was located before its removal. Electron microscopy of the interface confirms the tissue to be a mass of proliferating axonal dendrites and synapses, suggesting some form of a neural network had formed with the object before its removal.

Price returned the sheet to the desk and closed his eyes. He scratched absent-mindedly through the fabric of his shirt at the stellate scar indelibly etched across his chest. While he did not understand the complex medical terminology, the message was clear. The conclusions he had drawn after his conversation with Natacha seemed to prove that there was an inextricable link between the Esoteric Brotherhood and Pearly Black.

Now, with the pathologist's suggestion that an object had been implanted at the base of Black's brain and then subsequently removed at the time of his death, it was precisely as depicted in Bosch's paintings. As to the nature of the object or how it functioned, he could only speculate. Bosch had referred to the item as the Stone of Madness, but Price knew that, whatever else, Pearly Black had not been insane.

Price opened his eyes. Great swathes of tiredness washed over him. He was deeply troubled by this strange object and realised that if he was to solve the mystery, the recovery of the only other copy of Piotrowski's manuscript was now more important than ever.

13

THE STONE OF MADNESS

Atropos

PRICE SLEPT UNEASILY, TOSSING and turning but never attaining the rest his tired body craved. Troubled dreams intertwined with memories of the previous day's disturbing events wove into an intricate fabric of fiction and reality. In the moments before waking, he dreamt of Saskia, her happy face looking down on him as he lay caught in an inextricable mesh of wire. He desperately wanted to ask her something, but no matter how hard he tried, the question eluded him. Throughout the dream, Saskia never spoke but smiled beatifically at him, something he found both reassuring and disconcerting in equal measure. At last, he awoke feeling tired and frustrated and gave up on further attempts at sleep with much to do in preparation for the forthcoming day.

The morning of the Council meeting convened by Isaacson had finally arrived. As usual, it was to be held at Internal Security headquarters, and once the meeting was over, he had a plane to catch for Amsterdam. He had dined with Lily the previous evening but his sombre mood had ensured the conversation was sparse, and he was acutely aware that he had managed to evade all of her probing questions. Lily had reiterated her concern about his trip abroad and attempted to persuade him to allow her to accompany him, but he had remained resolute and would not be swayed by her attempts to play on his emotions. The recent bitter recounting of Saskia's demise had been all that was needed to reaffirm his decision to refuse her demands.

Price got up and packed some personal belongings in an aged, brown leather holdall. He showered and dressed, but before he left, he glanced around the bedroom, dwelling briefly on a picture of Saskia looking longingly at him from the bedside table. As he studied her face, he groped once more for the question he had been trying to ask her. Eventually, he gave up in frustration and descended the stairs to the hall, where he deposited the bag before setting off for the kitchen in search of breakfast.

It was early, and Price was surprised to see Lily already seated at the kitchen table. He sat down opposite her and picked up a brimming coffee pot, proffering it in her direction. She responded with a nod from beyond an ancient-looking tome and Price filled her cup before pouring some of the aromatic liquid for himself.

Mrs Brimstork was busying herself at the sink with some washing-up while aimlessly looking through the window. She had not seen Price come in, but when she turned round to find him sitting there, she mumbled an excuse and bustled out of the kitchen.

Lily was deep in concentration, and not wanting to disturb her, he drank his coffee in silence. He noted with approval that she was reading an ancient text of great importance by the Swiss psychologist, Carl Jung, entitled *Alchemical Studies*.

Lily eventually looked up from the book, her piercingly blue eyes looking dull and tired. She smiled wanly, but Price could see that she had been crying from the blotches around her eyes.

'Do you believe in alchemy as a practical or psychological science?' Lily enquired.

Price returned her smile, realising her ploy; she was avoiding the subject of his imminent departure by launching into what appeared to be a straightforward question. He immediately understood, however, the barbed nature of the question and inwardly rejoiced that she was prepared to engage him in conversation.

'I'm sure you've already discerned that Jung viewed alchemy from an entirely psychoanalytical perspective. He saw transubstantiation, not as the changing of physical, but of psychological, matter. He taught that self-development comes through the process of individuation and that this is achieved via the intermingling of alchemy and psychoanalysis. It is a rather simplistic view, of course.'

Lily smiled thinly at the contradiction in her father's words but did not interrupt.

'You already know from your lessons that alchemical science is a fusion between the physical manifestations of what is achievable and the internal power of the psyche.'

Lily looked puzzled but waited patiently for an explanation.

'The relationship is complicated and is difficult to define. It's no surprise that only a handful of alchemists has the ability to create demonstrable effects through the fusion of these intangibles.'

'Are you saying that our powers are unique?'

'Yes, I suppose I am. Despite my belief that there are many people with the intelligence to learn the intricacies of alchemical science, there are few remaining who know how to apply that knowledge. There seems to be a schism, in a way I can't explain, between the assimilation of learning and the ability to internalise and channel the skills that are necessary to produce the demonstrable effects that you and I take for granted.'

'Is that why so few people are studying at the Academy these days?'

Price shook his head. 'There's more to it than that, Lily.'

Lily raised her eyebrows but did not probe any further. 'Can I go there to study when I'm older?' she enquired.

'Perhaps, we'll see. Why do you ask?'

'I enjoy studying here, but I'm sure learning with people of my own age would make it more stimulating.'

'I understand that, Lily. It's just that the Academy may not be the right place for you. Now's not the time to discuss it, though; perhaps when I get back?'

Lily did not reply. Price knew that she was fed up with him always postponing their discussions. It was a delaying tactic of his, and he could tell she resented him for it. A palpable silence lingered before Price stirred and got up from the table, having drained the dregs from his mug. 'I have to leave now,' he said, looking uncomfortably at his fob watch. 'I hope to be back in a few days. Make sure you work hard, and when I return, we can spend some time together.'

Lily's smouldering look remained, but she still got up from the table to hug him. 'Be safe,' was all she said.

After an awkward silence, Price kissed her once on the cheek before leaving the room without a second glance.

*

Price stood on the footbridge looking across the grand old river that bisected the capital like a serpent sidling through an overgrown jungle of concrete. He stared with unseeing eyes at a giant dredger in the middle of the river and the surrounding buildings that rose like statues against a backdrop of leaden skies; the heart of the city was a pattern as unique as any fingerprint, but with his mind elsewhere, it hardly registered. He lifted his head and felt a cool breeze purge the sense of emptiness he had awoken with. He glanced down at his watch and realised with a start that if he did not leave now, he would be late for the meeting.

He hesitated, reluctant to move on from the bridge he and Lily referred to as Saskia's Bridge because of the time they had spent watching the architectural marvel take shape before her death. He had always felt a special affinity with the place and took comfort from the eye-pleasing shape of the curvilinear suspension bridge. The avant-garde design looked majestic even on a blustery day like this, but that was nothing compared to the hours of darkness when the bridge was lit up like a blade cutting a swathe across the river. He finally tore himself away from the unfathomable depths flowing silently below him and moved briskly towards the city.

*

The alley was gloomy and damp. Price looked up and caught a glimpse of a forbidding sky high above the sheer brick walls that rose above the claustrophobic confines of the narrow enclosure. He could barely make out the outline of the door at the far end of the alley such was its length, but when he reached the barrier, he halted and waited patiently without knocking. In the moments that followed, he marvelled at how this place could exist within such a busy part of the city and yet go unnoticed. He could not comprehend how the populace in their thousands passed the alley on a daily basis, yet seemingly failed to observe the comings and goings that marked the entrance to the headquarters of the clandestine organisation known as Internal Security.

He knew his approach would not go unnoticed, and when the heavy metal door eventually opened, a small, shifty looking man was waiting there to greet him. He ushered Price into a further, dimly lit, corridor that was so old and crumbled, it made him imagine that he was passing through a miner's tunnel hewn from rock. The walls were damp and the atmosphere musty, and it was no surprise that the man leading the way repeatedly coughed, a harsh echoing sound that reverberated unnaturally within the confined space. At last, the tunnel came to an abrupt end at yet another heavy door, allowing access to a more welcoming inner courtyard.

'You know your way from here, sir,' said the man matter-of-factly, slamming the door shut behind him before slipping into a snug security cabin abutting the entrance.

After the unpleasant humidity of the corridor, the courtyard was surprisingly light and airy, with a central, neatly manicured square of grass surrounded by cloisters that was more in keeping with an ancient seat of learning rather than the covert organisation associated with Nicolas Fox. He headed across the deserted courtyard to a corridor leading into a maze of tightly packed buildings. He followed the passage until he came to a set of double doors. He stopped to compose himself before he entered the spacious, wood-panelled chamber that habitually hosted the monthly Council meetings. He opened the doors but did not go in, standing in silence at the threshold while observing his fellow Council members. No one seemed to notice his presence and he realised with some disquiet that the men were separated into two disparate groups at opposite ends of the room. Isaacson, however, sat alone, concentrating on a great sheaf of papers laid out on the table in front of him.

While he waited, Price reflected on the changes that had taken place since the Council had first convened over fifteen years previously. The venue was the same, but some of the personnel had changed leading to a shift in balance. At the outset, the Council had thought and acted as a united body, but with time, it had become subject to extraneous political influence, and more recently, its decisions had been dogged by internal factions, each with their own ulterior motives that did not always necessarily serve the Council's best interests.

Price surveyed the room. Isaacson was sitting at a large round table, looking as aloof as ever. Nicolas Fox was standing behind him deep in conversation with General Ian McKenzie, no doubt discussing military matters as was their wont. McKenzie was the senior military advisor to the Council, and with years of experience, he was a voice of reason and pragmatism. Fox, so aptly named for his wily nature, had managed to hang on to his position as Chief of Internal Security, despite the blunders he had made in the events Price had recently witnessed through the Historoscope. The debacle surrounding that evening had culminated in a review of Internal Security's jurisdiction, and had, rather perversely, led to a strengthening of Fox's position and the resources available to him.

A group of three men was talking animatedly on the opposite side of the room conveniently out of earshot of the others. Abel Strange, alchemist and leading academic, looked uneasy. His bulbous eyes accentuated by the thick lenses of his glasses were flitting back and forth between his co-conspirators, who seemed to be arguing about something. William Olberry, the celebrated architect, builder and entrepreneur, whose visionary skills had left an indelible mark on the cityscape, also looked flustered. Olberry was tall and distinguished, but his face was unnaturally red, a reflection, no doubt, of the vehemence of the conversation he was holding with Sir Robert Lec, erstwhile politician and, more latterly, diplomat. Sir Robert, as usual, wore a haughty, austere expression and did not seem in the least perturbed by whatever they were discussing.

Price felt his stomach lurch as he looked in Lec's direction. Although he did not wish to admit it, he realised that the queasy sensation arose from the resemblance Lec shared with his daughter, Natacha, despite the stark contrast in their personalities.

Lec placed a hand on Olberry's shoulder in an attempt to diffuse the palpable tension that arose from their discussion, but Olberry was having none of it, and casually brushed the hand away.

Price made his way into the room, and as he strode towards the table, the sounds of idle chatter dwindled into an unnatural silence, interspersed by his own clipped footsteps. Fox was the first to react and came round the table to greet him.

'Ah, Henry, welcome,' Fox said, shaking Price's hand in a cursory manner. 'Isaacson's performed miracles in bringing us together at such short notice. I'm sure there must be a good reason ...' he added, his words trailing off but with the implication clear.

'There is indeed, as you'll see, but we're still one light, I believe,' replied Price, scanning the room.

'Mr Fielding will be with us presently,' Isaacson called out from the opposite side of the table. 'In the meantime, perhaps I could offer you some refreshment, Professor?'

Price politely declined and shook hands with McKenzie before crossing the room to greet the other men, who had dispersed from their clique and were making their way towards the table. The room fell once more into a profound silence as the men sat down and waited eagerly for the meeting to start.

'I hear you met with my daughter,' said Sir Robert, breaking the silence with his assertive voice.

Price felt a sudden rush of concern before he managed to regain his composure. 'Yes, and extremely helpful she was too,' he replied noncommittally, trying to quell the fear that Natacha had shared their conversation with her father.

'What on earth was my dear Natacha helping you with? I can't imagine what you'd want with her; she's an artist for goodness sake,' continued Sir Robert.

Price inwardly breathed a sigh of relief. The question implied that Sir Robert had no idea what their meeting was about; either that or he was playing one of his surreptitious diplomatic games. 'I needed some historical information, that's all. I believe Cornelius spoke to you about it,' he replied evasively.

'So he did,' boomed Sir Robert, 'but I'll be damned if he let on what it was all about. I presume you're about to enlighten us?' he continued.

Before Price could answer, the doors flew open, and Montague Fielding, editor-in-chief and owner of *The Daily Sting*, entered the room. All eyes turned towards Fielding as he limped painfully across the room carrying a wad of papers. Price could not miss the wince that flitted across his face each time his foot met the ground.

'Damnable gout,' said Fielding miserably. He sat down, scattering a sheaf of papers on the table in front of him. 'I do hope this meeting will be worth the effort. It's taken a hell of a lot of trouble to get here, I'll have you know. I have a newspaper to run,' he said irately, looking at Price.

Price ignored the comment and waited patiently for the meeting to begin.

'Ahem,' said Isaacson, clearing his voice. 'Now that we're all here, perhaps we could start.

'As you're all aware, this extraordinary meeting was convened at the behest of Professor Price,' he said, gesturing to Price seated to his left. 'I thank you for the effort it has taken you to fit this meeting into your schedules. I know time is short so I suggest that I hand over to Professor Price to explain the urgency himself.'

The room fell into an expectant silence as Isaacson sat down.

'Thank you,' said Price. 'I'll delay you all no longer. I called this meeting after the recent theft of a book I acquired from the Ambrosian Library in Milan many years ago. It is for this reason that I believe we're facing an imminent threat. I'm afraid I don't have all the facts at my disposal as yet, but I'm concerned that events may rapidly unfold. I hope you all understand the reasons why I felt the need to brief you at short notice.'

'Please continue,' said Isaacson.

After a brief pause to collect his thoughts, Price began with the break-in, focusing on the essential facts as he saw them. He started with an account of the unique locks protecting the house before describing the thief's brief foray into the building to steal Piotrowski's manuscript while ignoring the many more powerful and expensive items he could have taken. He also described the petrification spell the thief had cast, explaining that this was something only a handful of powerful alchemists could perform.

He related what he had learnt of Piotrowski and his links with the Esoteric Brotherhood. He also broached the subject of the second, if slightly different, copy of the manuscript purportedly containing a section written in indecipherable code, and once the subject of Pearly Black's interest.

He spoke calmly and logically throughout, relating his train of thought that linked the Order of Eternal Enlightenment with the Esoteric Brotherhood, thus suggesting a possible resurgence of the Order. When he had finished, there was a stunned silence. Price was well aware that he had not revealed everything he had learnt, including the discovery of Bosch's association with the Brotherhood and the grisly disturbance of Black's body following his death, but he still anticipated that what he had told them would be sufficient to support his claims. He waited patiently for the inevitable questions that would follow.

'I can see why you've reached this conclusion, Henry, but it seems that much of what you've just told us is based on conjecture,' said Fox. 'What makes you so sure the Order is behind this theft?'

'I'm not, is the simple answer,' replied Price, regarding Fox evenly, 'but there are certain facts that we can't afford to ignore. Cast your mind back to when the Order first appeared. The signs were there then, but they were not heeded, certainly in some quarters. I wouldn't wish for that to happen again. Are you prepared to take the risk, Nicolas?'

'Are you implying Internal Security was responsible for allowing the Order to flourish all those years ago?' said Fox, bristling at the perceived affront. 'It was impossible to predict exactly how the Order's activities would escalate. Surely you must remember that?'

'I'm suggesting nothing of the sort, Nicolas,' replied Price, with a dismissive wave of the hand. 'All I'm saying is that we must take this chain of events seriously. Don't forget, I was right before, and I fear I may be right again. There are far too many coincidences for my liking. Unquestionably, there are gaps in what I've told you, but now's the time for vigilance. We must not turn a blind eye as we did before.'

McKenzie stirred in his seat. He was an impressive man, particularly when regaled in his military uniform. The gold crown insignia over a star and crossed sabre and baton on his sleeve glistened in the hazy sunlight pouring through a vaulted glass skylight towering over the table. He stroked his pencil-thin moustache thoughtfully, and looked, first at Fox, and then Price, as if weighing up their comments before he responded. 'I'm prepared to accept your theory thus far, Henry,' he said, his greyish-blue eyes sparkling intelligently. 'Perhaps you'd be kind enough to explain why you consider a resurgence of the Order a possibility when their talisman has been dead for so long? I always thought it safe to assume that the Order's aspirations perished along with their leader.'

'I agree with your logic, General, but when the goal is as significant as I fear, then who knows what the outcome may be—'

'And just what is it you fear, Henry? I'm concerned you're holding something back,' interjected McKenzie.

Price looked the General in the eye. 'I've told you all I know,' he said in a voice that was unwavering, 'but in answer to your question, it's the second copy of this book that worries me most. I acquired my own copy many years ago because of a rumour that a dangerous secret was concealed somewhere inside it, yet no matter how hard I looked or how deeply I probed, I always drew a blank.'

'Surely if *you* couldn't find this secret then no one else will,' said Mackenzie.

'How I wish it were so, General. After years of scrutiny, I decided that the manuscript was just another false trail, but I was wrong. I'd always assumed that Piotrowski's manuscript was unique, but now I learn of another copy that's not the same as my own.'

'What difference does that make?'

'It changes everything. I fear the Brotherhood used a time-honoured ploy favoured by certain cabals that existed at the time to hide a most powerful secret. Imagine two near identical books containing a handful of differences. It raises the possibility that one book holds a key that will enable a code in the other to be deciphered. It's like having two halves of one whole where the integral parts are of no use, but when held together ...' he said, allowing his voice to trail off.

'You're not making yourself clear, Price,' snapped Fielding. 'What are you suggesting?'

'All I'm saying is that each copy of the manuscript is useless on its own, but when held in tandem with the other, it may hold the key to a powerful secret. Can we afford to take that risk?' he added rhetorically.

'Do you have any idea what this book is hiding?' said Fox.

Price nodded circumspectly. 'Perhaps, Nicolas, but remember this is pure speculation.'

An expectant hush fell inside the room.

'The Brotherhood was a powerful sect rumoured to have made discoveries rivalling some of the great alchemists of earlier ages. Indeed, some have gone as far as to suggest that the Brotherhood was successful in the quest for the fabled living stone, although in what respect or guise, I simply don't know.'

'Yes, but if the Brotherhood discovered the secret of the living stone, then why did they elect to withhold it? Surely it would bring great fame and wealth to whoever made the discovery?' said Fielding.

'I have no easy explanation for this, but perhaps the discovery was as much to be feared as it was revered. Maybe the Brotherhood decided to keep it hidden until a time when it could be put to better use.'

'But surely if this secret was so well guarded, then eventually it would have surfaced once the custodians felt the time was right,' said Olberry, shifting his bulk uncomfortably in his chair.

'You may be right,' agreed Price, 'but what is unclear is the eventual fate of the Brotherhood. We have no idea if the Brotherhood dwindled out of existence or whether it still continues under some other guise today.'

'Some cataclysm must have befallen the Brotherhood,' concluded Fox.

'What makes you so certain, Nicolas?' said Mackenzie.

'If Piotrowski's manuscript was hiding some unimaginable secret, then it makes no sense for the books to find their way to libraries in Milan or Amsterdam. It also explains why the secret has remained hidden for so long; simply put, there was no one left to pass it on to.'

'That certainly seems to make some sense,' agreed Sir Robert sombrely, his deep sonorous voice startling Strange and Fielding on either side. 'Assuming this secret fell from all knowledge, someone somewhere has rediscovered the trail. As you suggest, Henry, Black was interested in this book over ten years ago, hence supporting a link with the Order.'

'Er, yes, but that in itself proves nothing,' announced Strange suddenly. 'Just because Pearly was interested in this book doesn't mean we're on the verge of a revival of the, er ... Order. It's a leap of faith that's tenuous at best. Don't you think you're being a little premature in your assumptions, Henry?'

'Let me ask you this, Abel. What makes you think that this theft is not connected to Black's supporters? We know they vanished the moment he died. Who's to say that they've not regrouped at a time when our defences are at their lowest ebb? You're an alchemist of repute; how can you explain the petrification spell the thief cast?'

Strange looked queasy. When he replied, he spoke with his

bespectacled eyes fixed on the table in front of him. 'I, er ... knew Pearly well,' he began, his voice quiet and unsteady. 'Simply put, Pearly *was* the Order, its, er ... raison d'être, if you like. Without him, the Order never was nor ever will be.'

'You speak with a certain amount of assurance if you don't mind me saying so, Abel,' said Fox.

Strange fiddled with his glasses nervously. 'All I'm, er ... suggesting is that, er, even if Pearly's followers were considering reforming the Order, their chances of success without him to guide them would be, if you ask me, non-existent.'

'But do you think that this theft could be linked with one of Black's associates?' said Price.

'Er ... possibly,' Strange replied reticently. 'I agree that transforming organic into inorganic material could only be performed by a powerful alchemist. Indeed, it's true that there are a few of Pearly's allies who could do such a thing, but so could a handful of people not associated with the Order. No, Henry, I still, er, think that you're making far too many assumptions here.'

'Very well, Abel, but I still don't believe we can ignore the threat that arises from whatever's hidden in the manuscript,' said Price.

'I think we can all see that,' interjected Fox, noting the assenting nods around the table. 'So, what would you have us do, Henry?'

'First and foremost, be vigilant. Nicolas, you have your contacts at Internal Security; use them, particularly those on the side of the criminal fraternity. Listen to the gossip and the rumours and see where it leads.

'The same applies to you, Monty. I'm sure you have an extensive network of sources in your pursuit of truth and justice,' Price continued without irony.

'And the rest of us?' said Sir Robert.

'You've all been in this situation before. You know where your strengths lie and how to put them to good effect. All I ask is for your support. These are dangerous times.'

'And you, Henry. What will you do?' queried Sir Robert.

'I feel somehow responsible in letting Piotrowski's manuscript slip from my grasp. I must go and see this other copy for myself.'

'How do you, er, think that will help?' enquired Strange. 'You've already said that each book on its own is useless. Why waste your time on a fruitless journey overseas?'

'I'd have thought that much was obvious, Abel. Even if this second copy yields no more than the first, at least I can ensure that it doesn't fall into the same hands that procured my own.'

'And how do you hope to, er, achieve that? Surely the curator of this library won't just hand the book over to you.'

'That I do not know, Abel, but we'll see. What is certain is that I cannot wait any longer; I intend to leave for Holland the moment this meeting is over. I've already delayed for far longer than I'd have liked, but it was imperative the Council met before I went. Now, are there any other pressing matters?' said Price, eyeing the men circumspectly.

In the silence that followed, Price mulled over the responses to his news. He seemed to have support in some quarters, but others had received his views with suspicion. Nonetheless, he had planted the seeds in their minds. All he could do now was to wait and see how they reacted; it would tell him a great deal about the Council and how it might function in the future.

Eventually, Nicolas Fox cleared his throat. 'I think there's something I ought to bring to your attention,' he began nervously. 'I didn't think it was relevant until I heard Henry's news, but now I'm not so sure. The problem is ... well ... I'm afraid that one of my men has gone missing.'

'Surely not, Nicolas?' said Olberry mockingly. 'How can that be possible in an organisation such as yours?' Olberry smiled menacingly, enjoying Fox's disquiet. 'As interesting as this news is, Nicolas, what's it got to do with the theft?'

'For someone to go missing like this is most unusual,' replied Fox defensively. 'Nevertheless, the circumstances surrounding the disappearance of this man, is, to say the least, concerning.'

'What do you mean?' said Price.

'Michael Styx is a gifted cryptographer. In fact, he's probably the most talented we have. He joined us just over a year ago and he's already made a big impression. He has an incomparable talent for deciphering codes from ancient texts that were previously considered unbreakable. He's already conducted vital work for the organisation and is currently working on a code of his own, which, I'm led to believe, is being touted as unique. He's formulated a potentially unbreakable code that may herald an unprecedented breakthrough in modern cryptography.'

'He sounds like an intelligent young man, Nicolas. Someone you should nurture,' said Olberry with a liberal dose of sarcasm.

Fox ignored the slight. 'Unfortunately, Styx went missing just over a week ago. We've no idea where he went. He seems to have vanished into thin air.'

'It's not like you to have so little information, Nicolas,' said McKenzie genially.

'No, indeed,' replied Fox. 'He should've come into work as usual after the weekend.'

'Young men go missing all the time, Nicolas. If he's only been gone a few days, what's there, er, to worry about?' said Strange casually.

'Surely his family can help with his whereabouts,' interjected Sir Robert.

'Therein lies the problem,' said Fox. 'Styx lives with his mother. She's his only living relative. She requires regular nursing care when he's at work and relies on him totally the rest of the time. We know enough about Styx to appreciate that he wouldn't just disappear like this. He's devoted to his mother. What's more, when he failed to turn up for work, we began to make enquiries. It appears he was in dire financial straits and was borrowing heavily to pay for the cost of his mother's medical care. I'm afraid he was unable to meet the repayments.'

'Do you think he's been compromised?' asked Price.

'We strictly vet all of our employees before we recruit them, and so I didn't initially, Henry, no, but now, having heard your tale, I'm not so sure. It seems too much of a coincidence that a gifted cryptographer goes missing at around the same time as this manuscript of yours.'

'It certainly seems worrying,' said Price grimly. 'You must do everything you can to find him, and as quickly as possible.'

'Of course,' replied Fox, 'I'll get on to it immediately.'

'It would appear, Henry, that you've no time to lose if you're to get hold of this book before anyone else does,' said McKenzie. 'I believe we should draw this meeting to a close.'

'Is there anything else?' said Isaacson.

As Price rose from his chair, Fielding cleared his throat. It was an unpleasant, guttural sound that reminded Price of the behemoth of a dredger he had observed on his way to the meeting, ceaselessly furrowing a navigable channel along the river.

'I think we ought to take a moment to sort out the Council vacancy,' said Fielding. 'I know this isn't a scheduled meeting, but in light of these developments, it strikes me as even more important that the position is filled. It's been some time, after all, and I'm sure we could do with a full complement if, as you suggest, we're facing a new challenge. What do you think?'

Several heads on Fielding's side of the table nodded their assent. Price withdrew a pocket watch and glanced at it apprehensively. 'I need to be at the airport by early afternoon, but I suppose there's time. I know today's meeting was rather ad hoc, but I see no reason why we can't conduct the vote now. Isaacson?'

'Well ... it's a little unusual, but so long as everyone else is in agreement.'

Fielding's eyes narrowed. 'If you're in a hurry, Price, I'm sure we could conduct the vote without you,' he said, the look of chronic pain on his face metamorphosing into one of sly cunning.

Price gave Fielding a tired smile. 'That won't be necessary, Monty. It won't take long, after all. I think we should proceed,' he said, nodding at Isaacson.

Isaacson rose and opened a curtain behind him to reveal a door. 'As per Council protocol, each of you must enter the anteroom alone. You're required to choose either a black or white ball and place it in this bag,' he said, brandishing a Hessian cloth sack that he had miraculously procured out of nowhere. 'As you recall, the vote is to fill the vacancy that arose following Sir Roger Blake's untimely death. We debated the issue at the last meeting and only one name was deemed worthy of our consideration—Hermes Bing. His election must be unanimous with a black ball equating to a refusal. Now, does anyone else wish to say anything before we vote?'

'All I would say,' suggested Fox, 'is that we must deliberate carefully. Although we're one short of our full complement, it doesn't mean to say that we should just fill the vacancy regardless.'

'Agreed,' said Fielding, 'but Bing is a powerful man. He'll bring experience and expertise, not to mention connections. He's well-placed to bring even greater strength to the Council and is like-minded … well, at least to some of us here.'

'So you keep telling us, Monty,' said McKenzie, 'but don't forget, his father was an ally of Black's.'

'Pah! All I keep hearing is this obsession with a dead man. Move on is what I say,' Fielding replied.

'Your position interests me, Monty,' said Price smoothly. 'If we're to believe those reliable publications, the *Comet* and the *Sting,* you and Bing will be at one another's throats on almost any subject you care to mention.'

'Don't believe everything you read in the press,' Fielding replied with a sardonic smile. 'Bing and I agree on more things than you might imagine.'

'Perhaps that's what concerns us!' said Olberry in a mocking tone.

'Now, now gentlemen,' interjected Isaacson. 'Unless anyone has anything else of value to add, I suggest we begin. Is everyone agreed? Now—'

At that moment, the double doors burst open and a bedraggled-looking man rushed in, leaving Isaacson's words hanging mid-sentence. The man looked ill at ease and was gasping for air.

'What is it, Staghorn?' said Fox irritably. 'You know you're not meant to disturb us.'

'S-sorry, sir,' the man replied, wheezing audibly, 'but, I'm afraid this is urgent. Professor Price, there's a call for you. Please, you must come now.'

Price immediately thought of Lily and felt his stomach lurch. 'What is it?'

'The phone … a woman … Atropos, I think she said … sounds like someone's in trouble,' Staghorn blurted out, still fighting for his breath.

'Atropos? I'm not sure I understand,' said Price, sounding bemused, but quick as a flash, he was on his feet and rushed towards Staghorn. 'Which way?' he demanded as he reached the corridor.

Staghorn pointed towards a small office on the opposite side of the passage.

Price hurried through the door. The telephone receiver was lying on the desk amongst sheaves of papers. He lunged towards it, scooping it up in an ungainly motion. 'Yes?'

There was a moment's silence before he heard the unmistakable voice of a woman.

'Price, is that you?' she whispered.

'Yes, who's this?' he replied. A chilling sensation ran down his spine arising from a nagging suspicion that he had heard this woman's voice before.

'To some I'm known as Atropos,' the woman replied.

'Atropos?'

'You heard what I said. Now listen carefully, Price. The life of your friend, Cornelius Spydre, is hanging in the balance.'

'Cornelius? What's happened? Is he all right?'

'That depends on you,' the woman replied enigmatically. 'If you wish to help, I suggest you shut up and listen,' she snapped.

'I don't know who you are, but if you've—'

'If I've what?' interrupted the woman, her voice still sounding detached and remote. 'I don't believe you're in any position to dictate. Now, take my advice and listen if you wish to reach your friend in time,' she said in a commanding voice. 'I'll not repeat myself.'

Price remained silent despite his eagerness to hear the woman out. After a pause that seemed to go on forever, the woman eventually spoke again, this time with a rasping edge. 'Hot as a hare, blind as a bat, dry as a bone, red as a beet and mad as a wet hen,' she said.

'What are you talk——?' said Price, cutting his words when the call was terminated. He turned on his heels and almost knocked Staghorn over who was standing behind him.

'Is everything all right, sir?' said Staghorn.

'No, I'm afraid it's not,' replied Price gravely, still vacantly holding the telephone in his hand. He rapidly dialled Spydre's number and waited with a burgeoning sense of unease. The engaged tone rang out.

He turned to Staghorn still waiting patiently behind him. 'Could you organise a taxi to pick me up? Oh, and tell them to make it snappy. Just one more thing, Staghorn,' he continued as he rushed towards the exit, 'tell Isaacson I've had to leave. You can also tell him that I'm happy for the vote to proceed. He'll understand.' And with that, Price was gone.

14

The Gates of Delirium

THE TAXI PULLED UP outside the row of four-storey buildings located in the exclusive Mayfair district. Price jerked the door open and called out the destination's address. 'I'll pay you well if you get me there in double quick time,' he snapped as he leapt inside the vehicle.

Without a second glance, the cabbie gunned the vehicle and set off.

The trip to Spydre's bookshop was a fraught affair as Price willed the battered cab towards its destination. The busy late morning traffic hindered their progress at every turn and the journey seemed to go on forever. As the taxi weaved in and out of the slow-moving traffic, Price recalled the conversation he had held with the mystery caller. He still had an uneasy feeling that he had heard the woman's voice somewhere before, but he just could not recall a time or place.

'To some I'm known as Atropos,' he mouthed quietly to himself, repeating the words the woman had used to introduce herself.

Atropos. He wondered what it could possibly mean and whether the caller had been toying with him. As the taxi lurched violently one way and then the other, he tried to summon up the distant memory of Greek mythology he had learnt at school.

He recalled that Atropos was the oldest of the Fates, the three female gods who supervised, rather than determined, destiny. She was also known as the 'inflexible', choosing the mechanism of death of every mortal and cutting the thread of their life with her abhorred shears.

Price shook his head. He was not sure what awaited him at Spydre's bookshop, but as the cab traversed short-cuts and back streets he did not recognise, a feeling of dread manifested in the pit of his stomach.

After what seemed like an age, the black cab swung into Curiosity Street. The vehicle's wheels screeched in protest as the driver hauled on the steering column and braked hard to avoid an unsuspecting pedestrian who had ventured into the road.

'Anywhere in particular, gov?' the cabbie called out cheerfully as if nothing untoward had happened.

Price pointed to a spot a short distance along the street. 'Just there'll be fine. How much do I owe you?' he said, reaching into his pocket.

Price was out of the taxi the moment it halted. He paid the man well, handing him a hefty tip for the swiftness of the journey. He headed for the bookshop and glanced at the filthy window that was still masking the same old books that had been on display just a few days before.

Price scanned the door for signs of forced entry, but all appeared intact apart from some scuff marks on the bottom rail where visitors had used a well-placed boot to push on the door. As he stepped across the threshold, an object caught his eye, glinting in the sunlight. Pinned to the door jamb was a large, distinctive moth with striking rows of brown, yellow and blue stripes running along its abdomen. Its upper wings were shades of shimmering browns that contrasted starkly with lower wings of vibrant yellow. Price frowned at the sight of the strange specimen skewered through its thorax but immediately identified it as a Death's-head Hawkmoth. The moth was a rare visitor to the British Isles and had a sinister reputation as an omen of death, causing the dread he had felt earlier to return with a vengeance.

He entered the vestibule and waited, listening for sounds of life from inside the shop. He suppressed an urge to cough in the musty atmosphere that habitually pervaded the place before passing into the tightly enclosed bookshop. The room was deserted, yet Spydre's overburdened desk remained the same, hemmed in on all sides like a tiny island amidst a sea of books. He noted with a humourless smile that the whisky bottle and glasses were gone. The book displaying the brightly coloured plates of reptiles and lizards had also disappeared, and in its place was an encyclopaedia carefully propped open to reveal an illustration of the same moth he had just seen pinned to the door. An insidious chill seeped into his bones as he stared in horror at the caption below the beautifully adorned picture. *Acherontia atropos,* it read. There was that name again: Atropos; first the mystery caller and now the moth sharing a name inextricably linked with death.

He stifled a further cough as he examined the dusty bookshelves in search of the passageway Spydre had used to enter the room. He spotted a thick bell rope crudely nailed to an upright, and a shaft of light penetrating a small gap between two adjacent bookcases. He gave the rope a stout tug, and the bookcase slid smoothly towards him, allowing a swathe of artificial light to flood the room.

'Cornelius,' he called out as he hurried along a passageway that sloped gently down to a voluminous room stacked with mountains of books haphazardly arranged from floor to rafters. A narrow shaft of sunlight filtered through a window high on the opposite wall, illuminating a low archway visible through a cloud of dancing dust motes. Price sprinted towards the arch, drawn by a rhythmic knocking emanating from the room beyond.

As soon as Price entered the cramped office, he knew that something was seriously wrong. Spydre lay slumped across the desk, instruments and papers strewn haphazardly about him. His body twitched uncontrollably in tandem with his wristwatch repeatedly striking the desk.

Tap ... tap ... tap. The sound was like a harbinger of doom.

Price's boots thudded on the wooden floorboards as he rushed towards his friend.

Spydre stirred and looked up to reveal a lop-sided, brightly flushed face. He stared blankly at Price through widely dilated pupils and feral, unseeing eyes. 'Who is there? Is that you, Luschka?' he croaked in a voice that was hoarse and strained. 'The crows have escaped ... come with me, I will show you,' he said, struggling out of the chair.

Spydre staggered to his feet and swayed unnaturally, flailing his arms as he vainly tried to steady himself. He fell back into the chair, overwhelmed by a bout of insurmountable vertigo that only served to increase his agitation.

Terror was etched on his face as he looked beyond Price. 'See, there they are. Those demonic beasts,' he rasped, pointing at the dim, yet perfectly still space above Price's head.

Price edged towards his friend and laid a reassuring hand on his shoulder. 'Don't be frightened, Cornelius. It's me, Henry,' he whispered, but the effect was anything but calming and sent Spydre into a fury of agitation, thrashing his arms wildly about him.

'Look! He is amongst them. Do not let them fool you. See ...' Spydre said, pointing once more into the empty void.

'What is it, Cornelius?' Price asked.

'It is the Raven King. He holds the key in his vicious talons! There, see, he leads them. Do not let them approach. If they breach the gates, then I am doomed. Pleeeease, help me!' Spydre cried plaintively.

Price stood rooted to the spot, helplessly confused by his friend's futile pleas.

'Aaaagh! The gates have fallen,' Spydre screamed. With sudden finality, his head lurched forwards and struck the solid oak desk with a loud thump. After a brief spasm, the tremor was banished from his tormented body as he lapsed into the depths of unconsciousness.

Price leant over and stroked Spydre's hot, dry face, and noted with dismay that he had a raging fever.

You poor old man. Who's inflicted this mischief on you? he silently asked his immobile friend.

'Think!' he said as he slid a hand onto Spydre's neck, feeling for a pulse, which was thready and fast.

'Hot as a hare, blind as a bat, dry as a bone, red as a beet and mad as a wet hen,' repeated Price inanely. The mystery caller had predicted everything he was witnessing, albeit in riddles. Now, looking at Spydre, he intuitively guessed that his friend had been poisoned.

As he considered this, Spydre's pulse began to race, and after a flourish of impossibly rapid beats, the pulse vanished, a herald that was both ominous and final. Moments later, after a great heave of his chest, Spydre stopped breathing.

Price knew that his friend was dying. If he was going to save him, he had to act now and with absolute conviction. He lifted the old man from the chair and laid him flat on the floor in the confined space of the office. He knelt down beside him and removed the shirt loosely draped around Spydre's torso. He placed the flat of a palm onto his friend's exposed chest and closed his eyes, allowing his consciousness to flood into the body spread-eagled before him. From the first intimate touch, his fears were confirmed. He sensed the taint of corruption coursing through Spydre's poison-wracked body, a man teetering on the brink of mortality.

The root of the problem—the poison—would have to wait; first, he had to negate its effects. He tried to think logically, analysing all the clues the woman had left for him. He had felt the increasing hammering in Spydre's chest preceding the loss of a pulse and quickly deduced that the poison had caused the heart to beat faster and faster until it was completely overwhelmed; because of this, the heart was now beating in an uncoordinated fashion, and no blood was perfusing Spydre's brain.

There has to be an answer, he told himself, desperately trying to recall distant lessons of *physiologia* from his days at the Academy. He had learnt that an electrical discharge originating from nerve-bundles deep within the heart caused its muscles to contract in a synchronised way, and extrapolating from this, he deduced that he had to interrupt the random pattern currently driving Spydre's heart to return it to its regular rhythm.

As he racked his brains, he quickly determined what he must do. He lifted his hand and steadied it inches above Spydre's chest. He began to focus deep within himself. He had done this many times before, and now, reflexively, it came effortlessly. He visualised the tiny charged bundles of matter coursing through his body, and drawing on his innate power, he displaced a mass of electrons from their random activity into an ordered stream of movement thus creating a potential difference in his arm. By fashioning the end point in his hand, an electrical charge slowly built there. Price felt the power grow, until eventually, with his fingers tingling unpleasantly, he lowered his arm. The moment his fingers touched Spydre's skin, a current flowed from his hand. Spydre tensed then jerked spasmodically, but when the discharge ceased, his body sagged to the floor like a limp rag doll.

Price reached out and felt for a pulse but immediately knew he had failed. Perhaps Spydre was just too old or there was too much poison in his body, he reflected.

With time running out, he had to keep trying. Price compelled the charge to coalesce in his arm once again, and as the electricity built, so did the pain, yet this time he did not act. At last, when it felt as if he could bear it no longer, he lowered his hand, but even before his fingers connected with Spydre's skin, there was a phosphorescent flash. Energy arced from his fingertips, and, as the electricity surged from his hand, Spydre recoiled, lifted from the ground in a spasm of temporary reanimation.

Price held his breath, not daring to look. Then, with a surge of relief, he discerned the almost imperceptible rise and fall of Spydre's chest. He was breathing! Price bent forwards and checked for a pulse. There it was, fast and thready, but undoubtedly present. It had worked!

Despite this, Price knew that it was still not over. He could sense the strength of the poison, and did not doubt that the enfeebled old man might yet succumb. He had bought himself time, that was all; he had to think.

The woman, Atropos, had left clues to help him save Spydre. But why? She had implicitly forewarned him that Spydre was in danger, and even told him what to expect when he arrived. First, there was the moth pinned to the door, and then, the book on the table, and the incontrovertible link with the name, Atropos.

Atropos! Of course! It came to him in a rush; she had poisoned Spydre with atropine!

Price cursed himself; the clues had been there all along. Atropine came from the herbaceous shrub, deadly nightshade, and its Latin name, *Atropa belladonna*, was derived from Atropos. It was one of the most toxic plants known to man with dark, sweet-tasting berries renowned for their fatal effects.

It all fitted perfectly; he had just not seen it. When ingested, atropine produced dilated pupils, dry skin, rapid pulse, disorientation, hallucinations, and finally, coma; symptoms that had all been manifest in Spydre.

Price rechecked the body. Spydre was unconscious, yet his chest was rising and falling in tune with rapid, shallow breaths. There was no time to lose. He had to neutralise the poison. He reached for the desk and lifted the telephone lying askew on its cradle. He rapidly dialled a familiar number.

'Come on, come on,' he said, thrumming his fingers impatiently on the desk while waiting for someone to pick up the phone.

'Hello. Can I help you?' a voice said brightly.

'Lily, quick. I need your help. Cornelius' life depends on it.'

'What! I thoug—'

'I'm sorry, I don't have time to explain,' Price cut in. 'Just, please, do as I say. Go down to the laboratory. Look for two flasks in the reagent store: Indian snakeroot and Calabar bean. They should be close to one another. Grab them and bring them to Cornelius' shop. Get here as fast as you can. I'll be waiting. I'm relying on you, Lily.'

Lily immediately hung up, sensing the urgency in her father's voice.

Price returned to the body still lying prostrate on the floor. Spydre had not stirred following the convulsion that had restored him to life. His face was deathly pale and his breathing barely perceptible.

Price laid a hand on Spydre's brow and gently stroked the deformed face of his friend. 'Hold on, Cornelius, you can do it.

You're as tough as an ox. Help is on its way,' he muttered as much to himself as to the old man.

He had done all he could. He squeezed Spydre's hand, willing him to hang on. All he could do now was wait. He just hoped that Lily would get there before it was too late.

15

Bibliotheca Philosophica Hermetica

L IQUID LEX SLIPPED QUIETLY into Holland, arriving at a time
when he was most likely to avoid the attention of the local
authorities. He was travelling on one of many false passports, but
because of the nature of the assignment and the equipment he was
carrying, he remained wary. He had avoided the usual major ports
and airports, and opted to travel via a circuitous route to minimise
the risk of an impromptu search.

Lex had begun the journey by persuading a local fisherman in
Harwich that a quick trip across the North Sea was far more
financially rewarding than scraping a living from the ever-
decreasing fish reserves the man's livelihood depended on. Lex
almost changed his mind when he saw the ship—a decrepit fishing
smack that looked more suitable for the scrap heap than the open
seas. The wily captain somehow managed to persuade Lex of the
vessel's seaworthiness, and promised an uneventful passage,
despite Lex's unwavering suspicion that the vessel would sink with
the first big wave to cross its bows.

Lex spent the crossing in a small berth below decks, preferring
the disgusting blend of diesel oil and stale fish to the sight of the
little boat labouring against towering waves that threatened to
engulf it at any moment. He passed the time reading the *Racing
Post* and reviewing a selection of recent betting slips—losers every
single one—and although this merely added to his discomfort, he
managed to take solace from the boat remaining afloat.

The boat moored in The Hook after a longer crossing than the captain had promised and Lex disembarked the moment the boat was secured. He slipped ashore with a cargo of illicit goods safely packaged within a nondescript, black metallic case. He had hoped for some sleep during the crossing, but the thought of the unstable goods in his possession rolling around with the incessant pitch and fall of the boat somewhat tempered his desire for rest. As an expert in explosives, Lex knew that the liquids carefully secured and insulated within the case were far more stable than the prototypes he had used in his early years as a thief. Nonetheless, he could not help wonder whether passport control would have been a safer option than the risk of plummeting to the depths of the North Sea after a brief show of pyrotechnics.

At last, thankful to find himself safely, but a little unsteadily, on terra firma, Lex paid the fisherman handsomely for the crossing and agreed to rendezvous in a week's time. After a short bus trip up the coast to The Hague, he took the train to Amsterdam.

Following his arrival at the Centraal station, he set off on foot through the charming old city, crossing several canals on the way to the Jordaan, a sprawling, provincial district lying to the west of the Grachtengordel and the main canals of the central city. Here, he found a comfortable yet unobtrusive hotel overlooking one of the city's many waterways in preparation for his assault on the Bibliotheca Philosophica Hermetica.

Lex had not skimped on his research before setting off from London, working on the old adage of 'know your enemy well', where, metaphorically speaking, the library was his enemy. The library was the personal collection of Joost Ritman and consisted of over 20,000 printed books, manuscripts and incunables, making it the world's largest collection of works devoted to the Hermetic tradition. The library had opened its doors to the public in recent years to reveal a collection of rare and valuable books on the subjects of Hermetica, Alchemy, Mysticism, Rosicrucianism, Kabbalah, Freemasonry, Theosophy, Anthroposophy and Esotericism, to name but a few.

Lex wondered what all the fuss was about over a library

crammed full of stuffy old books, and with no fabulous jewels or fine art to whet his fancy, he could not work out the appeal of dusty old tomes on subjects he considered, quite frankly, bizarre. Still, a book was a book, and one he was committed to recovering. In order to finalise his plan, Lex was keen to discover the interior set-up of the library, the location of Piotrowski's manuscript and the security arrangements of the building—a major problem owing to his reluctance to enter the library for fear of being recognised by a sharp security guard; after all, his face was extremely well known to Interpol. He was also worried that the library had been primed about the interest in Piotrowski's manuscript thanks to the meddling of Price and his Council cronies, and so despite usually preferring to work alone, Lex elected to gather information from an insider, despite knowing from bitter experience that this would only increase the possibility of ending up in a stinking Dutch prison, an option not particularly high on his agenda.

Lex began a covert surveillance of the library immediately after checking into the hotel, and soon established the comings and goings of two security guards working there by day. Each evening after the library shut its doors to the public, the guards retired to a local bar to relax after a day of unrelenting boredom. Dressed in their smart, black uniforms, the men stood out like sore thumbs amongst the early evening masses. Lex soon discovered that the men were employed by a private security firm—ARC International—as evidenced by a small logo fashionably emblazoned on the breast pocket of their jackets.

On the fifth evening after his arrival, the guards ambled a short distance from the library on Bloemstraat to a bar on the adjacent Prinsengracht where they began to unwind over a few cold beers. The men chatted amiably against a backdrop of the early evening water traffic meandering along the nearby canal and they did not stop to draw breath when Lex slid surreptitiously behind a table within earshot of their own.

Although the conversation was little more than light banter, everything changed with the arrival of a man he had not seen during his reconnaissance of the library. The man was scruffily dressed in a pair of faded denims, and following his reluctant acceptance into the party, there was a distinct change in the nature of the conversation. As the evening wore on, the exchanges gradually became more heated, and although the men spoke rapidly in Dutch, Lex gleaned that the newcomer was a disgruntled ex-employee of ARC. The discussion eventually degenerated into a full-blown argument over the man's recent dismissal, despite the guards having heard it all before, and it was not long before they made their apologies and left the man to quietly seethe over the perceived injustices of his life.

On a whim, Lex opted to stay put and concentrate on what he intuitively saw as the likeliest source of the information he desperately craved. He watched the man drain his beer in double quick time then return to the bar to order another. On his way back, Lex jumped to his feet, seemingly heading for the exit past the disgruntled man. With a feigned stumble that would have graced the Maracanã, Lex expertly dislodged the contents of the man's brimming glass onto the floor, causing the man to flare up in a further show of fury.

'That was my beer!' he shouted indignantly, squaring up aggressively to Lex.

Lex smiled with nonchalant grace. He held up two hands to pacify the man and accompanied the gesture with the most disarming smile he could muster. 'I'm so terribly sorry, I'm English,' he said, in a halting yet passable Dutch, as if this was a reasonable excuse for the accident. 'Let me buy you a drink,' he added in his native tongue.

The man's ruddy complexion paled and his shoulders relaxed, seemingly appeased.

Seizing his chance, Lex held out a hand. 'My name's Leonard Lincoln,' he said, introducing himself with the alias inscribed in his passport. 'My friends call me Len,' he added amiably.

The man studied Lex as the prospect of another beer quickly calmed his rage. 'And my name's Thjiis ... Thjiis Ackerman,' he replied, in a softly spoken manner belying his recent behaviour.

Without hesitation, Lex pulled up a chair and hailed the waiter.

He ordered two more beers and began a slow but meticulous softening-up process, painting the picture of himself as a hapless tourist before starting to gently probe the unsuspecting Thjiis about his circumstances. It was not long before the men were happily ensconced in conversation as if they had known each other for years, kindred spirits of sorts, following Lex's sorry admission that he had embarked on his travels after losing his job following a dispute with his employers.

Thjiis frowned briefly at this juncture before he launched into a vicious diatribe about his own recent bitter experience, having been dismissed from his post at the library after fifteen years of unwavering service because of a disagreement over the time he had spent smoking a cigarette during an allotted break.

'Have you heard of the Bibliotheca Philosophica Hermetica?' Thjiis naively enquired.

When Lex shook his head with a suitably puzzled expression, he was treated to an unrelenting fifteen-minute lecture on the wonderful world of Ritman's library according to Ackerman.

It was apparent from the way Thjiis spoke that he had been happy working at the library and immensely proud of the responsibility invested in him as a guardian of all the treasures it housed. He spoke of the books with eager pleasure bordering on reverence, and, judging by the way he recounted the subject, he was clearly a disciple of the Hermetic tradition.

Lex allowed the man to speak without interruption, and as Thjiis' confidence grew—in direct correlation with his blood alcohol level—Lex knew it was only a matter of time before he could prise the information from his victim to help him get the book. He feared Thjiis' increasingly droopy eyelids and slurred speech was a herald of alcohol intoxication, but as Thjiis continued to take regular draughts from his glass, it only seemed to increase his vigour. All Lex had to do was to ensure Thjiis' glass remained full while maintaining his own sobriety, which he surreptitiously managed by tipping his beer into a large earthenware pot next to the table, only adding to the vim of the plant and its green, sharply serrated palmate leaves elegantly draped over the table. 'Pot' being the operative word, Lex considered, recognising the vegetation's distinctive appearance as almost impossible to mistake.

After Thjiis' eloquent oratory regarding the library's treasures, Lex casually enquired about the various sections of the building and the locations of the books it housed. It was like lighting the blue touch paper and retiring, allowing Lex to sit back and let the information flow. It was not long before he had learnt the entire layout of the library from top to bottom as Thjiis divulged where various sets of books were housed from Rosicrucianism, Anthroposophy and Theosophy on the ground floor to Hermetica and Alchemy on the first and second floors, and most crucially, the location of a collection of rare books on the third floor.

Following the conclusion of Thjiis' discourse, Lex smiled reassuringly. 'It sounds like a treasure trove, this library. You must miss it.'

'It's just not fair,' Thjiis replied dolefully. 'I worked there for fifteen years and just because of one small lapse, they got rid of me, just like that. I hate those smug so-and-sos at ARC.'

'ARC did you say?' Lex said in surprise, raising his eyebrows in a none too theatrical manner.

'Yes. They're a stupid, small-minded company run by a bunch of over-inflated egos. Why do you ask?'

'What a coincidence!' Lex replied, exaggerating a look of astonishment. 'I was recently doing some consultancy work for ARC myself. I'm afraid things didn't work out. I was developing a security system for them in the Middle East. Unfortunately, the contract fell through. ARC lost a lot of money, and guess what?'

Thjiis nodded knowingly.

'Yep, they blamed me. Made sure I'd never work in the security business again.'

'Typical!' said Thjiis. 'What did you do after you lost your job?'

'Well, here I am. I had a bit of money saved up, so I decided to do some travelling ... at least until I could think of something better to do. Sounds like we both owe ARC, eh?'

'I'd do anything to get back at them,' Thjiis replied, staring dejectedly into the depths of his glass.

Lex paused dramatically for a moment before he pounced. 'I can think of a way.'

Thjiis regarded him with mounting excitement. 'How?' he exclaimed a little too loudly for Lex's liking, causing a group at the next table to turn round and see what all the fuss was about.

Lex surreptitiously touched an index finger to pursed lips.

Thjiis dipped his forehead in acknowledgement and leant conspiratorially over the table to hear what Lex had to say next.

'Do you know anything about the library's security system?' Lex enquired.

'Of course,' Thjiis replied, whispering now. 'Why do you ask?' he added suspiciously.

'Let's just say I know some people who'd be *extremely* interested in that kind of information.'

'What! They're not planning to steal something, are they?'

'Of course not. What sort of people do you think I'm acquainted with?' Lex replied with a look of affront etched on his face. 'No. Let's just say that, having worked in the industry for many years, I know some people who'd be very interested in the kind of security system ARC utilises. ARC has a reputation for state of the art technology. If you could tell me some of the, er, shall we say, more advanced aspects of their hardware, I'm sure we'd get a good price for our trouble. A little bit of industrial espionage might be very rewarding for us both. It sounds like we could both do with the cash, and don't forget who's responsible for the predicaments we find ourselves in!'

Thjiis nodded his head slowly as scepticism gave way to greed. 'How much do you think we'd get?'

'Enough to keep me travelling for another six months and you in plenty of these,' Lex replied, lifting an empty beer bottle from the table.

'But we could get in trouble,' Thjiis replied, a little more circumspectly.

'Who would ever find out?' Lex said nonchalantly. 'No one would ever make the connection, particularly if we never meet again. Just leave me your bank details, and I'll wire the cash as soon as I get it. It's as easy as that.'

Thjiis started to mouth a protest, but Lex forestalled him with a placatory smile and a shake of the head. 'You've nothing to worry about, Thjiis. After all, ARC owes us, remember?'

Thjiis nodded in meek acquiescence before proceeding to speak for the best part of an hour with not so much as a second thought, oblivious to Lex pouring another beer into the, by-now, wilting pot plant.

Lex felt a glow of pride as he sat back and listened to Thjiis wax lyrical about perimeter locks, window alarms and interior sensors before completing his dialogue with the whereabouts of a safe in the curator's office on the third floor. When he had finished, Thjiis wrote down his bank details on a shabby beer mat, which Lex accepted with relish. After offering Thjiis his hand, Lex got up and left the bar without further ado.

On his return to the hotel, Lex smiled to himself as he screwed up the piece of card inscribed with Thjiis' sort code and account number. With a quick turn of the head to ensure he was alone, he tossed the crumpled beer mat high into a starless sky and watched it fall onto the inky black waters of the nearby canal and drift silently away.

*

The rain had well and truly soaked through Lex's supposedly waterproof coat and cast a chill deep into his bones. He pulled up the collar of his dun-coloured raincoat and tipped his beret to prevent the steady trickle of rain running down from his sprawling hair onto the back of his neck. He shivered involuntarily. Despite the low cloud that had not shifted all day, his spirits were high. He had spent most of the morning loitering outside a telephone kiosk waiting for a call while doing his best to discourage the occasional passer-by from entering the booth. Fortunately, no one had challenged him, mainly thanks to the threatening manner he had displayed whenever anyone came near.

Lex had contacted Aurelia the moment he had arrived in Amsterdam, and she had greeted him with the unwelcome news that Price was also planning a visit to the city, suggesting that the 'great man' deemed the theft of the manuscript important enough to track down the second copy for himself. It also implied that Price had tipped-off the library about the Order's interest in the book, raising the possibility that the curator might move the book to somewhere secure, an eventuality Lex had been hoping to avoid. Because of this, Lex had been tempted to make an immediate move, but he had held his nerve, resulting in the invaluable information he had gleaned from Ackerman.

Lex had subsequently spoken with Aurelia on a daily basis and had chosen the kiosk just in case the hotel was monitoring his calls, hence the last few hours spent dawdling in the soaking drizzle. When the phone eventually rang, Lex jumped two feet in the air in his rush to answer it, almost knocking a passing cyclist into the nearby canal. The cyclist managed to swerve at the last minute, cursing Lex with a few choice words barked angrily in Dutch.

Lex barely noticed as he grabbed the receiver and called out, 'Yes,' in a breathless frenzy. Much to his relief, it was Aurelia on the other end of the line bearing the exceptional news that she had managed to delay Price by another twenty-four hours on his journey to the city. It was just what Lex was hoping for, thus giving him free rein to break into the library without interference from Price.

He looked melancholically at the kiosk, knowing he would not need it again, and set off for the hotel. As he strode purposefully along Bloemstraat, he could not resist a smile at this fortunate turn of events. Once safely ensconced in the hotel, his thoughts returned to the small matter of retrieving the book.

At eight p.m., much to the surprise of the desk clerk, Lex checked out of the hotel and set off in search of a café in the cosmopolitan area of the Jordaan. En route, he passed the tall, imposing four-storey frontage of the Bibliotheca Philosophica Hermetica, and noted with satisfaction that the library was already shrouded in dark.

Lex was travelling light, having replaced the metallic case with a compact rucksack safely strapped over his shoulders. The holdall looked far lighter than its contents gave credit for, jammed with all the tools he had selected for the job, including a bespoke assortment of painstakingly packed instruments and volatile chemicals. Lex walked steadily upright to avoid the risk of a fall; he was no physicist but understood the concept of critical mass should he stumble.

The debonair café Lex chose for a leisurely supper was just a few minutes' walk from the library and was bustling by the time his Dutch pea soup arrived. A pretty waitress had taken his order thirty minutes earlier when the restaurant was quiet, and rather than being dismayed by the slow service, he had been content to sit and watch his fellow diners socialising and enjoying their food.

Lex took his time eating the thick, green soup, which was hot and appetising in equal measure. After drinking a stimulating cup of strong Dutch coffee, he left the café and was pleased to note that the surrounding district was already showing signs of quietening down.

He scouted the streets for almost an hour before making for the library, having planned to enter just after midnight when the streets would be deserted—the perfect time to scale the walls, break-in and acquire the book. If all went to plan, he would be out in time to catch the early morning train and keep his rendezvous with the skipper. All being well, if the crossing were a little more favourable than the outward journey, he would be back in Blighty before anyone realised the book was gone.

Lex was alerted to the appointed hour when the bell rang out from the nearby Westerntower, twelve loud chimes to signal the end of one day and the beginning of the next. He looked up and squinted, barely able to make out the silhouette of the tower set against a jet-black sky. As he turned into Bloemstraat from the intersection between Rozengracht and Prinsengracht, he pulled up the collar of his coat. He turned towards the library, awash with a dull glow from the neon streetlights, and tipped the peak of his baseball cap, casting his features into shadow. The street was empty, but Lex had no intention of breaking in from here; it was far too vulnerable to prying eyes.

Lex scrutinised the three asymmetric, interconnected buildings that comprised the library. It was the first and tallest of the buildings that interested him most, consisting of an attic and three floors nestled beneath a steeply curving roof that resembled an old warehouse. The rarest and most valuable books were located on the third floor, and this was where he expected to find the manuscript, either on the shelves or in the safe.

He ambled nonchalantly past the library and turned into an alley deeply cast in shadow. After a few loping strides, he halted at a tall iron gate nestled between sheer brick walls. He peered upwards and eyed with dismay the unscalable tangle of barbed wire sitting on top of the gate.

He unstrapped the backpack and set it down at his feet, freeing the clips to reveal an array of miscellaneous tools, meticulously stowed in exactly the right order. He withdrew a sturdy metal vacuum flask brimful of liquid nitrogen. He pushed the canister's long, thin nozzle into the cylindrical lock, and gave the controlling lever a squeeze. The liquid vapourised into clouds of nitrogen gas that billowed from the nozzle, hissing like an alley cat, and once he was confident that the metal pins had frozen, he shoved a pencil-thin screwdriver into the keyhole. After a hefty twist, the lock shattered like glass. He was not called Liquid Lex without good reason, and with a wry smile, he retrieved the rucksack and shouldered the gate.

Lex hurried through the gap into a deserted courtyard abutting the library's towering rear wall and slipped off his heavy woollen overcoat, bundling it into a pile at the foot of the wall before rummaging through the backpack for a bizarre pair of fabric gloves and overshoes. He huffed and puffed as he squeezed the unyielding material onto his paws, but eventually, and with some trepidation, he slipped his arms through the straps of the pack and began to climb. Like a besuited Peter Parker, he reached out, tentatively at first, pulling himself skywards along the library's sheer wall, and after leaving a first-floor window in his wake, his confidence soared.

As he climbed, he marvelled at Abel's ingenuity in providing him with such a wondrous new accoutrement to his villainous trade. Abel called them his 'Gecko Gloves', and as Lex edged closer to the library's summit, he even had time to reflect on Abel's baffling explanation of how the gloves clung to masonry as if stuck with glue.

When Abel had visited him two weeks earlier bearing gifts that would allow the scaling of buildings with consummate ease, Lex had struggled to contain his excitement. After all, he had performed similar feats in the past with nothing more glamorous than a grappling hook and rope, and he could remember all too well the time he had toppled fifteen feet to the ground when a parapet on the rooftop of a Parisian art gallery had given way. A fractured radius was one thing, but smuggling objects another, and not having to acquire additional equipment on his arrival in Amsterdam had been a major boon.

Abel had excelled himself this time in fabricating the Gecko Gloves there was no doubting it. Despite his fumbling exterior, he had once again demonstrated the brilliance of a mind few could aspire to. He had explained that the unique material, fabricated in the Academy's laboratory, was based on a gecko's remarkable gravity-defying ability to climb walls. Unfortunately, when he described how the microscopic elastic hairs covering the lizard's toes were split into terminal spatulas, allowing the gecko to hold onto surfaces because of van der Waals forces, the weakest of all intermolecular attractive forces, Lex soon lost interest.

During Abel's subsequent discourse on the alchemical process required to synthesise a polymeric material of multi-walled carbon nanotube hairs, Lex's mind was already elsewhere, imagining the dastardly applications to which he could put the amazing gloves and shoes; scaling walls and hanging from ceilings to name but two. Lex did not care about the large surface area of the flexible structures that demonstrated strong nanometre-level adhesion forces two hundred times greater than the hairs on a gecko's foot. All that mattered was that they worked, and here he was in the heart of the city scaling a one hundred-foot building because of a force named after a former Professor of Physics at the University of Amsterdam! How ironic, he thought as he pulled himself over the gable end of the roof wearing Abel's Gecko Gloves in all their adhesive glory.

After clambering onto the rooftop, Lex relaxed, safe in the knowledge that he was no longer visible to anyone on the ground. He glanced at the gently glowing hands of his wristwatch and smiled. Twenty past midnight; plenty of time to break in, find the book and escape. Demonstrating dexterity borne of daily Yoga routines, he stashed the Gecko Gloves in his backpack and set off across the steeply pitched roof towards an angled skylight barely visible in the low light.

Lex edged carefully towards the window, slipped the backpack from his shoulders and wedged the straps between two conveniently crooked slates. He rifled through the bag for a powerful torch and began a systematic evaluation of the window. Just as Ackerman had described, there was a magnetic contact switch on the frame and foiling inside the glass. Any attempt to open the window would separate the contact from the magnet and release a lever that would break the circuit to set off an alarm. Additionally, a thin piece of foil ran around the perimeter of the glass and inserted into two terminals to form a closed electrical circuit, thus breaking the glass would tear the delicate foil, and once again, the alarm would trigger.

Armed with this information, Lex knew that he could neither open the window nor break the glass without setting off the alarm, but this did not deter him; after all, he had done this many times before. Using a thick black crayon purloined from a nearby kindergarten, Lex began to draw. Round and round he went, marking a perfect circle in the centre of the glass an inch wider than the girth of his waist. Leaving the circle free, he systematically reinforced the surrounding glass with duct tape. Then, with fastidiousness bordering on obsession, he scored the circle using a diamond-tipped glass-cutter, tracing and retracing the line in a leisurely manner. With each passing rotation, the glass gradually weakened. Finally, he took a blob of modelling clay and adapted it carefully against the unadulterated inner circle of glass.

He took a deep breath, and with the precision of a surgeon, he lightly tapped all the way round the score mark with a dainty silver hammer while pressing an ear to the glass. He had performed this action many times before, and with his hearing attuned to the task, he could detect any slight change in sound that would forewarn him of a poorly propagating crack.

Tap-tap … tap-tap … tap-tap … and then, suddenly, the glass gave way, spiralling earthbound in a trajectory of eccentric beauty. The duct tape had done its job, leaving the window perfectly intact apart from a gaping hole in its centre. Lex watched in fascination as the glass tumbled towards the attic floor, even failing to shatter as it hit the rafters due to the retentiveness of the clay. He waited with bated breath for the sound burglars know and love so well—silence.

He tossed the rucksack through the window and followed feet first with all the elegance of an Olympic gymnast. He bent his legs, landing perfectly on two feet with barely a sound. He smiled. He was in! He retrieved the torch and sent a powerful beam of light flitting back and forth across the steeply sloping roof. There, nestled between two large storage boxes fifteen feet away, was the hatch Ackerman had described that led down to the library.

The air in the confined space of the attic was dank, and as Lex crawled along creaking rafters, myriad cobwebs danced around his face like a curtain of shimmering gossamer. By the time he reached the hatch, the urge to cough was overpowering, but rather than yank open the communicating door for the fresh air residing on the other side, he spent some moments recalling Ackerman's description of the room situated twelve feet below his current position.

The library's third floor reading room was a simple rectangular affair with a trapdoor in the ceiling conveniently opening into the centre of the room. Rows of books adorned the walls with infrared motion security alarms protecting the stairwell at one end and a small office at the other. He had seen it all before in various museums, banks and art galleries around the world, and like all the other heists he had previously orchestrated, this would be no different. The alarms were perfectly placed to intercept an unwary burglar approaching from downstairs but they had not been positioned with an approach from the roof in mind. Lex shook his head in disgust; sometimes it was all too easy.

He rummaged inside the rucksack and withdrew an elongated pair of odd-looking goggles, slipping them onto his forehead and tightening the elastic to ensure that they would not fall down over his eyes. Lex was especially proud of the goggles, having purloined them from the desk of a military bigwig while rummaging through the drawers in search of a top-secret document for Pearly. He had picked the goggles up on a whim because of their curious appearance, and although he had not realised it at the time, he had serendipitously procured a set of the most up-to-date night vision devices known to the army.

After foolishly asking for a demonstration of how the goggles worked, Abel's subsequent discourse on infrared image intensification tubes that focused light onto a photocathode plate, causing the emission of electrons to strike a second plate, thus producing an image recognisable to the human eye, was all but lost on Lex. Nevertheless, it took him no time to realise how useful the goggles would be, no more so than in the next few minutes.

The neglected trapdoor creaked in protest as Lex hauled it open. He poked his head through the gap and peered into the pitch black room below. He pulled the goggles over his eyes and the view changed in an instant. The motion sensors at opposite ends of the room emitted narrow beams of infrared light that were invisible to the naked eye, but shone with a sickly green hue through the viewfinders of Lex's goggles to illuminate the room as clear as day.

Lex dispensed with the torch and lowered himself from the attic, swinging like a lemur as he dropped to the floor. He looked around in wonder at the thousands of books surrounding him, orderly arranged by subject, and after orientating himself to make sure he did not encroach on the alarms, he began a systematic evaluation of the room. He started with the ancient wooden bookcase housing books under the subject heading of Alchemy, but after withdrawing and carefully reading the title and author's name of every single book, he found no trace of Piotrowski's work. He moved on to the adjacent bookcases. Anthroposophy ... then Freemasonry ... Gnosis ... followed by Grail, Hermetica, Kabbalah, Knights Templar, Mysticism, Rosicrucianism, Sufi, Theosophy. Nothing! The book was not there.

He approached the only bookcase he had not already searched. Western Esotericism. Lex nodded confidently, recalling Piotrowski's association with the Esoteric Brotherhood. He trailed a finger methodically across the spine of each book, alphabetically arranged by the author's name: Faivre, Guénon, Hanegraaf, Lévi, Papus ... Schuré. A space! There was a gap barely wide enough to house a single book. He stared in horror and cursed. Piotrowski's book was missing!

Lex cast aside his disappointment and looked at his watch. There was no time to lose. He strode towards the office, stopping short of a criss-crossing network of beams that traversed the room and blocked his path to the door. The infrared lights originated from a trio of small transmitters embedded in the wall, crossing the room at various fixed angles to strike strategically placed mirrors on the opposite wall. From the mirrors, the beams of light were reflected back to photoelectric receivers adjacent to the transmitters, thus protecting the office behind an invisible fence of infrared light, ready to alarm the moment the light was interrupted.

Lex withdrew a dental mirror from his jacket pocket and edged forwards, holding the mirror immobile inches from his chest. He closed his eyes and steadied himself with deep, cathartic breaths, his nostrils flaring like a thoroughbred. He relaxed his muscles by drawing upon daily routines of yoga and meditation and held himself perfectly still. Suddenly, with the voracity of a striking snake, he thrust out the mirror and held his hand unwaveringly. Lex could barely draw breath as he stared at the mirror interrupting a beam of light and reflecting it back to its corresponding sensor, albeit now over a shorter distance. In this way, he had created a window beyond the beam through which he might pass without setting off the alarm.

Inch by inch, Lex rotated his body about the mirror, performing a hypnotic, slow-motion, sideways limbo. With neck arched and back extended, he stepped gracefully over the beam below his waist with the finesse of a ballerina while instinctively avoiding the light that passed a hair's-breadth above his head. He edged towards the office and steadied himself. Following a final deep breath, he yanked the mirror towards him with a sudden snap, allowing the light to regain its former trajectory and pass unhindered as if nothing had happened. He had done it!

Once safely ensconced between the sensors and the office door, he sighed in relief. He smiled as he inspected a highly-polished, brass plate bolted to a solid wooden door bearing the name of one Marcus De Wolff. He studied the door, and in a flash, he found what he was looking for. There in the gap adjacent to the architrave was the shadow of a contact switch. It was a similar arrangement to the roof skylight with a magnet on one side and a switch on the other. As with the window, any attempt to open the door would separate the components and trigger the alarm, but this time, there was no choice, he had to open the door.

He removed the rucksack and unearthed a powerful magnet, which he secured on the architrave with a large blob of clay. He nodded appreciatively after ensuring that the magnet was positioned in precisely the right position. He took a set of lock picks from the rucksack, stood bolt upright and cracked his knuckles. He was ready to go.

Lock-picking was therapeutic for Lex in a way that hobbies and pastimes were to others. Abandoned by parents who did not care for him, Lex was raised by vagabonds and thieves on streets that became his home, learning many obscure skills normally considered rather unusual for one of his age.

At the age of six, a circus arrived in town, bringing untold opportunities for a young, would-be thief like Lex. The billboards advertising the spectacle optimistically hailed the top of the bill, Marco Zabini, as the greatest escapologist of all time. Late one evening, just as the show was closing for the night, Zabini spotted a shabbily dressed street urchin shamelessly picking pockets.

Overcome by pity, Zabini took the young boy under his wing, happy to pass on all the tricks of the trade to his newly appointed apprentice.

To this day, Lex could still recall Marco's words as he watched him demonstrate the fine art of lock picking. Since then, each time he worked the magic Marco had taught him, those words came flooding back in a wave of nostalgia.

'Never forget that lock picking requires great skill and expertise,' Marco enthused. 'For success you must combine mechanical tactility with manual dexterity, and visual awareness with analytical thinking. If you excel in these areas, Lex, you will grow in many ways.'

Lex never forgot his old guru, and as he grew in maturity and wisdom, he realised how prophetic Marco's words were. The time he spent learning the practical skills to master the art of picking locks also taught him the importance of patience and humility. Ironically, the acquisition of these attributes ultimately generated a yearning for greater depth and balance in Lex's life, culminating in a fascination with enlightenment through spiritual contemplation.

As Lex flicked through a vast selection of strangely shaped picks, he felt an inner calm wash over him, a man at complete ease with the task in hand. He worked the lock with a hand-fashioned pick he had painstakingly ground from a steel street-cleaning bristle acquired from the gutters that had once been his home. He tactilely adjusted the pick with exactly the right torque and pressure to align the pins utilising a technique Marco had described as 'scrubbing'.

As the minutes ticked by, Lex pictured the internal mechanics of the lock in his mind's eye, until finally, there was a muffled click as the tumbler rotated inside the keyway to release the lock. With a gentle push, the door swung open. Lex held his breath and craned his neck, listening with trepidation. Silence. By overriding the switch with an even more powerful magnet, the circuit remained unbroken, even with the door open; the magnet had done its job.

He stepped into the office, pushed the goggles from his eyes and retrieved the torch. The room was a rather sparse affair with a small, tidily arranged desk in the centre and a large wooden cabinet in the corner. Lex yanked eagerly on the cabinet door to inspect the contents and breathed a sigh of relief; he had found the safe.

The battered block of metal that masqueraded as a safe was a sad reflection of its unimportance, and to Lex, it was nothing more than a relic harking back to a bygone age, instantly recognisable for its simplicity by a lock and handle as the only external features to its door. The lock secured a strong bolt inside the door, and by simply rotating a key, the handle would turn and release the bolt. The sight of the ancient safe filled Lex with a sense of nostalgia, but times had moved on. He shook himself down and dismissed the bout of melancholia; it was time to finish the job.

After a fruitless search for the key, he returned to the safe, and although he had encountered infinitely more sophisticated locks in his time, after all the obstacles he had overcome, he suddenly felt an overwhelming sense of gratitude; it had been a rather long day, after all.

Although the safe was a rather basic design, it still took considerable know-how to open it, particularly as he could ill-afford to damage the contents. He considered picking the lock, but the safe was no push over, and after glancing nervously at his watch, he knew that time was running out. He also had a reputation to keep, and while a 'Liquid Lex explosive' would point the finger of suspicion in his direction, he did not care. It would take the authorities many days to establish him as a suspect, and by then, he would be long gone.

He gathered up an ancient typewriter sitting on the desk and hauled it over to the cabinet before carefully extracting a featureless box from his rucksack. He opened the box and peered excitedly at a glass phial brimming with a colourless liquid securely sealed with a taped rubber bung.

Lex always transported his precious chemicals with all the care of a doting parent, safely packaging them in separate compartments to reduce the chance of inadvertently blowing himself up. While back in the hotel bedroom, he had carefully unpacked the various reagents and spent the afternoon mixing them into the requisite phial. He began with one part aluminium powder to five parts ammonium nitrate before adding the resultant mixture to twice the volume of anhydrous hydrazine. The brisk reaction liberated a large billowing cloud of ammonia, which he quickly dispersed by opening a window before anyone came to investigate the strong pungent odour emanating from the room.

This simple chemical combination yielded Lex a solution of hydrazonium nitrate, a compound grandiosely described as one of the most powerful explosives in the world. Lex had developed a particular penchant for this liquid, courtesy of its ease of manufacture and the spectacular results it had previously afforded him. He had learnt of its existence from an old lag and physicist who had been happy to forgo his signature on the Official Secrets Act in exchange for a large wad of Lex's cash. The man had been discredited for embezzling funds from the military, and in revenge for the years he had languished in prison, he had been happy to provide Lex with the details of a compound developed, not as a weapons-grade explosive, but as a rocket propellant!

Lex lifted the bottle from its protective packaging. Taking great care not to agitate the liquid, he slid the tube into the safe's keyhole and secured it with a marble-sized plug of clay. Next, he tucked a small electric blasting cap into the clay, ensuring the detonator passed all the way through to the phial. He secured the typewriter to the safe's handle with a thick piece of rope, leaving it dangling in mid-air. He unrolled the wires from the detonating cap and scampered across the room, positioning himself behind the desk after he had calmly tipped it over with a strategically placed boot.

He smiled nervously, made the sign of the cross on his chest and flicked the detonator switch. The fuse wires in the cap immediately vapourised, firing the initiator explosive, which in turn triggered the output explosive, shattering the phial and exposing the contents to the detonating force of the cap. The gentle tinkle of breaking glass was merely a herald to the loud report that followed. The hydrazonium nitrate split like an exploding Mount St. Helens, blowing the lock asunder. Vast plumes of nitrogen and hydrogen were released in a gaseous outburst of nebular proportions as the bolt was freed from the restraining lock. The handle turned under the dead weight of the typewriter hanging by its rope, and as the smoke cleared, the door swivelled open. Lex was in!

Lex emerged from behind the desk now pockmarked with shrapnel and calmly brushed away the debris that had settled on his jacket. He looked in satisfaction at the black scorch marks around the lock and gazed expectantly into the safe at the only item of any size amidst several unimportant looking documents. Lex reached out in eager anticipation for the deeply tanned, leather-bound book with no obvious clue to its nature. He cradled the book in his arms like a long-lost friend before setting it down on the floor to inspect its pages by torchlight. The words set boldly in black ink were a little faded on the remarkably well-preserved vellum pages. Lex sat down and crossed his legs, composing himself before he read the introductory words penned many centuries before.

The circle has no beginning or end, and so it has always been thus for those who seek enlightenment through the teachings of the Esoteric Brotherhood of Men. Singularity is the path to darkness and eternal ignorance. Alone and you will surely fail.

On Frankl's instruction, Lex had committed these words to memory, and re-reading them now merely confirmed he had found what he had come for. He looked fleetingly at his watch; three a.m., it read. He bundled up the manuscript, tucked it safely under his jumper and lowered the goggles over his eyes.

After further careful contortions and the use of an implement miraculously pilfered from beneath a rubber dam during a course of root canal treatment, Lex wriggled safely beyond the beams of infrared light. He donned the Gecko Gloves in anticipation of escape, but his first ascent of the wall ended in disaster when the adhesive gloves pulled several books from their shelves, causing him to topple ignominiously to the floor. He cursed as he struggled to separate a seemingly irreversibly bound copy of *Plinchy's Esoterica* from the palm of a hand, but when finally free of the cursed book, he carefully confined his climb to the fixed wooden struts of a bookcase. After inching across the ceiling like a manifestation of Kafka, he reached the hatch and hauled himself into the attic. He scurried along the rafters and pushed a begoggled head through the carefully cut aperture in the sloping skylight, emerging like a mole from a tunnel. He doffed the goggles and stashed them carefully inside the rucksack. He slid across the roof, slipped over the parapet, and with his eyes firmly fixed on the wall, he set off towards terra firma.

Once safely returned to the ground, Lex retrieved his coat and slipped the book into a deep, inner pocket. Faint streaks of light were visible in the sky hinting at incipient daybreak, and after a pleasant stroll to the station, he even contemplated having time for breakfast before boarding the train. Lex smiled in a way that only someone who had just committed the perfect crime could. He swaggered self-assuredly through the gate and felt his elation soar from the misguided notion that, after all he had been through, nothing could now possibly go wrong.

Lex was a professional and not a person usually prone to overconfidence, but as he eased his way out of the shadows onto Bloemstraat, he missed the blur of movement that signalled he was no longer alone. Before he could react, a man jumped out in front of him brandishing a gun. The pistol flapped menacingly in the man's trembling hands, but Lex did not doubt that it was levelled directly at him. At first, he did not recognise the man barring his way, but as his eyes accommodated to the dull neon light, the unmistakable face of Thjiis Ackerman took shape. Following this disturbing realisation, Lex recognised two other things at once. Firstly, Ackerman's face carried the same ruddy complexion that had been apparent at their first meeting, undoubtedly a sign of alcohol intoxication. Secondly, the pistol waving awkwardly in Ackerman's hand was a Luger P80 semi-automatic, and not a particularly good specimen at that.

'You lied,' cried Ackerman with the neglected pistol still shaking in his hand.

Lex shifted uneasily on his feet, suspecting Ackerman had never handled a gun before. 'You're mistaken, Thjiis. Look, we can talk this over. Just put the gun down and we can—'

'You must take me for a complete idiot,' Ackerman cut in. 'When I woke up this morning, I realised I'd been duped. I couldn't believe what a fool I'd been.'

Lex smiled nervously. 'You're mistaken, Thjiis. Let me explain. Look, I haven't taken anything. See for yourself,' he said glibly, exposing empty hands. 'I just wanted to try out the security system for myself. I—'

'Stop lying!' Ackerman screamed in a voice that was steeped in anger and self-loathing. 'Do you *really* expect me to believe you now? I may look stupid, but it wasn't difficult to check your credentials. I still have some contacts at ARC, you know. The company has never operated in the Middle East and probably never will.'

'Okay, okay, maybe I wasn't entirely truthful the other night, but look, I haven't got anything to hide. Why don't you search me?' replied Lex.

Ackerman shook his head uncertainly.

'Come on, Thjiis, let me explain,' continued Lex in a placatory tone. 'I just wanted to break in, that's all. I work for Sinclair Security. Surely you've heard of them? They're one of ARC's rivals,' said Lex, rapidly thinking on his feet. 'It would be very embarrassing for ARC if someone broke in and bypassed their systems. It would mean a lot more contracts for my company. Look—'

For once, Lex's smooth words and charming manner only seemed to inflame the situation further. Ackerman, ill at ease from the outset, hopped from one foot to the other. 'I don't believe you! Just shut up!' he bellowed, the gun now shaking uncontrollably in his hand. 'Lie after lie, it all comes so easily to you,' he continued, and for once he was right. 'I trusted you, but you lied to me. I decided to keep an eye on this place and I was waiting for you when you arrived last night. You never saw me, but I followed you through the gate and watched you scale the wall like a blinking spider. I bet you've stolen something priceless from in there,' he said, beginning to sound a little unhinged as he brandished the pistol in the direction of the library.

The moment the gun veered off target, Lex saw his chance. He lunged for Ackerman's outstretched arm, but as he dived towards him, Ackermann pulled the trigger. There was a blinding flash and a reverberating boom as the ancient pistol exploded in flames.

The bullet tumbled from the weapon at a speed more akin to an arboreal sloth than the terminal velocity of a projectile exiting the barrel of a semi-automatic firearm, yet the missile still hit Lex squarely in the chest with sufficient force to lift him off his feet and send him flying backwards through the air towards the library wall.

As the echo dissipated, Lex struck his head on the solid brick wall and tumbled to the ground. When the smoke cleared, Lex remained spread-eagled where he had fallen, a small, charred entry portal the only clue to the bullet that had passed through the heavy-duty cloth of his overcoat. As he lay immobile, perhaps teetering on the brink of mortality, a paradoxical wave of euphoria poured over him in the brief moments before he lapsed into the depths of unconsciousness.

16

Poison or Antidote?

CORNELIUS SPYDRE SAT UP in bed, sipping gingerly from the mug Mrs Brimstork had deposited on the bedside table while he had been napping. The hot, steaming infusion gave off aromatic vapours smelling vaguely of pine, and as soon as the viscous green liquid touched his lips, he began to feel rejuvenated. His memory of the past few days was hazy, and he could recall little, if anything, of the time he had spent in Westminster Hospital prior to his discharge. Henry Price had insisted that he return home with him to recuperate, and despite not wishing to impose on his old friend, Spydre had been delighted to accept.

Spydre looked up from the mysterious liquid and caught sight of his reflection in a mirror at the end of the bed. His grizzled, semi-paralysed face looked tired and drawn, and his stretched, paper-thin skin was whiter than ever, giving the impression of a man who had cheated death once too often. He smiled lopsidedly at his mirror image and mused ruefully that his failing body could not tolerate many more injustices like this.

The sound of footsteps on the stairs followed by a circumspect tapping at the door jolted him from his thoughts. 'Hello,' he called out in a croaky voice despite the revitalising effects of Mrs Brimstork's concoction.

A face hidden in shadow appeared around the door, but Spydre immediately recognised the unmistakable outline of Lily's hair silhouetted against the glow rising from the stairwell. 'Come in, come in,' he said eagerly. 'I was wondering when you were going to come and see me,' he added without reproach.

'I wasn't sure whether you were resting,' said Lily in a voice little more than a whisper. 'Are you sure you're all right? I hear you're getting better but you need time to regain your strength,' she said sheepishly.

'Pah!' replied Spydre. 'It sounds like your father has been keeping you from me, the old rogue. I am fine. I will be back on my feet before you know it, and just you watch me then!'

Lily beamed. 'I know I haven't been in to see you, but you were still quite poorly when you arrived, and I was under strict instructions not to disturb you. Let's get this straight, though; you're not fine, and there's no excuse for you to behave irresponsibly, you old rascal,' she said.

'Now, come in properly,' Spydre ordered, ignoring the rebuke, 'and turn on some light, for goodness sake, so that I can see you.'

Lily switched on the bedside lamp. She sat down on the edge of the bed and Spydre could sense her baulk as she took his limp hand in her own.

'I know I may not look my best,' he said full of humour, 'but just look at you. As wonderful as ever, I see.'

'And it's good to see you looking so well, too,' she replied.

Spydre could sense the lie, particularly having just witnessed his haggard face in the mirror.

'You know how I love your company, Cornelius.' She leant forwards and kissed him on the cheek. 'I could also do with someone to confide in,' she whispered conspiratorially in his ear. 'It's not always easy with my father.'

Spydre gave her a reassuring smile. 'You can always come to me, Lily.'

'I know,' Lily said, nodding.

They sat together on the bed, enjoying the solitude and one another's company before Spydre eventually spoke. 'I believe I have you to thank for a part in my recovery, Lily.'

'Not really. It was my father who saved you. I just did as I was told. I brought the reagents he asked for.'

'Ah, but how magnificently and quickly you responded, my girl. Now, see if you can find me some whisky.'

Lily shook her head. 'You don't expect me to—?'

'Worth a try,' said the old man, interrupting Lily before she could finish her sentence, 'but rest assured there will be no one to stop me when I get home. I thought you would be a little more understanding than that irascible old housekeeper of yours.'

'You're incorrigible,' she said, laughing at his impertinence. 'Do you realise how close you were—?'

'Do not waste your breath, Lily,' Spydre cut in again. 'All the more reason to enjoy a good drink while I still have some breath left in me. Ah, well, never mind, it will just have to wait. But what of you, my girl, how are you?'

'Me? I'm all right,' she replied noncommittally.

'It does not sound like it to me. Now, what exactly is the problem?'

Lily's smile reappeared but quickly faded. 'Oh, I don't know ...' she faltered.

Spydre had always been perceptive when it came to interpreting Lily's moods, and he could read her in ways that her father never could. 'This is to do with your father, I take it?'

Lily nodded.

'Look, Lily. He has your best interests at heart, whatever you may sometimes think. I know it brings you into conflict, particularly as you are growing up so quickly, but he realises this, and I think it frightens him a little. Never forget that he has been through a lot himself, which is why he could not bear to leave you any more vulnerable than you already are.'

'What do you mean?'

'I mean that these are dangerous times. Just look at me.'

'I'm not sure I follow, Cornelius.'

'Come now, Lily, surely you realise that what happened to me was because of my association with Henry?'

'What! You mean that's why you were poisoned?'

'Of course! I take it your father has not spoken to you about this?'

'No, he has not!' she replied indignantly. 'Don't you see? It just proves my point. What actually happened to you?'

Spydre sighed but managed a wan smile. 'This should be a matter between you and your father, and not for me to discuss with you, but I believe you have a right to know what has been going on, particularly as you may be under threat yourself.'

'Me, under threat? How come?'

'I shall come on to that presently, but first, let me recount my tale. My recollection of what happened is still a little hazy, you understand, but bear with me. Henry has filled in many of the details relating to my visitation,' he said dispassionately.

'Come on, Cornelius, spill the beans,' Lily said eagerly.

'Very well, my dear. It all began with the arrival of a woman I had never met before. I was in the shop, as usual, and ironically enough, I was in the middle of unearthing some information for your father. Call me an old fool, if you will, but this woman bowled me over the moment I laid eyes on her. She was beautiful, but there was something about her that I could not put my finger on. I should have realised something was amiss when she enquired about an ancient book on Pagan magic. A particular interest of mine, you see, but as I said earlier, an old fool ...' Spydre allowed his words to drift as his mind began to wander, but after a brief pause, he continued with the account. 'We became embroiled in a fascinating discussion on Pagan rituals. She was either well acquainted with the subject or she had done her homework.'

'What did she look like?' said Lily.

'As I said, she was beautiful, beguiling even. Dark hair, so black, yet it held such lustre, it seemed to radiate a luminescence that lit up the stuffy old place that passes for my bookshop. Her eyes were captivating—so dark and so wide—I felt as if I could see into the depths of her soul. Her skin was smooth and unblemished, and her scent, ah yes, her scent ... I should have known better. I wonder now whether she somehow bewitched me.'

'Why? What happened?'

'I invited her to sit down while I searched for the book she had asked about. When I returned with some refreshment, we talked for what seemed like hours, although exactly what about I cannot remember now. It must have been while we were talking that she slipped something into my drink, because, all of a sudden, I began to feel unwell. I am afraid my memory fails me at this point, but I do recall developing an unquenchable thirst, although the more I drank, the worse I felt. I dare say I was drinking more of the poison she had administered,' he added bitterly.

'My vision became blurred and I was unable to focus on the print in the book. My heart was racing so fast, it felt as if it would explode. After that, I cannot recollect much, except the dreams, of course. I suppose I was hallucinating, but I have never experienced anything that was so terrifyingly vivid before.'

'You don't have to go on, Cornelius,' said Lily kindly.

'There is not much more to tell, in truth. I was at a desolate place I have visited in my dreams before, but never so real. My task was to defend the gates of a kingdom from a terrifying manifestation known only as the Raven King. I was with an old friend of mine, Luschka,' he said, unable to mask an expression of longing on his face.

'Alas, even in my dreams I could sense I was failing. I somehow knew the outcome of the dream was inextricably linked with my fate, and that when the gates fell, as they inevitably would, so my life would also end.'

'What were you poisoned with?'

'An extract from a plant known as deadly nightshade, I believe. Belladonna to some, but I prefer to call it the Devil's Herb. It contains a mixture of, amongst other things, atropine and hyoscyamine, drugs that are commonly used in medicine, but when taken in excess, are almost invariably fatal. Had it not been for your father's timely arrival, I am not sure I would still be here with you now.'

'I don't understand how he knew what this woman had poisoned you with,' said Lily, looking bemused.

'I cannot help feeling disappointed that he has not discussed this with you. Perhaps he has been meaning to, I do not know, but this is very important,' said Spydre.

'Why?'

'Because, Lily, as I said earlier, I am concerned for you. Let me explain. Several clues were left for your father alluding to the nature of the poison that this woman administered to me. It is clear that whoever poisoned me not only wanted him to find me but also for him to have a fighting chance of saving my life.'

'But who would do anything like that?'

'Someone who had good reason to want to stop him from travelling to Amsterdam on the day the attack occurred.'

'But I thought he was only going there to see a copy of the manuscript that was stolen.'

'You are right, Lily, but I am afraid that this second manuscript is every bit as important as his own. The night he was due to arrive in Amsterdam, the only other copy of Piotrowski's manuscript was taken from the Bibliotheca Philosophica Hermetica,' said Spydre solemnly. 'Whoever was involved in the theft knew of your father's travel arrangements. The attack on me was merely a diversion to ensure that he would not set off on the day in question, thus allowing the thief free reign to proceed without fear of being disturbed by someone as powerful as your father.'

'But who would do anything as evil as that, Cornelius? You nearly died.'

'Quite so, Lily, quite so. These people, I am afraid, will not allow anything to stand in their way. They would see the death of an old man as inconsequential compared to the prize they seek.'

'But why on earth would anyone want two copies of the same book? It doesn't make any sense to me.'

'It appears that the books are not quite the same. Alone and they are useless, but together, they hide a powerful secret, which a group called the Esoteric Brotherhood buried long ago, and, I believe, never wished to see resurface.'

'And now that the books have been reunited ...' Lily let her words trail off as the implications of the news sank in.

After a few moments' reflection, Lily queried, 'Tell me, Cornelius, why are you so worried about me?'

Spydre hesitated, weighing up exactly how much to divulge. 'I do not want to make your relationship with your father any worse than it already is.'

Lily glared at him. 'Come on, Cornelius. If I'm in danger, I need to know about it.'

He sighed and then nodded, if a little reluctantly. 'Have you ever heard the name Aurelia Nightshade mentioned before?'

Lily nodded tentatively, looking as if she was not sure she wanted to hear what he was about to say. 'She was a friend, an accomplice, I think, of Pearly Black after ... after my mum stopped working with Black,' she said uneasily.

'That's right, Lily. She was a very influential member of the Order of Eternal Enlightenment, and central to Black and his plans. When the Order was at its peak, there were some suspicious deaths of prominent people who opposed Black. At the time, the deaths were put down to natural causes. Eventually, though, the Council became suspicious. The bodies were exhumed, and after toxicological tests, I am afraid a grisly pattern began to emerge. We now know for certain that at least two of the individuals had traces of atropine in their body at the time of their death. It was obvious they had been poisoned. Of course, it was all hushed up at the time, but there was no doubt in your father's mind that the person behind these misdemeanours was Aurelia Nightshade.'

'Why wasn't she punished?' said Lily indignantly.

'I am afraid the evidence was circumstantial at best. Nightshade was linked with both of these men around the time they died, but nothing could ever be proved.

'Your father was convinced of her guilt, but he knew there was never a chance that she would be convicted. What made it worse was the way she goaded him. She knew full well that by using an extract of deadly nightshade, suspicion would fall on her by dint of her name and her connection to the men. It was as if she was advertising her involvement, but the only thing your father ever had to go on was his unshakeable conviction of her guilt, and she knew it.'

'Were there any more deaths after that?'

'Yes, but atropine was never used again ... up until now, of course.'

'So I assume it was this woman who visited you a few days ago,' said Lily, aghast.

'Yes, I am afraid so. It all fits. I could kick myself for not recognising her, although, to be fair, I have never met her before. I have seen pictures, of course, but it was all such a long time ago. My eyes are failing, and the light in the shop is poor. It never crossed my mind to suspect this woman, and I am afraid it so very nearly cost me.'

Lily stroked the back of his hand. 'Don't blame yourself, Cornelius. You weren't to know.'

'Maybe not, though it matters little now. What *is* important, however, is what happens next.'

Lily regarded him carefully as if trying to read his thoughts. 'I thought Nightshade and the rest of the Order disappeared after Black's death.'

'Quite so, Lily,' allowed Spydre pensively. 'What you must realise about the Order, however, is that it consisted of a disparate group of unsavoury individuals united by one particularly charismatic man. When Black died, the bond that united them evaporated. Oh, they tried to regroup, but amidst an atmosphere of mutual suspicion and recrimination, they were doomed to fail. By the time the Council began to flex its muscles, backing for the Order was already on the wane. Eventually, when news of the Order's nefarious activities emerged, any remaining support vanished overnight, leaving Black's closest confederates isolated and vulnerable. Not surprisingly, most of them, including Nightshade, went to ground. That was the last we ever heard of her ... until now, I'm afraid.'

'How can you be so sure that it was this woman who visited you?'

'Oh, I am sure all right. Although my recollections are vague, there is no doubting it. Your father managed to unearth some old photos of her, and I can assure you it *was* her.'

'But why now?'

'I only wish I could tell you, Lily. All I can say is that something strange and powerful is afoot. It all points to a resurgence of the Order because of whatever is hidden in Piotrowski's manuscript.'

Lily looked baffled. 'Do you have any idea what it is they're after?'

'Me, personally, no ...'

'But ...?'

'I believe your father has recently received some information that has caused him to speculate on this very subject.'

'And what is that, Cornelius?'

'I am afraid, Lily, that I must draw the line at this point. You must put your differences with your father aside and discuss this matter with him.'

'If only I could,' Lily snorted. 'Don't forget that he's the one who never confides in me. After all, who am I, apart from his daughter?' she added sarcastically.

'I feel like banging your heads together. You are both so alike. It is hardly surprising you have come to such an impasse. If there is one thing I aim to do before I leave this house, it is to ensure that you talk to one another.'

'I'll believe it when I see it,' she said, now smiling, her small, perfectly straight teeth shining like pulsars. 'Come on, Cornelius, you must be able to tell me something,' she added pleadingly.

Spydre's disfigured face softened. He had never been able to resist Lily no matter what trouble it got him into with her father. 'Very well,' he returned, accompanying his words with a defeated sigh. 'It is not as if I know that much anyway.'

'Tell me what you know!' Lily said excitedly.

'Your father thinks that this secret has something to do with the quest for immortality.'

A faint gasp escaped from Lily's lips. 'What do you mean?'

'This time, I really cannot answer you, for the simple reason that I do not know. As I said earlier, it is about time you had a frank discussion with your father.'

'Okay,' she said with a nod, 'but you said earlier that the attack on you was a smokescreen to prevent my father from travelling to Amsterdam.'

'Just so,' Spydre said noncommittally.

'Working on the assumption that the Order has reformed, then how did they know of his plans?'

'A good question, Lily, and the answer explains why I am worried about you.'

'Go on,' Lily prompted.

'Only a handful of people knew he was planning to travel to Amsterdam. He announced his intentions to the Council just a few hours before he was due to leave. It would not have been possible to get a message out of that meeting and for Nightshade to arrive on my doorstep when she did. No,' he said, shaking his head. 'It would appear that the diversion had been planned for some time. I am afraid that the only people who knew of your father's plans before that meeting, apart from me, of course, are linked with this household. It seems that, sadly, we have a mole in our midst!'

The colour drained from Lily's cheeks. 'I don't believe it!' she cried. 'My father trusts the staff implicitly. They're almost part of the family. Both Albright and Mrs Brimstork have been around since he was a child and they're totally loyal to him. The only other people to come and go with any regularity are my tutors, and while I may not always see eye to eye with them, my father has known them for years as well.'

'I would not disagree with you, Lily, but just think about it. How did the thief break into the house so easily? The simplest explanation is that they had help from an insider. It would also explain how Nightshade knew of your father's trip, and in sufficient detail to arrange a little visit to my shop.'

'I don't believe it,' said Lily, shaking her head vehemently.

'Whatever the case, Lily, this is one subject I suggest you do not broach with your father as I know to my cost. No. You must keep it to yourself and be vigilant. Keep your wits about you and, most importantly, trust no one. Do you understand?'

Lily nodded but remained silent, deep in thought.

'Now, perhaps it is time for you to fill me in on some details that I would like explaining.'

Lily frowned. 'What do you want to know?'

'You are not the only one that your father is reluctant to discuss matters with at the moment. I realise he is preoccupied, but I would like to know exactly how he managed to save me from the effects of the Devil's Herb.'

'I'm not sure I can help, Cornelius. All I can tell you is that he asked me to deliver some reagents he keeps in the basement store.'

'What were they?'

Lily thought for a moment. 'Extract of Indian snakeroot and powdered Calabar bean. I've never encountered either of them during my studies before.'

Spydre regarded Lily pensively. 'Ah! How very interesting.'

'Don't keep me in suspense!' she said reproachfully.

'Very well, but before I explain, just answer me this. What did your father do with the reagents when you arrived at the shop?'

'He was waiting at the door when I got there and took me straight through to the office. It was awful, Cornelius. You were lying on the floor. At first, I thought you were dead. You looked terrible, and you were barely breathing.'

'What did your father say?'

'Nothing. He was in such a hurry and he was in no mood to answer my questions. He took a teaspoonful of each of the reagents and placed them in a bowl. He mixed them into a fine paste with some hot water from the kettle and then diluted the paste with some cold water from the tap before transferring it to a drinking cup.'

'And then?'

'We propped you up against the wall, although you were barely conscious, and he forced the foul-looking brew into your mouth. You could hardly swallow, and I thought you might choke, but he wouldn't stop until you'd drained the lot. I didn't realise it at the time, but he was convinced that your life depended on whatever was in that awful concoction. After that, we just waited. You were still unconscious, yet your body was afflicted with muscular spasms that kept coming and going. Fortunately, by the time the ambulance arrived, the convulsions were subsiding.'

'Thank you, Lily. At last, I am beginning to understand,' said Spydre, shuffling into a more comfortable position. 'It is ironic that Nightshade chose to use that particular poison. Perhaps it is her warped sense of humour that compels her to select a compound that shares its name with her own.'

'But such a horrible poison, Cornelius. Why?'

'Well, as I have already said, Lily, I believe she used it for two reasons. Firstly, to prevent your father from travelling to Amsterdam, and secondly, because she wanted him to know just exactly who the perpetrator of this evil misdemeanour was. It is her calling card, you see! Belladonna ... how fitting. Do you know what it means?'

Lily shook her head.

'Beautiful lady! Can you believe the audacity of the woman? Ladies of court once used it to dilate their pupils as a way to enhance their beauty, but this particular beautiful woman seems to use it for far more deadly purposes.'

'What exactly does it do?'

'Now that I can tell you. I have had the chance to do some research since I came here,' he replied, procuring an old, tatty pharmacopoeia from beneath the bedclothes. 'I had Albright fetch it for me from the library. I have to hide it from Mrs Brimstork, you understand, or she would unquestionably confiscate it.

'Atropine acts on the nervous system by blocking a naturally occurring chemical, acetylcholine, thus producing profound effects throughout the body.'

'Acetylcholine?' Lily asked, nodding tentatively. 'Ana's taught me about it as part of my neurophysiology lessons.'

'Yes. It is a neurotransmitter that is released in minute quantities at nerve endings and is particularly important in the parasympathetic autonomic nervous system.'

'Yes. The parasympathetic nervous system is responsible for vegetative bodily functions such as controlling heart rate and producing secretions,' said Lily eagerly.

'And atropine acts by blocking the effects of these nerves. You already know what happened to me: racing pulse, dilated pupils, dry skin, and so on.

'Acetylcholine is also an important neurotransmitter in the brain, thus accounting for the hallucinations that tormented me.'

'So how did the reagents counter the drug's effects?'

'Your father's qualities never cease to amaze me, Lily. His quick thinking undoubtedly saved my life. I know he experiments with chemicals, but even I bow to his knowledge in this area. I would never have considered the Calabar bean as an antidote to atropine, for it is a potent poison itself.'

Lily looked aghast. 'And he gave it to you!'

'Indeed,' replied Spydre, accompanying his words with a wry smile.

'What do you know about it?'

'All I know is its reputation for evil. It was used in African witchcraft as a poison and in the trial of those caught transgressing tribal laws. It was administered to the victim by forced ingestion. If they vomited and lived, they were deemed not guilty. If they died, as they usually did, it was considered that they had received a fitting punishment for their crime.'

'And my father chose it as an antidote?' said Lily, shaking her head.

'Hmm. I would agree that it hardly seems appropriate,' replied Spydre contemplatively.

'Maybe it formed a compound with the other reagent. What do you know of Indian snakeroot?'

'Again, not much. It is a herb that derives its name from its reputation as an antidote to the venom of certain snakes. It has been used in India for thousands of years. I also know it has tranquillising effects. Eastern spiritualists utilise it as an aid to their meditation, I believe.

'I think we should do some research of our own, Lily,' he said, holding up the book. 'Let us see if we can find the answers in here.'

Spydre's twisted hands shook with a fine tremor as he turned the pages, looking for the relevant entries. 'Ah, here we are,' he said eventually. 'Now, Lily, pass me the magnifying glass,' he added, pointing to an object that lay out of his reach on the bedside table. 'The text is far too small for me to read with these ancient eyes of mine.'

Spydre thumbed back and forth between pages. At last, he set the book down on his lap and closed his eyes following the exertion. 'You know, Lily, your father really is a genius,' he said eventually.

'Why, what does it say?'

'It only confirms what I already knew about your father's encyclopaedic knowledge. The Calabar bean is from the genus *Physostigma*. It contains a drug called physostigmine, which antagonises atropine by negating its effect on acetylcholine.

'Similarly, Indian snakeroot contains reserpine, which counteracts the effect of atropine in a slightly different way.'

'How does it work?'

'Reserpine lowers blood pressure, reduces fever and acts as a tranquilliser; actions that are contradictory to atropine in every way.'

'It's incredible that he knew how these agents would work,' agreed Lily.

'Not only that, Lily, but what astonishes me most is that these drugs are both extremely potent poisons in their own right. Henry undoubtedly had to ensure that he used exactly the right dose, particularly as he elected to use them in combination. I do not doubt that either of these drugs is capable of resulting in death, and it is entirely possible that, rather than saving my life, they could just as easily have hastened my demise!'

Following a loud rap on the door, Mrs Brimstork came bustling into the room. Spydre had just enough time to hide the book under the bedclothes before the housekeeper looked in his direction.

'It's about time you took a rest, sir ...' said Mrs Brimstork, 'and you should be getting on with your studies, young lady,' she added, looking at Lily disapprovingly. 'Mr Mirkstone has been waiting for you downstairs for a while now and you should not be disturbing the gentleman like this. He needs to recuperate.'

Lily got up from the bed, nodding in acquiescence at Mrs Brimstork while still managing to cast a furtive smile in Spydre's direction before making her apologies and heading downstairs.

17

Styx's Legacy

AURELIA NIGHTSHADE HAD NOT been idle in the weeks following receipt of the black pearl that had summoned her to Riddlescombe, and despite her initial scepticism at Frankl's revelations, she had spent more and more time reflecting on the events of that day. She had tried to be objective and cast aside her loathing of Frankl—a throwback to his obsequious behaviour around Pearly—but the more she thought about it, the more she was intrigued.

Pearly had always been obsessive in his quest for power verging on a psychotic megalomania, but his other motives had been about as clear to her as the fog that had lingered over the capital for the past few days. Pearly had been driven by an unquenchable thirst for knowledge, and it seemed reasonable to assume that Frankl's quest was inextricably linked with whatever Pearly had been fixated on at the time of his death.

She knew Pearly had spent much of his time delving into obscure alchemical secrets, fervently believing that they held the key to both his future and that of the Order, but to what end? Was it power or wealth, or some other mystical panacea he had been searching for? She did not know, but Pearly had become increasingly distracted in the months leading up to his death, and whenever she had tried to question him, all he would say was that it was a matter of life or death.

And now, she had an irksome hunch that Frankl was on the

verge of discovering the truth behind Pearly's secret. This thought thrilled and appalled her in equal measure, kindling her interest to the point that she was prepared to play along with Frankl's plan. It galled her to think, however, that Frankl was the prime mover in recent events, and she cursed herself for her lassitude following Pearly's demise when she should have been searching for whatever had energised him rather than wallowing in self-pity. This realisation had, rather belatedly, galvanised her into action, and for the time being, she would continue to flatter Frankl and play along with his scheme. Beyond that, well, she would just have to wait and see.

For starters, she had been happy to play her part in stalling Price, and she had taken a perverse pleasure in reverting to her old ways. The success of the scheme that had almost seen the end of the doddering bookseller had taken her back to the days of the Order when she had organised and executed Pearly's plans with a thrilling exhilaration, a feeling she had not experienced in years.

She was flattered that Frankl had given her free rein to accomplish the job in her own inimitable style, and she had set to it with all her usual gusto. Following some simple but discreet surveillance, she had soon established the connection that existed between Price and his friend. She knew from her scrapes with Price in the past that if anything posed a threat to an ally, he would do everything in his power to help them out. Some would see this as enviable loyalty, but to Aurelia, it was a sign of weakness and one that she was happy to exploit. Even she had been surprised by the effortlessness of her plan, and the fact that the old man still lived was irrelevant. No. What mattered was that she had kept Price out of the way, allowing Lex to proceed with what he excelled in best, not to mention the not-so-subtle announcement that she was back.

Aurelia always knew that Price would do everything in his power to track her down after Pearly's death. She had spent many years on the run, only ever managing to stay ahead of her pursuers by expending vast amounts of cash secreted in numerous vaults and safety deposit boxes scattered around the globe. Her ability to bribe, corrupt and blackmail had never been more useful, and while her dwindling cash reserves was a source of considerable irritation, it had helped to keep her safe from Price and the far-reaching tentacles of Internal Security.

Following the attack on the old man, it was inevitable that Price would rekindle his efforts to find her, and so she had returned to a favourite haunt, one of several safe houses based around the capital. The small, deceptively spacious town house located in a quiet, fashionable part of the city was a place where Price would never find her. The house was a stone's throw from the upper reaches of the Thames, an area beloved of rowers, lovers, starlings, joggers, film crews, students, fishermen, exhibitionists, and in Aurelia's case, fugitives. The area attracted an eclectic mix of wealthy inhabitants like magnets to a pole, drawn by various opulent boutiques, restaurants, cafés and wine bars located there. In an area frequented by tax evaders, gamblers, property developers, city boys, embezzlers, corporate lawyers and fraudsters, Aurelia could not fail to blend in. Such a unique ecological niche also afforded her the luxury of living with profligacy and anonymity borne of the ill-gotten wealth that somehow seemed to flourish there.

The house was set over three floors, as luxurious inside as it was nondescript outside, and the place to which Aurelia always returned when there was work to do. The quiet, walled enclosure at the back of the house was nothing more than a pleasant inner city garden to the casual onlooker, but to Aurelia, it was a source of some of the deadliest concoctions she had ever cultivated. The house was nestled amidst a row of strikingly similar terraced houses with a small strip of garden suggesting nothing more than a pleasant sanctuary in a thriving community. On the property's south-facing rear wall was a well-established wistaria with bare, gnarled intertwining vines looking like the ancient limbs of a misshapen old man, and despite the plant's opulent appearance when in full splendour, its seeds harboured a toxic glycoside sure to incapacitate when appropriately administered. The wistaria was merely an entrée to some of the more lethal contents of the garden, including wolfsbane, cowslip, hemlock, lobelia, foxglove, moonseed, oleander, mandrake, cocklebur and the star lily, all innocently growing in a veritable conglomeration of murder and mayhem. The garden was Aurelia's very own potion store, readily available for use at a moment's notice, but apart from a subtle disturbance of soil around the base of a tall herbaceous perennial— a rather fine specimen of deadly nightshade—the garden had lain dormant for some time.

In the aftermath of Frankl's seaside sojourn, Aurelia had given up her coastal retreat for the city with the intention of finding out what he was up to and to start some preparations of her own. She had kept in touch with Lex during his trip overseas until the day of the theft but had heard nothing of him since. She had scoured the news for days, looking for any hint of his demise, until finally, she had come across a few lines in the foreign section of the *Comet* detailing a break-in at a not-so-important library in Amsterdam. The brief article made little significance of the theft of a worthless manuscript, but on the basis that the perpetrator had not been apprehended, Aurelia was prepared to bet that Lex had met with his usual success. She assumed, therefore, that he was already on his way home, raising the prospect that Frankl would soon get his grubby hands on the manuscript. If she was right, Frankl would be in touch very soon, and so she needed to be ready.

She began by concocting a diverse selection of unsavoury potions in the property's beautifully fashioned laboratory. The secret room adjoining the kitchen was home to a vast array of chemical equipment in which her supply from the garden could be pounded, mixed, heated, condensed and distilled into whatever took her fancy.

After hours of painstaking labour, Aurelia was delighted with the outcome, ranging from a colourless, odourless fluid that killed silently in minutes, to a supply of white granular crystals that, on contact with the eyes, induced temporary blindness in seconds. After whiling away the days in unbridled satisfaction, manufacturing a pharmacological arsenal of incapacitation and death, she knew that the inevitable call would come. In the meantime, she was happy to continue with her preparations so that when the summons came, she would be ready.

*

Liquid Lex's European excursion did not end as he had anticipated thanks to the sudden appearance of an aggrieved Ackerman looking like a gun-toting cowboy swaggering out from the O.K. Corral. Lex's recollection of what happened next was vague, and after attempting to wrest the gun from his assailant, it all went black. He could distinctly recollect the deafening sound of a discharging gun, and knew it had been pointing directly at him at the time. He also recalled a hefty blow to the chest that had sent him careering into a solid brick wall, but after that, nothing. The next he knew was a slow return to consciousness and a splitting headache that made him wince every time he moved.

As he came to his senses, he expected to see a pool of warm, sickly-sweet blood gathering around him, but apart from an uncommonly large egg on his head, there was barely a mark to see. As he staggered fitfully to his feet, he dared not stop to question his good fortune. He stepped around Ackerman, who was groaning incomprehensibly on the ground while clutching his face with soot-blackened hands, and left without further ado.

Despite the indeterminate period of catalepsy, Lex still arrived with time to spare to catch the first train out for The Hague and thence The Hook, where he gratefully rendezvoused with the skipper as previously arranged. The wily old sea dog immediately sensed something was amiss, and refused to embark until Lex, much to his chagrin, was forced to pay a hugely inflated price for the crossing.

Lex only unfurled his overcoat and fished out the stolen manuscript in the seclusion of his cabin once the boat was out to sea. To Lex, the manuscript looked like any other ancient, weather-beaten tome, identical to the book Frankl had extravagantly brandished in the cave a few weeks earlier. As he strained to inspect the book in the dim light, his eyes were drawn to a small, irregular hole passing through the front cover, scorched and blackened around its margin. He ran a finger across the imperfection and was astonished to see a sooty deposit come away on his hand. He was sure the blemish had not been there before, but in a flash of inspiration, he understood—it was a bullet hole! He beamed at his luck. He opened the book and re-read the obscure statement written on the first page and noted a small hole running through its centre. He wondered what Frankl would make of the adulteration to his prized possession, but he was relieved to note that the bullet had not passed beyond the first few pages. He removed the projectile and held it up to the light. He could not believe it; he had been saved by a stolen book!

Lex flicked indiscriminately through the book, and to his uneducated eye, he wondered what all the fuss was about. With its archaic language and bizarre symbols, the book had been written in double Dutch for all he knew, and after a few minutes' perusal, he quickly lost interest and returned it to his coat.

Lex spent the remainder of the journey cooped up in the claustrophobic berth trying to suppress the seasickness that continually threatened to engulf him, and after a crossing that was marginally less disconcerting than the outward trip, the boat struck land in a brackish backwater a few miles along the coast from Harwich. After boarding a freight wagon laden with cargo destined for the city, Lex returned to the bedsit he rented in a run-down area of the East End just shy of two weeks after his departure.

When he finally crawled up to his room in the early hours, he was reassured to espy the delicate piece of tape he had left hidden between the door and the jamb still safely secured in place. He unlocked the door and trod on a note lying on the doormat hastily written in Abel's spidery scrawl requesting the delivery of the book the moment he returned. He smiled at the thought of turning up on Abel's doorstep at four in the morning, and without a second thought, he went straight to bed and slept until lunchtime. After a leisurely bath, he caught a bus to the Academy and dropped the book off with Abel after a curt exchange of words. It was time to celebrate, and after a quick scout of the neighbourhood, he found the nearest hostelry, the rather inappropriately named Scales of Justice.

The weeks that followed went from one mind-bending hangover to the next, and while Lex heard nothing from Frankl, he was happy to combine days spent gambling with evenings of unbridled alcoholic excess. Despite an encyclopaedic knowledge of the horses and a never-ending supply of inside information gleaned from stable hands, jockeys, trainers, tipsters and owners, Lex's long-running and extremely unlucky losing streak continued as if he had never been away.

Barely a month after his return, he reluctantly opened his eyes and snapped them shut again. He pulled up the bedclothes to shield his eyes from the late morning sunshine streaming in through the half-drawn Venetian blind. He ruefully recalled the moment the blind had frozen after the cord had jammed, leaving the material sadly dangling halfway across its frame. The blind was swaying in a gale passing between the sash and its warped wooden frame, and as he ventured from beneath the sheets, his head spun with the kaleidoscope of light that accompanied the oscillating blind. His mouth felt as a dry as the Sahara, and as he peeled his tongue from the roof of his mouth, he recognised the familiar manifestation of alcohol-induced dehydration. He had drunk at least a pint of Scotch judging by how he felt, but as to where and with whom, he could not recall. He groped in vain for the bedside table and the packet of cigarettes he hoped, rather than expected, to find there, only to dislodge an empty liquor bottle onto the floor. He watched in dismay as the bottle rolled across the floorboards gathering speed as it went before colliding with the skirting board to shatter into myriad pieces.

After washing and dressing in a vain attempt to dispel the perennial headache that had dogged his return, he thought about where to go for a late breakfast followed by that elusive winner and a gentle slip back into oblivion. After all, he had fulfilled his side of the bargain, and now it was someone else's turn. In the meantime, well, there was always one more drink to be had.

*

Abel Strange's glasses slipped unceremoniously towards the bulbous tip of his nose, teetering on the brink of an inglorious fall onto the faded pages of the manuscript that lay open on the desk in front of him. He pushed absent-mindedly on the glasses so that they came to sit more comfortably on the bridge of his nose, an innocuous gesture habitually performed due to the weight of the thick optical prisms his short-sighted vision depended on.

He looked up from the manuscript with eyes that were strained and weary after an unbroken spell studying the hand-written words. He sighed and looked aimlessly through the window, only to be startled by a hideously deformed, demonic silhouette of a gargoyle leaping out from the shadows of the crenellated stonework. Strange's pulse slackened once the penny dropped that the waning sunlight was playing a trick on his eyes, seemingly bringing the gargoyle to life. As he stared through the window, he looked back on his progress, or more accurately, the lack of it, over the past few weeks.

While Lex was in Amsterdam, Strange had not been idle, diligently scrutinising the cipher to look for the keyword even before the second book arrived. Just before his death, Styx had explained that by undertaking a frequency analysis of the encrypted passage, the keyword could be determined. Nevertheless, despite looking for patterns of repetition using a complex mathematical formula, Strange soon realised that the technique was flawed, because, quite simply, the number of encoded letters was too small to allow such a sophisticated analysis.

Once the manuscript arrived, Strange set to work amidst a frenzy of expectation, locking himself away in a dormitory high up in one of the countless towers that dominated the Academy's skyline. The Academy had once been overwhelmed with students, but in recent years, numbers had dwindled to little more than a handful of classes, leaving students in the unenviable position of being outnumbered by the teachers who had made the decaying edifice their home. The countless vacant rooms of the once-thriving institution were ideal for Strange to pursue his meticulous evaluation of the near-identical copies of the book, and as Chief

Mentor, it was his privilege to have unhindered access to abandoned areas of the building free from interruption and away from prying eyes.

Initial progress was both rapid and fruitful, but eventually and to considerable frustration, his work soon came to a grinding halt. As luck would have it, it was not a difficult task to determine the keyword through a painstaking comparison of the books. During his evaluation, he noticed that, at various intervals, a word was repeatedly omitted from the text. In one copy, Piotrowski continually made reference to 'the Esoteric Brotherhood', whereas in the other, on five occasions, it was 'the Brotherhood', leading Strange to suspect that 'Esoteric' must be the keyword. With a creeping sense of anticipation, he paired the keyword with the cipher and input the pairs of letters into a Vigenère table constructed in the way that Styx had described. He felt a thrill in the pit of his stomach as the plaintext took shape, but elation soon gave way to disappointment as the letters coalesced into the same gobbledegook he had begun with.

After a moments' dismay, he recalled Styx's description of the Caesar shift and how the table could be constructed with twenty-six possible permutations depending on the position of the alphabet within the table's axes. He knew it would take time, but on a whim, he began with a Caesar shift of five, based on the number of times the presumptive keyword had been dropped from the manuscript. This time, as he wrote out the letters, he stared in amazement as the deciphered letters merged into a recognisable sentence.

'The secret is deeply buried within the covers of the book,' he read out over and over again, each time with an increasing sense of dissatisfaction and disappointment. Yes, he was relieved at finally breaking the cipher, but all he had achieved was to confirm what Pearly and Frankl had suspected all along.

Following the false hope of a breakthrough, Strange went back to the manuscript time and again, searching in ever more ingenious ways to uncover the secret the message alluded to, but all to no avail. He tried to convince himself that there was further code enmeshed within the text, but no matter how hard he looked, he could not find it. It was like searching for a grain of sand on a beach, continually re-examining the book looking for patterns in the words and in the construction of the sentences in the vain hope of uncovering something he must have missed, but the more desperately he searched, the more impotent he felt. The prospect of failure hung over him like a black cloud, and in frustration, he even questioned Frankl's overzealousness at disposing of Styx.

Strange realised he had been daydreaming and shook himself free of his musing. He looked away from the gargoyle and returned his attention to the book, accompanying it with a sigh at having reached such a frustrating impasse. He switched on a reading lamp, illuminating the desk he had been slumped over for as many hours as he cared to remember. He returned his attention to the manuscript and regarded it with a combination of exasperation and despair. In a sudden act of defiance, he slammed the pages shut, scattering sheaves of notes across the room. He leapt up from the chair, desperately needing to escape from a room that had become a prison cell. He knew he could ill-afford it, but perhaps a break would allow him to return refreshed, ready to face the many hours that unquestionably lay ahead. It was only a matter of time before Frankl turned up to assess his progress, and after the repulsive man's increasingly frequent phone calls, Strange had struggled to reassure him that everything was proceeding as planned. He dared not imagine the ignominy that Frankl would heap on him should he fail, and he was determined not to let that happen.

In a sudden fit of pique, he picked up a candle and a box of matches and turned his back on the desk while silently cursing the Academy's ancient electrical wiring system. He strode from the room and set off down a spiral staircase that led towards numerous vacant dormitories. He passed through long-forgotten halls exuding desolation and neglect, chilling him to the core, and along indistinguishable corridors bound by cool walls as smooth as marble, damp with the ever-present trickle of decay.

At last, Strange saw a distant glow of light ahead and slowed his pace. He halted, turning his head towards the sound of carefree voices drifting back towards him along the corridor. In his black mood, Strange had unknowingly found his way through a maze of passageways to the students' common room. The sound of idle chatter took him back to a forgotten time when he had also been a student at the Academy, doting over his friends like a faithful dog. He pictured Pearly and Henry sitting together as he looked on, silently torn between his loyalty to each man, observing their discussion gradually evolving from friendly banter into something far more menacing. Henry had been, ostensibly, such a dark and brooding young man, yet undeniably also capable of kindness that often went unnoticed by others. Pearly had been intelligent, articulate and captivating, and admired by one and all. These two men had been the closest of friends and the most profound of enemies from the moment they met, and despite this baffling dichotomy, it was no surprise that, finally, it had ended with him, Abel Strange, caught in the middle.

He laughed, cold and hollow, still unsure even now of where his true allegiance lay. To Pearly, a man who had been dead for ten years? Or to Henry, who had done so much for him in recent years? The debate had been raging inside his head for as long as he cared to remember, yet no matter what, it all seemed in vain. And now he was embroiled with Frankl, a man he detested, but what choice was left to him if he was to unravel a secret that had accompanied Pearly to the grave?

Sitting on the cool stone floor, Strange recalled the anger and despair that had threatened to overwhelm him following Pearly's demise; resentment at being left alone and sorrow for the loss of a man he had loved. While these feelings had dwindled with the passage of time, he had never come to terms with them. He supposed it was inevitable that Henry had been linked with Pearly's death, but as to who was culpable, he had never dared to speculate. It was also hard to believe that Pearly had, in some way, been responsible for Saskia's death.

He shook his head. He had never been privy to Pearly's darkest secrets, and even now, he suspected that Frankl was holding something back, but whatever it was, he was determined to find out. He closed his eyes and let his recent struggles wash over him. He licked his fingers and doused the candle, pitching the corridor into darkness. The babble of voices gradually dipped as the pupils headed for their dormitories, and as the sound of footsteps on the stone flags dwindled into an eerie silence, he was left feeling utterly alone and forlorn.

He rested in the corridor until he lost all track of time, focusing on the solitude as he sought to purge the thoughts that threatened to engulf him. Whether he slept or rested, he did not know, but in the darkness and isolation, he finally found some harmony as all thoughts were vanquished, leaving his mind an empty canvas.

Strange suddenly sat bolt upright. At first, it began as nothing more than a distant notion, but gradually, his thoughts coalesced into something more tangible, a bright and all-defining light, a revelation of infinitesimal dimensions. That was it. He had it. He had solved the riddle of the manuscript!

'The secret is deeply buried within the covers of the book,' he cried out, only to hear his words reverberate around him, exacerbating his excitement even further.

He laughed. How could he have missed it? It was all so glaringly obvious!

He picked himself up in a sudden frenzy, desperate to return to the tower. He knew he was right; he was sure of it. He fumbled in his pocket for the box of matches, and after rekindling the candle, he set off, rushing headfirst to his apartment to collect the implements he was sure to need.

Fifteen minutes later, breathless and in a whirl of anticipation, Strange crossed the threshold to the dormitory and made for the small desk. He stooped to inspect the manuscript still lying where he had slammed it shut, regarding it now with excitement rather than the despondency of earlier. He sat down with a magnifying glass and scrutinised the cover, immediately finding what he was looking for.

Piotrowski's manuscript was typical for its era, comprising of groups of eight pages of vellum, bound together and hand-stitched into the bindings. The book's front and rear covers were constructed of thin, rectangular pieces of wood protected by leather jackets. Strange felt his pulse quicken as he focused the lens on the bullet hole. At last, he knew he was right! Rather than a single sheet of wood making up the front cover, there were two, but even now with the aid of a powerful lens, he could barely make it out.

'The secret is deeply buried within the covers of the book,' he repeated inanely, this time with a wry shake of his head. He finally realised that the sentence he had puzzled over for so long was merely a statement of fact; a piece of paper was hidden inside the book's front cover!

He picked up a stiletto and worked it assiduously around the margins of the cover to peel back the leather that had encased the wood for almost five centuries. He placed the sharp point of the blade between the two pieces of wood, and with a quick twist, the conjoined twins parted to reveal a single sheet of vellum. He removed the paper and held it up to his eyes, smiling with relief as he stared at the reams of letters, small and neat, and quite obviously and incoherently written in code.

18

Wren's Cache

JOSEF FRANKL PULLED UP the collar of his ankle-length overcoat and huddled back in the doorway to shelter from the incessant rain. He shook his head disconsolately, struggling to accept that even now, in the early hours of the morning, the storm had not abated. He looked up to espy water spilling out of a blocked gutter and collecting in a seething puddle at his feet. He followed the water's progress as it flowed in great rivulets across the pavement before gushing into the road. Here, the water was building into a swirling vortex above a storm drain clogged with debris. He shivered involuntarily and, for the first time, questioned the prudence of going ahead with the meeting he had convened for the remainder of what had once been the Order of Eternal Enlightenment.

It was a week since he had received the news that Strange had finally cracked the secret of Piotrowski's manuscript. After visiting the Academy to see the astounding revelation for himself, he had spent the next few days absorbing the implications of Strange's discovery before dispatching the black pearls that would convey the instructions of where and when they were to meet.

He had followed Pearly's age-old tradition and chosen a typically dangerous venue for the meeting after receiving the dubious assurance from the meteorological office that the current downpour he was witnessing from the confines of the shelter would miss the capital, but once again, they had got it wrong. He briefly wondered whether to postpone the meeting, but after straining his eyes to examine his wristwatch, he realised it was already too late; he could not back down now.

He slipped from the doorway and looked up to leaden skies. The oppressive atmosphere endured, and although the rain was slackening, it continued to fall in a steady drizzle. He shook his head like a dog, expelling raindrops from the few remaining strands of his hair. He pulled up the hood of his coat before heading eastwards along The Strand towards a deserted Fleet Street. It was several years since he had last visited this area, but his destination was one of Pearly's favourite haunts, and on this day of days, he was well aware of how fitting that would be.

He checked he was alone before turning off Farringdon Road into a neighbourhood of narrow alleys and passageways, and after losing himself in a maze of frighteningly similar streets, he came to a halt. He craned his neck to examine a street sign on the adjacent wall, dimly lit in the neon light. Old Seacoal Lane, it read; a throwback to the distant past when coal barges from the north had sailed up the Fleet River. It was hard to comprehend that the river had once flourished here, passing beneath the gates of the notorious prison that had shared its name. In days gone by, the river had been a dumping ground for the murdered and slain, yet even now, the tightly-knit tenements still retained a dubious reputation as a haven for gangsters and thieves. Although the river had long since disappeared, Pearly had always loved this part of the city from the day he had been born into it.

Assured of his bearings, Frankl pushed on for Saffron Hill, implausibly named because of the herb that had once grown on the riverbanks of the lost river. The place was now nothing more than a featureless alley lined by tall, imponderable buildings. His vision settled on a fashionable inn. The faint sound of laughter issuing from beyond bolted doors and shuttered windows suggested it was still busy, even at this hour. The sorry looking building next door was Frankl's destination, and in stark contrast to the inn, its windows were boarded and defaced, yet he still felt a thrill of expectation as he withdrew a key and placed it in the lock. It had been over ten years since he had last visited this place, and as he stepped over the threshold, he paused for a moment to listen. All was silent bar the faint scurrying of mice, and after shutting the door, he strode along the hallway and entered a bare room save for a generator sitting precariously on rotting floorboards. Despite the contraption's shabby appearance, it was well lubricated and fuelled thanks to the recent attention of a lackey Frankl had dispatched to service it. The machine was simple in its construction, consisting of an internal combustion engine powered to rotate a set of coils inside a magnetic field that would generate sufficient electricity for the property's meagre needs. As one of the Order's safe houses, Pearly had always taken the utmost care to avoid prying eyes, even from the likes of the electricity board.

The floorboards creaked as Frankl tiptoed gingerly into the room. He leant on the generator's crank handle, and the engine powered up. With a nonchalant flick of a wall switch, the light bulb dangling precariously from the ceiling spluttered pathetically into life, bathing the room in a wavering glow of artificial light. Once the machine was up and running, he vacated the room, closing the door behind him to muffle the sound of the engine's gentle chugging.

He hurried along the passage to a door nestled below a rickety set of stairs that looked as if they would collapse at the first sign of trouble. He stooped to pass through a low entryway onto a flight of steps that led down to a dark, musty cellar. He was approaching a subterranean room Pearly had always referred to as 'the vault', and judging by the dank, still air, it was likely that no one had visited the room in years.

Pearly had purchased the property at the height of the Order's pomp fifteen years earlier via a string of intermediaries to conceal its true ownership. It had quickly become one of his favourite haunts, largely because of where it was and what it led to. Like the surrounding district, the building had a rather surprising past, and with Pearly's research so intimately intertwined with the past, it was inevitable that, from time to time, he managed to unearth fascinating historical discoveries like the hidden gem on Saffron Hill.

During the nineteenth century, the house had belonged to the Metropolitan Board of Works as accommodation for itinerant workers brought to the capital to deal with the increasing problem of the city's sewage, which had always drained as untreated effluent into local cesspits and thence the Thames. With the inexorable growth of the city, disease inevitably flourished, including several outbreaks of cholera and the resultant loss of life. The final outrage was the 'Great Stink' of 1858, when, due to a combination of untreated sewage and the unprecedented heat of the summer, the House of Commons was forced to make a rapid U-turn by reinstituting a sewage policy previously devised by Joseph Bazalgette, Chief Engineer to the Metropolitan Commission for Sewers. Soon after, intercepting sewers were built to the north and south of the Thames to divert waste to pumping stations in the east at Beckton and Crossness.

The house on Saffron Hill was a doss house for a crew of labourers partly responsible for the three hundred million bricks or so that were laid in seven years during the construction of the monstrous underground wonder. The property was purchased on behalf of the Order after Pearly had discovered a portal in the cellar leading to the subterranean course of the long-buried Fleet where the navvies had once moved silently from bed to work and back again, never seeing the light of day for weeks on end.

Pearly quickly developed a fascination for the rivers, culverts, conduits, channels, spillways, tunnels, drains and sewers that formed an endless maze of interconnecting passages beneath the city. With unhindered access to an underground lost world, Lex was the most to benefit from the silent and near invisible mode of travel the tunnels allowed, and he soon began to pass undetected into some of the most secure areas of the city, well beyond the scrutiny of Internal Security, thus propelling his status amongst his fellow criminals to that of a god-like phantom. Access to the hundreds of miles of underground sewers also led to the discovery of Pearly's most favoured meeting place, and the destination to which Frankl was presently heading.

Wren's Cache was a storm relief drain that was part of Bazalgette's Northern Outfall Sewer, designed to divert flow away from the Fleet on its journey from Hampstead to the Thames. At times of heavy rainfall, Wren's Cache was at risk of flooding, inevitably increasing Frankl's unease following the rain that had fallen during the past twenty-four hours.

Frankl hesitated at the top of the stairs and looked nervously at his watch. He was due to meet with his compatriots in less than an hour and envisaged the effect it would have on them by holding the meeting in Wren's Cache. With the electrifying information he was about to reveal, he could not cancel now. Pearly had always held his meetings in the most dangerous surroundings for the loyalty and unity they instilled, and he would not renege on a principle that his former boss had laid down when the Order was first established.

Wren's Cache was a name guaranteed to instil fear in anyone with links to the Order after the gruesome outcome of a meeting in which a cohort of Pearly's thieves, inevitably led by Lex, were planning an audacious heist of the nation's most beloved treasures from the National Gallery. Unfortunately, the meeting ended in unmitigated disaster due to the combination of a full moon, a spring tide and an unusually heavy rainfall for the month of June. Not long after the group's arrival, Wren's Cache was submerged in a deluge of floodwater, and although most of the men were flushed into the Thames below Blackfriars Bridge, they still had to swim from the swollen river and claw their way up the sheer walls of the embankment to make good their escape.

It was some time before anyone realised that Lex's trusty lieutenant, Club Patterson—so named for his injudicious use of said weapon—had not been so lucky. Club's body was never found and no one knew what had befallen him until a subsequent meeting held in Wren's Cache when his sorry fate was laid bare for all to see. No one dared to mention the sight of Club's infamous toupee dangling from a metal pipe high up on a wall for fear of upsetting Pearly, and for the rest of the meeting, the water-sodden wig remained where it lay as a grisly testimony to a fallen comrade.

Frankl dismissed these unnerving memories as he traipsed down the stairs into the vault. He could barely see more than a few paces in front of his feet in the dull light of the small windowless space, but after uttering a few words in his native tongue, an unnatural glow issued forth from his hands to reveal a heavy metal grille recessed in the stone floor. As he strained to lift the dead-weight, a sweat broke out on his brow, yet his unhealthy appearance belied a great physical strength, and all in a flash, the cover heaved open.

Frankl set off down a spiral stairway that led into a seemingly bottomless pit. After an uncomfortable descent with his perverted radiance highlighting the way, the steps finally gave out onto a small platform that led into a low tunnel and the distant, yet ever-growing, sound of flowing water. He clambered through the narrow passageway, and after a dozen strides, he emerged into a wider space that signalled his arrival at the Fleet Sewer.

He paused to stare in wonder at the circular walls that encased the Fleet. The river had once been clear and free-flowing but had slowly dwindled into a filthy trickle. The mills, abattoirs, and tanneries that had once prospered on the riverbanks had expelled their effluent into the river without cease, and as the increasingly populated city outgrew its cesspits, the Fleet had gradually been transformed into an open sewer. Frankl peered circumspectly into a river whose name had become synonymous with squalor and degradation, and as he stared into the river's inky depths, he imagined that he caught a glimpse of the city's distant past. He shook his head; it was hardly a surprise that the Fleet had been bricked over and incarcerated, and much to his astonishment, he was left with a sense of melancholy at the corruption of the age-old river.

He shook himself free of his reverie and set off southwards along the path amidst a confusing maze of intertwining tunnels. At intervals, the red-bricked walls were interspersed with monumental floodgates and sluice channels, an ominous reminder of what lay on their other sides. The smell of filth was overpowering, forcing him to pull a neck scarf over his nose while treading carefully on the slimy path underfoot. At last, there was a sudden change in the colour of the wall from red to yellow brick, highlighting the tunnel he was searching for. He stopped and unfurled a fist to cast a glowing ball of heatless flame into the air; a signal to mark the way and a beacon to aid his return. The small circular tunnel that branched off the high-arched passage encasing the Fleet looked much the same as the others he had passed, but without hesitation, he left the towpath and disappeared through the entrance, stomping through the murky black effluent that spilled over his boots.

After a short march, the narrow tunnel opened into a vast, vaulted space that was oddly out of place after the claustrophobic passage. Frankl looked around with the same sense of wonder he always experienced whenever he entered Wren's Cache. In the murky light, it was difficult to appreciate the high-arched ceiling that towered above a circular amphitheatre set around a central channel. He looked nervously towards a voluminous inlet pipe that protruded through the opposite wall, spilling water into the channel, and was delighted to note that the flow was little more than a trickle, suggesting that the excess rain of the past twenty-four hours had been diverted elsewhere.

He marched to the midpoint of the head-height conduit where metal ladders on opposing walls led to a semi-circular stone platform on one side and tiers of terraced steps on the other. He looked up towards a tangle of interconnecting pipes that ran along the wall beyond the steps. In the dim light, the pipes looked like a writhing mass of serpents, filling him with dread. Here, dangling on a large metal tap, poor Club's toupee had once been found, ominously suggesting the height to which the water had risen on that fateful occasion.

He clambered up the ladder and scrambled onto the dais. He withdrew a handful of sturdy candles and placed them in a circle around him, lighting up the chamber with flickering candlelight that created an element of theatre just as Pearly would have liked. His work now done, Frankl sat down on the platform, closing his mind to the constant sound of running water while he waited apprehensively for his guests to arrive.

19

Acta Neurochirurgica

DROPLETS OF SWEAT RAN down Henry Price's brow as he stooped to retrieve a crucible from the furnace. He shied away from the blistering hot, noxious vapours that billowed from the shimmering surface of the molten alloy nestling in the bottom of the receptacle. He set the crucible down on the bench and leant over to inspect its contents, nodding appreciatively at the amalgam as it coalesced in the cool laboratory air. He stared transfixed at the solidifying metal and failed to hear Albright's steps on the stairs as he descended into the smoky depths of the laboratory.

'There's a visitor for you, Professor. I believe you were expecting a Dr Asquith. He's waiting for you in the sitting room,' Albright announced.

Price stirred from his deliberation. 'Thank you, Albright. Tell him I'll join him shortly. I need to change out of these clothes. Perhaps you'd ask Mrs Brimstork to provide us with some refreshment?'

'It's already done, sir,' replied Albright sombrely, who had turned and was on his way back up the stairs.

Ten minutes later, Price opened the double doors to the sitting room and joined Asquith, who was sitting by the fire staring pensively at the glowing coals.

'Abram, welcome. Thank you for coming at short notice. I know how busy you are,' said Price, startling the seated man, who was deep in thought.

Asquith was a respected member of the Royal Society by dint of his reputation as a distinguished neurological surgeon and had met Price on several occasions. He was a tall man and looked ungainly as he struggled out of a low chair to greet his host.

Price held out a hand. He baulked at the sight of Asquith's spindly fingers despite the digits being entirely in proportion with the rest of the man's wiry frame. His thin face was dominated by a bulbous nose that supported a pair of half-moon spectacles. The glasses were positioned so improbably on the end of his nose Price wondered how on earth they managed to stay there.

'What can I do for you, Professor?' said Asquith brusquely as the men shook hands.

'I need your help with a medical matter,' replied Price, who reached into his jacket and withdrew the typed post-mortem report on Black.

Asquith's bony hand jerked out and took the papers like a praying mantis snatching its quarry. He unfurled the pages and raised his head, bringing the spectacles on the end of his nose to good use. 'May I ask the source of this report?' he asked after several minutes scrutinising the notes.

'It was undertaken by a Home Office pathologist who, unfortunately, is no longer with us. I believe Dr Cantonus was a man with flawless credentials. He was a former president of the Royal College of Pathologists, no less.'

Asquith nodded. 'An eminent fellow, indeed.'

'I'm afraid that this is a rather delicate affair, and I must ask that the details of our conversation remain confidential, but I'd like your opinion on the mysterious object described in the report,' said Price.

Asquith appeared taken aback but nodded perfunctorily. 'Very well,' he said, perusing the notes. After a few minutes, he set the papers down on the arm of the chair and looked inquisitively at Price, waiting for the inevitable interrogation.

'What do you make of it, Abram?'

'It's certainly most intriguing, Henry. I've never encountered anything like it before. Could you tell me when the post-mortem was carried out? I think it may be important.'

'About ten years ago,' replied Price. 'As you can see, these notes are incomplete and do not relate the cause of death. Black died as a result of other injuries, but we believe that an accomplice removed the object the report alludes to soon after death.'

'Do you have any more information on what was removed?'

'I'm afraid not. I was rather hoping you might be able to enlighten me.'

'I see,' replied Asquith noncommittally. He paused to digest what he had just read before he responded. 'The first thing I would say is that the method of fixation used to stabilise the vertebral column may be significant.'

'Go on,' Price encouraged.

'It appears that the initial procedure to access the brainstem was carried out by a surgeon with specialist skills. Exposure of this area is hazardous, and in the wrong hands, such an approach would almost certainly result in death or debility. Only a surgeon well-versed in neurosurgical technique would be capable of placing the implant. It's a standard surgical approach to the area. I'm intrigued, however, by the method that was used to stabilise the vertebral column after the bone was removed.'

'I'm not sure I follow,' said Price.

'The vertebral column is made up of twenty-four bones linked by strong ligaments extending from the base of the skull to the sacrum, yet its articulations allow the body to bend, flex and rotate, in fact, move in almost any direction without risk of damage to its contents. It provides vital protection along its length to the spinal cord, which is a delicate structure comprising of an intricate mass of sensory and motor nerve tissue.'

'Yes, I understand all that,' said Price impatiently. 'What of the surgery, though?'

'Well, you can see from the post-mortem that bone was removed from the back of the upper two cervical vertebrae,' said Asquith. He picked up the papers lying on the arm of the chair and passed them back to Price. 'The pathologist refers to these vertebrae by their medical names—the atlas and axis—the two most specialised, and perhaps, important, of the vertebrae.'

'What makes them so important?'

'Damage to the spinal column at this site would inevitably result in death. Bone was removed to access the spinal cord and brainstem, but in doing so, it rendered the area unstable. If no further steps had been taken to stabilise the vertebrae, the moment the person awoke from the anaesthetic, they'd have been pithed, resulting in immediate death. Instead, an arthrodesis was performed.'

Price frowned.

'An arthrodesis is the fusion of two bones. It's usually carried out to abolish or minimise movement when stabilising a joint that's causing pain.'

'But not in this instance,' Price stated.

'No, indeed. What's most interesting, though, is that the bones were fused utilising a laminar screw fixation method. I remember quite clearly the surgeon who described this technique; it was published some years ago in a neurosurgical journal, *Acta Neurochirurgica*.'

'What makes this procedure so important?'

'That's the whole point, Henry. Nothing! Although the method has certain advantages, it never gained credence. Additionally, the man who first described the technique no longer practises.'

'Mm,' said Price pensively. 'What was this surgeon's name?'

'Luca Nexus. He once held rooms in Harley Street, but he's not been heard of for many years.'

'What became of him?'

'That's what interests me most in the context of this report. Nexus was not well-liked amongst his peers, and it was no surprise when he was discredited and forbidden from practising.'

Price inclined his head quizzically. 'What happened?'

'Some of Nexus' research was exposed as being, er, shall we say ... somewhat unethical. Boundaries in medicine are occasionally blurred, and while innovation is essential to achieve enlightenment, there are certain lines that should never be transgressed.'

'And Nexus crossed one of those lines,' said Price eagerly.

'I'm afraid so.'

'What did he do?'

'My recollections are somewhat hazy,' Asquith said reticently.

'This is important, Abram.'

'Of course,' he said, nodding pensively. 'Research in neuroscience is, by necessity, observational. Take the example of a tumour in a particular part of the brain. On the whole, the growth will produce predictable effects based on the anatomy and physiology of the central nervous system. Greater understanding has arisen from animal experimentation, and sometimes, in extreme circumstances, interventional procedures carried out on patients. This work is of fundamental importance to the medical profession, but it inevitably generates considerable antipathy in those who fail to grasp the importance of such research. Unfortunately, some of my, shall we say, more zealous colleagues, have, on occasions, gone too far.'

'And?' Price prompted after an uncomfortable silence.

'What I'm trying to say is that some individuals overstep the mark. As I recall, Nexus was a fanatic who believed passionately in his work. His field of study was the human brain, and, as I'm sure you appreciate, Henry, this is a domain in which observation and animal research can only go so far. I'm afraid that Nexus took the indefensible step of performing research on his patients. He managed to keep it quiet for some considerable time, knowing full well the penalty if his secret were ever revealed. He had to be clever, though, selecting his subjects from the seedier parts of the community. Down and outs, ne'er do wells and the like, the sort of people who are desperate for money but will not be missed. I'm afraid I'm not proud of what some of my colleagues have done in the name of science, but there you have it.'

'You seem to be a little reluctant to part with all the details, my friend.'

'With good reason, Henry. I was not party to the hearing that resulted in Nexus' fall from grace. The trial was conducted behind closed doors. All that emerged was that Nexus was banned from medical practice with immediate effect. He disappeared soon after and, I believe, has not been heard of since.'

'Surely you must have *some* idea of what he was up to?' demanded Price.

'All I know is based on rumour and hearsay. Nexus was found guilty of the greatest transgression of the Hippocratic Oath, namely that he conducted unethical experimentation on his subjects to further his research.'

'Come now, Abram, is that all you can tell me?' said Price in exasperation.

'I understand your disquiet, Henry, but I'm afraid that if you want to learn more, then I suggest you discuss it with the man who led the enquiry.'

'And who was that?' snapped Price.

'Rather unusually, the chair of the disciplinary panel was not a medical man.'

'Spit it out, Abram.'

'The hearing was led by Sir Algernon Caruthers.'

'Caruthers! Why on earth was he involved? He's a civil servant, for God's sake!'

'Precisely. The government got involved because of the sensitive nature of the hearing. They were worried about the possibility of a backlash against senior figures who had provided Nexus with financial backing.'

Price's face flared. If the government knew about this, then why was the Council not briefed? He reached out for a decanter on the table next to him and proffered it to Asquith.

'Not for me, Henry. I've patients to see this afternoon.'

Price filled a glass and took a gulp of port to calm his nerves.

'I presume from your reaction that the Council was not involved,' said Asquith.

Price set the glass down, ignoring Asquith's statement. 'When did all of this happen?'

'It must have been about twelve years ago, maybe more.'

Price nodded. 'Yes, that would fit. Do you know who else was involved with Nexus?'

'No. As I mentioned before, he had some powerful backers; people with the financial clout to provide him with the resources he needed for his research, which is why the government got so windy. I'm afraid I don't know any more than this, but perhaps it explains why the hearing was so political. I suggest you take this up with Caruthers. He'll be able to tell you more,' said Asquith finally.

Price nodded. It was clear that this line of questioning had gone as far as he could take it. He paused for a moment, mulling over what he had just learnt. It was odd that the Council had never got to hear of this as it was just the sort of thing that should have landed on his desk. No matter, it would have to wait. He would track down Caruthers and question him further.

Price picked up the crumpled papers from his lap. 'Can we go back to the post-mortem?'

'What else do you want to know?'

'What do you make of the object the report refers to?'

Asquith smiled uncertainly. 'That's what's so interesting. It seems that whatever it was must have been there for some time. Look at the pathologist's comments. He says that the regeneration of bone was well established. For this to make any sense, the implant must have been there for some years. Microscopical examination of the tissue taken from the cavity margin revealed a mass of nerve tissue, also supporting this hypothesis. What fascinates me most is the implication that the object had integrated with the nervous system.'

Price looked aghast. 'Have you ever come across anything like this before?'

Asquith shook his head. 'Never. Certain materials such as metal plates and screws used for the fixation of fractures are known to integrate with bone, but in my experience, I've never seen anything like this before. The pathologist even alludes to it in his report where he states that the object had formed a symbiotic relationship with its host by developing what he refers to as a neural network.'

'What did he mean by that?'

Asquith rubbed his chin pensively. 'Hmm. The fundamental structure in the nervous system is the neuron. As a single entity, a neuron shows minimal demonstrable effects when acting in isolation, but when a group of neurons function together as an integrated unit, they exert their effects in many different and tangible ways.'

'Could you expand on this, Abram? I think it might be important.'

'Neurons communicate with one another via cellular appendages known as dendrites and synapses, turning an individual cell into a syncytium of many, forming the so-called neural network the pathologist refers to. What's interesting about this arrangement is the network's ability to function so much more effectively than the sum of its parts, which is why the ultimate of complex organisms, *Homo sapiens*, demonstrates higher activities such as intelligence, logic or even abstract thought, not to mention some of the abilities that even physicians can't explain.'

'Such as?'

'There are many things in medicine that we still struggle with. Take memory as an example. It perfectly illustrates just how little understanding we have of the brain's ability to store both short and long-term data. Yes, we can appreciate where memories are kept from an anatomical standpoint, but just how they are retained at a cellular level is beyond our grasp, which brings us back to the neural network the pathologist was referring to. Nerve cells communicate with one another by synaptic connections that convert electrical activity into chemical messages, thus creating a specific effect on an adjacent cell in the network, and so on. We think that the pattern of synaptic activity within a neural network enables a particular memory to be coded. In this way, the brain retains information and makes it available for subsequent retrieval. A good analogy is the way binary code is used to store data.'

'I see.'

'Let me give you an example from your own area of expertise.'

Price raised an eyebrow but passed no comment.

'Alchemy is still an ultra-secretive realm of study, open to a privileged few amongst the cognoscenti. You've previously enlightened the Royal Society with examples of your startling achievements, and although such wonders are beyond medical reasoning, as a rational man, I try to see them in physiological terms. Now, although you may disagree, I believe the abilities that you've demonstrated are purely manifestations of the untapped reserves of the human nervous system.'

'I wouldn't disagree, Abram, for there's still much that we don't understand, but I fear we're digressing here,' replied Price. 'You said earlier that the implant had integrated with the host's nervous system. Perhaps you'd care to speculate on this?'

'I fear that this issue is inextricably linked with Nexus. It's far too coincidental that a talented surgeon like Nexus, a man who was prepared to risk his livelihood in pursuit of some abstruse goal, should vanish not long before this body appeared. I would hazard that these two matters are in some way related. My advice to you, Henry, is to find Nexus as quickly as possible if this is as important as you suggest.'

Price nodded solemnly. 'I'll do as you say, Abram. First, I'll approach Caruthers. Perhaps he can help with Nexus' whereabouts.'

Asquith got up and made to leave, but Price forestalled him, ushering him back into the chair. 'Perhaps I could trouble you over one further matter.'

Asquith glanced at his watch. 'I should be back at my rooms ...'

'It won't take long, fifteen minutes, perhaps. I'll make sure that Albright has transportation ready the moment we finish.'

'Very well. How can I help?'

'What can you tell me about trephination?'

'Trephination?' repeated Asquith, sounding taken aback. 'Well, it's a technique that's utilised to relieve pressure on the brain and is practised when there are signs of bleeding.'

'Can you tell me how it's performed?'

'The surgeon determines the site of bleeding by careful evaluation of the patient's physical signs. A hole is drilled through the skull at exactly the right point to allow evacuation of a clot and cautery of the bleeding point. Surgery of this nature is usually undertaken in extremis. It is yet another instance when the surgeon's knife holds sway over the healing ability of the physician.'

'Yet this method has been practised for centuries and has not always been undertaken for this purpose,' said Price evenly.

'You're right, of course, Henry. Trephination has been performed for medical reasons across the ages, but also for more esoteric and mystical reasons we don't fully understand. The technique was first conducted on a skull believed to be over seven thousand years old. Anthropologists have found evidence of this practice in skulls unearthed from sites of early civilisations as diverse as Africa, South America and even the Melanesian Pacific Islands.'

'Do you have any idea why it was performed?'

'Well, there are several theories, all based on conjecture.'

'Go on.'

'Many ancient civilisations based their beliefs on superstition, and within tribal societies, religious chiefs, shamans and healers yielded considerable power over their subjects. It's quite possible that trephination was carried out for relatively simple medical problems such as headaches or convulsions, conditions that we now treat with pharmacological remedies.

'Trephination was also carried out as an adjunct to the treatment of various forms of mental illness. Indeed, there are records of it being undertaken for this reason during the Renaissance.'

'Would you care to elaborate on this?' Price said urgently.

Asquith raised his eyebrows at the sudden interest. 'Of course,' he replied. 'During the Dark Ages, mental illness was often interpreted as being possessed by evil spirits. Hearing voices, experiencing hallucinations and becoming delusional are all manifestations of mental illness, but consider how less well-advanced societies perceived these symptoms. This behaviour was often construed as evidence that an individual was under the influence of a supernatural entity. Frightened kin would send the possessed for healing, either by exorcism or other ways aimed at banishing the demonic control held over them. Trephination taken in this context does not necessarily seem so ridiculous.'

'Put like that and I wouldn't disagree.'

'During the Renaissance, evolving religious and medical beliefs were vying for attention with long-held superstitions and persistent pagan dogma, but these old attitudes still held considerable sway. Healers still believed that people showing signs of mental illness had stones in their brains and that successful removal of these stones would cure them.'

'I don't suppose anyone has ever proven the presence of these mythical stones, but is there any evidence that this treatment was ever successful?' enquired Price excitedly.

'It would be very simple to discount this treatment given our present understanding of medicine. On the whole, it seems that claims of this nature were usually made by charlatans. It's easy to understand why ever more outrageous procedures were devised to treat the poor souls who were thought to be possessed, particularly when you consider that if they died, it was deemed a cure. The healers couldn't lose!'

'So am I right in assuming that this procedure never gained credence?'

'I didn't say that, Henry. I know of at least one healer who practised in Europe during the early part of the sixteenth century and carried out this procedure with some apparent success.'

Price sat forwards in his chair, eager to hear more. 'Go on.'

'He studied medicine at the University of Basel and was adept in many surgical procedures, but especially this one.'

'How can you be so sure?'

'That's easy, because, in this instance, his work was well-documented. The man was a disciple of the great Swiss physician and alchemist, Paracelsus. They worked together for a while, although they eventually fell out.'

'What happened?'

'Paracelsus wanted to publish details of the procedure, and despite his colleague's resistance, he went ahead and described it in his most famous medical publication, *Opus Chirurgicum*. Perhaps you're familiar with it, Henry?'

Price shook his head. 'I recall much of Paracelsus' wisdom pertaining to alchemy, but not this. Remind me, what does it say?'

'Paracelsus wrote a detailed report of the procedure in which his colleague cured a madman of his insanity by the process of trephination and the extraction of a stone from the man's brain.'

'What! Where did this happen?'

'Somewhere in Holland, I believe.'

'Holland!' exclaimed Price, who was sitting on the edge of his seat, tightly clutching the arms of his chair. 'Do you remember the man's name?' he demanded.

'Of course, it's documented in Paracelsus' book.'

'Well?'

'If I recall correctly, his name was Alfons Piotrowski,' replied Asquith calmly.

20

Here Comes the Flood

AURELIA NIGHTSHADE WAS BECOMING increasingly nervous the longer she waited. She knew Lex had returned to the city after receiving several cryptic messages he had left for her at one of her favourite haunts, but that was weeks ago. So why the delay? Maybe Abel had been unable to decipher the code or perhaps Frankl had decided to continue his scheme without her. She was almost on the verge of contacting the obnoxious Frankl when a grubby street urchin knocked on her door and deposited an unaddressed envelope into her mitts. Her heart leapt when she opened the package and a marble-sized pearl tumbled into the centre of her palm.

She laid the jet black pearl down on the kitchen worktop and looked at it in trepidation before she finally dared to touch it while uttering the word she had shared with Pearly all those years ago. The pearl shimmered as if in the midst of a heat haze, and as the transformation took place, she marvelled at how a message could be passed on like this; she was a botanist and not an alchemist after all, but just how alchemy could be performed by proxy was beyond even her scientific mind. She craned her neck so that her eyes came within inches of the slowly morphing pearl, feeling the heat emanating from the chemical reaction as the pearl seemed to melt and coalesce into a perfectly formed piece of paper.

She unfurled the tiny note and squinted at the handwritten message. 'Shit!' she screeched. Of all the places Frankl should choose, it was the one place she had always refused to go, even daring to risk Pearly's wrath at her perceived mutiny by mollifying him with her charm. She should have guessed. By implication, whatever Frankl had discovered, it must be something momentous. She vacillated over whether she should go, but in the end, there was no choice; she had to find out.

Two days later, she set off nervously across the city. Even after arriving at the decrepit building on Saffron Hill, she was convinced that the meeting would be cancelled as a result of the continuing rain, but when she found Lex and Abel waiting for her in the vault, she knew that she was seriously mistaken.

Lex led them in silence through an open grille into the fathomless depths, and after a journey scampering through darkness and filth, Aurelia sensed that they were getting close when Lex took a sharp turn into a tunnel highlighted by a flare hovering unnaturally in mid-air. When they emerged into a voluminous chamber, Lex's torchlight settled on a bulky figure smiling down at them from a dais that towered over a central culvert.

'Well met, my friends,' Frankl announced, waving his arms grandly. 'How convenient that you should travel together to our most honoured meeting place. I'm so glad you could join me. Do come in and make yourselves comfortable.'

'Hardly comfortable,' replied Aurelia acerbically, making an exaggerated show of looking about her. 'I know of this place, Josef. Don't waste your time humouring me. I'm well aware of what happened here. After all this rain, I assumed you'd see sense and arrange the meeting elsewhere. No doubt you'll tell us that you have a very good reason for choosing this place.'

Frankl smiled, his megalithic teeth flashing in the candlelight. He descended the ladder, his feet squelching in the steady trickle as he traversed the channel to greet them. 'As ever, you're right, Aurelia, but when you've heard what I have to say, you'll understand,' he replied, allowing his smile to morph into a steely glare. 'I suggest we make a start. The sooner we finish, the sooner we can leave. I suspect the dearly departed Club would agree, don't you think, Lex?'

'You're right, Josef, although I'd rather not think about it,' replied Lex solemnly.

'And you, Abel, I trust you're well? Come in and sit down,' Frankl said, ushering the trio towards the ladder that led up to the terraced steps.

As they sat down, Frankl clambered up the ladder on the opposite side of the channel, and after briefly composing himself, he stood soberly facing them from the dais across the divide. His face flitted in and out of shadow in the glimmering candlelight, giving him an otherworldly appearance. He glanced at his watch before clearing his throat, a strange guttural sound that echoed unnaturally in the high-arched space. 'Thank you for joining me,' he began earnestly. 'Wren's Cache was always Pearly's favoured meeting place for his most trusted allies. Naturally, it is fitting that we should meet here to honour him and cement the destiny we must now face together.'

'Er, quite so, Josef,' replied Strange uneasily. 'I'm sure our, er, presence affirms, at the very least, our desire to find out what you've discovered. Please, though, we must not linger any longer than is necessary. The sluices and floodgates that dictate the flow of water through these tunnels are unpredictable at best, but with the recent rain, it's anybody's guess what may happen. Don't forget that this culvert is a, er, storm relief drain.'

'Thank you for your rational words, Abel ...' replied Frankl, 'as if I'd forgotten,' he added sarcastically. 'We're safe here, and in any case, this won't take long.

'Now, firstly, let me say how grateful I am for all your aid in the acquisition of Piotrowski's manuscript. Aurelia, for the beautifully wicked way you thwarted Price; Lex, for your sublime skills in acquiring the book; and finally, Abel, in deciphering the secret of the Esoteric Brotherhood. It exemplifies the solidarity we once displayed when the Order was in its prime, and augurs well for its resurrection. Listen carefully to what I have to say. There will be no dissenting voices by the time I've finished,' he announced with supreme confidence.

'Go on then, Josef, get on with it,' said Aurelia.

'Firstly, I'm pleased to report that, as we hypothesised, the Esoteric Brotherhood was successful in discovering one of the fundamental principles of alchemy, the living stone. Sadly, their secret was flawed and led to terrible consequences, forcing the Brotherhood to bury their secret until a time when they could perfect it. And so it was that Alfons Piotrowski devised a plan to hide the secret in two near identical manuscripts, one containing a codeword, and the other, a string of encrypted words.'

'Yes, yes, we know all that,' said Aurelia impatiently, 'can't you just get on with it?'

'Please, don't interrupt, Aurelia,' Frankl snapped. 'My preamble is necessary for you to fully understand. Now, where was I? Ah, yes. I was referring to the same discovery that Pearly made some years before his death, yet ultimately failed to unravel. It has taken me all of this time to uncover the convoluted trail that Pearly left for me, and, at last, discover the secret that, somehow, he also acquired for himself.'

'What are you talking about, Josef?' said Aurelia.

'I believe that Pearly managed to uncover the very same secret as the Brotherhood, but by alternative means.'

'I would, er, agree with your deduction, Josef,' said Strange. 'The secret compartment in the book showed no trace of tampering, suggesting that the piece of enciphered text had lain undisturbed since the time it was placed there.'

'If so, then how did Pearly also discover this secret?' enquired Aurelia.

'That must, for the time being, remain the subject of our speculation, but for now, I suggest we concentrate on the secret itself,' replied Frankl.

'Come on, Josef, don't keep us in suspense,' said Lex, unable to contain himself. 'Besides, despite your earlier assertion, the flow of water is already increasing,' he added, inclining his head towards a stream of filthy black water that was tumbling out of the inlet pipe into the channel.

'Very well. I shall be brief. You'll recall our speculation regarding the Brotherhood's secret and their pursuit of the living stone. The information that the Piotrowski manuscript yielded confirms we were correct.

'Abel could bore you witless with a description of the documents written during the Middle Ages purporting to describe methods of distilling the stone, yet despite numerous attempts to replicate these techniques by some of the greatest alchemists of our era, it has never proved possible to validate this early experimentation. No doubt many of these alchemists believed that they had created the mythical substance that could transmute base metal into gold or purify and rejuvenate the body, but their methods have never withstood modern scrutiny. Piotrowski's secret notes are assuredly different, and having analysed them at great length, I believe they're genuine.'

Strange nodded vigorously. 'You already know my, er, thoughts on this matter, Josef. Piotrowski's technique to prepare the stone is extremely long and, er, arduous, but it's like no other I've ever seen. While it will take many months to replicate, I too have read enough to convince myself that what he describes is authentic.'

'And what exactly makes you think that his method is any different from all the others?' said Aurelia.

Frankl nodded to Strange. 'Please, Abel, if you will.'

'The answer is somewhat convoluted, but bear with me. Until now, we knew little of, er, Alfons Piotrowski, but I've filled in the gaps in his life with the extraordinary revelations in his text,' said Strange. 'Piotrowski was born in Amsterdam towards the end of the fifteenth century and spent most of his life there. Like many startling discoveries, luck often plays its part, and Piotrowski was the subject of a rather fortuitous visitation that ultimately resulted in dramatic consequences. Piotrowski was well-established within the higher ranks of the Brotherhood, but he'd been struggling for many years with his alchemical experimentation until, one day, an acolyte from Spain mysteriously appeared on his doorstep.'

'Spain?' repeated Lex.

'Yes. The link with Spain was not unusual as the Netherlands during Piotrowski's lifetime was part of the Habsburg empire, and consequently under Spanish rule. The Spaniard claimed to be a descendant of a man known as Maestro Canches.'

'Oh, for goodness sake! The floodwaters could come pouring in at any minute while you relate the story of Don Quixote; is this really necessary, Abel?' burst in Aurelia, huffing impatiently.

Strange looked hesitantly to Frankl, who returned him a curt nod, suggesting he should continue. 'I'm sorry, er, Aurelia, but I believe this is, er, important,' he replied, sounding even more flustered than usual. 'I realise you've never heard of, er, Maestro Canches, but it's vital in, er, understanding precisely how Piotrowski stumbled on the information that transformed his work.'

Aurelia shook her head but passed no comment.

'Canches' descendant related the story of a Parisian bookseller by the name of, er, Nicolas Flamel, who lived and worked in France during the fourteenth century. Flamel was, first and foremost, a scribe, but he had also developed a passion for the Hermetic art through his love of books. He began plying his trade by opening a humble bookstall on the market next to, er, Saint-Jacques la Boucherie. Through hard work and diligence, he saved enough money to purchase a property on the Rue de Marivaux, which he converted into a bookshop. One night, soon after moving into the new premises, he had a vivid dream in which he was visited by an angel bearing a fabulous book. The angel commanded Flamel to remember the book, foretelling that, one day, he would own it, although he would not understand its contents.

'Many years later, a man desperate for money visited Flamel in his shop bearing a curious manuscript. The book was magnificent to behold with archaic bindings of worked copper engraved with strange diagrams, runes and, er, hieroglyphs. It was written, not on parchment, but on the bark of a young tree in a language Flamel could not discern, but he, er, immediately recognised it as the book the angel had prophesied he would one day own. Flamel paid the man well for the manuscript and spent many years dedicated to uncovering the hidden meaning of the text. From his research and what the angel had told him, Flamel was convinced that he had found one of alchemy's ancient fabled texts written by a man known only as Abraham the Jew.

'For twenty-one years Flamel attempted to unravel the secrets

303

hidden in the book, but despite consulting some of the greatest minds of his generation, he failed to discover the true meaning of the text. He eventually learnt that the book was written in, er, ancient Hebrew and that he would have to seek the aid of the Jews who had been persecuted and driven from the land.'

Aurelia could sense herself becoming increasingly immersed in the curious tale. 'Where did he go, Abel?' she asked.

'Flamel set out for Spain hoping to find a Jew schooled in Kabbalah who could translate the Hebrew and help interpret the ancient text. Unfortunately, the people he met refused to discuss the book and would not say why. After months of fruitless searching, he decided, er, rather despondently, to return to France.'

'Another dead end,' Aurelia said, shaking her head.

'Ah, yes, but miraculously, on his return journey, Flamel met a French merchant in Leon who knew of an old Spanish sage named Maestro Canches, whom the merchant thought could help. The pair tracked down the recluse and arranged an audience, and although it took a considerable time to persuade Canches of his trustworthiness, when Flamel produced excerpts from, er, Abraham's book, the meeting was transformed.'

'What happened?' said Aurelia.

'To Flamel's amazement, Canches knew of Abraham the Jew and recounted his story as a Kabbalist of no equal who had recorded his knowledge and testament in a long-lost book. After Abraham's death, the book had been passed down from generation to generation, always seemingly falling into the hands of the, er, person destined to receive it. Finally, after many aeons, the book disappeared from all knowledge.'

'Did Canches help Flamel?' said Aurelia.

'He did. Canches was convinced by the authenticity of Flamel's notes. Together, the men translated the ancient Hebrew and deciphered the symbols originating from Babylon. Unfortunately, Flamel had only brought fragments of the book with him, and to his dismay, it was insufficient for Canches to unravel all of the book's hidden meanings.

'By then, Canches was captivated, and at once agreed to accompany Flamel back to Paris, but the old man was frail and fell ill in Orleans on the arduous journey north. On his deathbed, Canches revealed the whereabouts of his son, a man also schooled in Kabbalah, and urged Flamel to make contact with him. He also advised Flamel how he should dispose of the book after his death.

'Flamel returned to Paris alone, and armed with the knowledge gleaned from Canches, he finally unearthed the secrets hidden in the book.'

'What happened to Flamel?' said Aurelia.

'That much is known,' boomed Frankl. 'Despite his new found wealth, Flamel did little to change his frugal lifestyle, apart from the purchase of a new shop in his old stamping ground on the rue Saint-Jacques la Boucherie. He spent his money on the poor, building houses and hospitals, and endowing churches, and lived out his life in great happiness with his wife, Pernelle, while whiling away the time writing books on alchemy. He died peacefully at the age of eighty and was buried under the nave of Saint-Jacques la Boucherie.'

'Following his death, rumours abounded about Flamel's great wealth and alchemical prowess, suggesting that he had mastered the transfiguration of mercury into silver, and thence into gold, and that he had also transmuted his soul.

'Not surprisingly, the places he had lived were ransacked, and even his tomb despoiled, but despite the archaic symbols and runes inscribed there, no sign of Flamel's body or the book were ever found,' said Strange.

'Was anything ever found of him?' said Aurelia.

Strange smiled nervously. 'Er, not until Canches' descendent turned up on Piotrowski's doorstep.'

'Go on,' Aurelia urged.

'Piotrowski was already familiar with the story of Flamel but was astounded to learn that he had never been, er, buried in Saint-Jacques la Boucherie. In anticipation that his final resting-place would be desecrated, Flamel had arranged to be buried in the Cemetery of Innocents. The only person who knew of this was Canches' son, whom Flamel had contacted just as he had promised.'

'What did Piotrowski do?' said Aurelia.

'He immediately dispatched one of his most trusted agents to Paris. Under cover of darkness, Flamel's final resting place was located in the Cemetery of Innocents, and the body exhumed ... or not as it turned out. There was no trace of, er, Flamel's body in the stone sarcophagus, but the legendary book of Abraham the Jew was there, which was spirited away into Piotrowski's eagerly awaiting hands.'

'What did he do with it?' said Aurelia.

'Piotrowski was, er, patently a learned man. With the Brotherhood's network of influential European scholars to call upon, it was a far easier task for him to unlock the secrets hidden in the book. Armed with the mythical information the book yielded, Piotrowski eliminated the earlier mistakes he'd made in his quest for the stone, and within a few years, he'd replicated Abraham's process to create the pinnacle of the Brotherhood's dreams— their very own living stone!'

'You said that Pearly also managed to acquire this knowledge for himself,' said Aurelia excitedly, turning her attention to Frankl.

'Yes, but, as to how ... well ... that remains a mystery,' replied Frankl circumspectly. 'Now, please, let Abel finish.'

Aurelia shook her head but kept her counsel.

'I won't bore you with the details regarding Piotrowski's, er, technique,' continued Strange, 'but I've already begun the arduous task of replicating the process, and have, so far, encountered no obvious anomalies. It will take many months to complete the work, and I will, of course, er, keep you updated as I progress, but it's a laborious process involving twelve steps, each taking a variable amount of time. First, there is calcination, and then, in the strictest of order: congelation, fixation, solution, digestion, distillation, sublimation, separation, ceration, fermentation, multiplication, and finally, projection, culminating in the production of the, er, Star Regulus of Antimony and Iron.

'This substance is amalgamated with silver to create the Lunar

Regulus to which is added a triple distilled quicksilver to produce a mercury capable of dissolving all metals, including gold, the so-called "cauda pavonis", which translates to "the multicoloured tail of the peacock". It goes by this name because the distillate hardens into a solid that's as dark as pitch, but coalesces through many stages from grey to blue to green to white to orange, until finally, all that is left is a stone that is as, er, red as blood; this, my friends, is the living stone!'

'Thank you, Abel,' said Frankl, breaking the stunned silence that followed. 'I'll continue the story from here.'

Strange nodded, looking relieved that his speech was over.

'So it appears that Piotrowski successfully recreated the living stone just as Flamel had done by following the method described in Abraham's book,' said Frankl. 'It would be nice to think that the story ends there, but like everything else, I'm afraid it's not so simple. Despite Piotrowski's conviction that he had fabricated the living stone, the Brotherhood were less inclined to accept the veracity of this momentous discovery. Not one to give up, Piotrowski continued with his experimentation in secret, determined to prove that he was right.'

'What did he do?' asked Aurelia.

'Piotrowski's interpretation of the book in conjunction with the opinions of the experts he'd consulted, was that the stone could accrue or imbibe an individual's characteristics if used in the correct way.'

'I'm not sure I follow,' said Aurelia.

'Piotrowski deduced that the stone had to be incorporated into a person's body to form a symbiosis with the recipient.'

'Symbiosis?' said Lex.

'Yes. It describes a relationship that is mutually beneficial to two organisms, but without resulting in harm to either. There are many examples in nature where plants and animals demonstrate this interaction. I suppose, here, it's slightly different, but by placing the stone in proximity to the brain, Piotrowski believed it would somehow integrate with a person's nervous system.'

'What exactly do you mean by "integrate", Josef?' asked Aurelia, eyeing him suspiciously.

'Ah, that's the crux of the matter, Aurelia, and perhaps the most difficult question to answer. If I explain how Piotrowski went on to use the stone, then perhaps all will become clear.'

'Go on,' she prompted.

'Piotrowski was a trained physician as well as an alchemist, and with the help of a medical colleague, he performed a craniotomy on, of all things, his pet dog, Richelle.'

'His own dog?' said Lex incredulously.

'Yes. Richelle was a wily old creature and had learnt many tricks during its ten long years of life. It was an ideal choice for the unique experiment Piotrowski was planning.'

'And what exactly is a craniotomy?' Lex enquired.

'It's a surgical term for the process of creating an opening in the skull. Piotrowski placed the stone into a pocket he had fashioned inside the dog's Dura Mater—the tough protective lining that separates the skull from the brain.'

'What happened?' said Lex.

'Amazingly, the dog survived and lived out its life. When it died, Piotrowski retrieved the stone and kept it safe for the next stage of the experiment.'

'Which was what?' Aurelia asked.

'He implanted the stone inside the skull of a puppy.'

'How perfectly barbaric. What was the outcome?' said Aurelia.

'The transformation was instantaneous. The dog immediately displayed identical traits to Richelle, even answering to the former dog's name whenever it was called and performing tricks a puppy of its age could never have learnt. You may wonder whether this was a coincidence, and I suspect even Piotrowski harboured some doubts, but one final encounter convinced him that the stone had somehow subsumed the soul of his previous pet to flourish within the puppy.'

'What happened?' said Lex.

'Piotrowski was called away on business shortly after he had performed the operation on Richelle. He left the dog in the care of the physician who had aided him with the surgery, a cruel man by the name of Leer. Leer mistreated the dog, leaving it without food and beating it when it complained. On Piotrowski's return, the dog was a cowering wreck. Piotrowski was furious at how the dog had been treated, and after a harsh exchange of words, he expelled Leer from his house with the instruction never to return.

'Several years later, Piotrowski was out on the streets taking the puppy for a stroll. All of a sudden, the dog began to strain on its leash and whimper as if in great pain. Piotrowski could not understand what was wrong, but when he looked up, he spotted Leer strolling towards him. Piotrowski promptly turned on his heels, and as he retreated, the puppy instantly calmed down and regained its former benign disposition.'

'The final piece of evidence Piotrowski needed to convince himself that the soul of Richelle lived on in that of the puppy!' Strange exclaimed.

'Exactly!' Frankl concurred.

'What did Piotrowski do next?' said Aurelia.

'He implanted the stone into the brain of a human!'

The expectant silence that followed was interrupted by a distant rumbling as of thunder.

Aurelia shuffled uncomfortably on the wet stone slabs and looked uneasily at the large inlet pipe in the dim, guttering candlelight. 'I think there's more water coming out of the pipe,' she said.

'You're mistaken, Aurelia. Now, I've almost finished,' said Frankl dismissively, quickly resuming his narration. 'After performing the recondite alchemy to produce a fresh stone, Piotrowski began the search for a suitable recipient. He selected an ageing disciple from the Brotherhood's ranks for whom the offer of immortal life was too much to forego. We do not know how long the man survived or whether he saw out the natural conclusion of his life, but Piotrowski reclaimed the stone less than a year after it was placed. He then offered a large sum of money to a beggar by the name of de Groot to be the next recipient of the stone. Not surprisingly, the man did not refuse.

'Unfortunately, the result of the operation was not as Piotrowski had anticipated and led to terrible consequences. It is, perhaps, best if I read Piotrowski's observations of what happened,' said Frankl, retrieving a piece of paper from inside his coat. He leant forwards to peer at the notes in the dim light and began to read.

'I conducted the chirurgery in the same fashion as I had before, exposing the skull through a small incision in the scalp and performing a trephination to expose the brain. I developed a pocket beneath the Dura into which I delivered the stone. The wound was closed with the finest of thread and doused liberally with iodine to prevent sepsis. Although de Groot had been sedated with a large dose of alcohol, it was not long before the effects of the chirurgery became discernible. Almost at once, as he aroused from his slumber, de Groot clutched at his head and moaned as if in great pain. He clawed at the wound like a mangy animal and flailed his arms, attempting to undo the good work I had performed on him. It took two of us to restrain him, but this had little effect on the distress he was experiencing. At first, I wondered whether the reaction was caused by the firewater he had ingested, but it soon became evident that something profound was occurring. It was as if a battle was being waged deep within the man's head. I immediately concluded that I was witnessing a confrontation between the soul trapped within the stone and the mind of de Groot, a battle for supremacy if you will. I am afraid I had not anticipated this, nor could I have foreseen what would happen next. De Groot began convulsing like a man possessed, and when the paroxysm passed, he threw off the bonds that restrained him. As he approached, I looked deep into his eyes, but all I saw was a feral intensity, hinting at inchoate madness. He pushed past me with an unnatural strength the equal of a dozen men and escaped by dislodging a sturdy wooden door. Despite my fervent attempts to follow, de Groot disappeared into the narrow city streets as if he still retained the streetwise sense he had acquired through years of living as a vagabond. After hours of futile searching, I returned, disconsolate at my folly and the loss of this madman.'

'You're not trying to tell us that this is another of your wild goose chases, are you, Josef?' said Aurelia irritably.

Lex furrowed his brow. 'I hope recovering the manuscript was not in vain,' he said, challenging Frankl to prove his fear unfounded.

'I'm afraid it doesn't get any better,' replied Frankl matter-of-factly. 'Two days after de Groot escaped, a vicious murder was committed. Piotrowski thought nothing of it, but when a witness came forward bearing the description of a man looking uncannily like de Groot leaving the scene of the butchering of an innocent citizen, he had no choice but to go to the Brotherhood elders and explain what he'd been doing behind their backs. The Brotherhood was desperate to hide the truth, knowing there would be repercussions in light of Piotrowski's necromancy. They launched a frantic search for the madman, and fortunately for them, they apprehended de Groot before the city protectorate could get their hands on him. The elders immediately commanded Piotrowski to prepare de Groot for surgery. Remarkably, once the stone was removed, de Groot's demeanour immediately returned to how it had been before the operation, and despite having no recollection of the macabre events that had taken place, it was as if by removing the stone, he had been cured of a temporary madness.'

'What did the Brotherhood do?' said Lex.

'Not surprisingly, the elders decided that further experimentation was too dangerous to contemplate. They elected to preserve Piotrowski's knowledge for a time when greater wisdom would allow them to proceed without further misfortune. They forbade Piotrowski from concluding his work and made him conceal what he knew in an unbreakable cipher. Whether the Brotherhood ever intended to resurrect Piotrowski's terrible secret, we do not know, for Alfons Piotrowski disappeared without trace soon after he'd finished writing.'

'What happened to the manuscripts?' said Lex.

Frankl shook his head. 'We do not know. How they got to where we found them is not clear.'

'It makes no sense to me. If, as you say, these books were so important, the Brotherhood would have kept them hidden–' said Lex.

'Er, yes, or they would have had them destroyed if they never had any intention of utilising the information they contained,' Strange cut in.

'Yes, but we have no idea what happened to the Brotherhood,' said Frankl. 'Some say that the Brotherhood endures, but if, as I suspect, it died out, then who knows what may have happened to their secrets?'

'Perhaps you're right, Josef, but I, er, remain unconvinced. It puzzles me that Piotrowski disappeared soon after he concealed the secret. The assumption has always been that he was murdered, but a man driven by an obsession with the stone would not give up. Piotrowski knew that he had lost the Brotherhood's support. He would also have known that his life was in danger. Perhaps he manufactured his own disappearance so that he could continue with his work in secret. This seems a far more, er, plausible explanation to me,' concluded Strange.

Once again, there was a distant rumbling, but this time, it was accompanied by a palpable shaking of the chamber.

'What was that?' Aurelia screeched once the noise had abated, looking uneasily around her.

'You're worrying unnecessarily, Aurelia,' Frankl replied. 'Tell her, Lex. There are always strange noises down here,' he said unconvincingly.

'Hmm. You may be right, Josef, but never anything like that. We'd better get out of here,' Lex replied.

'There's not much more to discuss, as a matter of fact,' said Frankl. 'Just a few more minutes.'

'Well, get on with it, will you?' said Aurelia. 'Whatever happened to Piotrowski is irrelevant. What's more, Josef, you bring us here on the pretext of a momentous discovery then tell us that the manuscript reveals nothing. How much longer do we have to endure this charade?'

Frankl's stared menacingly. 'Charade? You'll hear me out, Aurelia!' he commanded.

The chamber remained eerily silent once the reverberating boom of Frankl's voice had died down.

'Er, please continue, Josef,' said Strange eventually.

Frankl nodded. 'I admit that the quest to find Piotrowski's secret has been a disappointment, but it made me realise what Pearly was trying to tell me on the night that he died. If I take you back to the events of that evening, all will become clear.'

'The sooner you explain yourself, the sooner we can all get out of here,' said Aurelia, looking apprehensively at the water now flowing freely from the pipe.

'On the night in question,' Frankl began, speaking more quickly now, 'Lex and I accompanied Pearly to a factory in the East End on a simple errand. Internal Security must have been tipped off because they were swarming all over the place as soon as we broke in. We were worried about how it would all end, yet it didn't seem to bother Pearly; it was almost as if he knew what would happen. He expected Price to come; it was just a question of when. He dispatched Lex up to the roof with the instruction to call him the moment Price arrived.'

'I remember it well,' said Lex, nodding his tousled head in corroboration.

'Once I was alone with Pearly, his composure evaporated,' Frankl continued. 'He became more and more agitated, although at first, he wasn't prepared to talk. All he did was prowl back and forth, mumbling to himself as if he was deliberating over something. I didn't dare approach him. You know how unpredictable he could be when overcome by one of his dark moods. He eventually reached a decision, and with it, his anxiety evaporated. He called me over, and we sat in silence in a corner of that miserable factory, until, at last, he began to speak. It was as if he had an inkling of what was about to happen, although quite how is beyond me. I've thought about what transpired many times since, but I still can't imagine what was going through Pearly's head.'

'What did he say?' said Aurelia.

'Quite simply, he told me what I had to do if he died.'

'He knew?'

'I don't think so, but he must have considered it a possibility,

313

otherwise, he would never have brought it up. You can imagine my reaction. We all knew what Pearly was capable of, and although the thought of him dying was inconceivable, he was insistent.'

'What did he tell you?' said Aurelia.

'That I had to recover an object.'

'So why have we never learnt of this before?' said Aurelia.

'Pearly made me swear not to divulge anything until I'd worked it out for myself ... it's only now, after all these years, that I've finally reached that point.'

'Go on,' she prompted.

'I admit Pearly's behaviour confused me, and I had no idea what he was talking about, so I just asked him straight out. He reacted by showing me a scar on the back of his neck. In all the time I'd known him, I'd never seen that scar before. He assured me it had been there for several years. Perhaps you were aware of it, Aurelia?'

Aurelia shook her head. 'Er, well ... no, as a matter of fact, I wasn't,' she said uncertainly.

Frankl smirked in self-satisfaction. 'Pearly explained to me that he'd had an implant surgically inserted next to the base of his brain. He said it was imperative that I retrieve it in the event of his death.'

'Did he tell you anything else about this, er, implant?' queried Strange, excitement tingeing his voice.

'I'm afraid not, Abel. Naturally, I asked him, but he steadfastly refused to answer.'

'Er, why?' Strange pressed.

'I do not believe that Pearly seriously considered he would die that night, hence his reluctance to tell me much about the implant and why it was placed there. All he would say was that it was crucial I recovered what he referred to as "the stone". He was determined that it should not fall into Price's hands.'

'What were you meant to do with this *stone*?' demanded Aurelia.

'He said I was to guard it in a place where no one would ever find it. He also hinted at some vital information hidden in a secret cache of his. After his death, Internal Security went through every place he was known to have frequented, looking for evidence to justify their persecution of the Order. We were in disarray and our supporters long gone. I didn't dare begin the search for whatever Pearly had been safeguarding until the furore had died down.'

'I presume you eventually found this cache?' Lex asked.

Frankl nodded. 'Pearly told me to seek out Abel. He wouldn't tell me the exact whereabouts of the cache other than that it was located at the Academy, but I had to wait until it was safe. I laid low after Pearly's death, hiding as best as I could, trying to stay ahead of the detestable Fox. I left the country to regroup, and it was several years before it was safe enough for me to return. By then, Abel had wheedled his way back into Price's confidence by convincing him that he knew nothing of the Order or its machinations, and that he'd been little more than Pearly's puppet. In this way, Abel kept his position at the Academy and even managed to inveigle his way into Price's beloved Council.'

'Where did you find the cache?' said Aurelia.

'The Academy is a rabbit warren full of secret rooms, vaults, tunnels, catacombs and chambers, any of which could have been Pearly's hiding place. I searched his old lodgings until, at last, I uncovered a cunningly hidden passageway leading down to a crypt in the darkest depths of the building. After hours of fruitless searching, I began to suspect that the wretched place was empty. I assumed that whatever was hidden there had been magically concealed, but despite exploring the room on many different planes, I found nothing. Ironically, I finally succeeded in a way that I had not anticipated. I located a small niche in a corner of the room that was oddly bereft of light. The place was dark in no ordinary manner, though, and would allow light neither in nor out. There, I found a box wrapped in a sheet of material like nothing I'd ever encountered. I'd seen Pearly render objects invisible by alchemical means before, of course, but such an action inevitably leaves a trace of energy that can be sniffed out by a powerful alchemist.'

'How did he do it?' Aurelia asked.

'Pearly had fabricated a unique material with no overt signs of his power. It was remarkable. Wrapped in this material, the box was invisible. In retrospect, I suppose I should've guessed he'd have done things in his own inimitable fashion.'

'What did you find in the cache?'

'There were countless papers written in Pearly's hand. The notes covered all sorts of alchemical learning and only began to hint at the depths of lore he had acquired through meticulous study. What was interesting, though, was a name that appeared as a recurring theme. Pearly had made prodigious notes on the life of Alfons Piotrowski and the contents of two similar manuscripts he'd written. From that point on, I was committed to the task of finding these books. I knew of the manuscript in Amsterdam, of course, but it took me some time to track down the other copy, which, of all places, was under our noses in the house of that meddling old fool, Price.

'During this time, I began to speculate on the true nature of the stone, but I couldn't fathom out what Pearly had been planning and what he expected me to do with it.'

'Did you reach any conclusions?' Aurelia demanded.

'None of us were party to Pearly's motives, and I can only speculate, but knowing him as I did, I believe he foresaw the actions I'd take, despite having explained so little to me.'

'You're telling me that Pearly knew what you'd do?' said Lex incredulously.

'Not exactly, but I think he had a pretty good idea. He understood how I'd piece together all the information he'd left for me, and by extrapolation, what I might do with it. It's only now, after unravelling the riddle of Piotrowski's work that I've finally come to understand what his intentions were.'

'Don't keep us in suspense, Josef,' Aurelia urged.

'By whatever means, ladies and gentlemen,' he said melodramatically, 'I believe Pearly managed to unravel the mystery of the living stone before he died!'

As Frankl's echoing words slowly faded, the auditorium fell into a stunned silence.

'But I thought you just told us that Piotrowski's work was flawed. Surely this stone you speak of is useless?' said Aurelia.

Frankl shook his head. 'A wrong assumption, Aurelia. You're presuming that Pearly followed Piotrowski's methodology.'

'I'm not sure what to believe, Josef,' she replied with a sigh.

'Pearly led me to Piotrowski merely as a way to explain what he'd already discovered by alternative means. You knew Pearly as well as anyone. Do you suppose he'd waste our time on a false trail such as this?

'Nor do I,' continued Frankl in response to the silence that followed. 'I've made some assumptions during this quest, I admit, and it's taken me many years to assemble the requisite pieces of this intricate jigsaw, but now, at last, I finally know what we must do.'

The air hung with an expectant silence as Frankl inhaled deeply as a prelude to the moment of truth. 'My friends,' he began flamboyantly, 'I do not believe Pearly expected to die on that night, thus explaining why his preparations were both hasty and ill-conceived. You may wonder why he took so many risks—a question I have asked myself many times since—but all I can assume is that his supreme self-confidence and vanity were responsible for his downfall. He believed he was untouchable, overcome by his own arrogance. It was his one great weakness, but when faced with a threat to his mortality, he finally realised he could not achieve all he had set out to alone. Almost as an afterthought, he confided in me about the stone and left me with a cryptic message that would lead me to his personal notes. He knew I'd find the references to Piotrowski and his thoughts on the living stone, and once I'd put the two together, I'd begin the quest to recover Piotrowski's manuscripts. He also knew that, once I'd deciphered the secret, I'd also deduce what I had to do.'

'So what *do* you intend to do?' Aurelia demanded.

'Very well, Aurelia, I shall tell you, but before I do, you must all agree to some simple tasks I have for you.

'Shall I take your silence as a tacit agreement?' said Frankl, inclining his head. 'Well?'

'If you must,' said Aurelia.

'Men?'

'You can count on me,' said Lex.

Strange nodded, somewhat reluctantly. 'Er, what would you have us do?'

'Very well. Abel, you must return to the Academy and carry on with your routine. Wait for my call as it is central to our plans that you have access to our enemy's thoughts.

'As for you Aurelia, well, I have a slightly more demanding task.'

Aurelia gave an exasperated sigh. 'And just what is that?'

'I'd like you to bring someone to me,' he said, looking expectantly towards her.

'Who do you have in mind?'

'Henry Price,' Frankl replied evenly.

'Price! You expect me to kidnap Price?' Aurelia screeched.

'Oh, you'll find a way. I know how resourceful you are. I'm sure you won't let me down.'

'Hold on a moment,' shrieked Aurelia, the sound of her mellifluous voice rising by an octave. 'Give me one good reason why I should.'

Frankl bared his teeth in a malevolent grin. 'Oh, I'm sure you'll understand when you learn what I'm planning.

'Now, as for you Lex ...' he continued, but as he spoke his words were drowned out by a loud noise that sounded like the grating of a heavy metal door.

'What was that?' said Aurelia, turning her head in alarm towards the inlet pipe.

As the ominous noise subsided, silence reigned for a few glorious moments, but then, increasing by degrees as if something was moving inexorably towards them, a thunderous roar echoed around the chamber accompanied by a freshening of air.

'Water! The sluice gates ... er, the sluice gates are open!' Strange yelled, his words almost overwhelmed by the sound of the approaching tsunami.

The dumbstruck group turned towards the inlet pipe and looked in horror at the sudden surge of water pouring into the chamber.

'Run!' Aurelia screamed as the memory of Club's fate flooded over her like the incoming torrent surely would. With a jump akin to a migratory salmon, she leapt into the channel and set off towards the tunnel. Lex was next, vaulting after her like a gymnast, then Abel, moving as fast as his feeble frame would allow. Finally, Frankl lumbered ungainly behind them, disappearing into the tunnel like a fleeing refugee, leaving the rapidly-filling chamber behind.

Aurelia rushed headfirst towards the beacon that marked the end of the tunnel with the deafening sound of rushing water urging her on as fast as her legs could carry her. She reached the shining light almost as the tidal wave was upon her, and with an unimaginable leap, she emerged from the exit. She turned upstream and sprinted along the towpath until, finally, she halted. She heaved, fighting back waves of nausea while gasping for air. Finally, fearful of what she might see, she dared to look back. There, in a blur of movement, two figures burst from the tunnel. Lex was first, soaked to the core, followed by Abel, staggering like a blind man, arms outstretched and glasses gone. The men had barely time to turn towards her before the tidal wave struck, spewing from the tunnel in a foaming jet of awesome force.

The bedrock shook below Aurelia's feet such was the water's terrible power. She stared in grim fascination as the water gushed inexorably into the channel, commingling with the Fleet into a flood that plunged pell-mell towards the Thames.

Once Abel and Lex had caught up with her, she pulled herself away from the chilling spectacle and headed upriver as fast as her leaden legs would allow, never daring to stop, terrified that the backflow would yet send her tumbling into the torrent.

At last, she arrived at the spiral stairs and clambered to the top, pushing aside the grille and diving headfirst into the vault. The men followed her into the cellar and sat down next to her in stunned silence, chests heaving in unison as they fought to regain their breath.

They stared pale-faced at the circular opening, waiting in dread anticipation. The minutes ticked away until, slowly but surely, the unpalatable truth dawned. They had seen the power of the water and could only tremble at the thought of being caught up in the flow. Cold and shivering they kept their counsel, deeply lost in thought at the fate of their missing comrade, Josef Frankl.

21

Through the Glass

RELATIONS WITH HIS DAUGHTER had become increasingly strained in recent months, and Price did not doubt that it was his fault. He had neglected her because of his preoccupation with the theft, and he had also avoided discussing it with her, not because he did not trust or doubt her abilities, but from a misguided notion that he was protecting her. Not surprisingly, his behaviour had only served to alienate her further, and it was only now that he realised he had let her down. The opportunity to seek redress had not arisen during the past few days, mainly due to the distraction of a forthcoming Council meeting, but once it was over, he was determined to put things right.

Price was anticipating that this morning's meeting would be as unproductive as the last, despite the consolation that the recently appointed Hermes Bing would be present. While Price had never been a proponent of Bing's methods, he did not doubt the value of his sly cunning and bombastic style, attributes that had turned Bing's journalistic empire into what it was today. He hoped that Bing's presence would provide a welcome fillip to Council proceedings and go some way to stirring up the factions that had recently dogged its progress, but when Price entered the boardroom later that morning, he was disconcerted to find that Bing was not there. When the media tycoon eventually sauntered in fifteen minutes late, he greeted Price with such a ferocious glare, it was enough to suggest that it was going to be a long and arduous meeting.

It was no secret that Bing harboured a lifelong grudge against Price, blaming him through some kind of twisted logic for the downfall of his father. With most of the Council seeing Bing's appointment as yet another weakening of Price's increasingly tenuous grasp on its leadership, it seemed inevitable that Bing would allow his hatred for Price to cloud his judgement and oppose his objectives, but as it turned out, nothing could have been further from the truth.

Isaacson opened the meeting by asking Price for an update on the missing manuscript. Purely for Bing's sake, Price began with a précis of the theft followed by an account of what he had discovered about the manuscript, and how he had been lured away to a stricken Cornelius Spydre at the end of the last meeting. Price recounted the references to Atropos and the clues that had been left for him, and how he had finally worked out what Spydre had been poisoned with. He also gave a rational explanation as to why he believed that the vile misdemeanour had been perpetrated by Aurelia Nightshade. Most of the Council greeted his assertion with reservation, apart from Fox, and of all people, Bing, whose backing for Price was met with incredulity from everyone around the table apart from Price himself.

When the Council vacancy had arisen, there had been a long and heated debate about the qualities needed to join such an august body of men, including morality, honesty and a sense of justice (ironic, considering some of those currently seated around the table). The prospective candidate was also required to have connections that would enable them to influence events and opinion at the highest level.

Fielding and Olberry were Bing's principal backers, but the rest saw his nomination as an attempt to balance the disparity between factions. As it transpired, the votes were cast after Price had unexpectedly been called away at the end of the last meeting, and despite some earlier opposition, not a single black ball materialised once Isaacson emptied the bag. As per Council protocol, Isaacson was tasked with offering Bing the position, and to explain his duties and obligations should he accept. There were those who thought Bing would instantly decline given Price's status on the Council, but, much to general surprise, Bing jumped at the chance. Strangely enough, Price had been anticipating this, and although he had not shared his thoughts with anyone else, he was secretly delighted with the outcome.

Although Price was fully aware of Bing's antipathy towards him, having been on the receiving end of numerous vitriolic attacks in the editor-in-chief's various publications, he had followed his rising career with more than just a passing interest. Price saw in Hermes Bing a singularity and ruthlessness that was never evident in his father, Dionysus, leading Price to believe that Bing would act as his own man, putting any personal vendetta aside in favour of a moral pursuit of truth and justice. In fact, Price had been so concerned that Bing would not accept the Council's offer, he had done everything in his power to ensure that he would.

It was a dangerous game that Price had played, but he smiled to himself now at the ploy that had undoubtedly influenced Bing's decision. After Bing's name had first been proposed, Price made an anonymous call to the newspaper's headquarters to tip him off, reasoning that if Bing suspected Henry Price of being behind a conspiracy to exclude him from the Council, then, should the chance arise, he would accept the offer unflinchingly. As it transpired, this was how it had all panned out, and Price could not fault himself for his successful Machiavellian scheme. Political intrigue had never been a forte of his, but after years of dealing with devious politicians, it was simply a case of, 'if you can't beat them …'

After his conclusions at the previous meeting relating to the manuscript and its link to the Order were so coolly received, Price was reluctant to divulge any more of his suspicions, particularly where Black was concerned. He made the decision not to overly expound on the conversation that had taken place with Asquith, and only briefly mentioned the name of the disgraced surgeon, Luca Nexus, but the moment he voiced the surgeon's name, Sir Robert Lec was overwhelmed by a sudden coughing fit that brought the conversation to an abrupt halt. Sir Robert's puce face and bulging eyes suggested he was in danger of asphyxiation, but Isaacson immediately leapt to his aid with a glass of water, allowing for a serendipitous break in proceedings while Lec recovered.

When the meeting reconvened ten minutes later, much to his relief, Price's reference to the previous matter was long forgotten. The subsequent items on the agenda passed in a blur of irrelevance, apart from Fox's continued failure to locate the missing Michael Styx, which only served to increase Price's discomfort and consolidate his decision to pursue his investigations alone.

Following the meeting, Price took the train to Oxford for a meeting with Sir Algernon Caruthers. Price had been noncommittal when securing the appointment, and although Caruthers had retired from political circles some years previously, he was more than happy to meet, if only because of Price's reputation. Caruthers offered to host the meeting at his club, and after leaving the station, Price took a short taxi ride from Park End Street to a row of expensive-looking, three-storey Georgian town houses not far from the university colleges.

The taxi driver pointed Price in the direction of the building, and it was only as he approached a set of imposing iron railings that he observed a small brass plaque discretely set to one side and engraved with the words, 'The Stiletto Club – Members Only'. Price had barely reached out to knock on the door before it opened, and a formally dressed doorman ushered him inside without enquiry after his name or business. Price deposited his belongings at the reception and followed the man towards the rear of the establishment into a cosy bar with an ambient atmosphere of decadent leather armchairs and low-lights suffused with Montecristo cigar smoke and peaty single malt whisky. The room was empty apart from a single occupant seated in a club chair with his back to the bar. The man stubbed out his cigar in an ashtray on the occasional table next to him, got up slowly and waited for Price to join him.

The man was tall with sharp, distinguished features, framed by receding grey hair. 'Care to join me in a glass?' he said in a softly spoken voice. He lifted a decanter from the table. 'Scotch. Not too early for you, is it?' he added as they shook hands.

'It's tempting after the day I've had, but, no, thank you,' Price replied, declining with a shake of his head as he sat down opposite Caruthers.

After taking a sip, Caruthers smiled. 'Now, what can I do for you?' he asked.

Price elected to opt for a direct approach, and admitted he had come looking for information regarding Luca Nexus, but the moment he mentioned the disgraced surgeon's name, Caruthers' attitude immediately changed.

'Never heard of the fellow. If that's all you've come for, then I'm afraid you're wasting your time,' Caruthers boomed, replacing the sycophantic charm of earlier with unpleasant belligerence. 'Now, if you don't mind ...'

Price shook his head dejectedly. It was obvious that Caruthers was lying, and he could sense that if he were to glean any information from this objectionable man, he would have to employ alternative means to extract it. Price was always reluctant to utilise his innate alchemical talent, but for once, he could see that this was the only choice. He knew that Caruthers was an arrogant, pompous man who had built his career as a high-ranking civil servant on the success of others, and so the moment Caruthers began to display hostility, Price leapt from his chair and laid a hand on the man's wrist, clutching it tightly while summoning an essence of pure energy.

The vital, seething electric blue power that poured forth from Price's hand bit deeply into Caruthers' skin. 'W-what the hell do you think you're doing?' he said, flinching.

'This is nothing, my friend, only the beginning,' said Price, making sure that Caruthers' arm did not slip from his grip. 'Now do be a good chap and answer my questions,' he added blithely, increasing the power emanating from his hand.

Sweat poured from Caruthers' brow as the current surged through his arm in intolerable spasms. He looked into Price's eyes and shrank back from the menacing stare that contradicted the softly spoken words. Any resolve Caruthers harboured in resisting the request quickly dissipated, and the man palpably diminished before Price's eyes as he degenerated into a quivering wreck, willing to do anything to halt the pain.

'As I mentioned a moment ago, I'd like to know about Luca Nexus,' began Price. 'Firstly, why were you chosen to preside over the hearing?'

'I ... what? I c-c-can't think clearly ... the p-pain ...' stammered Caruthers.

'Well, I suggest you try,' replied Price coolly. 'I'll not slacken my grip until I get some answers.'

Caruthers shifted uneasily in his seat, looking around him forlornly for help. The club was typically empty during the early part of the afternoon, and now was no exception, apart from the barman who was disinterestedly cleaning glasses oblivious to what was happening behind the high back of Caruthers' chair.

Rivulets of sweat trickled down Caruthers' temples onto his reddening cheeks as he struggled to pull away from the unbearable stimulus. 'P-please, s-s-stop,' he cried plaintively.

Price reduced the power flowing from his hand, easing the pain just enough for Caruthers to gather his thoughts.

'L-look, I've got nothing to hide. Just let go and I'll tell you all I know,' Caruthers said belligerently.

'Nothing could be easier than to repeat the exercise,' Price said assuredly, releasing his grip. 'I suggest we continue our conversation without further interruption. You've merely witnessed the least of my abilities. Do not doubt my capacity to overpower anyone you may call to your aid,' he added confidently, glancing briefly in the direction of the barman, who continued to go about his duties blissfully unaware of what was happening directly under his nose.

Caruthers nodded, shuffling uncomfortably in his chair. 'I don't doubt your capabilities,' he replied resentfully, scrunching up his eyes into narrow slits. 'I guarantee you've just made some powerful enemies by threatening me like this. I realise I've no option but to comply with your demands, but rest assured, this won't be the last you hear of this.'

'Very well. That's a consequence I'll just have to live with,' replied Price evenly. 'Now, perhaps you'd be kind enough to answer my questions?'

'What do you want to know?' Caruthers snapped.

'As I've already said, tell me of Nexus and your role in his trial.'

'I presume you're already familiar with the reports that appeared in the press? The matter was given some attention at the time,' said Caruthers, slowly regaining his composure.

Price nodded. 'Yes, but the information was limited. The hearing was held in privacy, if I recall. Nexus' experimentation was a gross contravention of medical ethics, as I understand it, but the details were never made clear. Perhaps you'd be kind enough to enlighten me?'

'I was chosen to preside over the hearing because I was trusted to be discrete about the outcome. It was a sensitive matter,' Caruthers replied.

'Go on.'

'Nexus had been performing illicit medical research.'

'So I was informed, but what exactly was he up to?'

'He was interested in cryonics.'

'Cryonics? The freeze preservation of cells, you mean?'

'Yes, that's right. He began by experimenting on the nerve cells of rats, envisioning that one day he could apply the technique to the entire nervous system of the poor brutes. No one believed him, of course. The medical profession thought he was quite mad and turned a blind eye.'

'And?'

'He eventually started experimenting on patients, choosing his victims carefully so that they would not be missed. He believed, through a misguided notion, I suppose, that one day he would be able to prolong their lives … prolong their suffering, if you ask me.'

'What happened?'

'He developed a cryoprotectant, a chemical mixture of sorts, that allows the brain to be frozen without damage to its cells. He believed he could preserve the organ forever. You can see where all of this is leading, can't you?'

Price nodded gloomily. 'The panacea that misguided souls have sought through the ages. Eternal life!'

'Yes, although Nexus was not the only one involved. When the press got a whiff of what he was up to there was a furore, but it all died down very quickly. Nexus had contacts in high places because someone hushed up the details of his work. I suspect that was why I was put in charge of the hearing. I was tasked with ensuring that as little as possible emerged; damage limitation, I suppose you'd call it. I was to make sure that Nexus was banned from medical practice with as little fuss as possible, and without any details creeping into the press. It was as simple as that.'

'A cover up, you mean,' said Price evenly.

Caruthers smiled. 'You know how things work, Price.'

Price shook his head in disgust. 'You said earlier that Nexus was not the only one involved.'

'Nexus had some powerful backers, but when the news broke, he was left to face the music alone.'

'Who else was involved?'

'I don't know, and before you try another of your tricks, trust me, I *really* don't.'

'Hmm. I can see that,' said Price sensing the truth in Caruthers' words. 'Who was your contact?' he asked, changing tack.

'You don't know, do you?' replied Caruthers, allowing a thin smile to pass across his lips.

'What do you mean?'

'Have you ever wondered why the Council was not involved?'

Price shook his head and frowned, suddenly feeling a deep sense of unease.

'I was merely an intermediary. Someone purposefully excluded the Council from the loop,' said Caruthers glibly, exuding enjoyment at Price's disquiet.

'What! Who?'

'Let me finish and I'll explain.'

'Well, get on with it, man!' replied Price, his anger rising.

Caruthers glared at Price. 'I knew nothing of what was going on at a higher political level, and I purposefully chose not to ask.

My remit was simple. I was to make sure Nexus was banned from medical practice and to prevent him from performing any more of his dubious research. My political masters assured me that they would be satisfied with nothing less, and so I created a smokescreen to allow the hysteria surrounding Nexus to die down. As it happened, the whole thing went off with a whimper. On the final day of the hearing, strings in high places were pulled to ensure that another story broke with the sole purpose of overshadowing what was going on with Nexus. Politician's misdemeanours are by no means infrequent and inevitably make for headline news. It was a simple task to hold back such a transgression for the appropriate day. As I remember it, Nexus' trial barely made the papers on the day the outcome was announced. It was no surprise that he disappeared into obscurity.'

'Someone high up must have been embroiled in all of this,' stated Price, looking nonplussed.

'You're right,' replied Caruthers, allowing an obsequious smile to return to his lips.

'So who was your contact?' demanded Price.

'My contact was … Sir Robert Lec,' announced Caruthers theatrically.

'Lec! Are you sure?'

'Of course. It seems you can't even trust your allies,' said Caruthers triumphantly.

'How was Lec involved in all of this?' Price demanded.

'I've told you before. I made certain I knew no more than I needed to.'

'You must have some inkling,' insisted Price.

'All I can tell you is that someone coerced Lec into ensuring the whole business was brushed under the carpet. It was obvious in my dealings with him that he was under considerable duress. As to how that was achieved, well, I wouldn't wish to speculate. Now, if you'll excuse me, I've other business to attend to,' said Caruthers, getting up quickly and crossing to the bar.

'Call me a taxi, Smythe, I'll be leaving promptly,' Caruthers said, addressing the barman.

Arrogant bastard, Price thought. He had a good mind to teach him a lesson but he had better things to do than deal with a reprehensible lowlife like Caruthers. He just wanted to get home to Lily. He got up from the chair and brushed past Caruthers. After collecting his belongings, he hurried from the club while reflecting on the unsavoury information Caruthers had just relayed.

Two hours later, Price surveyed the English countryside as it rolled serenely by from the comfort of the train compartment. Dry, warmer weather had replaced the continuous rain of the past month, but here and there, pools of water were still visible in the fields, a dwindling reminder of the floods that had beset the country. It had been a long and arduous day, and Price was looking forward to returning home. He removed a fob watch from his waistcoat pocket and flicked back the ornately monogrammed casing to check the time, but just as quickly replaced it, irritated that he had performed exactly the same manoeuvre barely a few minutes earlier. The train was due in at Paddington in under an hour, and Price was desperate to be home in time for supper with Lily.

It was not long before the sprawling suburbs of the capital replaced the open pastures of the Home Counties. As he contemplated the comfort of home, the sound of the door sliding on its runners suddenly broke his reverie. He jerked his head towards the door, half expecting to see the ticket collector, but he was surprised to see the emergence of a swarthy-looking man dressed in shabby denims as he made his way into the compartment. Price was puzzled by this man; the train had not stopped for some time and he could not help thinking that the interloper's ill-kempt appearance was not appropriate for the first-class compartment. The man's eyes were glazed, possibly as a result of intoxication, but Price failed to detect the smell of alcohol on his breath. The man sat down on the bench directly opposite and scratched involuntarily at patchy grey stubble on his chin, staring with a feral intensity that immediately put Price on guard.

'Price, innit? Looks just like 'er said ye would. Just don't look at me. Makes me angry, it does,' the man barked in a heavily accented voice while he clenched and relaxed his fists as if readying himself for violence.

'What do you want?' enquired Price levelly, while lowering his eyes to avoid further antagonising the man.

The man ignored the question and jerked his head in the opposite direction. 'Wha' was that?' he said as if someone had spoken directly into his ear.

Price saw or heard nothing and wondered whether the man was conversing with an imaginary person or, more likely, using a hidden communication device.

''Er says I shouldn't answer any of your questions and to watch out for yer tricks, so take my advice and shut it,' shouted the man aggressively. 'Now, look ya, see wha' I 'as 'ere in me 'and,' he continued. As he spoke, he thrust out a closed fist that came to rest barely an inch from the end of Price's nose.

'Now, don't ye be shy, come meet me little friend,' he said, unfurling his fist to reveal a small pile of fine white powder.

As Price recoiled, the man leant forwards and blew the powder into Price's face.

'Aagh!' cried Price, pawing helplessly at his burning eyes, but the more he rubbed, the more the discomfort intensified. He backed away from the inevitable assault but was surprised to hear the sound of the man flopping back into his seat.

'Worked just like 'er said it would, dinnit? Look at 'im. Can't see a blinkin' thing,' he said, chortling heavily. 'Now, wha' was I meant to do next?'

Price could almost sense the cogs of the man's mind ticking over at sloth-like speed, and although tears were streaming from his eyes, he could just make out the blur of movement as the man got up from his seat. Rather than coming towards him as Price expected, however, the man advanced towards the window and stretched out a hand. Then, with a sudden yank, he pulled on the communication cord with such force that he almost wrenched it from its housing. The train lurched as it slowed down, causing the man to topple back into his seat while his maniacal laughter rose in tandem with the screech of the train's brakes. Sparks flew from the track illuminating the compartment in a coruscation of light, and the train came to a jerking halt amidst a flourish of billowing smoke that rose up and cloaked the carriage in a thick veil of fog.

Price tried to focus his stinging eyes on the great hulk seated opposite, and as his blurred vision slowly cleared, he was greeted by the sight of the man's smirking visage staring intently back at him.

'Now, If I 'ave this right, all I 'ave to do is wait,' the man said, scratching his head. 'And ye sit still and don't move,' he added, pointing at Price.

Price regarded the man levelly, not able to fathom his purpose. The tanned, leathery skin of the man's face was marked with livid bruises across his forehead and cheeks, suggesting recent violence. From his bizarre behaviour, Price deduced that he was taking orders from someone, and bearing in mind the way he had used the powder, he wondered whether this was another of Aurelia Nightshade's charades. He glanced away from the man and fixed his eyes on the smoke, which was slowly dissipating to reveal an expanse of deserted sidings. He looked on with bewilderment at debris strewn across the tracks, and dilapidated buildings in the distance in various states of disrepair.

The man made no further attempt to speak, but when Price got up, he quickly jumped up too, barring the exit. 'Now just ye be patient and sit there like a good 'un, and let me see yer 'ands. I don't want none of them tricks I bin warned about,' he said aggressively.

'I don't have much time for this nonsense,' replied Price calmly. 'The guard will be here any minute to find out why you pulled the cord, so I suggest you let me pass. It'll only make it easier for you in the long run,' he continued, taking a further step towards the door.

Quick as a flash and with an agility that belied his lethargy of mind, the man was upon him, grabbing his hands and pinning them behind his back before thrusting him back into the seat.

The man shoved his face inches from the end of Price's nose

and hissed uncompromisingly, 'I warned ye once, an' I won't do it again. Next time, I'll break yer fingers. Savvy?'

Price pulled away involuntarily, overcome by the man's foetid breath, but he still managed a cursory nod to confirm his acquiescence.

'An' don't expect no 'elp to be comin' yer way. The guard's locked in 'is van, an' I don't suppose 'e'll get out for a while.'

Price sat down and looked out of the window into a wasteland of disused tracks and decommissioned engines, deliberately avoiding the hoodlum's threatening stare while calmly appraising the situation as best he could. He was unsettled and puzzled by this man, who had apparently been sent to keep him in the compartment of a stationary train, but to what purpose? Was he waiting for someone or was there some other reason?

Price was not sure, but he was not prepared to sit idly by and wait. Whatever else, he had to get away. He had already been caught unawares by the man's startling turn of speed. From his appearance and the way he spoke, he assumed that he had no knowledge of alchemy, yet this was merely a hypothesis, and if he was wrong, it might result in fatal consequences. No. He wasn't going to make that mistake. If he were going to escape, he would have to use his guile.

Price relaxed back in the seat and closed his eyes, but rather than resting as he hoped it would appear, he focused his mind on the complicated action he was about to institute. He recalled the many times he had taught Lily to channel her inner energy in preparation for the manipulation of one physical form into another, and considered the analogy of a converging optical lens focusing parallel beams of light into an infinitesimally small point of unimaginable concentration.

Price inched his hand towards the opaque, scratched window of the locomotive and felt the clinical coldness of the glass. With the contact came a barely discernible hum as energy flowed from his fingertips. The thug opposite briefly stirred, but Price dampened the power stemming from his hand, causing the sound to immediately cease. The man closed his eyes, suggesting that, to his primitive senses, nothing had changed, and Price could almost sense the thug dreaming about the money he had been promised and all the ale it would buy.

Imperceptibly at first, the glass shimmered with a soundless resonance as its molecular structure shifted, and by allowing the energy to incrementally grow, Price avoided any surge in power that would overwhelm and shatter the glass, until finally, he reached the point that would allow the transubstantiation to take place.

For an accomplished alchemist, glass was an almost perfect substance for molecular transformation, being an amorphous amalgam of silica fused with phosphate and borate arranged into a vitreous mixture that was neither solid nor liquid. As he worked, Price pictured the cohesive molecular units that were responsible for the rigidity of the glass. Yet this was also the key to the change, and by modifying the relationship, he gradually transformed the unyielding glass into a malleable, thixotropic gel.

If the laggard opposite had cared to look while Price had been working his alchemical magic, he would have seen the window shimmering like a waterfall touched by the first sun of spring. As it was, the man remained glassy-eyed, staring vacantly ahead, looking, but definitely not seeing.

Price held the glass in an amorphous state while preparing for the challenging step that lay ahead. Suddenly, with an acrobatic leap, he flew from the seat towards the glass. The window moulded around his outstretched hands before bending like a sheet of elastic as his palms passed deeper into the glass. Then, with an indiscernible pop, first fingers, then hands, and finally forearms melded with the glass before passing directly through it. The momentum of his dive sent him forwards in a blur of head, torso and legs as he exited seamlessly through the glass while his assailant watched helplessly by. The glass rapidly closed behind him as he flew from the train before he hit the ground, spraying shingle all around him. The impact left him momentarily stunned, but there was no time to lose. He sprang to his feet, quickly shaking off the disorientation from the blow to his head while glancing back towards the compartment. Price locked eyes with his assailant and smiled in response to the astonished look on the man's face as he pawed helplessly at the window. Try as he might, he could not follow Price through the glass, and the man slumped back in his seat, defeat written irrefutably across his face. Finally, still unable to comprehend what had happened, the man got sluggishly to his feet and headed for the door, belatedly beginning his pursuit at a pace suggesting that he already knew it was too late.

Price sprinted as fast as he could, dodging this way and that around skeletal remnants of burnt-out carriages, rusted engines and hulking containers. He looked over his shoulder at regular intervals, but eventually, he allowed his pace to slacken, safe in the knowledge that the lumbering giant had neither the stamina nor the wits to catch him. After losing his way amidst a maze of buildings and purposeless sidings, Price finally stumbled upon civilisation. The hope of a quick return home immediately evaporated with the sight of a vast ghetto of run-down terraces and tenement blocks. The place was deserted, but the occasional flick of a curtain hinted at unseen agoraphobics either too scared or too timid to venture onto the uninviting streets. The few people he met consistently ignored his request for directions, shuffling away uneasily without reply. He looked down and noted the filth he had picked up from his fall, and the tears in his clothes, courtesy of the barbed wire on the fence he had clambered over to escape from the interminable sidings yard. His dishevelled state did not exactly invite people to help him, he supposed.

After an age aimlessly wandering along one frighteningly similar street after another, Price finally blundered into a run-down row of shops, padlocked behind heavy metal shutters. He found a late-night liquor store that was open, presided over by a portly man who spoke with a sharp Eastern European accent. The shopkeeper eyed him suspiciously, and it took all of Price's powers of persuasion to get the man to phone for a taxi after they had bartered over the cost of the call.

'Ze taxi vill be here in sirty minutes. Now, perhaps you vould like to purchase somesing vile you vait?' the shopkeeper announced after he had made the call.

Price felt duty bound to pay an exaggerated price for a bottle of water, which he duly drank in silence while waiting impatiently for the taxi to arrive.

It was almost an hour before a battered car passing itself off for a taxi came to pick up its ride. The driver would not allow Price into the vehicle before he had paid the exorbitant fare in full for the fifteen miles or so it would take to get him home.

Neither party spoke during the journey and when the taxi pulled up outside Price's house next to the common, dusk was beginning to fall, accentuating a building that was oddly devoid of light.

He jumped from the car and fumbled at the gate before striding towards the door. He placed his palm on the locking mechanism, eager to enter the house as quickly as he could. As he worked through the resonances, he jumped back in shock when the door suddenly opened to reveal Albright standing before him looking pale and drawn. One glance at his servant's face was enough to suggest that something was terribly wrong.

'What is it, man?' Price demanded, fear rising from the pit of his stomach.

'It's ... L-Lily ...' Albright began, seemingly lost for words.

'What is it? Come on, spit it out, man.'

'It's ... Lily,' he repeated inanely, 'she's ... she's gone!'

22

A Question of Parentage

LILY STARED AT THE droplets of rain clinging resolutely to the dormer window of her father's attic study. She had slept fitfully and listened for most of the night, or so it seemed, to the incessant pitter-patter of rain striking slate as she tossed and turned amid dreams she could no longer recall.

She had breakfasted alone apart from a brief conversation with her father before he left for yet another of his interminable meetings. He had announced that he expected to be home at a reasonable time and astonished her with the promise that he would update her regarding the theft the moment he returned.

Lily wondered what had caused this change of heart but could only speculate that Cornelius' influence lay behind it. She missed the irascible old man and had got quite used to his company during his period of recuperation after the attack. He had returned to the bookshop that doubled as his home a few days earlier, and it was no coincidence that Lily's melancholia stemmed from that time. The disparity between the way Cornelius treated her compared with her father had only been accentuated during the time of his stay. For a start, Cornelius was always happy to listen to what she had to say without making excuses that he had to leave for nebulous reasons, but whenever she tried to talk to her father, she always felt that while he appeared to listen, he never seemed to take it in. She knew her father had important commitments, but she could not accept that they were justified reasons for neglecting her.

337

Lily peered through the window. The early morning drizzle had given way to a depressingly low mist that obscured the zenith of the bridge's abutment, despite her attempts to view it through her father's binoculars. Even with the lenses, the bridge appeared strangely incomplete, disappearing half way across its span into a stark wall of mist that obliterated the far bank of the river from view. She sighed and sat down at the desk. The mist outside mirrored her sombre mood, and the distant view of the ghostly bridge had failed to lift her spirits as it so often did.

She glanced at the debris strewn across her father's desk and caught sight of a large book that had not been there on her last visit. To her disappointment, it was a treatise on the works of Hieronymus Bosch, an artist she knew nothing about. She flicked disinterestedly through the pages depicting bizarre images and sneezed unexpectedly from the invisible cloud of dust that spilt from the book as she snapped it shut. She looked at the clock and noted with a start that she was late, but even then, she did not rush. She was not looking forward to yet another Latin lesson with Victor Mirkstone and did not know what was worse, Classics or her boring old tutor.

Lily trundled lethargically down the stairs and entered the first-floor classroom, which was a small and rather sparse affair compared to all the other grandly furnished rooms in the house. A pair of desks sat facing one another, and with the exception of a blackboard and a couple of shelves populated with a meagre collection of textbooks, the walls were bare.

Lily felt only the slightest sense of relief when she arrived before her tutor. She sat down at her desk and lifted its top to retrieve a book she had deposited there at the end of the last lesson. Presently, the unmistakable sound of Mirkstone's diminutive feet trudging up the stairs preceded his appearance at the door. He crossed the room and gave Lily a cursory wave before sitting down without a word.

Mirkstone was a tiny, fat man with a balding head offset by a full beard that was black around the jowls but shockingly white on the point of his chin. He always wore the same pressed, formal dark suit, starched collar and black tie, and walked with a waddling gait, inevitably reminding her of a penguin. He never addressed her unless it related to what he was teaching, and with such a lack of rapport, Lily could not fail to dislike him. Mirkstone's attitude was in stark contrast to Anatoly Volkiev, with whom she had always enjoyed a much happier relationship, but the prospect of seeing Volkiev after lunch was little compensation for the tedious hours that lay ahead.

The morning's lessons dragged interminably, and Lily's mind began to wander while listening to Mirkstone's voice as he droned on about the gerund, a grammatical concept she neither wished nor intended to grasp. History followed, which was only marginally more entertaining. After several hours of unbroken boredom, it was time for lunch, and Lily could barely hide her relief when Mirkstone gathered up his belongings and nodded dismissively to bid farewell, even if it was only for another twenty-four hours.

She made her way to the kitchen and picked up a small package of sandwiches and fruit that Mrs Brimstork had left for her on the worktop. She entered the garden and sat on an old, wooden bench, enjoying the late winter sunshine and the company of a robin that hopped brazenly towards her across the lawn in search of some crumbs.

To Lily's dismay, her lunch break was over all too soon. She glanced towards the gate at the end of the garden and felt a thrill in the pit of her stomach as she briefly contemplated heading off in search of Aedh and Seoc. With a disgruntled sigh, she rejected the idea when she imagined how her father would react to the news that she had skived off to visit friends he would undoubtedly disapprove of. No, she was not going to jeopardise her forthcoming conversation with him, and reluctantly, she made her way indoors and up the stairs to the classroom where she waited for Volkiev to arrive.

She sat at her desk listening out for the telltale sound of her tutor's footsteps but she nearly jumped out of her skin when a gnarled hand fell on her shoulder. Her heart was pounding when she turned to face the intruder but was astonished to see Volkiev beaming back at her as if his unforeseen approach had somehow pleased him. How he had managed to sneak up on her, she did not know, particularly as she had been learning how to discern whoever approached by the characteristic sound of their steps. After her father's introductory lesson on the art of psychic defence, she had already begun to grasp how a seemingly insignificant sign could be used to great effect, including an awareness of who approached. Since then, she had continually practised the skill, and this only made Volkiev's approach all the more disconcerting.

She cast aside the thought and opened her mathematics book. Volkiev smiled amiably, his lined features exuding a warmth that contrasted sharply with Mirkstone's habitual glower. 'Ah, Lily, how are you today?'

'I'm fine,' Lily replied curtly, still a little nonplussed. 'And you, Ana?' she added a little more politely.

'Yes, I too am well. Now, I suggest we continue with Boolean algebra and explore its applications in electrical circuit theory. I believe this will tie in nicely with some of the more, er, practical applications you've been learning from your father.'

Lily briefly wondered how much her father discussed with her tutors and Volkiev's comment suggested a level of collusion that she had previously underestimated. Nevertheless, the reference to her father sparked an increase in her concentration that carried her through the lesson in growing anticipation of his return.

Thankfully, the afternoon passed considerably quicker than the morning, and Lily was astonished when Volkiev gathered up his books in preparation to leave.

'Okay, Lily. You've worked extremely well today, and as a reward, I think we can finish early. What do you say?'

Lily returned Volkiev's smile and nodded excitedly. She jumped up from the desk before her tutor changed his mind.

'Now, before you go, perhaps you'd be kind enough to do me a favour?'

Lily hesitated, suspecting a catch that would see the end of her burgeoning plans for what remained of the afternoon.

'Could you drop this off in your father's study? It's a book I promised him,' Volkiev said.

Lily relaxed as she accepted a book entitled *Mathematics in the Fourth Dimension*. 'What's it about?'

'Nothing for you to worry about, Lily. Now run along before I find another job for you.'

'See you tomorrow, Ana,' she said, turning quickly on her heels while clutching the book. She was surprised when Volkiev did not reply, and as she left the room, she glanced back to see that he was no longer looking in her direction. He remained seated and was staring into space, apparently lost in thought with a sad expression etched indelibly across his face. Lily promptly cast the memory aside and took the stairs two at a time in her hurry to reach the study. With her father not due home for several hours, she would still have plenty of time for a game of marbles or a cup of tea with the boys.

She burst into the attic, eager to deposit the book and get away as fast as she could, but as she crossed the room, she came to a shuddering halt when she noticed that the instruments and books on her father's desk had been disturbed. Inevitably, her gaze fell upon the largest gadget amidst the clutter, the Historoscope, which lay askew on its stand. She instinctively reached out to reposition it, but as she did, the gold and silver veins coursing across its surface burst into life, pulsing with light. Although her father had never allowed her to use the Historoscope, she had watched him operate it, and she knew that it should not behave in this manner. She raised it off its stand and weighed it in her hands. The metal veins continued to flash, throwing off beams of light in all directions, and Lily felt a barely discernible vibration coming from the instrument that sent a thrill of expectation flowing up her arms.

Without a second thought, she raised the Historoscope and pressed the lens to her eye. She almost recoiled when a maelstrom of bright, swirling colours appeared on the screen. Even as she questioned how this could happen without the use of the skullcap, she was transfixed by the beauty of the kaleidoscopic images

341

materialising before her. She stared in surprise at the blurred lights as they coalesced into a coherent image of her father sitting alone by the fireside. She flinched when he turned to look in her direction as if she had somehow disturbed him from the reams of paper lying in front of him. He was sitting in the drawing room downstairs, and Lily gasped when he got up from the chair, set the papers down on the armrest and made his way towards where she imagined her own ghostly image was floating in mid-air. She was relieved, however, to see him pass beyond her viewpoint and open a window. Lily knew that the scene was merely a record of a past event stored inside the Historoscope, but she could not understand how the image had appeared without her activating the machine; whatever else, this was not how it was supposed to work.

Lily watched her father return to the chair only for a gentle breeze to lift the sheaves of paper from the armrest and scatter them onto the floor. As he scrabbled around on his hands and knees to pick them up, it dawned on her that she was viewing a scene that had taken place many years ago. Her father looked much younger, his long, straight hair free from the telltale streaks of grey she had come to know so well. The furrowed brow and crow's feet around his eyes were absent, replaced by a carefree expression Lily had rarely seen in the time since her mother's death.

As she viewed the scene, she felt a pang of regret at the loss of the father she had once known, and mournfully realised that he had changed forever from that fateful moment, as undoubtedly, she had too. She found it absurd that, with the passage of time, they had slowly drifted apart despite the shared bond of their loss. She also felt guilty for prying on her father in such a voyeuristic fashion, but with the reassuring weight of the instrument in her hands, she realised she was watching no more than an imprint of a memory. She briefly wondered whether the scene was just an irrelevance, but when her father sat down and rearranged the papers, there was an urgent rap on the door that made her sit up and pay attention.

'Come in,' her father called out.

The double doors opened, and Albright shuffled into the room. Judging by the careworn expression on his habitually placid features, her father's manservant carried the weight of some burden on his shoulders. 'It's Miss Schalk, sir. She's at the door. She seems to be a little distressed.'

'Saskia? Show her in at once, Albright,' said Price, sounding shocked.

Lily clutched the Historoscope tightly and watched transfixed as she witnessed the events unfold. She wondered when this meeting had taken place and was greatly puzzled by the look of astonishment that had appeared on her father's face in response to Albright's announcement.

A few moments later, Albright ushered a figure, clad from head to foot in a long, sweeping cloak, into the room. The hood was up over the woman's head, obscuring her features from view, but the ease and familiar grace with which the woman deported herself left Lily in no doubt that the image was that of her mother. Lily's heart was pounding as the woman lowered her hood. She felt a sudden, unexpected rush of emotion, and gasped as she looked at the face of her long-dead mother. While Saskia appeared younger than at any time Lily had known her, she looked tired and drawn and her eyes were puffy, suggesting she had been crying.

'Henry, please forgive me for coming here, but I ... I had nowhere else to go,' she said in a voice quivering with emotion.

Price looked at her with a mixture of puzzlement and concern. 'You know you're always welcome,' he said matter-of-factly. 'It's just that I wasn't expecting you. After all, it's been a long time,' he said, moving slowly towards her as if he was unsure how to greet her.

He stood uncomfortably a few feet away before eventually ushering her towards the chair he had just vacated. He offered to take her cloak, but she shook her head resolutely, pulling it tightly about her as if it afforded some sort of protection.

Saskia sat down and stared melancholically at the fire. 'I know I haven't been in touch since I left the Academy but you made it pretty obvious how you felt. I didn't want to make matters any worse than they already were, especially as I left with Pearly,' she said in a voice little more than a whisper.

Lily could see her father bristle at the mention of his rival's name but just as quickly regain his composure. 'And how's your work been going?' he said unenthusiastically as if he was reluctant to hear the answer.

'Well, thank you,' she replied, smiling for the first time since her arrival, 'although it seems to have reached a natural conclusion.'

'I'm not sure I follow.'

'Pearly doesn't need me any more. That partly explains why I'm here, but I'll come on to that later if you don't mind. I want to make sure I explain everything properly; it's the least I can do,' she added nervously.

'Very well,' replied Price, still looking bemused.

'You recall that I was collaborating with Pearly at the same time that we were working together at the Academy. In retrospect, I realise what a mistake that was, but I never appreciated the depth of animosity that exists between the two of you,' said Saskia as if she had carefully rehearsed her words.

'Perhaps you're right,' replied Price with a sigh, 'but that still doesn't explain where you've been and what you've been up to these past couple of years. I've not heard a thing since you left, and now you just turn up on my doorstep.'

'I know, Henry, and I realise how it must appear, but please, hear me out. I'm sorry to barge in like this, but like I said, I know how much I hurt you.'

Price raised his eyebrows but passed no comment.

'Don't forget that we had completed our research, whereas my work with Pearly was only just beginning. That's why I left with him, although I know you never saw it that way. As it transpires, perhaps you were right,' she added bitterly.

'What do you mean?'

'Let's just say that things didn't work out as I expected.'

'What happened? Is something wrong?'

'Far from it,' replied Saskia with an ironic laugh. 'The work yielded results beyond our wildest expectations.'

'So what's the problem?'

'As you warned me, Henry, the problem is ... well ... Pearly himself.'

Price looked on impassively, unable or unwilling to comfort the woman sitting opposite him as a single tear rolled silently down her cheek. He sat patiently, waiting for her to expand upon the missing time since they had last met.

Finally, Saskia drew herself up in the chair and wiped away the tear with an elegant flick of a fingertip. 'As you well know, I've always been interested in metals, and in particular, the fusion of metals as a means of storing information. One of the early spin-offs from this was, of course, the Historoscope. That was only the beginning as far as I was concerned, and I knew there was so much more I could achieve. You were so busy with everything else, and with your mind on other things, I turned to Pearly. I was flattered by his enthusiasm for my work. When he found out what we'd achieved with the Historoscope, he could hardly contain his excitement. He told me that he'd been carrying out similar research and wondered whether I'd be interested in collaborating with him. He convinced me that, by pooling our expertise, we'd achieve so much more together. Naturally, I couldn't help but be bowled over by his zeal. I immediately agreed to work with him when he left the Academy.'

'What were you working on?'

'Pearly was studying the transfer of information into something far more sophisticated than the Historoscope. He was looking to fabricate a vessel that could retain the memories and thoughts of a living person.'

'What! You mean by capturing the essence of a living soul?' said Price with a look of disgust.

'Maybe ... I don't know,' replied Saskia hesitantly. 'I'm not sure what he planned. I'm sorry. I was so taken in by it all. I just didn't think it all through. I suppose I got carried away.'

'What happened?' prompted Price.

'Pearly was experiencing considerable difficulties in the interpretation of an ancient alchemical text he'd managed to get his hands on. He saw in the work that you and I had carried out together the opportunity to resolve those issues.

'I hate to admit it now, but we formed a good partnership and collaborated well together. Initial progress was slow, but we gradually began to close in on Pearly's objective, although I still wasn't sure exactly what that was. Unfortunately, my relationship with Pearly deteriorated quite suddenly barely a few weeks ago.'

'Why?'

'I'm not sure I can answer you, Henry. Rather perversely, Pearly became more and more disinterested in our work, despite how well it was going. The change in his behaviour coincided with the appearance of another woman, and for whatever reason, he started spending more and more of his time with her.'

'What were they up to?'

'I don't know. He wouldn't discuss it with me.'

'Did you meet her?' demanded Price.

'No. Her name's Aurelia Nightshade. Do you know her?'

Price thought for a moment before he shook his head.

Lily detected no hint of recognition on her father's face as she continued to eavesdrop on the scene with deepening interest. She withdrew the Historoscope and considered the conversation she had just heard. She felt a growing sense of unease but was not sure where it stemmed from. She shivered involuntarily. Something was not right with her parents' stilted conversation, but she could not put her finger on it. There was no doubt that the meeting had taken place sometime before she was born, and her parents were behaving in a manner she had never witnessed before. Perhaps what was to come would provide an explanation. She lifted the instrument back to her eye and picked up the scene from where she had left off.

'It all came to a head this evening when Pearly joined me in the laboratory,' said Saskia. 'I don't know why, but he was in a foul mood. Not surprisingly, we began to row. You know how volatile he can be, and in the end, he just exploded and told me to pack my bags. I thought he was joking, but the look on his face told me otherwise. I was scared, Henry. I thought he might do something to me and ...' her voice trailed off and she bowed her head, making Lily suspect that she was crying.

Price regarded her quizzically but did not speak.

Eventually, Saskia looked up, wearing a puzzled expression as if she was weighing something up. 'I'm sorry for coming here like this, Henry, but I had nowhere else to go.'

'That's all right. It's ... it's nice to see you,' he replied hesitantly, but with a little more warmth than he had displayed earlier.

'Thank you, Henry, but before anything else, I think there's something you should know,' said Saskia quietly.

'Yes?' said Price, frowning.

Lily felt her heart thumping, sensing the scene was reaching its climax, and although the images on the screen seemed to blur at the edges, it did not detract from the events as they unfolded before her eyes.

Saskia did not reply but slowly rose from her seat. She untied the knot that had been holding the robe loosely about her neck. When it was free, she dropped her hands and allowed the garment to slip from her shoulders into a crumpled heap on the chair behind her.

Lily stared transfixed at Saskia's strangely calm expression, and as her eyes trailed down to take in the rest of her mother's appearance, she gasped at the sight of her tight-fitting blouse and the unmistakable smooth, round bulge of her abdomen. Lily glanced sideways and caught the dawning realisation as it appeared on her father's face. The colour drained from his cheeks as he stared at Saskia with an expression of pure horror.

'You're ... you're ...' he said, unable to finish the sentence.

'Yes,' replied Saskia levelly. 'I'm having a baby ...'

The scene was wrenched from Lily's view as the Historoscope spiralled from her hands, striking the wooden floorboards with a resonant thud. She stood there for a few moments, unable to grasp the meaning of what she had just witnessed. She stared vacantly at the now motionless instrument. Her head wheeled in a rush of nausea as she fell back into her father's chair. She did not want to think about what she had just seen, but the implications were clear. Henry Price was not her father! There could be no other explanation. Even worse was the overarching sense of terror regarding who her true father must be. She did not want to believe it, but she had seen the evidence for herself. She had to get away. Her father—no, how could she call him that?—would be back soon, and she could not face him now.

That was it; she needed time to think. As she stumbled towards the door, she thought about the way her father had treated her since her mother's death, and she began to sense the inherent truth of what she had just witnessed.

Lily forced her mind to empty; this was no time for reflection, she told herself as she flew down the stairs. She dived into her bedroom, grabbed a rucksack from the end of the bed, and without a second thought, filled it with a random assortment of clothes plucked from a multitude of drawers. Just before she left, she went over to the bowl of seashells perched on the windowsill and carefully unravelled the contents, one by one, until she spotted a chocolate brown shell speckled with brown and white spots—a Snakehead cowrie—the shell she had found with her mother all those years ago. She scooped the tiny object into her hand and slipped it into a pocket before leaving the room without a second glance.

Lily swept down the gently curving staircase into the hall. She moved cautiously, hoping to avoid Albright and the probing questions that would undoubtedly arise courtesy of the rucksack strapped securely across her shoulders. She tiptoed into the kitchen and was greeted by the unmistakable sound of Mrs Brimstork singing (the housekeeper cooked like an angel, but sang like a wailing banshee). She crept furtively towards the door, sneaking behind the cook's ample frame as she kneaded dough while singing Puccini's 'Butterfly Chorus', a feat quite marvellous to behold were it not for Lily's dark mood. She slipped soundlessly through the door and checked all around her before darting across the lawn. She pulled up the collar of her denim jacket to shield herself from the raindrops that tumbled as she brushed past the foliage, and cursed herself for forgetting to oil the hinges that creaked as she opened the gate at the bottom of the garden. She made off along the path but suddenly froze at the sound of a snapping twig. She spun round and stared into the dwindling light then chided herself for her edginess. Of course there was no one following her; why on earth would there be?

Lily strode purposefully towards the old railway embankment, passing through the previously bent railings and onto the path that led towards the canal basin. She broke into a run, eager to reach her destination as quickly as she could for the refuge she was sure the boys would offer her. The overhanging branches tore at her clothes as she fought her way along the overgrown path. Finally, with a flurry of swinging arms, she burst into the clearing beside the canal, but just as quickly stopped stock-still. Panic welled up inside her as she turned her head, first one way and then the other, but no matter which way she looked, she could not avoid the indisputable fact that the boys and their boat were nowhere to be seen.

23

Na Cruacha Dubha

L ILY SPRINTED TOWARDS THE canal desperately hoping she
would find her friends somewhere nearby. She had been so
preoccupied with the theft that she had not been down to visit the
boys and with this thought came a sudden surge of remiss at
neglecting them. Nonetheless, Lily could not accept that Aedh and
Seoc would just up and leave without a word of goodbye. She
approached the spot where the narrowboat had been moored and
feverishly scouted the area for clues suggesting why, or even when,
the boys had left. There was no discernible evidence that a boat
had ever been there, but she soon found the telltale signs of a
smouldering fire next to the towpath, raising her spirits that she
had stumbled into the clearing not long after the boys' departure.
She even raised a smile when she spotted a glass marble lying in a
small patch of grass adjacent to a gaming circle the boys had carved
on the surface of the towpath. Her amusement turned to concern
when she realised that the beautifully ornate, multicoloured
marble was Seoc's most prized possession, one he had proudly
won from her in a mammoth encounter a few months earlier. She
could still recall the whoops of joy that had emanated from the
young boy's mouth when, for once, he had got the better of her.
With a jolt, Lily realised that something was amiss; Seoc would
not have misplaced this trophy without good reason. There was
no time to lose; she had to find the boys.

Lily knew that the boat would make slow headway on the

overgrown waterway, and if the boys had only just left, she would still have every chance of catching them once they stopped for nightfall. She immediately set off at a steady pace, but a sudden rustle from a copse of trees made her jump and spin round. She sighed in relief when a wood pigeon emerged from the trees and flapped harmlessly over her head. She wondered whether she was becoming unnecessarily edgy, but then recalled the sound of a snapping twig when she had left the garden. She shuddered involuntarily; perhaps someone was following her after all.

As she rushed to catch up with the boys, Lily kept her senses heightened, utilising the techniques she had learnt from her father while on the lookout for any other clues the boys might have left for her. Her anxiety eased as she made progress along the towpath, but here and there the track was blocked by lush undergrowth, and in one place, the path had disappeared where the canal wall had collapsed into the water. After a long sweeping bend, she was amazed to see a variety of objects protruding through the water's surface. There was no sign of the boat, and she wondered how the boys had managed to steer the craft through the partially submerged debris that made the canal look like a bizarre obstacle course comprising of man-made icebergs. She stopped and gazed uncertainly at several smaller tributaries leading away from the canal's main trunk, doubting whether any of them were navigable given the rubbish blocking their entrances. She opted to follow the main route, but by now, the light was beginning to fail. With a shiver, she realised that she had to find the boys or risk spending the night outdoors, which was not an attractive proposition bearing in mind she had left without any suitable clothing and had nothing to shelter in.

Lily's resolve started to falter when she followed the channel into a deep cutting where long, eerie shadows obscured the path. She thought she caught a glimpse of a flashlight behind her and turned to stare fixedly into the twilight, scrunching up her eyes to pierce the darkness that was rapidly gathering about her. Strange, nocturnal noises replaced familiar daytime sounds, only serving to heighten her unease, and when the light failed completely, panic welled up inside her that rivalled the moment she had viewed her parents' shocking confrontation through the Historoscope.

Lily desperately tried to keep moving, but an overcast, moonless night hampered her progress even further, and she nearly toppled headfirst into the water when she tripped on a hidden branch. Still she stumbled blindly on, ever hopeful that she would be greeted by the welcoming lights of the boat that she hoped, rather than expected, to find safely moored around the next bend.

Lily tried to quell her plummeting spirits and ploughed on steadfastly as the temperature dropped, but as the prospect of finding the boys gradually dwindled, the harder it became. Once again, she thought she saw a light behind her, reaffirming the frightening prospect that she was not the only one out and about on the canal.

Just then, an arm shot out in front of her, pulling her into the undergrowth. As she fell, she felt another hand wrap around her mouth, stifling her cries. She thrashed her arms, desperate to escape, but she soon realised she was not strong enough to break free from this powerful assailant. Panic welled up inside her, and a terrifying thought flashed through her mind that whoever had grabbed her meant to kill her here and now. She resisted the urge to fight back and called up a force deep inside to repel the attacker, yet perversely, as she relaxed she felt the muscular arms around her also slacken. She sensed the warmth of a man's breath next to her ear, and as he began to speak, she immediately recognised the voice.

'Shh, Lily, don't say anything, just listen ...'

Those simple words were the most beautiful thing she had heard all day; it was the gentle voice of Aedh, and not the deadly assassin she had supposed it to be! She had found the boys after all, or rather, they had found her. She did as Aedh bade and waited for him to continue.

'Seoc and I have been watching you for some time now. A man was following you,' Aedh whispered. 'We had to make sure he didn't see us, so we waited until dark. Seoc was hiding by the canal when you went past, and when the chance arose, he cut in between you and your pursuer. Seoc led him off in the opposite direction. Your tracker's now in pursuit of Seoc, thinking he's still following you. Seoc will take him on a wild goose chase, just you wait and see! He'll meet us back at the boat as soon as he can; it's hidden just a couple of miles away. Come on.'

'How can you be so sure Seoc's all right?' whispered Lily nervously.

Even in the dark Lily could tell that Aedh was smiling, simply by the tone of his voice. 'Oh, don't you worry about him. Seoc can look after himself. He's the best tracker I've ever seen. He can appear and disappear at will in this environment. Come on, Lily, there's no time to lose. Let's get going before your stalker realises he's been duped. He's sure to come back this way once he does.'

'What's been going on? I—' Lily began, but Aedh forestalled her with a finger to his lips.

'I'll tell you when we're safely back at the boat, but for now, make sure you don't waste any more energy other than on following me. Come on …' he said, and with that, he set off confidently, ridiculing the dark Lily had found so hostile.

Aedh set an exacting pace, and Lily soon lost all sense of direction as the route he set weaved first one way and then the other. She assumed that they were no longer following the towpath, judging by the haphazard directions Aedh took. Now and again, he whispered to warn her of some unforeseen obstacle. Lily wondered how he managed to see so well in the dark and supposed it was because of the tracking and hunting skills he had acquired while fending for himself and his brother.

Eventually, after almost thirty minutes of relentless marching, Aedh's pace slackened. 'We're almost there now, Lily,' he announced. 'Wait here while I check the boat. I need to make sure we've had no unwelcome visitors.'

While Lily waited, she heard the distant call of an owl immediately followed by a much closer reply, and once more, her feeling of vulnerability returned, making her fervently wish that Aedh would be back soon.

She was not disappointed when Aedh appeared a few minutes

later. 'Come on, Lily, the boat's just round the corner,' he said, and with a tug on her sleeve, they were off.

Aedh was now confident enough to strike a match, which he held aloft in front of his face to guide them the last few strides towards the boat. As they edged forwards, Lily could still not see the outline of the boat, which was expertly tucked behind a clump of bulrushes that gently rustled in the breeze. Aedh parted the tall stems to reveal the prow of the boat, and on its hull, the name Lily had longed to see ever since she had arrived at the canal basin to find the boys missing.

'Na Cruacha Dubha,' she said, almost reverently.

'Follow me,' said Aedh, heading towards the stern. 'Let's go inside and wait for Seoc. I don't think he'll be long.'

Aedh and Lily were soon safely ensconced in the warm, comfortable interior of the boat. Aedh lit an old but perfectly functional oil lamp and placed it on a small table, amply illuminating the galley in a dull, warm glow. The blinds had been drawn, and Aedh assured her that no one would see the light from outside.

While Lily sat waiting nervously for Seoc to return, Aedh busied himself by preparing a wonderfully hot, spicy herb infusion, which the pair held cupped between their hands and drank in silence. Lily could feel the oddly aromatic liquid revitalising her after a single sip.

'So what's been going on?' asked Lily as soon as she had drained the dregs of the strange, green liquid.

'I could say the same to you, Lily,' returned Aedh with a cadence in his voice that sparkled with amusement.

Lily studied the features of her friend in the dimly lit cabin. His hair was its usual untidy mess, falling in tangled knots onto his shoulders. His bright hazel eyes shone with warmth and enthusiasm, and she realised just how much she had missed the company of her friends. After the earlier troubles of the day, Lily felt herself relax despite the circumstances. 'I ... I was just coming down to see you.'

Aedh smiled. 'I know you well enough by now to realise there's more to your story than that, but no matter, it can wait. Let me tell you what happened to us while we wait for Seoc to get back.'

Lily was horrified. 'Seoc! Of course, we should be out looking for him. He could be in trouble.'

'Relax. Seoc's more than capable of looking after himself. What you need to realise, Lily, is that Seoc and I are used to the odd scrape or two, and while Seoc may look young, he's mature beyond his years. We've had to fend for ourselves for some time now. I trust Seoc, as you should too. He'll be back soon enough. Now, while we wait, let me explain what's been going on.'

Lily nodded, if a little reluctantly. 'Yes ... of course.'

'The morning started much the same as usual. Seoc went to check the traps while I went off to fetch some water. We'd just lit a fire and hadn't been back on the boat for long when we heard footsteps. As a matter of fact, we both wondered whether it was you as you'd not been down to see us for a while,' he added without any hint of reproach.

'I ...' began Lily sheepishly.

Aedh held up a hand to forestall her. 'It's no matter, Lily. We hold no sway over when you visit, but when you do, it's always a pleasure,' he said kindly. 'Now, where was I? Ah yes, footsteps! We realised someone was coming, and moments later, there were some loud whacks on the galley door. It sounded like they wanted to smash it down.'

'What did you do?'

'I opened the door and came face to face with a very unsavoury looking man.'

'What did he want?'

'He was very aggressive and told us we were trespassing. He ordered us to clear off in no uncertain terms.'

'And did you?'

'You know me, Lily. I just laughed. I told him we'd been moored up for months without harming anyone or anything. I also told him that I couldn't possibly see how a canal could be on private land.'

'What happened?'

'He just got angry and told us we were no more than common criminals. He issued us with an ultimatum: either clear off or face the consequences.'

'What did you do? I can't imagine you letting someone intimidate you like that.'

'Under normal circumstances you'd be right, but when he pulled a gun on me, it didn't really leave me with much choice.'

'What!' said Lily aghast.

'I'm afraid so, Lily. He pointed it right at me, and I certainly didn't feel compelled to argue. Whether he'd have used it, I don't know, but I didn't want to find out.'

'So what happened?'

'I told him we didn't want any trouble and I agreed to do as he said. He told us that he wouldn't leave until we'd gone. We had no choice.'

'Yes, I can see that,' said Lily, nodding her head in earnest.

'It didn't take long to pack up, and we were ready within the hour, but while we gathered up our belongings, Seoc and I had the chance to talk.'

'Planning something, no doubt.'

'Aye. We'd both already come to the same conclusion. There was something strange about this man, and his story didn't add up. Don't forget we've been moored on that stretch of the canal for the best part of six months and we've never seen sight nor sound of anyone like that before. It just seemed odd for him to show up like that and start behaving in such a threatening manner.

'We decided that we wouldn't just take off as he suggested. We agreed that, once we were out of sight, I'd take the boat and hide it safely downstream while Seoc doubled back to follow the man and find out what he was up to.

'Once I'd found a decent spot for the boat, I went back to meet Seoc. That's when it all started to get interesting.'

'Why?' enquired Lily, eyeing Aedh inquisitively.

'Seoc didn't have to follow him very far. The man led him directly back to your house!'

'No!' gasped Lily in astonishment.

'The man was stationed in a hideaway with a direct view of the back of the house. By the way he was set up, Seoc reckoned he must have had the place under surveillance for at least a couple of days. From time to time, the man made forays around the house to look at it from different angles as if he was waiting for something.

'After watching him for several hours, Seoc came back to rendezvous with me at the canal. We decided that we'd try and get word to you, but that was when events overtook us.'

'Why? What happened?'

'I think you probably know the rest. We headed back to the house, but as we sneaked towards the garden, we realised something was already going on. Fortunately, we saw you coming before you saw us, and we guessed, correctly as it turned out, that the man was following you. We returned to the canal assuming you were on your way to visit us. Seoc had the presence of mind to drop a marble he'd won from you. He knew you'd realise it was a sign that all was not well. We couldn't chance intercepting you there and then, particularly as the man was armed. That's why we decided to wait until it was dark before we put our plan into action. I think that just about brings us up to date.'

'That explains the snapping twig. I thought someone was following me. What does this man look like?'

'Swarthy features, possibly Mediterranean. In his fifties, I would hazard. Deep-set, cold eyes, and a nasty, livid scar across his cheek that looks like it may have been recent. Also, he hadn't shaved for a few days,' Aedh added as an afterthought.

'Doesn't ring any bells,' said Lily, shaking her head. 'You say he hadn't shaved ... that would support Seoc's view that he'd been watching the house for a few days. What do you think he was after?'

'I don't know, but the fact that he set off after you seems to suggest that it has something to do with you.'

'What on earth could he possibly want with me?'

'I'm not sure, but maybe Seoc can tell us. He'll be back any minute.'

'How can you possibly know where Seoc is?' said Lily with a combination of excitement and astonishment.

'Did you hear that owl hoot again a moment ago?'

'Er, yes, I think so.'

'It was Seoc. Listen, that'll be him now.'

Just then, Lily caught the sound of the bulrushes parting, and moments later, Seoc's beaming face appeared at the galley door.

'Ah ... you both ... made it!' Seoc called out gleefully amidst great heaving breaths.

'Looks like you're out of shape, little brother. Look at the colour of your face!' said Aedh, obviously pleased to see him. Aedh draped an arm around his brother's shoulder and pushed the bolts across the door to lock it securely behind him.

'What happened?' said Lily.

'Led him right round the houses, I did. We won't be seeing him again before the crack of sparrows,' said Seoc jovially. 'Now, what about some nettle beer?'

'Come on, Seoc. Tell us what really happened. I'll get you a hot drink; now's not the time for beer.'

'You're such a bore,' replied Seoc, pulling a face behind his brother's back as Aedh filled the kettle. 'Very well then, keep your pants on. Sit down, and I'll tell you.'

When the three friends were comfortably seated around the table with mugs of steaming cocoa in hand, Seoc began to recount his tale.

'I managed to nip in between Lily and that old fool following her,' he said, revelling in their rapt attention. 'It wasn't very difficult to lead him astray once it got dark; he wasn't very good at tracking, if truth be told.

'I led him to a derelict worksite a couple of miles from here. I've been there a few times, and I know the place like the back of my hand. It's a bit of a death trap if you don't know your way round. There's all sorts of rubbish 'n stuff scattered all over the place.'

'The kind of place you have a habit of exploring,' said Aedh, smirking at his brother.

Seoc returned the gesture. 'I led him towards an old shaft of sorts, and before he knew where he was, he'd stumbled right into it!' he said triumphantly.

Lily frowned. 'Was he hurt?'

'I'm surprised you're bothered, Lily. I suspect this man meant you harm, so I wouldn't worry about him, if I were you,' replied Seoc dismissively.

Aedh cast his brother a reproachful look.

'Keep yer hair on, you two. He didn't fall very far; 'bout ten feet or so, I would hazard. Heard him moaning but I didn't hang around to offer him a hand out,' he added sarcastically. 'Don't think he'll be troubling us again this evening, though.'

'That's good,' said Aedh. 'Well done, Seoc, you did a grand job.'

'Did you hear that, Lily? Rare praise indeed, eh bruv?'

They all laughed before Lily downed the dregs of her cocoa and felt the last vestiges of her earlier anxiety dissipate.

'So, Lily, were you coming down to see us when that idiot set off after you?' said Seoc.

Aedh cast his brother a reproachful look. 'Maybe we should discuss this in the morning,' he said, butting in before Lily could reply.

'No, it's all right, Aedh. You both deserve an explanation. It's the least I can do after all you've done for me. The truth is ...' said Lily, hesitating, 'well, the truth is, I've run away from home!'

The cabin remained silent for a few moments before Aedh spoke. 'You're welcome to stay with us for as long as you like,' he said as Seoc beamed at Lily over his brother's shoulder.

'Why did you—?' began Seoc, but Aedh thrust a hand unceremoniously over his brother's mouth, blurring the words into an unintelligible splutter.

'I'm sure Lily doesn't want to talk about it at the moment, Seoc,' Aedh said, still holding a hand firmly over his brother's mouth. 'There'll be plenty of time to discuss this once we're underway tomorrow. I think we should aim to be off at first light. I don't want to risk anyone finding us here. The boat's reasonably well hidden, but if someone really wants to find us, I don't think they'll have much trouble during daylight. Come on,' he said, finally releasing his grip on Seoc's mouth. 'It's time to get some sleep. We need to be up early tomorrow. Seoc, why don't you take Lily to the prow? She can have the bunk there. Oh, and Seoc, no more questions!'

Seoc glared at Aedh, and as he ushered Lily through the bulkhead to the sleeping area, he whispered to her out of his brother's earshot, 'I do have one question, Lily.'

'What's that?' she replied with a frown.

'Can I have my marble back?' he said with a beaming grin.

24

The Baobab Tree

ABEL STRANGE LOOKED UP at the sign swinging lazily above his head and squinted. The poorly-lit, cobbled alley made the sign difficult to see, and he could barely make out the silhouette of an odd-looking tree with a tall trunk and sparse foliage set against the backdrop of a barren landscape. The Baobab Tree. How strangely incongruent to name a pub after a tree of the African savannah, particularly in such an insalubrious part of town, he observed, but at least he was in the right place. He pushed on the heavy wooden door and made his way into the tavern's gloomy interior.

Strange's thick-lensed glasses misted over the moment he edged into the densely packed room. He removed the spectacles to wipe away the condensation but then struggled to discern the blurred outline of the person standing in front of him. He replaced the glasses, and immediately, the inhospitable features of a harsh-looking woman came sharply into focus from the other side of the bar.

'Yes?' she demanded.

'I, er, am looking for …' he spluttered.

Before he could finish, the woman held up a hand and pointed towards a dimly lit cubicle in the corner of the room. ''E's over there. Now, what you be drinkin'?' she said, scowling.

Strange ordered a half pint of beer, much to the woman's disgust. She turned her back on him and filled a glass from an oaken cask, and when she thrust the tankard down on the bar, half of the contents slopped over the side. She stared intently at Strange, challenging him to complain, but he looked demurely away. He paid the woman an over-inflated price for the cloudy ale and made off in the direction she had indicated.

Strange squeezed into the space between an old wooden bench and a small square table, but in the murky light, he had to squint to discern who was sitting opposite. It was a man he was both expecting and dreading to see in equal measure. Josef Frankl sat smiling grotesquely back at him, a small, empty glass and a bottle of cheap whisky inches from his hand.

'This is about the best this place could manage,' Frankl said, gesturing with a nod in the direction of the bottle.

As Strange settled down on the bench, he realised with a start that a second man was seated at the far end of the table hidden in a small alcove, his face obscured by shadow. From where Strange was sitting, he could not get a clear view of the man's face, but he could tell from the silhouette of straggly, unkempt hair that the man nodding amicably in his direction was Liquid Lex.

Strange smiled at Lex then regarded Frankl uneasily. 'I was worried you hadn't, er, made it, Josef.'

Frankl raised his eyebrows. 'You didn't seriously think that I'd drowned in the sewers, did you? If I was going to die, I think I'd have chosen somewhere a little more fitting, don't you?' he said animatedly.

As Frankl spoke, a small gob of spittle escaped from beyond the confines of his megalithic teeth. Strange flinched involuntarily as the projectile flew towards him, but to his relief, it passed him by and landed harmlessly on the wall behind. 'I ... er ... we ... er, all did, yes,' he replied unconvincingly, casting a glance in Lex's direction for support.

'Well, I hope you weren't disappointed,' replied Frankl with a mocking smile.

'I'm well aware of your, er, abilities, Josef, but I feared for your safety. With the force of the, er, water, it seemed impossible that anyone could survive ... even you,' he added as an afterthought.

'I'm disappointed you should doubt my talents, Abel, but nevertheless, here I am,' replied Frankl with an extravagant flourish of his arms.

'As I assumed when the black pearl arrived at the Academy this morning. I did not doubt who'd sent it, but for the sake of, er, completion, tell me, Josef, how *did* you escape?'

'Now that *is* a question! Lex has been very patient waiting for you to arrive, and now that you're both here, I'm sure you won't be disappointed.'

Frankl refilled his glass and took a slug of cheap liquor. 'It was rather unfortunate that our meeting in Wren's Cache was curtailed. It was just as well we'd almost finished our conversation, although there were a few outstanding issues to discuss. I'll come on to those presently, but first, let me explain how I escaped.'

Strange nodded unenthusiastically.

'When I saw the water heading our way, I cannot deny that I feared for our fate. The memory of Club still lingers, after all, eh, Lex? Fortunately, I was never so vain as to wear a toupee,' he said, patting his bald head.

A palpable silence followed Frankl's pitiful joke, yet he continued his narration undeterred. 'I knew I could never keep up with Aurelia once she'd disappeared into the tunnel,' he said proudly, resting a hand on his corpulent belly that spilled over his trousers. 'I had little choice but to use my singular skills to extricate myself from the deluge. Though I say it myself, my solution was far more elegant than fleeing like a bunch of sewer rats.'

The men ignored the slur and waited expectantly for Frankl to continue.

'It wasn't easy raising such power with millions of tons of water bearing down on me, but rather than take flight, I summoned a source of plasma to protect myself by fashioning it into a bubble to act as a shield.'

Strange felt his stomach lurch. He had heard of alchemists performing such feats before but never anything of this magnitude. Students undergoing the rigours of alchemical training at the Academy were inevitably taught defensive spells, but something of this complexity was beyond the capabilities of even the most talented tutor. Plasma could be contained within an electromagnetic field and used as a buffer, but to use it in this fashion was a different matter entirely.

'What are you talking about?' said Lex, looking nonplussed.

'Plasma is a gas of ionised, free electrons,' Strange explained. 'At exceedingly high temperatures, it's viscosity is so great, no other matter can pass through it. The ability to produce and contain such a force is unheralded and has only ever been used to repulse a projectile such as a sword thrust or bullet. It's unheard of for anyone to effect control over power of this nature for a prolonged period, yet that is what was necessary for Josef to protect himself,' Strange extolled, suddenly regarding Frankl in a new light.

'I couldn't have explained it better myself, Abel, and it's heartening to see you're impressed. I'd like to say it was nothing, but as you well know, it was indeed a momentous achievement.'

'So how did you get away from Wren's Cache?' Strange enquired.

'Contained within my protective shell, I rode the wave, buffeted by the tunnel walls on my perilous journey to the river. It was difficult to concentrate for so long, but with certain death at every turn, it sustained me while I was carried like a ball on the waterspout of a whale. When I neared the Fleet, I glimpsed three figures scurrying upriver as I emerged from the tunnel. The flood took me in the opposite direction with the rest of the flotsam, and soon enough, I found myself dumped unceremoniously into the river,' Frankl said theatrically, revelling in the rapt attention of a starstruck audience.

'Utterly exhausted, my power faltered and I tumbled headfirst into the river, or rather, I should say mud as it was low water. I eventually emerged from that pit of filth covered from head to toe in cloying muck and stumbled up the embankment looking like a clay golem. Fortunately, there were few onlookers at that early hour apart from a ragtag bunch of ne'er-do-wells and vagabonds, who turned and ran at the alien vision they saw approaching.'

Nothing usual in that then, Strange thought as he surveyed the hideous bulk of the man seated opposite.

'Three days it was before I managed to eradicate the last traces of that infernal mud, not to mention the bruises from the battering I took in the fall.'

'Ah, yes, Josef, but look at what you, er, achieved,' said Strange, fighting to contain his admiration for a man he had always loathed.

'Yes,' added Lex, nodding hesitantly, as if he was not entirely sure that what he was hearing was the whole truth.

'Indeed, my friends, indeed,' replied Frankl. 'I know, of course, that you all made it safely back; but what of your actions since?' he added, allowing his effusive mood to evaporate into one of threatening malevolence.

Strange looked flustered. 'I ... well, er ... we didn't know what to do. We waited for news of you.'

'You mean you waited for my bloated body to turn up on the Isle of Dogs,' said Frankl darkly.

'No!' cried Strange loud enough to be heard above the hubbub coming from the bar. A group of unsavoury looking men turned round to see what all the fuss was about but quickly lost interest and returned to the pressing engagement of supping their ale.

'Lex returned to the sewer the following day to see if he could find any sign of ... your ... er ... I mean ... what happened to you.'

'And rather unpleasant it was, too, going back so soon,' said Lex. 'You can imagine what I expected to find after all that rain.'

'We had men scouring the riverbanks and visiting your usual haunts, but we found nothing,' said Strange. 'It was as if you'd vanished into thin air. The river's currents are notorious and the tides treacherous. Bodies take weeks to wash up, and often many miles downriver. We feared you'd drowned, and the longer we waited, the more likely it seemed. And now you turn up wondering what we were doing. What did you expect us to do, thinking you were dead? You've kept your plans hidden from the outset. It's about time we had some answers,' said Strange, feeling emboldened by the ale.

Frankl laughed, sending a further barrage of saliva in Strange's direction. 'Well, well, Abel, I do believe you're threatening me.'

Strange did not reply and turned to Lex for support.

'Abel's right, Josef,' said Lex. 'It's time we had some answers.'

'You'll have your answers this very evening,' said Frankl.

'Er, you mean you're actually going to tell us what this is all about?' said Strange uncertainly. 'Does that mean Aurelia's on her way, too?'

'Unfortunately, she's otherwise engaged. What is planned for us tonight does not require her sublime talents, although I do not doubt she'll be utilising her skills to the best of her abilities elsewhere at this very moment.'

'What are you talking about?' demanded Lex.

'You have a short memory, Lex. Have you already forgotten my last conversation with Aurelia?'

'You mean just before the sluice gates opened?' said Lex.

'Indeed! We're about to enter the final phase of my plan, but it's imperative that everything is timed to perfection.'

'So, er, what exactly is Aurelia up to?' said Strange, draining the dregs of ale from his glass.

'Do you recall Aurelia's less than enthusiastic response just before we were so rudely interrupted?'

Strange nodded. 'You mean, er, about abducting Price?'

'That's right,' said Lex. 'She wasn't too impressed, if I remember rightly.'

Frankl smirked. 'I contacted Aurelia some days ago, and I'm pleased to say that, after a brief conversation, she had a change of heart. She's currently in the throes of conducting the task I set for her.'

'But surely seizing Price is beyond even Aurelia?' said Lex.

'I think, perhaps, you underestimate her, Lex. She knows that every man has his weakness, and Price is no exception. She has no intention of going directly to Price, but believes—and in this I'm sure she's right—that he will present himself to her.'

'And what makes you think that?' asked Lex sceptically.

'Aurelia has managed to lure Price's daughter away from the house she shares with him and, as we speak, she's planning her abduction. With the girl as a bargaining tool, Price will do anything to get her back.'

'Er, yes, and that will undoubtedly make him more dangerous than ever,' said Strange.

'Perhaps, but like I said, don't underestimate Aurelia. Now that she realises what's at stake, she won't let us down.'

'Aurelia knows your plans?' said Lex, sitting bolt upright. 'It's about time you shared your thoughts with all of us. We're equal partners in this, I assume.'

'Indeed we are, Lex, indeed we are. Now drink up, men, it's time we were on our way,' said Frankl, peering at his wristwatch through the smoke infused atmosphere.

Strange raised his eyebrows. 'Where are we, er, going?'

'We're off to visit Dr Lucas Neil. His premises are just round the corner. Come on,' said Frankl, struggling to lift his bulk off the stool.

Strange looked confused. 'Er, what on earth do we need to see a doctor for?'

Frankl leant forwards and whispered conspiratorially in Strange's ear. 'You may know him better as Dr Luca Nexus, but he no longer practises under that name for reasons perhaps even you might recall, Abel,' he said acerbically. 'Now, if you wish to be involved, I suggest you follow me.'

'That's exactly it, Josef. Involved in what?' said Strange, making no move to vacate his seat.

'You still haven't got it, have you? For a man of such prodigious intelligence, Abel, you sometimes display a complete lack of common sense. Go on, Lex, tell him,' he said, finally defying gravity and pulling himself up from the stool.

'Tell him what?' said Lex, shaking his head vacantly.

'Very well,' said Frankl, and as he shuffled towards the exit, he grabbed Strange by the arm, pulling him forcibly from his seat. 'Come on, men, we're going to visit an old friend of ours. You won't want to miss this!' he cried with a look of frenzied excitement on his face. 'We're off to see Pearly!'

25

THE STONE OF MADNESS

The Shaman

STRANGE RUBBED WARILY AT his arm after being yanked unceremoniously to his feet. He was still unsure of what Frankl had in store for them, and it took him a moment to catch up with Lex, who had set off after Frankl along the narrow cobbled street. It felt chilly after the warm ambience of the tavern, and Strange shivered due to a combination of the unseasonably low temperature and Frankl's final words as he was leaving the bar.

'Ah, I see you've decided to join us,' said Frankl. 'Come on, it's not far.'

'B-but … ' spluttered Strange.

'Hurry up, and you'll see,' Frankl said impatiently.

The two men followed Frankl in silence through a neighbourhood of depressingly similar streets until he pointed towards a terraced house that was entirely in keeping with the equally shabby properties surrounding it. The paint was peeling off rotten wooden window frames, and the rickety front door hung askew, indicating that the house was desperately in need of maintenance.

Frankl strode confidently up to the front door and gave it a loud rap with a wooden cane that he was carrying to support himself. Strange wondered whether the door would splinter from the force of the blow, but the tone rang out resonantly, suggesting the door was far sturdier than it looked.

The door opened to reveal a tall man whose face was hidden

in shadow. He invited them in without reservation, confirming that he was expecting them, and one after the other, the men marched silently inside.

The man bolted the door behind his guests then flicked a switch to illuminate a surprisingly spacious antechamber plushly decorated in a manner that contrasted strikingly with the property's exterior. The men craned their necks at expensive artwork adorning the walls and marble busts nestling on sturdy columns as they followed their host into a larger, but equally luxurious, room towards the rear of the property. The room was lined with bookcases housing a vast range of medical literature, and in a far corner sat an oak desk with several large books open on stands, displaying grisly anatomical plates.

'It hasn't changed much,' Lex whispered to Strange, shivering involuntarily.

'You've been here before?' Strange asked behind Frankl's back.

'Ten years ago,' Lex affirmed.

Frankl turned round and glared. 'Shh!' he said, ushering them forwards.

'Abel Strange, I presume. Pleased to meet you, my name's Luca Nexus,' said the householder, extending a hand in Strange's direction. 'And, of course, we've already met,' continued Nexus, shaking hands with Frankl followed by Lex. He directed the men towards a sofa adorned with opulent drapes and fashionable cushions. 'It's a pleasure to welcome you all here at last. I've been waiting a long time.'

Nexus was wearing an exquisitely cut Italian silk suit that fitted him perfectly. He had an angular, gaunt face framed by groomed, shiny black hair and a neatly cropped goatee, which he stroked methodically as he spoke. Strange estimated that Nexus was in his early fifties, but his effortlessly manicured appearance was deceptive; he could easily have passed for ten years younger.

'Can I offer you some refreshment before we begin?' Nexus said in a slightly clipped, foreign accent that Strange found difficult to place.

'That won't be necessary, Luca,' replied Frankl on behalf of his comrades. 'I think we should get down to business.'

Nexus nodded. 'Of course.'

'Now, there are a few things we need to clear up before we begin,' said Frankl. 'Lex, perhaps you'd like to start?'

Lex looked perplexed. 'I'm not sure wha—'

'Perhaps you'd like to begin with the night Pearly died. There are a few things Abel needs to know,' cut in Frankl.

'Ah, yes,' replied Lex with a look of dawning comprehension.

'What, er, are you talking about?' demanded Strange, frowning.

'Please don't interrupt, Abel,' said Frankl, holding up a podgy hand. 'Just be patient and let Lex continue.'

Strange glared at Frankl like a scolded schoolboy but kept his counsel.

'You probably know much of what happened that night, Abel, but there are certain things that you were never told.'

'What! Er, such as?' demanded Strange sullenly.

'I hardly know where to start,' said Lex. 'It was such an odd evening from start to finish.'

'In what way?'

'Well, for a start, I still don't know why Pearly came with us; it wasn't as if it was an important job, but he was determined to be involved. Internal Security were swarming all over the place as soon as we broke in, and from that moment on, Pearly's behaviour was very peculiar.'

'Why? Er, what did he do?' Strange asked.

'He knew it would've been risky trying to escape, but nothing's impossible; after all, he'd done it before. For some reason, though, he decided to stay put. He knew that Fox would send for Price, and for some reason, he was determined to wait. I was in the stairwell leading to the roof when Price arrived. I alerted Pearly and he immediately came up. After Price blew up the door, Josef and I tried to follow Pearly onto the roof, but he sent us back. We observed the proceedings from the hatch and watched in horror when Price sent Pearly tumbling over the parapet. My instinct was to run to his aid, but Josef dragged me back, reasoning that we had to get to Pearly before anyone else. We descended the stairs and found an exit where I took out the guard with one of Aurelia's beloved concoctions. We set off in search of Pearly, and by the time we found him, he was dead. Josef barely had time to retrieve the stone before one of Fox's men turned up. We only just managed to get away in time and return to a nearby safe house.'

'Is that, er, it?' said Strange.

'Not quite. Once we were at the house, it wasn't long before Josef ordered me back to the factory.'

Strange looked nonplussed. 'That's ridiculous! What for? I can't even remember why you went there in the first place.'

'A chemical for the doctor,' Lex said, inclining his head towards Nexus. 'Something fundamental to his research, I believe. Pearly knew exactly what to look for and where to find it, and although we had no intention of staying there for no more than a few minutes, Fox and his men arrived the moment we broke in. I still don't know to this day how they got there so fast. We must have been set up, I suppose, but we never found out who was behind it. With Pearly dead, anyone with ties to the Order scarpered quicker than ale turns to piss.'

'So why, er, exactly did you go back?' said Strange.

'For Pearly's body, of course!'

'His body!' Strange repeated. 'Er, what for?'

'All will become clear, Abel, but for now, hear Lex out,' said Frankl.

Lex cleared his throat. 'When I returned to the factory, I watched the comings and goings for some time. Price and Fox were with Pearly's body, and soon after, a pathologist joined them. They spent some time going over the body, but eventually, they bundled poor old Pearly into an ambulance emblazoned with the name of the old Eastern Hospital. I suppose it was the ideal place to take the body given the circumstances. It was originally built as an infectious diseases unit, but by then, it was in the throes of being demolished. I knew the hospital wasn't far, so I followed on foot. They took the body straight to the morgue, and after a couple of hours, the pathologist left the body in the care of a mortuary attendant with one of Fox's men standing guard.

'Fortunately, I still had a supply of Aurelia's darts, and so it didn't take much to take out the guard. The mortuary attendant was happy to turn a blind eye for a wad of cash, and he even lent me the keys to the ambulance. So off I went with Pearly's body.'

'Where did you go?' Strange asked.

'I thought you'd have guessed by now, Abel. I came here.'

'What!'

'That's right; those were Josef's instructions. I left the body with the doctor together with the vials Pearly had stolen from the factory, and I've never been back since … until tonight, that is.'

'So what, er, happened to Pearly's body?' said Strange.

'Why, the body's still here,' replied Frankl. 'Luca, please be good enough to explain what you've been up to these past ten years.'

Nexus rose from his chair, rhythmically stroking his beard while carefully appraising his guests. 'Before I start, I ought to tell you about my relationship with Pearly,' he said, looking down his thin, pointed nose at his audience. 'We became extremely close, you know.'

Strange raised his eyebrows but passed no comment while he waited for Nexus to elaborate.

'I came to his attention not long after he'd left the Academy because of my eminence as a neurological surgeon and my innovative surgical techniques. My groundbreaking research was respected the world over.'

'Doesn't think much of himself, does he?' Lex whispered to Strange behind the back of his hand. 'Not sure fame's the right word for it … more like infamy. Wasn't he struck off?'

Nexus glared at Lex but continued undeterred. 'Pearly was fascinated by my work, and in particular, a paper I'd written on a new stabilisation system for the cervical spine following exposure of the skull base. He was also interested in my work on cryonics,' Nexus continued, barely stopping to draw breath.

'Cryonics?' repeated Lex, sounding bemused by the complex medical terminology.

Nexus sighed. 'Cryonics is the freeze-preservation of tissue following death.'

Lex shook his head uncomprehendingly and looked around for support, but Frankl gestured for Nexus to continue.

'Pearly saw the potential in my work, which is more than can be said for those idiots at Queen's Square,' spat Nexus, exhibiting a brief show of rage. 'Pearly believed in what I was doing.'

'Even when you were struck off?' said Lex.

'I was struck off because of an orchestrated campaign led by ignorant fools in the medical profession,' replied Nexus, self-consciously rubbing at a tic that had appeared at the corner of his eye. 'By then, I'd been collaborating with Pearly for some time, and despite my erasure from the medical register, he was happy to provide financial backing that allowed me to continue with my work and still live comfortably ... as you can see,' he added, gesturing at the opulent surroundings. 'He also set up a research foundation that supported me after his death—'

'Explaining how you managed to carry on with your interest in cryonics,' interrupted Frankl.

'Exactly. Well before Pearly's death, my research had already broken new ground. After considerable success working with animals, it was a natural progression to begin trials on human volunteers. My patients were happy to act as guinea pigs, knowing that my research would not necessarily benefit them, but fervently understanding the long-term benefits for all of mankind. Somehow, word got out, and I found myself at the centre of a witch-hunt. Colleagues feigned outrage at what I'd been doing. They claimed my work was unethical, but they didn't understand. Once the press got wind of it, I was doomed. An enquiry was set up with an outcome that was inevitable, and after a hearing that barely lasted a couple of days, I was banned from practising medicine. I was hung out to dry.'

'What did your research involve?' enquired Strange.

'The extraction and preservation of nerve cells.'

Strange frowned. 'Was it successful?'

'To some extent, yes. Cells die when they're frozen because

of intracellular ice crystals that form during the process. The damage is irreparable, and this, in essence, is the conundrum associated with cryonics. I developed a mixture known as a cryoprotectant with the aim of preventing the damage that results from cellular freezing.'

Lex shook his head. 'I'm not sure I understand.'

'Hmph.' Nexus sighed again. 'I'm trying to explain as clearly as I can.'

'Go on,' Frankl prompted, 'but perhaps you could be a bit more simplistic ... for Lex's sake,' he added in an attempt to placate both men.

'If I must,' Nexus replied. 'For years, scientists have fervently believed that cryonics would provide the means to prolong life and that freezing cells would prevent the deterioration seen after death. In this way, a body afflicted by disease could be stored until a time when they might be cured. Unfortunately, cryonics was plagued by many obstacles and this was only made worse by the charlatans aiming to make an easy buck from the sick and the desperate. Not surprisingly, cryonics fell into disrepute, and the way I was treated bears testimony to this,' he added bitterly.

'However, toiling in secret, I overcame the many difficulties that had previously beset my work, slowly making many unique advances to counter the lethal effect of ice crystal formation by preserving the cells in a suitable medium prior to freezing, thus raising the possibility of returning them to full functionality at a later time.'

'And were you, er, able to accomplish this?' asked Strange.

'I believe my cryoprotectant will prevent cellular damage when the freezing process is reversed, yes ... although there is one major problem,' Nexus said guardedly.

'And, er, what is that?'

'The preservation of the brain.'

'As I suspected,' said Strange with a sad shake of his head, 'but if this is unachievable, then surely the problem is insurmountable?'

'Indeed, Abel, but we shall see,' Nexus replied enigmatically. 'Freezing is unrivalled at maintaining the structural integrity of any organ, and when thawed out, it is possible to return the organ to full functionality, but for one rather glaring exception. Just imagine the possibilities, however, if we could preserve a person's brain without disruption to personality, thoughts, memories … emotions even. It would allow the possibility of true revivification.'

'Revivification! I'm beginning to get an uneasy feeling here,' said Lex. 'I delivered Pearly's body to you ten years ago, and all we've heard so far is talk of cryonics, and now, revivification. What does it all mean?'

Nexus smiled nervously. 'Perhaps Josef will answer that for you.'

'All in good time, Luca, but for now, perhaps you'd be kind enough to continue.'

'Very well, Josef. I'm afraid, gentlemen, that the ultimate goal of preserving the psyche following death remains tantalisingly out of reach. The brain is decidedly different to other organs. Trying to maintain a network of neurons so that intangibles such as memories and thoughts are retained has, sadly, proved beyond my grasp.'

'Why?' asked Strange. 'If you can make it work for, er, other organs, then surely why not the brain?'

'The cell that is fundamental to the function of the brain is the neuron—a cell that is decidedly different from all others in the body,' replied Nexus. 'A delicacy exists between neurons that make them unique. They interrelate with cells of their own kind and communicate via dendrites and synapses to create a complex neural network, thus explaining their multifaceted abilities. It is also the reason why freezing has little chance of success in preserving the brain's functional integrity.

'It is only recently that we've come to understand the mechanisms that allow long-term memories to be retained in the brain. The hippocampus and limbic system are critical areas for storing memories, but just how are these memories stored? Through diligent research, I have demonstrated that when precise sequences of electrical activity pass between neurons in a part of the brain known as Papez's circuit, it creates memories by chemically encoding these patterns in discrete, spatially positioned cells. It's hardly surprising that freezing destroys such a complicated arrangement. No, I'm afraid, gentlemen,' Nexus concluded categorically, 'the central nervous system is such a delicate network of cohesive circuitry that it cannot be maintained in the way that I had once envisioned.'

'But surely Pearly must have believed differently? Otherwise, he'd never have invested so much time and money in your work,' said Strange.

Nexus shrugged his shoulders. 'Perhaps. We shall see,' he repeated in the same mysterious manner he had displayed before.

'Let me, er, get this straight. Pearly's body was brought to you on the night he died. So, are you, er, saying that his body is still here?' Strange queried.

Nexus smiled. 'Pearly's body is indeed still here, and I have preserved it in the exact same state as the night that Lex delivered it to me. It was the least I could do bearing in mind that Pearly died in the act of aiding my work.'

'What do you mean?' asked Strange.

'Pearly understood the problems I'd experienced with manufacturing a cryoprotectant. He helped fathom out where I'd gone wrong, and with his great analytical mind, he worked out what I needed to perfect the mixture. To my dismay, it was this very chemical that Pearly was in the act of stealing on the night that he died.'

Lex nodded. 'I always wondered what Pearly wanted from a refrigeration plant. He wouldn't tell us what was in the vials he took, and we never had the chance to question him.'

'For obvious reasons,' said Frankl scornfully.

'So, what exactly is this chemical?' asked Strange.

'N-methylformamide, which when combined with dimethyl sulphoxide and ethylene glycol, forms the perfect solution for cryopreservation.'

'So ... er ... what exactly have you done with Pearly's body?' asked Lex, sounding unsure of whether he really wanted to hear Nexus' answer.

'Nothing,' replied Nexus casually, 'apart from keeping it stored here all these years.

'Let me explain,' he continued. 'The biggest problem following death is that cells begin to perish the moment breathing stops. The brain is exquisitely sensitive to a lack of oxygen. Fortunately, it was a bitterly cold night when Pearly died and it was not long before his body arrived at the hospital for refrigeration. Just a few hours after Pearly died, Lex delivered his body to me in a near-perfect state, apart from the fatal injuries, of course. Lex also brought me the final ingredient for the cryoprotectant.

'We were lucky with how it all panned out. Pearly left explicit instructions outlining what I was to do should the circumstances ever arise, and so I did not deliberate.'

'So, er, what exactly did you do?' Strange enquired.

'I prepared the cryoprotectant and readied the machinery for vitrification.'

'Vitrification?' repeated Lex.

'Yes. It means "transformation into glass", and describes the process of lowering the body's temperature so that it hardens as it's frozen. By this method, the body's cells remain stable for thousands of years.'

'And that's what you've done to Pearly?' said Lex, looking as if he was about to throw up.

'When I received Pearly's body, I dealt with the injuries then removed what remained of his blood and replaced it with the cryoprotectant before rapidly cooling his body to its glass transition point.'

'What on earth is that?' queried Lex.

'Approximately minus 135 degrees Celsius, to be exact,' replied Nexus casually. 'The temperature at which all water solidifies.'

'Such rapid cooling cannot be simple,' said Strange, intrigued.

'Indeed, but by using a vapour of liquid nitrogen, Pearly's body has been kept safely frozen for these past ten years,' Nexus exulted.

'So what do we, er, do next?' said Strange, squirming apprehensively in his seat.

'That's for Josef to say,' said Nexus. 'I've done all that was asked of me, and while I can thaw Pearly's body out, his brain has no chance of recovery ... unless, of course, Josef can tell me otherwise ...' he said, allowing his words to trail off enigmatically.

Frankl eyed him uncertainly. 'Pearly never revealed the true nature of the stone, but I believe he foresaw a time that would culminate in this meeting.'

'Are you saying he, er, planned all this?' said Strange dubiously.

Frankl shook his head. 'No, not exactly, Abel. Although I *am* convinced that Pearly knew exactly what I'd do with the information he left for me. All he did was sow the seeds.

'Just think about it. He gave me barely enough information to start the ball rolling, yet he anticipated where it would all lead, which is why we're here tonight. Now, Luca, perhaps you can tell us what you know of the stone,' continued Frankl with a feverish anticipation shining brightly in his eyes.

Nexus nodded. 'Very well, Josef. Perhaps you're right ... we'll see,' he added pensively.

'I first met Pearly a couple of years after he'd left the Academy. He came to see me one evening with a beautiful woman in tow. Her name was Saskia Schalk. She was a woman of extraordinary talent and had been working with Pearly on a strange metal alloy fused by an obscure alchemical method. Although he kept the details from me, Pearly asked me to aid him in his work. I accepted without hesitation.'

'Why?' enquired Lex.

'You know how convincing Pearly could be. He offered me facilities and finance beyond my wildest dreams, and never asked anything of me in return ... that is, until some years later, when he appeared here unannounced requesting my aid in a most peculiar task.'

'What was this task?' said Lex.

'He brought with him a small, perfectly smooth, spherical metallic object, as red as blood, which he referred to as the stone. He asked me if I'd implant it into his brain. Naturally, I was perturbed. His request was unconventional, to say the least. I explained as best I could the grave risks that surgery of this nature would involve, but he would not be swayed. He led me to believe that the implant would boost his already considerable alchemical talent, and against my better judgement, I agreed to help. I didn't have much choice; like I said, Pearly could be very persuasive.

'Pearly had already funded a fully functioning medical facility on these premises where, it just so happened, I could conduct my work without intrusion. And so it was that I implanted the stone just as Pearly dictated. Fortunately, the surgery proved uneventful.'

'When, er, exactly did you perform this surgery?' enquired Strange.

Nexus hesitated. 'It was about seven or eight years before he died.'

'Where's the stone now, Josef?' said Lex.

'Safely here,' replied Frankl, tapping his breast pocket. 'And soon it will be back exactly where Pearly planned,' he added mysteriously.

Lex sighed. 'What are you saying, Josef? Surely it's about time we had some answers?'

'Very well, Lex. Since our last meeting, I've been busy making the final preparations for what is now so tantalisingly close. I began by coming here some days ago to explain to Luca what we must do with the stone.'

'Indeed,' said Nexus, nodding his head. 'I was always intrigued by the stone and found it unimaginable that Pearly, a man of such immense power, would put himself at risk for what appeared to be so little gain. In the years that followed the implantation of the stone, I got to know Pearly better, and he slowly came to trust me. Eventually, he gave me a more meaningful insight into the true nature of the stone, but I still harboured some doubts. Now, with the information that Josef has recently divulged, it goes some way to explaining why Pearly was prepared to take the risk.'

'Exactly! And if Pearly was right, then we sit on the brink of immortality,' said Frankl eagerly.

'Perhaps ... we'll see,' said Nexus, still sounding unconvinced.

Strange sighed. 'Why did you keep us in the dark for so long, Josef?'

'Oh, Abel, you're far too sensitive. It's only since I met Luca that I finally realised what Pearly's intentions were for the stone,' replied Frankl irritably. 'Once I'd learnt of Luca's involvement and what he'd done with Pearly's body, it all fell into place.'

'So what do we do next?' asked Lex uneasily.

'First the body will need rewarming, and then I'll replace the stone,' said Nexus. 'After that, I believe it's down to you, Abel.'

Strange glanced uneasily at Frankl. He nodded and bowed his head, lost in thought. The room remained eerily silent until he finally stirred. 'There's, er, just one thing that concerns me,' he said, addressing Nexus. 'You perfused Pearly's body with a chemical mixture to prevent damage during freezing. Surely the risk will be the same when you rewarm the body?'

'Very astute, Abel. Rewarming is even more problematic than freezing; this is known as the revitrification problem.'

'Which is what, exactly?' said Strange.

'The cryoprotectant doesn't prevent ice crystal formation on rewarming and so the risk of cellular damage remains.'

'You don't seem too, er, perturbed by this. How can you be so confident?'

'The damage can be prevented by rapid rewarming. I've designed a system utilising radio frequencies that allows the body to be rewarmed in seconds without damage to the tissues.'

'Is this something you've tested?' asked Strange.

'Of course. I've not been idle these past ten years,' Nexus replied waspishly. 'I've tested the machine on numerous occasions, thus allowing me to freeze and rewarm organs without detriment. I've no doubt it will succeed. If there are failings in what we are about to embark upon, believe me, Abel, they lie elsewhere …' he said, staring challengingly back.

'And what of the injuries Pearly sustained in the fall?' said Strange.

'That won't be a problem,' Nexus replied confidently. 'I dealt with them the moment Pearly's body was brought to me. Damage to the liver combined with multiple fractures caused massive internal haemorrhage. I evacuated the blood lying within the abdomen, repaired the lacerations to the liver and injected some stem cells for good measure. Fractures of the pelvis and lower limbs also required stabilising. It took some hours, but it was worth it. I didn't wish to delay freezing the body, but it didn't take long to infuse the cryoprotectant as most of the blood had already been lost.'

A look of revulsion appeared on Lex's face, but he passed no comment.

'Now, is there anything else?' continued Nexus, eager to press on.

'Yes. There's still more I need to know. Impressed as I am with how you dealt with the, er, injuries, if all the blood was replaced, what will happen when the body is rewarmed? Without blood, the organs will never function,' said Strange, unconvinced by Nexus' supreme self-confidence.

'Ah, yes, now I'm glad you brought that up. Even you will be impressed by this,' he replied patronisingly.

Strange raised his eyebrows.

'The principal function of blood,' began Nexus as if addressing a class of students, 'is the transportation of oxygen from the lungs to the tissues. Needless to say, carbon dioxide moves in the opposite direction. The erythrocyte, or humble red blood corpuscle, performs this function due to the haemoglobin it carries. This unique molecule binds oxygen and carries it through the bloodstream, where it releases it for cellular metabolism.

'Prior to meeting Pearly, I'd been working on replicating biological gas transfer by man-made means. There were many obstacles in creating an artificial mechanism that would work just as well, but with Saskia's help, I achieved this goal.

'She could work materials in ways I could not begin to comprehend. She had alchemical skills beyond even Pearly, and with her aid, I overcame the difficulties that had plagued the project to develop a prototype of the cell.'

'Why go to such bother?' said Frankl. 'Why not perform a blood transfusion after rewarming?'

'Because it wouldn't work,' replied Nexus matter-of-factly. 'A transfusion only works in a living organism. The blood would clot almost immediately and render it useless. No. I synthesised the only viable solution, and one that offers enormous benefits to the recipient—a mechanical replica of the red blood cell!'

Strange nodded thoughtfully. 'That sounds, er, intriguing. Please go on.'

'With Saskia's metallurgical know-how, we engineered the ultimate biocompatible cell: a spherical, hollow geometric lattice divided into three internal compartments to carry oxygen, carbon dioxide and water for ballast. Because the skeleton of the cell is composed of a strong organic geodesic matrix, it can transport gases at much higher pressures than normal, thus allowing physiological abilities far outweighing our own.'

'You seem to be implying that your cells confer superhuman powers on the recipient,' said Strange.

'Exactly!' replied Nexus jubilantly. 'These cells are almost six times more efficient in their oxygen carrying capacity than existing red blood cells. I've calculated the maximum dosage Pearly's body can tolerate based on his height and weight, and I aim to deploy one thousand trillion devices.'

'So what does it mean for whoever receives these, er, cells?'

'The recipient will be able to swim unprecedented distances underwater or run flat out for prolonged periods. Perhaps you now understand why I prefer my own method to something as crude as a blood transfusion?'

'Forgive me, but surely these, er, cells require an energy source to function?' said Strange sceptically.

'Again, you're correct. The cells contain chemomechanical turbines that generate power by drawing in glucose from the blood and combining it with oxygen they're carrying to power the various cellular subsystems. This allows the gases to be pumped in and out of the cell by mechanical sorting rotors in response to the gas saturation pressures of the tissues, and these are continuously monitored by onboard chemoreceptors situated on the cell membrane.'

Strange nodded sagely. 'A unique fusion of alchemy and medicine. Again, I'm impressed, but how are you so certain these cells—what do you call them?—will work?'

'Lucacytes!' replied Nexus, smiling at his play on words. 'They won't let me down, Abel. You'll just have to trust me.'

'Time will tell, Luca,' said Frankl. 'Perhaps we should see for ourselves.'

'Very well, Josef, follow me. I'll take you down to the medical facility,' said Nexus, getting up from the chair and heading towards the door. Frankl and Strange jumped up to follow him, but Lex remained firmly seated.

'I don't think you'll have need of my services,' Lex said. His face had turned a sickly green hue, perfectly matching the jade vase sitting on the occasional table next to him. 'I think I'd prefer to wait here. It was bad enough bringing Pearly's body here the first time. I'd rather not face it again.'

'Very well, Lex, you stay here, although why you'd want to miss this is beyond me,' said Frankl, shaking his head incredulously.

'Oh, you know me, Josef. I've always been a little squeamish. I'm happy to wait,' he said, sitting back in the comfortable chair and helping himself to a cigar from a box on the table next to him.

'That's a Cohiba Esplendido you have there, Lex. Just make sure you don't waste it,' said Nexus jovially as he entered the hallway.

Nexus walked past a triangular wood panelled space nestled beneath the stairs that ended at a small door. He fumbled for an oddly shaped key hanging on the wall, placed it in the keyhole and turned it through several rotations. The door grumbled in protest, hinting at a far more sophisticated mechanism than a simple mortise lock. The door slid open with a hydraulically-sounding hiss, and as Nexus crossed the threshold, the men peered over his shoulder, eager to see what lay beyond. Nexus led them down a flight of stairs where the air was cool and the steps slick with condensation, making for a treacherous descent despite a dull light spilling up from the chamber below. The men emerged from the cramped stairwell onto a semicircular balcony that overlooked a spacious operating theatre housing several tables variously festooned with medical paraphernalia and grisly looking surgical instruments. The men's eyes were inexorably drawn towards a rectangular glass case prominently positioned on a conveyor belt in the centre of the space. The glass was frosted, and in the dull, throbbing light, it was impossible to make out what lay inside.

'Is that, er …?' began Strange uneasily.

Nexus nodded, his mind elsewhere, already deliberating over his next move. His eyes darted back and forth at the equipment in front of him until they settled on a squat machine. He licked his lips feverishly as he reached out for the multiple gauges and knobs bedecking the panel. He hit a line of buttons in a seemingly random order, and immediately, three sickly-green lights flashed in quick succession as the device powered up.

Strange looked anxiously around, searching for the source of a deep, resonant hum that rose up from the chamber below.

'Perhaps you'd be kind enough to tell us what you're doing, Luca,' boomed Frankl, struggling to make himself heard over the slowly intensifying sound.

'Oh, yes, of course,' Nexus replied absent-mindedly. 'That's the magnetron you can hear. It'll take a few minutes to warm up. In the meantime, we wait …'

The lights flashed insistently, but Nexus' eyes never strayed from a conspicuous gauge in the centre of the console. The needle flickered hesitantly before it began to climb inexorably towards a bold red line unmistakeably marked with the word, 'DANGER'.

'We're almost ready!' Nexus called out suddenly.

Beads of sweat had gathered on Nexus' forehead, and the sickly hue of the console's lights reflected in the depthless orbs of his eyes gave him the look of an archetypal mad scientist.

'Now!' cried Nexus, striking a lever on the console with great gusto.

Strange felt his stomach lurch as he watched the glass case trundle methodically along the conveyor belt towards a thick-walled receptacle recessed in a small alcove. Moments later, the glass container disappeared from view.

'What's happening?' cried Frankl.

'The body's gone into the resonant cavity,' shouted Nexus, trying to make himself heard over the loud hum of the machine and the vibrations of a vast array of surgical instruments laid out on metal tables.

'This'll only take a few seconds,' he barked confidently. 'The radiofrequency generator can rewarm to rates of 100,000 degrees Celsius. It's timed to ensure that the mechanism cuts out once the body's temperature reaches two degrees below normal.'

Just as Nexus had predicted, the noise emanating from the machine suddenly died, and the vibrations ceased. Nexus pulled on the lever and the conveyor belt kicked into reverse.

Strange stared open-mouthed, waiting for the opaque glass case to reappear, but when a small, body-shaped form materialised from the machine covered in a simple linen shroud, he gasped.

'Come on, we have to move quickly now,' said Nexus, bounding down a short flight of steps into the chamber with Strange and Frankl following closely behind.

'Bring that pump with you,' Nexus ordered, gesturing behind him as he crossed the room to a stainless steel sink at the side of the enclosure. He grabbed a nail brush and began frantically scrubbing his hands.

Nexus donned a pair of gloves, picked up a small object from a tray of medical instruments and approached the table. 'First, I must insert a cannula into the antecubital fossa,' he said, brandishing a long, thin needle and lifting back the shroud to expose a ghostly pale arm. He worked with great dexterity and inserted the needle into the fleshy skin of the corpse. He grabbed a transparent tube dangling loosely from the pump that Strange had dragged across the room and connected it to the cannula. Without looking down, he flicked a switch on the pump with a deft kick of a boot.

'This shouldn't take long,' Nexus called out above the thrumming of the machine that was gently rocking back and forth. 'The apparatus will remove all the remaining bodily fluid. See, it's already collecting in the container,' he added, pointing to a bell jar attached to the pump into which droplets of a murky-looking fluid were beginning to condense.

'Surely, er, the pump cannot remove all of the fluid?' queried Strange.

Nexus shot off towards a corner of the room. 'It doesn't matter, Abel,' he replied, opening a small fridge and fumbling for a malleable bag filled with liquid.

'Anything left of the cryoprotectant will be of little significance. If we're successful, the small volume that remains will be excreted by the kidneys.'

The bag of fluid was transparent but simultaneously radiated a mesmerising array of colours that shimmered like a rainbow. Even after Nexus had suspended the bag from a drip stand, the liquid continued to swirl, suggesting it held a life of its own.

'We're ready,' said Nexus, disconnecting the tube from the pump and reconnecting it to the bag, still awash with colour.

'I'm about to infuse the Lucacytes,' he said while dexterously rotating a circular tap on the tube, allowing the solution to pool in a small chamber and drip slowly through the cannula into the body.

'The infusion's set for thirty minutes. The Lucacytes are suspended in a solution of dextrose saline that will provide sufficient energy to permeate every nook and cranny of the body. The cells are saturated with oxygen, and once they reach the capillaries, the gas will diffuse into the tissues and perfuse the body in preparation for the final stage.

'And now, while the body completes its final rewarming, it will leave me just enough time to replace the stone. Josef, if you please?' he said, turning to Frankl and stretching out a hand.

Frankl reached inside his jacket and hesitated. He reluctantly withdrew his hand, extending it slowly towards Nexus before unfurling his stubby fingers to reveal a blood red stone nestling in the centre of his palm.

Nexus stooped to examine the object. 'It hasn't changed since I last saw it,' he observed, reaching out. He weighed the stone in his hand and set it down on the table beside the body. He peeled back the shroud to reveal a body that was lying face down and swept back a shock of untidy black hair to expose a gaping vertical wound in the back of the corpse's neck.

'P-Pearly?' said Strange uncertainly.

'Of course. Who else were you expecting?' said Frankl.

Nexus worked in silence, alternating between an array of lethal-looking instruments laid out on a Mayo table next to him. He selected a retractor resembling two bent forks attached at the waist, which he placed parallel with the skin and ratcheted open, improving visibility and access in one fell swoop. His hands moved in slick, graceful motions, meticulously dissecting the inanimate tissue until he had developed a deep pocket in the back of the neck.

Suddenly, he pulled a hand from the wound without allowing his eyes to stray from the surgical field. 'Someone pass me the stone,' he commanded.

Frankl was the first to react. He reached out and picked up the stone and deposited it in Nexus' hand.

Nexus' hand trembled as it hovered over the body before he plunged it deep into the wound. 'There!' he cried triumphantly. 'That was easier than I expected. When I first placed the stone all those years ago, I had to fashion a small cavity at the base of the brain to secure it, but now ... well ... it fits perfectly!'

'Odd,' said Strange pensively. 'Why's that?'

'I'm not sure. Foreign material typically produces an inflammatory response inside the body ... but here ... well, if anything, I'd say it's the opposite. It's almost as if the stone had blended in with the surrounding tissue before it was removed. I've never seen anything like it!'

'Perhaps you were too quick to doubt, Luca,' said Frankl.

'We'll see,' replied Nexus, picking up a pair of needle holders.

Once he had closed the incision, Nexus set the instrument down, doffed his gloves and wiped the sweat from his brow. 'The infusion's almost through,' he said, watching the last drops of fluid empty from the reservoir into the cannula. 'I've done all I can. The body's just as I promised, Josef. It's up to Abel now, although I still have grave doubts about how any alchemical reinvigoration will work,' he said, craning his neck to admire the neat line of knots he had placed to close the wound.

'You'll see, Luca,' said Frankl, smiling grimly. 'Are you ready, Abel?'

Strange nodded slowly, deep in thought. Once he had deciphered the manuscript and learnt of Pearly's attempts to recreate the living stone, he had always suspected it would come to this. He still felt a lingering annoyance that Frankl had not told him about Pearly's body, but at least it answered the question that had troubled him most. Piotrowski's experiment had ended in disaster, but with Pearly's body as a viable option into which the stone could be reimplanted, everything had changed. Resurrection had always been one of alchemy's central tenets inextricably linked to the mystery of the living stone, and now, with the stone returned to Pearly's body, it was down to him, Abel Strange, to perform the ritual that would restore Pearly's body to life ... or so he hoped.

Strange's head wheeled with the enormity of what he was about to attempt. 'Er, perhaps you'd be so kind as to turn the body,' he said, closing his eyes and steadying his breathing.

While Nexus and Frankl were struggling with the body, Strange's mind drifted back to his time as a student at the Academy. He recalled the rapid blossoming of friendship between Pearly and Henry only for it to be supplanted by rivalry and jealousy. The young Strange had always been there as a buffer to his friends, forever the steadying influence, but while they had channelled their considerable talents into dark and mysterious alchemy, he had shunned those areas of lore for a greater understanding of spiritual learning and alchemical healing. On completion of his studies, Strange had travelled the world in search of mystical cultures to enhance his already encyclopaedic knowledge of healing. From the medicine men of the Oroqen and the sangomas of the Nguni to the shamans of the Inuit and the curanderos of the Amazon, Strange had never ceased in his quest for learning.

Soon after his return, he was called upon to demonstrate all he had learnt when a gang of Lex's men were ambushed during an attempt to replenish the Order's dwindling coffers. In the mayhem that ensued, one of the Order's men was shot, and although the gang escaped with the bleeding man in tow, it was left to Strange to save him. To Lex and his men as they stood back and watched, it looked as if Strange was simply laying his hands on the man's chest. In reality, he was utilising the mystical skills he had accumulated through years of study, channelling life-restoring energy into the exsanguinating man. With consummate ease, he stemmed the flow of torrential bleeding and recommenced the beating of a lifeless heart. Ten minutes later, the men stood and gawped when the fatally wounded man got to his feet and walked away as if nothing had happened.

From that moment on, the legendary status of Abel Strange as a man capable of miracles was born, and on many occasions since, he had demonstrated an astonishing ability to heal.

Yet what he was about to attempt was not the same.

With a jolt, he opened his eyes and looked at the face of a man he had never expected to see again. The shroud had been pulled back to reveal the serene features of a man who looked as if he was asleep rather than having lain undisturbed in cold storage for over ten years. Long, tousled hair fell about Pearly's tranquil face, which carried a hint of a smile suggesting that, at any moment, he might open his eyes to address them.

Strange swallowed nervously. He took a deep breath and stretched out a hand, laying it lightly on the cool, alabaster skin of Pearly's forehead. He closed his eyes and quietly chanted a mantra, allowing his mind to empty as he sought to raise a mystical energy to channel into the inanimate form. The process began with an infinitesimal spark of inchoate matter, somewhere intangible deep inside his body. The energy built like an oak from an acorn, gradually condensing into a force of unimaginable intensity such that he felt as if he would explode. He fought to restrain the burgeoning power, directing it along his arms and into his hands, and for the briefest moment, he held it in check. Then, with a jerk that sent a spasm shuddering through his body, the force leapt pell-mell from his fingertips into the corpse.

As power issued forth, Strange directed the flow, urging it along the pathways and meridians through which all qi must pass, seeking out the six key chakras located within the lifeless body. He lost all sense of time as the power grew into an irrepressible force. Gradually, by increments, he subtly orchestrated the life-giving qi, reinvigorating, repairing and healing the body's damaged tissues until the energy had engulfed every last cell, nudging and cajoling them back from their frozen dormancy of these past ten years.

Then, suddenly, out of nowhere, something foreign impinged on his awareness. His mind wavered while he battled for control of the energy still issuing forth from his fingertips, but the intrusion would not be denied, gently impacting upon his consciousness in a quiet, yet strangely insistent manner. He detected another presence—what was it? Yes, there it was again ... and then, with an overwhelming sense of wonder and fear, he finally understood. At first, chaotic and indistinct, the stone slowly materialised into his consciousness like a crystallising snowflake, pulsing like a distant beacon in a void of icy blackness.

With a sudden rush of excitement, Strange sensed the stone take over, acting as a conduit that enhanced the qi as it flowed through Pearly's body. But it was more, much more than this. There was rationality in the way the stone behaved, gradually superseding Strange's failing control until he was merely a helpless bystander, watching the healing force diverge into sundry levels that was anything but indiscriminate. Strange gaped in awe, as first, enzymes and proteins burst forth into action, a herald to the palpable presence of living cells. Next, a pulse of electricity coursed along a nerve, and then the twitch of a muscle, and finally, a single beat of Pearly's heart.

Suddenly, the connection with Strange was gone, and a force that was no longer under his dominion expelled him from the body he had set out to revive. He flew through the air as if struck by lightning, landing in an ungainly heap next to his colleagues. As he staggered to his feet, he looked back in astonishment at Pearly's body.

'What's happening?' called out Frankl in a voice laden with fear.

Strange stood motionless, dumbly shaking his head while pointing inanely back towards the body.

The men stared in amazement, watching the shroud gently rise and fall, imperceptibly at first, but slowly gathering momentum.

'He's ... he's breathing,' said Nexus uncertainly, reaching for Pearly's wrist. 'A pulse ... I can feel a pulse!'

After a brief flicker, Pearly's eyelids parted for the first time in ten years as if simply reawakening from a deep slumber.

As Strange raced across the chamber, any lingering doubt at what he had just witnessed was immediately dispelled as soon as he looked into the vivid ultramarine of Pearly's eyes and saw a fierce intelligence brimming with vitality shining brightly back at him.

26

Mickey Finn

L ILY'S HAND RESTED LIGHTLY on the tiller, occasionally adjusting the rudder in response to the pull of the craft and the gentle flow of the current. It was the fourth day following her reunion with the boys, and they had wasted no time in putting some distance between themselves and any would-be pursuer. They were relieved that they had encountered only a handful of people since their departure, and they had little reason to suspect that they were being trailed. Despite this, Lily still wondered why anyone would want to follow her. She assumed that it was linked with her father, and bearing in mind her pursuer's behaviour when confronting the boys, it seemed sensible to keep a low profile until they decided what to do next.

The narrowboat glided effortlessly along the broad expanse of water in marked contrast to the slow progress of the first few days negotiating the derelict canal. Aedh stood watching over Lily's shoulder as she steered the vessel. Much to her disgust, he leant over from time to time to make a minor adjustment to the line of the craft in the water by giving her hand a gentle push. It was the first time the boys had given her the honour of piloting the boat, and despite only a few hours' experience, she was beginning to think that she could do the job just as well as them.

The inviting aroma of frying mushrooms wafted up from the galley accompanied by the sound of Seoc whistling a mournful Gaelic tune. He had been up at first light to pick an assortment of odd-looking fungi, and despite the smell that was making Lily's mouth water, she still harboured a grave concern that they were all about to be poisoned.

'Don't you worry,' said Aedh in a reassuring tone, 'Seoc knows what he's doing. He's not quite as stupid as he looks,' he added, raising his voice over the background thrum of the engine.

'Oi! I heard that,' bellowed Seoc from below decks.

Lily laughed unreservedly, further enhancing the sense of relief she had felt since meeting up with the boys. She was doing her best not to think too much about what had happened. She was also thankful that the boys had not pressed her on her sudden appearance. For the most part, she was managing quite well, apart from wondering about the man and why he had abandoned the house in favour of following her. After all, she had always assumed that she was unimportant in her father's affairs. It just did not add up. Cornelius had alluded to a re-emergence of the Order of Eternal Enlightenment, even suggesting that she, too, was under threat. But why? She tried to consider all eventualities, including the unpalatable suspicion that her pursuer might be associated with the mole Cornelius had referred to. She also wondered whether it had something to do with Internal Security. Nicolas Fox's name had cropped up recently in conversations with her father, making her wonder if he might be involved in the whole sorry affair. The more she thought about it, the more it made her head spin, and no matter how hard she tried, she was not getting any closer to understanding what was going on.

'You've gone all quiet on me again,' said Aedh, interrupting Lily's train of thought.

She smiled. 'Oh … just thinking about the man who followed me.'

'Well, I've no idea what your father's caught up in, Lily, but it strikes me that he's the only one who might have some answers. Perhaps you should get in touch with him,' coaxed Aedh.

'No!' cried Lily.

There was an awkward silence before Lily spoke again. 'I'm sorry, Aedh,' she murmured, realising how harsh she had sounded.

'I need a bit more time to think. I know I'll have to face him again, but for the time being, I'd prefer to stay with you. Is that okay?'

'Of course. I won't mention it again until you feel ready to talk. Is that a deal?'

'Deal,' Lily said, nodding brightly.

Moments later, Seoc emerged from the galley bearing a large platter of mushrooms, fried eggs and bacon. 'Breakfast's ready,' he called out happily.

Aedh swept the tiller away from Lily and immediately steered the boat into the bank. He brought the craft to a standstill before leaping ashore to secure the moorings.

'Looks like you've done that before,' said Lily, impressed.

'Not had one of Seoc's breakfasts, have you?' he replied merrily.

They had all been looking forward to this moment ever since taking a detour the previous day to stop off at a farm known to the boys. Some uncompromising trading had taken place, and Lily still did not know what the boys had swapped with the farmer in exchange for the large volume of produce Seoc had come away with.

Lily was reticent to eat at first, despite watching the boys happily tucking into an enormous mound of food. She looked suspiciously at the odd array of fungi scattered around her plate, despite Seoc demonstrating an impressive knowledge by identifying each of the species to allay her fears.

'That's a Wood Ear fungus you're pushing around your plate,' he said, beaming at her. 'Tends to grow on trees, particularly elders. I found a bumper crop this morning, and I've got some drying below decks as we speak. It'll be in the rabbit stew tomorrow. It adds a delicious flavour, just you wait and see.

'And that one is *Tricholoma sejunctum*, better known as the Deceiving Knight Cap,' he continued as Lily skewered a more traditional shaped mushroom with her fork.

Lily held the olive-coloured mushroom to her mouth. 'I'm not sure I like the sound of that. Why exactly is it called "deceiving"?'

Seoc smiled mischievously. 'Some people confuse it with *Amanita phalloides*, and vice-versa.'

'Stop talking in riddles, Seoc. What are you talking about?'

'*Amanita phalloides* also goes by the colloquial name of the Death Cap because of its reputation as the deadliest of all fungi. It's killed many people in its time, either by accident or poisoning, including the Roman emperor, Claudius. It's sure to produce a slow, lingering death; liver and kidney failure, I believe,' he said in a dismissive tone.

Lily looked circumspectly at the mushroom hovering inches from her mouth. As she was about to return it to her plate, Seoc snatched the fork out of her hand and downed the specimen in a single gulp. 'Delicious!' he cried, followed by a loud burp, which caused some raucous laughter. 'You need to have a little more faith, young lady,' he said mockingly. 'Now, come on, no more messing around, tuck in or I might just turn angry.'

'Better do as he says, Lily,' Aedh advised.

'All right, all right. You obviously know what you're talking about, Seoc. I trust you, I just don't fancy the sound of liver failure, that's all.' With that, she picked up her knife and fork and proceeded to clear the plate.

After washing up together, they returned to the deck where Aedh unfurled a battered map at their feet. They all knelt down to study it, and Lily soon realised the wavy blue lines haphazardly criss-crossing the chart were waterways in and around the capital.

'It's a bit old now, I'm afraid,' said Aedh. 'A lot of the old routes shown here are no longer navigable, but it's proved very useful to us in the past. It's about time we decided where to go next.'

Lily realised that this was Aedh's way of asking her what she wanted to do. She thanked him silently for his understanding and squinted at the map in an attempt to decipher the complicated patterns that looked more like a tangled mass of spaghetti than a river map.

'We're here,' said Aedh, running a finger northwards along a ribbon of blue that stood out on the faded map. 'It's not too far before we reach the Thames,' he continued, pointing at a denser blue line snaking from east to west.

'How long do you think it'll take?' enquired Lily.

'The best part of a day,' replied Aedh, turning to Seoc, who nodded his head in agreement. 'We've still got three more locks to negotiate, but once we reach the river, we'll have a lot more options.'

'Such as?' said Lily.

'Until now, we've not had much choice with the route being pretty much predetermined. That's why I was so keen to press on. If anyone's on the lookout for us, they won't have to search very far. If they've any knowledge of the waterways, they'll know that where we set off from is effectively a dead end. It hasn't always been the case, I'm afraid, but many of the canals have fallen into disrepair, and the old ways are no longer safe for a craft of this size.'

'Let me get this straight,' began Lily uneasily. 'If whoever was following isn't working alone, they'll know exactly where to look for us.'

'Exactly,' replied Aedh sombrely.

'So what's our best option when we reach the Thames?' said Lily.

'I think we should make for the Grand Union,' said Aedh, pointing to a canal heading northwards. 'This gives us the choice of several different routes once we reach the Midlands.'

'Aye, no one will find us up there,' agreed Seoc, nodding sagely and looking twice his age.

Being serious did not suit Seoc, and Lily struggled to curtail a smile. 'Do you know what I think the best solution would be?'

'And what is that?' replied Aedh sarcastically. 'Don't tell me you're already an expert on the canals we've only come to know through years of travel.'

'Well ...' she began hesitantly, knowing the boys would not like what she had to say. 'You're only in this mess because of me. If you were alone, you wouldn't have to worry about anyone following you.'

Before she could continue, the boys had waded in with their protests, but Aedh's voice held sway over his younger brother.

'Don't even think about it,' he said in a tone of steely determination. 'We're in this together. No one's going off on their own, do you understand?' he added, holding her fiercely in his gaze.

'I don't want you involved,' said Lily, but Aedh held up a hand to forestall her.

'That's as maybe, Lily, but I'm afraid we already are, and as friends, we should stick together. That's our way, and no matter what you say, we won't change our minds.'

She nodded compliantly, knowing that further argument was futile but also feelingly secretly delighted.

'Now, I suggest we pack up and get underway as quick as we can. The sooner we reach the Thames, the better,' said Aedh determinedly, making it clear that the conversation was over.

Fifteen minutes later, the narrowboat was heading northwards along a deserted, tree-lined waterway. The sun was hidden behind grey skies, hinting at the prospect of rain. Lily suddenly shivered in the gentle breeze that accompanied the craft's momentum and cursed silently for not being more selective with her clothes when she had fled the house.

Nothing more was said after breakfast, and although Lily still felt responsible for dragging her friends into her affairs, she was equally glad of their company. She was also thankful that she had not developed any after-effects from the mushrooms and castigated herself for her lack of conviction in Seoc's foraging skills. The boys had shown unyielding faith in her when she had needed them most, and she was determined that she would not let them down again.

The narrowboat made steady progress throughout the morning, and it was not long before Lily alerted the boys to a set of lock gates looming in the distance.

'Highfield Gates,' Aedh called out, pointing towards the black and white striped beams ahead. 'We're almost halfway to the river. Seoc, are you ready?'

Seoc poked his head up from below decks, brandishing a right-angled metal implement with an open square socket at one end. 'I've got the windlass, or rather lock key to you,' he said,

THE STONE OF MADNESS

waving the instrument in Lily's direction. 'Come on, it's your turn. You've seen me do it a few times now. It's about time you had a go.'

Lily leapt eagerly from the boat and followed Seoc towards the lock.

'That's lucky. The water inside the chamber's already level,' Seoc observed cheerily.

Lily and Seoc swung the gates open, allowing Aedh to steer the boat seamlessly into the narrow enclosure. Once they had shut the gates, they headed off to prepare the paddles for opening at the other end of the lock. Lily manipulated the windlass in the way Seoc had previously demonstrated, placing it onto the axle and turning it carefully to open the gate. She stared transfixed at the glistening weed dangling from the ancient brick walls during the boat's steady descent into the murky depths of the lock.

'Just be careful now,' said Seoc, calling out to Lily over the noise of the water as it emptied from the chamber. 'Watch out for the pawl, it looks a little worn. The windlass engages with the teeth of the rack as the paddle gear rises, but if it slips, it'll fly from your hand and clock you one,' he said, pointing at the instrument in Lily's hand. 'What's worse, it might fly off and hit me,' he added with a toothy grin.

Once the water levels had equalised, they opened the gates and Aedh eased the boat forwards, guiding it serenely towards the bank while cutting the engine to wait for his companions. Lily and Seoc shut the gates, reset the lock and hopped back on board.

The afternoon proved as uneventful as the morning, and Lily was thankful for the paucity of water traffic, a sure sign she used to convince herself that no one was trailing them. They spied the occasional straggler walking along the towpath, accompanied by an unseen dog rummaging in the undergrowth, but other than that, they spent the day blissfully alone. As they approached the river, Lily felt the tension that had been hanging over them all day suddenly lift, making her realise that the boys had been feeling just as anxious as her.

It was late afternoon when Aedh signalled their arrival at the final obstacle before the river. 'Thames Lock,' he yelled gleefully, pointing into an eerie mist that had fallen with the failing light. 'Not a moment too soon,' he added in relief.

Lily squinted into the gloom, striving to see what Aedh was pointing at. When the boat slowed, she spied another boat moored on the reach before the lock.

'Looks like there may be a delay,' said Aedh warily. He steered the boat neatly into the bank, and while Seoc leapt off to secure the moorings, Aedh turned to Lily and whispered in her ear, 'Just wait here for a few minutes while I go and find out what's happening. Make sure you keep Seoc in check and he stays here with you. Okay?'

Lily nodded and watched with trepidation as Aedh disappeared into the swirling mist.

Seoc jumped back on deck moments later and threw Lily a quizzical look. 'Where's he off to?'

'He's gone to find out what's going on. We're to wait here until he gets back,' Lily replied, sounding as forceful as she could.

'Hmph. You've got to be joking,' replied Seoc, and before Lily could react, he had leapt impulsively from the boat and vanished into the mist in hot pursuit of his brother.

Without a second thought, Lily set off after him. She knew she was going against Aedh's wishes but she was equally sure that she did not want to remain on the boat alone. Despite the confusing haze, Lily soon caught up with Seoc and managed to haul him back by the tail of his shirt just in time to stop him from butting in on a conversation that was taking place up ahead of them.

'What's the hold-up? Is there a problem with the lock?' said Aedh, his disembodied voice addressing a third party hidden by the swirling fog.

'Aye, laddie, there is,' said a female voice in a soft, pleasant tone.

'West Coast of Scotland,' whispered Seoc indisputably. 'Fife, by the sounds of it,' he added, raising a smile from Lily at yet another of the boy's hidden talents.

'The pinion's jammed,' the woman continued. 'Looks like it's been tampered with, if ye ask me. Ah canna move it up or down. The paddle gate's nae gonna budge, and until it's sorted, ye'll nae be going anywhere, laddie.'

'I think I'll go and check for myself if you don't mind,' said Aedh.

'Do what ye want, laddie, but Ah wouldna waste yer time, if Ah were ye,' came back the reply. 'The mechanic's on his way. Promised me he'd be here by first light, and even if ye could pass the lock, it's too late now tae go any further, what with this haar. Take my advice, moor up and enjoy the evening. Ye alone?' she enquired, but even before Aedh could mouth a reply, Seoc had materialised out of the mist with Lily behind him desperately trying to yank him back.

'No, he's not,' said Seoc, beaming brightly at the attractive woman who had been deep in conversation with his brother.

The woman wore oil-stained overalls and heavy boots. Her silky black hair was tied up and held in place by a baseball cap, but despite several streaks of grime sullying her face, she still managed to look captivating.

Lily tried to guess the woman's age, but failed miserably, putting her at anywhere between mid-twenties and forty.

'And who's this wee laddie?' enquired the woman.

'This *wee laddie's* my brother, Seoc,' replied Aedh, sounding irritated and giving Seoc a surreptitious kick as he spoke. 'And my name's Aedh,' he added, almost as an afterthought.

'Pleased tae meet ye,' came the reply. 'Ma name's Michaela but everyone calls me Mickey ... and the lassie?' she added, peering round Aedh, who was purposely shielding Lily from view.

'This is ... er ... Eimile,' cut in Aedh, before either Seoc or Lily could reply. 'She's our sister,' he added as an afterthought.

A short squeak escaped from Seoc's lips in protest, but this was foreshortened by yet another furtive kick from the toe-cap of his brother's boot.

'Come on, let's take a look at those lock gates,' said Aedh, tugging forcibly, first at Seoc and then Lily, letting them know in no uncertain terms that they were to follow him.

'Let me know what ye find,' Mickey called out as they disappeared into the gloaming.

It didn't take the trio long to reach the lock gates, and despite the deepening gloom, Lily could clearly see the index finger that Aedh was holding up to his lips. 'Shh!' he whispered. 'What on earth do you think you were up to?' he hissed as quietly as possible while still managing to convey his deep disapproval at their behaviour. 'I thought I told you to stay hidden. We've no idea who this woman is. I wanted her to think I was travelling alone or at least that Lily was not with us. Safer that way, wouldn't you agree?' he added sarcastically.

'Oh, come on bruv, she seems all right to me,' said Seoc. 'She was right about one thing, anyway. Look, the whole thing's seized,' he continued, pointing at the paddle gear. 'The sprocket's jammed solid in the rack. It looks like it's been twisted somehow. There's no way it'll budge in either direction, and that means we can't open or close the paddle gate. We're stuck here until it's fixed, and we'll definitely need a mechanic to replace the sprocket; it's beyond repair if you ask me,' he said, running his fingers over the oddly deformed piece of metal.

'What I don't understand is who would do this?' said Aedh. 'This isn't just wanton vandalism. I've got an unpleasant feeling that whoever was responsible for this wanted to make sure that nobody went through the lock.'

There was silence for a few moments as Seoc and Lily digested the unsavoury implications of Aedh's comment.

'I could fix it,' said Lily suddenly, taking the boys by surprise.

'Lily, have you seen how bent the metal is? There's no instrument I know of that could straighten this out and make it work again. A mechanic, perhaps, but otherwise, forget it. Now come, let's get back to the boat,' said Aedh dismissively. 'At least we'll be a little less conspicuous there.'

Lily decided not to protest, despite being stung by Aedh's indifference. No, it can wait, she told herself, realising that now was not the time to reveal her alchemical abilities to her friends. The light had almost gone, and even if she had been able to repair the sprocket, it would be far too dark to travel any further tonight. She would hold her counsel for now, she decided. She trudged off after the boys, who were already heading back towards the boat.

'Fixed it yet?' Mickey called out with a sarcastic chuckle as they made their way past her boat. She had lit several lanterns on deck while they had been away inspecting the lock, and Lily was captivated by the welcoming appearance of the boat. The sides of the boat were adorned with intricate patterns, dazzlingly painted in swathes of bright colours, leading Lily's eyes towards the nameplate. Largo Law, it read, and Lily wondered what on earth it meant.

'You were right about the sprocket,' said Aedh disconsolately. 'Any idea how long it's been like that?'

'Ah got here this morning,' said Mickey. 'It didna take me long tae realise there was no way Ah could fix it. Ah went off up yonder tae look for help and found a lock-keeper's cottage nae far upstream, just before ye get tae the river. He put me in touch with a mechanic; he was busy today, but he's promised tae be here tomorrow. Better be anyway, Ah've got tae be in Oxford the day after.

'Look, why don't ye go back and get yerselves sorted out, and then come back and join me for a drink and perhaps a bite tae eat. Ah could do with the company; nae seen anyone aboot for days.'

'That's very kind of you, but ...' Aedh replied, but before he could continue, Seoc had stretched out a hand and covered his brother's mouth to drown out the rest of his words.

'We'd love to! We'll be back in a few minutes, and I'll bring some nettle beer,' said Seoc brightly. 'I don't think I could stand another night with my serious brother here. It's about time we had a laugh!'

Lily and Mickey beamed at Seoc's antics, and although Lily knew that Aedh would be furious, she was secretly glad of the opportunity for some light relief after the fear of pursuit that had hung over them all day.

Soon after, Lily and the boys made their way back to Mickey's boat. Seoc struggled with the heavy flagon of beer he had in tow while Aedh steadfastly refused to help him, still demonstrably seething at his brother's irresponsible behaviour. Aedh's usual mild-mannered nature had been sorely tested yet again by the carefree attitude of his younger brother, and even with Lily's support, it had taken some considerable persuasion to get Aedh to agree to go back with them. Lily was convinced that Aedh had only succumbed to their badgering so that he could retain some control over their actions, particularly if they were walking into trouble. Aedh eventually seemed to accept that Mickey was harmless, but not sufficiently to drop the charade of referring to Lily by her alias, reasoning that if anyone had been snooping around asking questions, Lily's name would be the first to crop up.

Mickey cordially welcomed them into the snug cabin of the Largo Law and bade them sit down around a small, rectangular table barely big enough to accommodate the boys on one side, and Lily and Mickey on the other.

'I couldn't help but notice the name of your boat,' said Lily, shuffling along the bench to make room for their host. 'What does it mean? Is it a place or something?'

'Aye, indeed it is, lassie,' Mickey replied with a wry grin. 'Largo Law's a ben that overlooks the place of ma birth—Lundin. They say it's an extinct volcano, but Ah wouldna ken. Always seemed a little grand tae think we've had volcanoes in Scotland if ye ask me.

'Bit of a coincidence that yer boat should be named after a range of mountains. Ireland, isn't it?' Mickey added, much to the boys' surprise.

'Ireland it is!' Seoc replied proudly. 'But how come you've heard of Na Cruacha Dubha?'

'Och, there's not many things Ah dinna ken,' Mickey replied mysteriously. 'Now come on, what would ye like tae drink?'

Seoc had placed the flagon of beer on the table as he entered, leaving little room for anything else. 'What say we start with my nettle beer? I guarantee you won't be disappointed. You'll never taste anything as good as this!'

'Ah'll get some glasses,' said Mickey. 'Ah can hardly wait!'

Seoc filled four tumblers that Mickey had laid out on the table, doing his best not to spill any of the precious fluid. He watched expectantly as they each took a sip of the cloudy ale, and was delighted when Lily and Mickey took further draughts from their glasses.

'It's delicious!' exclaimed Mickey. 'Just as ye said it would be. Ye must tell me the recipe.'

'Family secret,' replied Seoc, touching the side of his nose mischievously, 'but I'm sure I could make an exception for you. Pretty simple, actually. Nettles, lemon, ginger, dandelion, yeast, and the most precious ingredient of them all ...'

'Which is what?' Mickey enquired.

Seoc could hardly contain himself in his desperation to reveal the secret. 'Water, fresh from the mountains of MacGillycuddy's Reeks, of course!' he replied excitedly while raising his glass in anticipation of a toast. There was a resounding clink as the four tumblers met before they all drained the contents.

While the conversation strayed between topics, and the level of laughter rose in keeping with the volume of beer imbibed, Lily took the opportunity to take in the surroundings of the boat's interior. She could not fail to notice the various herbs and flowers that hung from the rafters, and despite her encyclopaedic knowledge of such things, she was puzzled by the number of items she did not recognise. A feeling of unease briefly surfaced but just as quickly evaporated as the nettle beer dulled her wits, enriching her with a misguided impression of well-being. She looked at the boys and seeing them laugh so freely only served to enhance her sense of security. Even when she noted the incongruently manicured fingernails of her host, neatly painted black, she failed to see the warning signs before it was too late.

'Now it's ma turn for a treat,' said Mickey, slurring her words. 'Just like Seoc, here, Ah've got ma own special brew. Come on, Ah'd like ye all tae try it. Just one glass, mind ye, and that'll be enough.'

'What issit?' cried Seoc excitedly.

Mickey squeezed out of the cubicle and retrieved a small

bottle hidden at the back of a cupboard cram-full of a variety of interesting looking provisions. The azure blue flask looked as if it had not been opened for some considerable time judging by the residue that had crystallised around the bottle's neck. They all stared expectantly as Mickey removed the cork and poured out a clear, viscid liquid into four tumblers. She came back with the glasses and carefully placed them into the three outstretched hands that greeted her return before depositing her own on the table.

'It's a mixture of several ingredients, much like yer own beer, Seoc. Smell it and Ah guarantee ye'll nae be able tae resist it,' she said, pouring herself a generous measure.

Lily held the glass to her nose and inhaled the heady mixture of exotic aromas she could not place. It smelt delicious, just as Mickey had promised. On a count of three, Lily and the boys raised their glasses and drained the contents in a single gulp while failing to observe that their host's glass failed to pass beyond her lips, caught up as they were with the sweet flavour and burning aftertaste of the imprecise liquor. The soporific effect of the drink did not take long to manifest combined with the beer they had already consumed, and within minutes, Lily's eyelids started to droop and her vision blur. She looked at the boys and was horrified to see them slumped forwards, soundly asleep with their heads resting on the table. She staggered to her feet, panic welling up inside. Her head was spinning, and she teetered ungainly before she toppled back into the seat. She threw out a trailing arm to steady herself, inadvertently clipping the empty glasses on the table and sending them spilling onto the floor.

Mickey got up from the bench, smiling smugly. 'You'll nae be waking soon,' she said, stroking the boys' hair in turn. 'And as for you,' she said, regarding Lily, 'look at the mess you've made,' she snarled, sweeping the broken glass under the table with a flick of a foot.

Lily scrutinised the woman with a combination of fear and loathing through eyes displaying twin images that swayed in and out of focus. 'W-what h-have you d-done?'

'What do you think, you stupid girl?' Mickey said in a voice that was strikingly bereft of a Scottish accent.

Lily shook her head as a sickening comprehension dawned on her.

'You've been slipped a Mickey—my very own Mickey Finn— and you were all too dumb to realise,' the woman said.

'A M-M-Mickey?'

'Exactly!' she trumpeted. 'I did tell you it was a concoction of my own making, didn't I? The drink's a blend of bloodroot, poppy and skullcap, not to mention a liberal dose of chloral hydrate I enlisted from an all-too-helpful pharmacist. The mixture ensures rapid catalepsy in anyone stupid enough to drink it, and while the boys succumbed almost immediately, I see you're made of sterner stuff. You better be sleeping before help arrives to spirit you away.'

Lily felt the urge to vomit. 'A-Aurelia?' she said, already fearing the answer.

'Well done! You got there at last,' she said, clapping her hands in mock applause. She parted the curtains and switched a torch on and off several times in quick succession.

Lily's head slumped forwards and struck the tabletop with a loud thump. She heard a vague sound as the cabin door opened followed by loud boots stomping on wooden floorboards.

'I've brought some bags for the boys,' a man said in a gruff voice. 'I'll get 'em tied up and weighted, and then I'll toss 'em overboard.'

Lily fought to keep herself awake, but it was all to no avail. The last thought she had as she lapsed into a deep and dreamless sleep was that she had led the boys into a trap, and they would pay for it with their lives.

27

Disturbing News

HENRY PRICE STARED VACANTLY ahead. Dark rings were gathered around his eyes like storm clouds, testimony to a chronic lack of sleep. His gaze was fixed on a patch of grass in front of him when a wren hopped into view, brazenly grabbing a worm from below his feet. He did not respond to the appearance of the small bird, unwilling or unable to break free from his preoccupation with recent events. It was much too cold to be sitting in the garden, but the chill wind that gnawed his bones was his way of assuaging the guilt that had lingered from the moment he returned to discover Lily gone.

Price stirred at the sound of footsteps squelching in sodden turf. He looked up to see Albright traipsing towards him, and noted the same careworn expression on his manservant's face that had blighted his own features since his return five days earlier.

'What is it, Albright?' he said testily. 'I thought I said I didn't want to be disturbed.'

'Indeed you did, sir,' replied Albright in his familiar deep voice. 'I'm afraid you have a visitor. She was most insistent that I came to look for you. I—'

'Is there news of Lily?' Price butted in.

'No, unfortunately not, sir,' Albright replied with a curt shake of his head.

A brief spark of hope immediately evaporated with Albright's words. 'Who'd come visiting at a time like this, Albright?'

'A Miss Natacha Lec, sir. I believe her father is a colleague of yours.'

Price was nonplussed. He had not been expecting Natacha and could not think why she would call unannounced. 'What does she want?' he enquired.

'She didn't say, sir. Would you like me to send her away?'

Price thought for a few moments. 'No ... no. You did the right thing, Albright. Tell her I'll be with her in a few minutes.'

Price rummaged through his pockets for a small band to tie up his hair. For the first time in days, he considered his appearance and rubbed his eyes as if this simple act would wipe away the fatigue that undoubtedly showed on his face. He felt like an old man as he struggled to his feet, and the effort it took to get up from the garden bench reaffirmed the exhaustion that seeped into the core of his bones.

On his return to the house, Price took a detour to the bathroom. He sprinkled liberal amounts of cold water on his face in the vain hope that it would dispel the mixture of guilt and fear indelibly etched there. When he opened the double doors to the sitting room, Natacha jumped up to greet him. As she approached, he was shocked to see a look of great anguish on her face and subtle smudges of mascara around her eyes.

'Natacha?' said Price uneasily. 'What is it? What's happened?'

'It's ... it's my father. He's ... he's dead!' Natacha blurted out.

Price hesitated before wrapping his arms around her. He held her in silence, comforting her as she cried until her shoulders relaxed and she pulled away.

'I'm so sorry,' Natacha murmured. 'I promised myself this wouldn't happen, but I just didn't know what else to do. I've come straight from my father's house. You were the only person I could turn to.'

'Come on, sit down,' Price said, guiding her to the sofa and sitting down beside her. 'Can I get you anything?' he said, offering her a handkerchief, which she gladly accepted.

Natacha shook her head and wiped away the tears. 'No ... no, thank you.'

Price waited for Natacha to compose herself. When she finally stirred, she met Price's gaze head on. 'I went over to see my father this morning,' she began determinedly. 'He called on me a few days ago, and I've been worrying about him ever since. When I arrived, there were two policemen at the door. They wouldn't let me in, but when I told them who I was, they let me pass. A man named Fox met me in the hall. I believe you know him?'

Price nodded. 'Yes. He's head of Internal Security. He's an associate of mine, and he knows ... er ... knew your father through his position on the Council,' said Price, immediately regretting his words. 'I'm so sorry,' he added remorsefully.

Natacha smiled weakly, giving Price a glimpse of the girl he remembered from their first meeting.

'Fox led me into the lounge and sat me down. I knew something awful had happened, but nothing could prepare me for what he had to say.'

She paused for a moment and licked her lips nervously. 'He told me he'd been contacted by the police after they'd received a call from the maid. She found my father's body slumped in a chair when she went in to clean the lounge this morning. He'd been dead for some hours, apparently. In view of my father's position, Fox was called in.'

Price wondered why no one had contacted him. 'What did Fox say?'

'He said they were treating my father's death as suicide. They think he took an overdose.'

'An overdose!' said Price, astonished.

'I thought that's how you'd react! Anyone who knew my father would also know that he'd never kill himself.'

'And did you explain this to Fox?'

'Well, no, as a matter of fact, I didn't. My mind was in turmoil; I didn't know what to think. There was also ...' Natacha began before she faltered.

'What is it?' Price prompted.

'I don't really know, but there was something about Fox that made me question his motives. I got the impression that he wasn't being completely honest with me. He told me a doctor would be taking blood samples for toxicology. He also said there'd have to be a post-mortem. I don't really know why, but it just seemed sensible to keep my thoughts to myself.'

'What made Fox think your father had taken an overdose?'

'There was a glass next to the body and an empty bottle of wine. Fox led me to believe that there was some kind of residue in the glass. He suggested my father had been drinking more than just alcohol and implied that he'd taken something with the specific intention of killing himself.'

'He seems to be making some assumptions,' observed Price. 'I wonder what makes him so certain that your father killed himself?'

'Apparently, my father was on his own last night. There'd been no visitors before he dismissed his manservant around 9 o'clock, and no suggestion that anyone called on him after that. Fox said that the obvious conclusion was that he took his own life.'

'And you don't think he did.'

'No. I think he was murdered,' she stated categorically.

'But why on earth would anyone want to kill your father?'

'As you well know, Henry, it's impossible for someone of my father's standing not to make a few enemies along the way.'

'Did he express any worries?'

'Not until two nights ago, no.'

'Why? What happened?'

'That's why I'm here, Henry. I believe this business has something to do with you.'

Price felt his stomach lurch. 'How?'

'My father turned up unannounced at my studio a couple of nights ago; this is rather unusual in itself, and I could tell something was bothering him. He began by enquiring about you. I wondered whether it was something to do with our recent meeting, but then he mentioned that you'd said something at the last Council meeting that was troubling him.'

Price tried to recall the meeting, but his memory was blighted by Lily's disappearance. 'I don't recollect anything out of the ordinary,' he said, frowning.

'My father's usually reluctant to discuss anything related to his work, but on this occasion, he told me about a mistake he'd made some years ago. He also added that it was not until recently that he'd realised its significance.'

'Mistake? What kind of mistake?' said Price, still unsure of where all of this was leading.

'At the meeting, you mentioned a name my father had long forgotten; a man by the name of Luca Nexus, I believe.'

Price recalled referring to Nexus in reference to his meeting with Asquith but had deliberately kept the conversation to a minimum. 'That's right. I remember now,' said Price, nodding, 'but I didn't mention anything other than the man's name. I also recall that it was a coughing fit of your father's that interrupted the proceedings. I was very grateful at the time as it deflected attention away from a subject I didn't really wish to discuss, but in light of what you've just said, perhaps the disruption was intentional. Did your father say anything more about this mistake?'

'He told me that Nexus had run into trouble some years ago. He'd been carrying out research that the medical authorities deemed unethical, but not everyone agreed. Nexus had support in high places, and once his political allies realised he was about to be struck off, they recruited my father to ensure that Nexus would be allowed to continue his work whatever the outcome of the hearing. They told my father that Nexus' work would have enormous benefits for mankind. I'm afraid he did whatever was asked of him to deflect attention away from Nexus. He also helped him to set up his work in secret after the hearing without any unwelcome intrusion from the medical profession or the media. My father had no reason to doubt the source of the information.'

Price nodded. 'Mm. It all seems to fit.'

'You know something of this?'

'I only recently learnt of your father's involvement in the cover-up surrounding Nexus. What I don't know is why. Maybe you can help me. Did your father say what became of Nexus?'

'No, I'm afraid not. I wished we'd discussed it in more detail now.'

'You said your father felt he'd made a mistake. Did he elaborate?'

'He told me that after Nexus' hearing, the man's name was never mentioned again ... until you brought it up at the recent meeting, that is. It came as a complete bombshell to him when you said that Nexus had been involved with Pearly Black. He swore to me he knew nothing of this.'

'And did you believe him?' said Price, scrutinising Natacha closely.

'I had no reason to doubt him. My father was always a principled man. I just think that, on this occasion, he must have got it wrong. By coming to me, it proves he was prepared to admit it,' she replied defiantly.

Price remained silent until he eventually asked, 'Was there anything else he said?'

'Yes, as a matter of fact there was. He told me that after the Council meeting, he made some enquiries. I believe the information he discovered corroborates your story tying Nexus to Black. He also told me that he'd arranged another meeting that would clear everything up.'

'Do you know who he was planning to meet?' said Price eagerly.

'No, I'm afraid not. I wish I'd been more insistent now, but my father thought it better that I didn't know any details. What he did tell me, though, was that he'd arranged the meeting for last night. As no one visited him before his servant left, I can only assume that the meeting took place after that—'

'Which would suggest that your father did not spend last night alone,' interrupted Price.

Natacha looked grim as she nodded.

'I just wish we knew who he'd arranged to meet,' Price continued. 'It seems distinctly possible that whoever it was could be implicated in your father's death. It certainly doesn't appear that your father's actions were those of a man about to take his own life.'

Natacha nodded. 'I'm glad you agree, Henry. Thank you,' she said, her words heavily laden with emotion.

Once Natacha had departed, Price shut himself away in the attic to reflect on yet another unwelcome turn of events. He looked dolefully through the dormer window at a row of dirty grey buildings lining the embankment that blended seamlessly with the sky. He smiled thinly at the way the leaden skies seemed to mirror the state of his own uncompromising mood following the news of Sir Robert's untimely death, only adding to the burden of guilt he was already carrying.

As it happened, Nicolas Fox was due to visit later that day to provide an update on the search for Lily. Price resolved to raise the issue of Sir Robert's death and to see if Fox really thought he had taken his own life. There was always more to the Chief of Internal Security than met the eye, and Price was well aware that what Fox had told Natacha may not have been the truth. Nonetheless, this did not explain why Fox would think that Sir Robert had killed himself; after all, he knew him as well as anybody else on the Council. On the assumption that Natacha had told the truth, and he had no reason to doubt her, it seemed far more plausible that the circumstances surrounding Sir Robert's demise were sinister.

Price concluded that Fox knew more than he had let on to Natacha and it was up to him to find out what he was hiding. While he pondered how he would go about this, his mind inevitably drifted back to Lily. He was well aware that their relationship had been strained, but he could not believe that she would just walk out on him. He was convinced that something had happened to make her behave in this manner, but despite repeatedly going over the events surrounding her disappearance, he still had no idea why she had left.

Price turned his back on the city vista sprawled out below him and strode purposefully to the desk. He sat down and looked at the chaotic mess of books and instruments strewn across its surface, and eyed the Historoscope suspiciously. The instrument had steadfastly refused to work from the moment he had found it lying on the attic floor on the night he had returned to find Lily missing. The malfunctioning Historoscope was the only clue he had discovered, and since he was sure that no one but Lily had visited the attic on that fateful day, he could only assume that she had left it there, cast aside and broken. He had done everything in his power to get the machine working again, but the damage was so extensive, it would probably take months to fix; time he did not have.

Price banged his hand on the desk in frustration. He winced as a sickly dull ache spread up his forearm. He had no idea why Lily had used the Historoscope or what secrets it may have revealed to her. All he had discovered was that she had set off towards the derelict canal, but from there, the trail had gone cold. He had also learnt that she had recently taken to skulking off from the house, yet no one seemed to know where she had been going or what she had been up to. How could he have been so remiss? he asked himself for the umpteenth time.

He withdrew his fob watch and rubbed wearily at his eyes. He still had an hour to kill before Fox was due, and rather than just sit aimlessly around doing nothing, there had to be something he could do. He glanced at the Historoscope and wondered whether he should try to inject new life into it, but after all his vain attempts so far, he knew deep down that it was likely to be futile.

As his hand reached for the Historoscope, he heard footsteps plodding laboriously up the stairs moments before his servant appeared at the door.

'What is it?' said Price, noting with trepidation the agitated expression on Albright's face.

'I have something for you, sir,' replied Albright, brandishing an envelope in Price's direction.

'A little late for the post, Albright.'

'Exactly, sir. The letter was hand delivered just moments ago.'

'What is it?' said Price, furrowing his brow.

'I don't know, sir, but the man said that I must hand it to you immediately.'

'Albright? What's the matter?' asked Price, reading the concern in his servant's voice.

'He said the letter has something to do with Lily. He just forced it into my hands and turned tail. I tried to stop him, but he was gone in a flash. I brought it straight upstairs.'

Price leapt from his chair and took the letter. He tore open the blank envelope and withdrew a single sheet of hand-written text, quickly reading it in open-mouthed horror.

I have your daughter. Travel by car to Up Wellow in the South Downs. Park in the village and enter the church. Arrive by 4 p.m. and wait to be contacted. If you are not alone or you are followed you will never see your daughter again.

'Is everything all right, sir?' said Albright.

'Perfectly,' replied Price, his voice cracking incongruently with emotion while he methodically folded the note and slipped it into a jacket pocket.

'Get the car ready, Albright. I'll be leaving straight away,' Price said, reflexively checking his watch.

'But, sir ...'

Price held up a hand. 'I know, Albright. Perhaps you'd be kind enough to contact Nicolas Fox and inform him that I won't be available this afternoon. Tell him something's cropped up, and that I'll be in touch.'

'What should I—?'

'I'm sure you'll think of something. Oh, and Albright, please make sure he doesn't follow me. I'm afraid this is rather important. Do you understand?'

Albright nodded. 'Of course, sir. I'll tell him that you've been called away on urgent business.'

Price nodded. Albright had faithfully served him for many years and was well versed in the art of discretion. He would not let him down. 'Good man,' he replied.

'Your vehicle will be ready presently,' Albright added, turning promptly on his heels and heading towards the stairwell.

'Oh, Albright, just one more thing. Did you get a look at the man's face?'

Albright thought for a moment. 'No, I'm afraid I didn't, sir. He was wearing a cap and it was pulled down over his face.'

'Is there anything else you can remember?'

'It all happened so quickly, but there *is* one thing that seemed a little strange.'

'What is it?' said Price, inclining his head quizzically.

'The man said that if I didn't hand the letter to you immediately, the lady would have his guts for garters. He made me promise I'd deliver it straight away.'

'Thank you, Albright,' said Price circumspectly. 'You've been very helpful.'

28

Ælfric's Jolly

PRICE'S ESTIMATE WAS UNERRINGLY accurate in predicting the time it would take to escape the sprawling city suburbs for the gently rolling English countryside. The traffic was light, and it was not long before he caught a glimpse of the South Downs rising in the distance well in advance of the deadline the note had set. He had committed the road map to memory before leaving London and had driven like a man possessed to the small village of Up Wellow, nestled in an isolated backwater of the Downs on the border between Hampshire and Sussex. The last few miles dragged interminably due to a gargantuan tractor that seemed to block his way at every turn along the single-track lane. A fine drizzle hampered his progress even further, and the overgrown hedgerows that straddled the lanes gave an ominous feel to the final leg of the journey.

Finally, the hedgerows broke, giving way to a row of dilapidated barns and isolated farm buildings on the outskirts of the small village. A sorry-looking sign hinted at what was to come, and it was no surprise to find the streets deserted. Price slowed the vehicle to a snail's pace while he peered through the steamed-up windscreen at the cottages on either side of the road. The village comprised of a score of small, squat stone dwellings overlooked by the square tower of a Norman church that slowly materialised through the misty rain as he pulled over and killed the engine.

He locked the car and set off along a muddy track that led to the church. The lychgate was choked with bindweed and ivy, and he had to push the dangling weeds aside to reach a small graveyard littered with crumbling tombstones. He looked on in dismay at the strangely forlorn place where ancient, misshapen yew trees cast dark shadows across the monuments in the oppressive light, making him wonder how long it had been since anyone had tended this sacred, yet oddly, neglected place. In the short time it had taken to walk from the car, the drizzle had seeped through his jacket, and he shivered involuntarily as he dived for cover under the arched entrance to the church. He glanced over his shoulder before turning the round metal handle of the wooden door and had to push with the full weight of his shoulder for the door to respond. He crossed the threshold and stood motionless, searching for anomalies that would alert him to the presence of anyone else. Energy licked reflexively over his fingertips as he readied himself for action, but the church remained peacefully quiet. He edged into the musty interior of the nave and headed along a narrow aisle bordered by a short row of pews. He crept towards the chancel in search of a hiding-place that would provide an unobstructed view of the entrance and settled on a cranny behind the choristers' bench where he sat down and waited.

Price barely had time to settle before footsteps rang out from the path and the door flew open. A thickset man entered the church muttering under his breath. 'Blasted weather,' he said, brushing the worst of the rain from his shoulders.

The man was dressed in tattered khaki fatigues visible below the hem of a shabby dun-coloured greatcoat. He scratched irritably at grey stubble on his weather-beaten face with filthy nails that protruded beyond the ends of fingerless gloves.

The man peered into the dim interior of the church, but his blank expression merely affirmed that he could not see what he was looking for. He ambled along the aisle, turning his head methodically, first one way and then the other, checking along each row of pews.

'Ye in 'ere?' the man called out. 'Seen yer set off from the village. Ye must be hidin' in 'ere somewhere.'

Price wondered whether he should just take the man out, but there was something about his demeanour that made him hesitate. He did not look a threat, and while Price could not be sure of his role in Lily's abduction, it would be safer to hear him out rather than do something he might later regret.

He remained motionless until the man was within a few feet of his crouched position. 'Looking for me?' he said, suddenly emerging from his hiding-place. He held his arms languidly to each side, feigning a relaxed attitude that was at complete odds with the enhanced state of readiness coursing through his body.

'Aye, I am that,' replied the man. 'I can see from yer appearance yer the man I was sent to meet. Not many of yer type with long hair an' flashy clothes round 'ere, now is there?'

Price nodded grimly. 'Where's Lily? If she's suffered any harm—'

'Don't know nought of this Lily yer talkin' abou',' interrupted the man. 'C'mon, I ain't got no time to waste, just gotta get ye somewhere, tha's all,' he said, turning on his heels and making for the exit on the assumption that Price would follow.

Price inherently knew that the man was telling the truth; he was someone who had been recruited to guide him and nothing more. 'Who sent you?' he demanded, grabbing the man's thick coat as he caught up with him in the churchyard, almost spinning him round with the force of his grip.

'Can't tell ye that, mate. Simple reason is I dunno. Got this message in the pub las' night that someone was waitin' for me outside.' He held up a hand. 'An' afore ye ask, it was dark an' I couldn't see 'er face. Told me to come an' meet ye 'ere today. 'Er said there'd be good money in it. Paid me fifty quid up front, 'er did, an' there'd be more to come if I did as 'er said. Now, let's be 'avin' yer. I ain't got no time for idle banter. Follow me. It ain't far.' With that, the man pulled free of Price's grip and set off from the graveyard at a good pace.

After passing through the lychgate, the man took off in the opposite direction to the village along a narrow path leading up a sharp escarpment. The track was slick with mud from the recent

419

rain, and Price frequently lost his footing as he tried to keep up while overhanging branches tore at his clothes. When the path finally emerged from an avenue of hedgerows into a grassy clearing, the man halted to survey the short distance that remained to the top of the hill.

'Where are we going?' Price demanded, slowly regaining his breath.

'C'mon, ye'll see. We're almost there now,' the man replied, setting off for the final ascent.

Minutes later, the men stood on the exposed ridge of a hill looking back at the tiny buildings of Up Wellow, set out below them like a model village. Price caught a whiff of tobacco emanating from the man's clothes as they stood in silence side by side, making him wonder what kind of life this man must lead.

'Lived 'ere all me life, I 'ave,' said the man as if he had read Price's thoughts.

'What do you do?' enquired Price, feeling a little more empathetic towards him.

'Not much. Makes me livin' off the land. Trappin' an' the like. Bit a poachin' an' maybe some beatin' in the 'untin' season.'

Price nodded. 'What's your name?'

'Owen,' he replied. His features momentarily softened before he turned his back on the village. 'C'mon, we need to go thisaway now,' he said, indicating with an outstretched finger towards a gently undulating plateau of pasture and scrub.

Price squinted through the murky light. He could just make out the outline of a building rising above the patchy vegetation, approximately half a mile distant. He rubbed his eyes, unable to believe what he was seeing. 'What on earth is that?' he said, staring in confusion at the towering structure that rose up like a finger pointing to the heavens.

'It's known as Ælfric's Folly. C'mon, ye'll see. That's where I'm takin' yer, an' I'd bet whoever's behind all this will be watchin' out for us,' replied Owen as he set off towards the tower.

Price caught up with the man after a few strides. He reasoned that if they were being watched, it would not be wise to dawdle, despite his determination to glean as much as he could from this man in preparation for whatever lay ahead.

As they drew nearer to the strange looking building, it took on the appearance of an oddly incongruent octagonal Gothic tower. Price counted five arched windows rising up the side of the sandstone tower, and he gasped in amazement when his eyes settled on an ominous crenellated battlement at the summit.

'I've never seen anything like it, and built in such a place too,' said Price between breaths, regarding a structure that rose over a hundred feet into the sky. 'What do you know of it, Owen?'

'Everyone round 'ere knows that story. 'Twas built by a man by the name of Victor Ælfric,' replied Owen without breaking stride. 'Poor sod 'ad just returned from them Opium Wars fightin' the blessed Chinkies. Ælfric was a naval marine officer; saw service under Bremer at the blockade of the Pearl River, 'e did. 'E was taken bad while 'e was out there an' was evacuated 'ome. Them doctors thought 'e'd contracted one of them foreign diseases, see, but eventually, they found out 'e'd got consumption. 'E was sent to one of them sanitoria they were buildin' at the time for the fresh country air. Anyways, ol' Ælfric didn't like it where they sent 'im, so 'e 'ad this tower built. It went up in under a year, an' just as well it did, 'cause the poor sod only managed to see out a few years before 'e died. 'Twas rumoured 'e slept on them battlements under the stars for the fresh air, but I dunno, must 'ave been flamin' cold if ye ask me.'

'What happened to him?'

'Got gallopin' consumption, but rather than let it take 'im, 'e threw 'imself from the top of the tower. After that, no one went near the place. As rumour 'ad it, Ælfric came back to haunt it. The tower fell into disrepair, but the fact that it still stands is testimony to them masons as built it. The place was bought up a few years ago, an' I 'eard some work was done on it, but tha's all I know. Wha' sort of state ye'll find it in, I dunno, but tha's as far as I'm goin',' said Owen, stopping dead in his tracks a hundred yards from the base of the stone monolith. 'All as I agreed was to bring ye this far. Now if yer don't mind, I'll be off.'

Price regarded the man levelly. He intuitively knew that Owen had been honest with him and that his motivation was purely financial. He had no reason to involve him in anything that was liable to get messy, and Price felt a great sense of relief when Owen turned to leave. 'Before you go, perhaps you'd consider doing something for me? I'll match whatever you've already been paid.'

Owen smirked. 'An' wha' might tha' be?'

'If my car's still in the village this time tomorrow, I'd like you to call this man. Here's his number,' said Price, holding out a card containing Nicolas Fox's details together with a neatly folded fifty-pound note.

Owen's eyes flicked nervously back and forth between the tower and the crisp note in Price's hand. He quickly came to a decision and snatched the items on offer before turning briskly on his heels without another word.

Price watched Owen head back along the path until he disappeared into the failing light. He wheeled round to face the tower, which was slowly turning to ruin judging by the state of its crumbling brickwork. He craned his neck skywards, scrutinising the column of high-arched windows cast deeply in shadow. He charged round the building until he came to a high-vaulted arch boasting massive oak doors set back in a gatehouse that abutted the tower. As he approached, there was a flicker of movement that caught his eye. He looked up and locked eyes with a demonic gargoyle staring menacingly down at him. The beast's wings were folded, but its forked tongue and bulbous eyes could not mask its diabolical intent, yet he still managed a humourless smile as a bat emerged from behind the statue and flitted off into the gloaming.

Price knocked on the door and waited, but the tower remained ominously silent. He opened the door with a twist of the handle and a gentle push. He passed through the arch and entered a short corridor that led to a metal postern gate blackened with age. He pushed on the door, but it would not budge, and a small, rectangular grille remained stubbornly shut despite his attempts to prise it open.

He shook his head; it seemed odd that he had been allowed to come so far only to be barred from entry here, but as if on cue, there was a faint click and the door swung open to reveal an octagonal hall illuminated by rows of candles mounted on sconces. The flames flickered from the sudden inrush of air, casting foreboding shadows across the walls. The room was empty apart from a marble bust that had toppled from its column, barely recognisable as a shattered head strewn across worn flagstones.

The door closed behind him as he hurried across the room towards a low arch that led to a circular turret housing a narrow staircase barely wide enough to accommodate his frame. It appeared that he was being shepherded upwards by whoever was holding Lily, and without hesitation, he ascended the sharply curving staircase. He halted at a cramped landing on the first floor and looked through the window. The night was drawing in and a dense mist rolled eerily across the landscape in great billowing clouds. He turned his back on the failing light and gave the opposing door a shove. The door was locked, and as he continued his climb, the doors on successive floors were barred.

The muscles in his legs rebelled as he hurried towards the summit, but the final rise of stairs was blocked by an impassable mound of masonry, preventing any possible ascent to the roof. He turned his back on the stairs, and much to his relief, the door on the landing was ajar. He peered through the gap into a small room illuminated by a shaft of light filtering through a narrow window high on the adjacent wall. The walls were caked with aeons of grime, and as he entered the room, he stifled a cough from the stale air thick with dust that filled his lungs. He looked up, drawn by the unremitting sound of water dripping from the ceiling; it was no wonder this place had done so little for Ælfric's health, he surmised humourlessly.

He crossed the room towards a heavy wooden door, which was locked, and after several unanswered raps, he turned his attention to an ornate goblet sitting atop a slip of paper on a round table next to the door. He lifted the chalice and looked suspiciously at the steaming, colourless liquid. He held the cup to his nose but immediately pulled away, eyes streaming. The pungent fumes billowing from the goblet smelt similar to the sal ammoniac he used for alchemical experimentation, and he had an uneasy feeling that the contents were intended for him. He picked up the note and read the words written in the same elegant handwriting as the letter delivered to Albright a few hours earlier.

Drink and you may enter, it read.

Price considered the words but instinctively knew that he had no choice. He seized the goblet, and without a second thought, he swallowed the contents in a single gulp. The acrid fluid burnt all the way down, and as he waited for the first signs of whatever poison he had doubtlessly ingested, the door flew open.

His head swam as the liquid took effect, but nothing could prepare him for the sight that greeted him as he stumbled through the door. A narrow arc of light surrounded by an all-enveloping darkness streamed down from a high ceiling, highlighting Lily propped up against the wall. Her mouth was gagged and her head lolled uncontrollably on her shoulders.

'Lily?' Price whispered, staring in horror at the metal shackles that bound her hands and tethered her to the wall.

Lily started at the sound of her father's voice. She strained to lift her head as if it was a dead weight, but as she opened her eyes and looked towards him, a woman stepped into the shaft of light to join her.

'At last! You arrive as a lamb to the slaughter,' the woman announced, spitting out her words with a combination of glee and malice. She leant forwards and tugged on the tangled strands of Lily's hair, jerking back her head to expose the pale skin of her neck.

Price immediately recognised Pearly Black's one-time accomplice and the attempted murderess of Cornelius Spydre. 'Aurelia, if you've—' he cried.

'Silence!' she commanded. 'We haven't harmed the girl, and if you wish it to stay that way, you'll have to be patient. Wait there and do as I say.'

Price frowned. It seemed odd that he had come so far only to be told to wait. In the ensuing silence, he took the opportunity to consider his surroundings, despite the conviction that whatever he had ingested was insidiously neutralising his intrinsic alchemical talent. He shook his head like a mangy dog in an attempt to prevent the blunting of his faculties before it was too late, and as he examined his surroundings, he immediately perceived an immense power perfusing the room. As he probed deeper, he sensed someone hiding in the shadows, manipulating an obscure, yet strangely exotic force. He blinked, unable to grasp the nature and magnitude of what was staggering in intensity yet impossible to comprehend. He had to find out more, and without hesitation, he stepped forwards, searching for the source of the power.

'I warned you! Stay where you are or I'll slit her throat,' Aurelia barked, brandishing a stiletto and thrusting the tip towards Lily's neck.

Price jerked to a halt, watching in horror as a drop of blood trickled from a tiny puncture wound in Lily's neck. 'Please ... put down the knife,' he said in as calm a voice as he could muster, holding up the palms of his hands.

'If you take another step, I *really* will use this thing,' Aurelia affirmed, holding the knife aloft. 'Now we wait,' she commanded.

Price nodded, bowing his head in feigned acquiescence. Whatever the reason for Aurelia's tarrying, she was granting him the opportunity to utilise what remained of his quickly-receding skill. He dared not approach her but perhaps there was something he could do about the poison.

Since he had swallowed the foul-tasting fluid, he had developed a tingling in his fingers and, with every breath, a tightening of his chest. As he turned his mind inwards to analyse the effects of the liquid, Aurelia threw him a wicked smile, rejoicing in the obviously discernible effects of her concoction.

'I'll save you the bother,' she gloated. 'You've ingested a naturally occurring neurotoxin, designed to cause muscular paralysis and much, much more. The inevitable conclusion, of course, is a lingering death by suffocation, which will be extremely unpleasant as you'll be conscious throughout the ordeal ...' she said, pausing theatrically. 'Unfortunately, the dose you've taken is insufficient to kill you … more's the pity,' she added with feigned disappointment. 'I have my orders, I'm afraid, but *that* pleasure is reserved for someone else.'

Price shook his head, yet despite the confirmation that the poison was not meant to kill him, in the time that Aurelia had been speaking, a malign burning had spread up his arms.

'No. What you've taken is sufficient to ensure that your abilities are neutralised so that you're powerless to interfere at this vital point in the proceedings.'

Price forced his chest to rise and fall in short, staccato bursts as if he was fighting for his breath. 'W-what … have … I … t-taken, Aurelia?' he said in as pitiful a voice as he could muster.

'A simple toxin,' she replied, effortlessly falling for the ruse. 'It's found in a type of phytoplankton that's a source of food for many marine animals. I isolated it from a shellfish that goes by the pleasant name of the butter clam; just a little more exotic than the poison I used on that friend of yours. What was his name? Spider or something, as I recall. He only just made it, I hear,' she added gleefully.

Price shook his head but kept his counsel, desperately trying to retain the vital information Aurelia was giving up in the hope that it might help him.

'The toxin is a competitive inhibitor of nerve conduction and binds to sodium channels, thus negating the effects of the neurotransmitter, acetylcholine. The result is that all muscle activity ceases once the nerve endings controlling muscular contractions are blocked. It also has the added benefit of nullifying your *so-called* alchemical abilities,' she continued, showing great delight in demonstrating her own natural brilliance and ingenuity.

'AURELIA!' a voice called out from the dark.

'You, wait!' Aurelia hissed, pointing authoritatively at Price before turning in response to the summons.

Underestimate me at your peril, Price thought, perceiving a dwindling of his singular skills yet rejoicing in the retention of his intellect. He urged himself to think, knowing that while this woman was happy to demonstrate her genius, she was also allowing him the time to act before it was too late. She had revealed that the poison was stifling every nerve in his body, stripping away his body's functioning, and as the final vestiges of his power slowly dwindled, he knew what he had to do. It was simple; by increasing the concentration of the chemical the poison was acting on, it would displace the toxin and negate its effects.

He could sense his mind slowing and his muscles failing, and it would not be long before he was completely incapacitated. He steeled himself, internalising his mind to seek out every nerve, synapse and gland in his body. Then, with his eyes tightly shut, he summoned a huge bolus of electrical energy, which he sent coursing down his spine, compelling an outflow of natural chemicals to flood his body.

Pain exploded inside him. Violent spasms afflicted his muscles, pulling and tearing at every ligament and sinew as if it would rip him apart. His spine arched and his body shook, yet he revelled in the agony, sensing the certitude of his actions. Gradually, the pain receded, and by degrees, the cramps ceased and his body relaxed. He looked around, and as his breathing eased and the pain ceased, his hopes soared. Aurelia was talking animatedly to someone in the shadows, oblivious to what had happened. With an exhilarating influx of lucidity, he sensed the last vestiges of the poison ebb away. He was free; now he could act!

Price looked at Lily but knew that there was nothing he could do for her until he understood the nature of the enormous power he had sensed when he entered the room. Even now, the bizarre energy force was still there, or was it? On the one hand, he sensed something mere inches in front of him, yet on the other, there was nothing there at all. The deeper he probed, the greater the inconsistency between something he intrinsically felt, but could not see. Then, with a giddy clarity borne of the poison he had banished, he knew. Whoever was hiding was wielding an inconceivable force of negative gravity and mass. It was hardly surprising that he had failed to grasp the incongruent nature of the force in his bewildered state, but now, with his perception restored, he felt the same tainted corruption of alchemical power permeating the ether as the trace he had detected when he had discovered the theft of Piotrowski's manuscript from his home.

Price barely had time to digest the implications of the frightening revelation when a blinding light flared in front of him accompanied by a tumultuous crack. He threw up his hands and reflexively backed away. The room shook and the air crackled as if its fabric was being torn asunder. A gaping cleft opened up before him, as black as death. The fissure erupted, releasing malign, flames of hellish red that coalesced into a seething vortex of exotic matter, circulating malevolently around a central empty void. He reached out oblivious to the scorching heat, entranced by the abyss that lay beyond the maelstrom.

'Stay where you are!' boomed the deep-toned voice of the hidden man.

'If you move another inch, I'll cut her throat,' Aurelia shrieked, drawing the blade theatrically across her victim's neck.

Price halted. 'No!' he cried, staring helplessly at the blade hovering inches above Lily's jugular.

'Do as you're told and you may yet avoid witnessing the demise of your daughter,' Aurelia commanded.

Price nodded. He could not risk compromising Lily but silently vowed not to waste the time Aurelia was gifting him. As he waited in mock subservience, he racked his brains, trying to recall all he could about exotic matter.

His thoughts turned to the Academy and a time when he had worked with his one-time friend, Pearly Black, in trying to raise a force of negative gravity and mass by alchemical means. After early experimentation dabbling with this paradoxical force, he had backed off, fearful of the devastating consequences arising from attempts to harness a power that underpinned the cosmos.

Predictably, Black was not so easily swayed, and after years of obscure experimentation in pursuit of some terrible goal, he made the breakthrough he alone had anticipated. Price could still picture him now, standing egotistically before an auditorium crowded with renowned alchemists and Cambridge dons, Nobel laureates and professors of particle physics, expounding on the complex mathematical equations and alchemical theorems few alone could comprehend. As a finale to his brilliant exposition, he had announced to a thunderstruck audience that an enormous proportion of matter constituting the universe could not be accounted for, and like Einstein incarnate, he had predicted the presence of invisible particles, heavier than protons, to account for the anomalous phenomenon of anti-gravity.

From that moment on, Black was not to be denied, and as he delved deeper, toying with an energy of negative density and pressure, he dreamt of bending space-time, and the panacea he sought—instant travel between distant points.

As far as Price knew, Black had never achieved this unimaginable goal, but now, at last, with his faculties fully restored, he perceived that the intangible mass of energy seething inches in front of him had been fashioned into a gate just as Black had envisioned—a portal destined to lead elsewhere.

Despite his predicament, Price marvelled at the achievement and wondered who was wielding this unimaginable force. Then, as if in response to his silent query, a voice called out from the darkness. 'At last, Price, we're ready. Step forwards and meet your destiny.'

He had no choice; he knew what he had to do. He closed his eyes, reached out to his daughter and prepared to meet his doom.

29

THE STONE OF MADNESS

Alone

IN THAT INSTANT, LILY felt the chill touch of another's thoughts intrude on her despair. She recoiled, straining against the bonds that tethered her, but then, just as suddenly, she relaxed. She had never experienced this sensation before, yet as a child, she had witnessed the silent communication practised by her parents, and now, as the words passed silently through the ether and materialised inside her head, she intrinsically knew that she was listening to the soothing, cajoling words of her father.

Listen carefully, Lily. Time is short. Remember, I'll always love you. In a moment, I'll be gone. Strike during the confusion and flee!

With these words, she felt her father's presence depart as he stepped forwards and disappeared into the whirling chaos that separated them as utterly as if he had never been there.

'No!' she bellowed, desperately trying to cling on to her father's touch, which had told her so much more than his silent words had conveyed. She had felt his love for her and the pain of his sacrifice, and the unequivocal proof that he truly was her father. She also discerned that he was fully aware of what he was doing as he stepped into the void, and if she had fully understood the emotions that accompanied the melding of their minds, he had quite possibly foreseen his own death. Yet despite all of these things, he had entered the void with a contented smile on his face that arose from the knowledge that he was doing it for the sake of his daughter.

Lily steeled herself. She would not waste her father's actions; she had to escape. She blocked out the memory of all she had witnessed, and turned her attention to her captors and the wild, dangerous energy flowing through the room.

'Josef, he's gone. It worked!' cried Aurelia as the gate flared in response to Price's passing, shimmering and glowing in a mesmerising show of pyrotechnics.

'Of course, it worked,' Frankl replied dismissively, at last visible in the corona of hellfire that surrounded the portal.

Lily regarded the man as he lumbered towards her. He looked haggard following the exertion of his effort with dark rings surrounding his eyes and heavy jowls masking his jawline.

'Price is a fool. He has no idea of what he's blundered into. Quickly, Aurelia, you must also follow him. They'll be waiting.'

Aurelia hesitated. 'But ... the girl?'

'Leave her to me,' snapped Frankl, licking his lips in sick anticipation. 'Go, Aurelia! The energy powering the gate is intrinsically unstable. It won't hold for much longer.'

'B-but ...'

'GO NOW!' he screamed, looking hungrily at Lily.

Aurelia hesitated. 'You're not planning—'

'GET OUT OF HERE!' Frankl commanded.

Aurelia fixed Lily with a look bordering on pity then turned away, unable to hold the young girl's gaze. She stepped forwards and followed Price into the void. The gate hissed malevolently as she disappeared, flaring in a conflagration of brilliant reds and yellows.

Lily groaned as grief threatened to consume her, yet she resolved not to waste the opportunity her father had gifted her.

Since she had been taken, her mind had wandered through brief periods of confused consciousness separated by long hours of drug-induced slumber. She had only fully awoken minutes before her father's arrival with a thudding headache and the first semblance of sanity. Perhaps in his twisted mind, the man creeping towards her had wanted her to witness her father's fate, and to be lucid enough for whatever wickedness he had in mind for her. No matter; it was the chink of light she had seized on from the moment her father's words had stung her into action, and now, with her mind no longer encumbered by the drugs Aurelia had imposed on her, she was free to act.

Lily closed her mind to the repulsive man edging towards her and sought the knowledge her father had taught her. Up until this point, she had never fully grasped the importance of the laborious alchemical exercises he had made her perform over and over again, but now, finally, she understood. She turned her attention to the cold metal of the manacles biting into her wrists and saw them for what they truly were: an amorphous complex of ferrous oxides masquerading as two rusted iron rings. In a rush of exhilaration, she poured her power into the metal, working her alchemical magic to transform iron into silicon. She felt the transition slide smoothly from one oxide into another—a metal transformed into glass. She smiled; could this be so easy?

Where once cold, hard metal had bound her wrists, all she felt now was the soothing touch of cool, smooth glass. She clenched her fists, causing the muscles of her forearms to impinge on the brittle bonds that restrained her. With a sharp snap, the shackles shattered, releasing her hands amidst a diaphanous cloud of glass shards that tumbled silently to the floor.

She watched the puzzled expression that flashed across Frankl's face before he shrugged his shoulders and continued his advance. As he approached, he slavered, displaying an eager greed in his beetle black eyes. He hesitated ecstatically before stretching out his bloated fingers to touch her face.

'Keep away!' Lily hissed, pulling away in revulsion at the stench of his foetid breath and the anticipation of his inevitable touch.

Frankl sniggered. 'You're hardly in a position to negotiate,' he replied dismissively, brushing the matted tangles of hair from Lily's eyes. 'You've already witnessed the power I wield,' he said, pointing grandiosely at the gate. 'What could you possibly do to resist me?'

'What have you done with my father?' Lily spat.

'Let's just say he's with old friends. There's nothing you can do for him now. He prepares for his death as we speak. Now hush, little girl, your time fast approaches too. If you resist, you'll only feel more pain,' he said, allowing his fingers to trail down Lily's face onto the smooth skin of her neck.

Any lingering fear that Lily harboured was washed away with Frankl's touch. She sensed the essence of his corruption and snarled at him like a feral dog. She could not bear his presence any longer, and with a sudden flourish, she brandished her hands and pushed.

The strength of a slight, teenage girl was no match for a man of Frankl's stature, but as Lily drove forwards, she did so as much with her mind as with her hands. With a sense of violence tinged with glee, she released the power coursing through her arms and sent Frankl toppling towards the seething void behind him.

Frankl barely had time to register a look of incredulity on his face before he crashed through the gate and disappeared from view. With his passing, the gate released an arc of flames that erupted high into the room like a solar flare.

Lily struggled to her feet, blinded by retinal burn. She staggered forwards, intent on following Frankl into the void, but as the blindness cloaking her eyes dispersed, she gawped helplessly at the empty abyss, dark and lifeless, where the gate had stood. She immediately understood that the portal had gone forever, and with it, her only chance of following her father. With an overwhelming feeling of despair, she fell to her knees, tears silently streaming down her face.

How long she remained there, alone and desolate, in the summit of the dark, cold tower, she did not know. When the racking sobs finally ceased, she pulled herself up, and after casting a forlorn glance at the spot where she had last seen her father, she fled the room as fast as her enfeebled legs would carry her.

30

Pearly Black

HENRY PRICE FLOATED WEIGHTLESSLY in the ethereal void where time held no earthly significance. It seemed like hours had passed in that grey and nameless place, but in reality, the time it took to traverse the gate was no more than a fleeting instant. He stretched his aching limbs and licked feverishly at his lips, head spinning. The stone floor felt cool and damp to the touch. His vision was blurred and insubstantial, but he could sense several indistinct figures standing around him beyond a circle of five stout candles that flickered uncertainly in a dank, windowless room. He hauled himself to his feet, but immediately collapsed back to the ground, restrained by an invisible barrier that held him in the cramped space into which he had materialised. He blinked away the rheum, and in time, his vision cleared to reveal the hazy outline of three figures.

'Welcome to the vault. I'm so glad you could join us,' said the man standing directly in front of him. The words were softly spoken and melodic, but sent a chill into Price's soul, for this was a voice he had not heard for many years. He squinted at the face of a man he had never expected to see again, and in truth, could not believe he was seeing now.

'You wouldn't believe the trouble we had in bringing you here, but such a convoluted trail was necessary, I'm afraid,' the man declared. 'Your allies were searching for your daughter everywhere, you see; we had to get her out of the city to a place they'd never find her. It was inevitable you'd follow her, which left us with the simple task of bringing you here.

'Now, I hope you didn't find the mode of travel too upsetting for your constitution, but even *you* must appreciate the beauty of utilising exotic matter in such a manner,' the man continued in the same hushed tone. 'You've just travelled through a Conjoined Spatial Gate. What do you think of the name, by the way? I thought of it myself, of course, but it could never do justice to the scale of my achievement. I always knew it was possible to create a tunnel through space, harnessing gravity to bend the very fabric of the universe, but as to creating a portal to allow passage, Henry, well who'd have thought it? But I digress, for I well remember how you dabbled with exotic matter, but it was just a little too sophisticated for you, wasn't it?'

Price stared in disbelief. He tried to respond but his throat was dry and all that came out was an unintelligible croak.

'With time, even you might come to understand how a tunnel linking two points in space can be stabilised by exotic matter. Naturally, you require two exceptional alchemists on either side of the gate to maintain the energy for long enough, but, as you can see, we've power here in abundance,' the man announced in a mellifluous tone.

As Price's vision gradually accommodated to the dim surroundings, the man's features coalesced into a recognisable form. What he saw only confirmed the fear that had grown from the moment he had heard the man's voice—a voice he had last encountered on the rooftop of a cold, deserted factory ten years previously.

'P-Pearly?' said Price incredulously as the man's piercing blue eyes locked with his own. Price stared open-mouthed at the man's face, still unsure of whether he could truly believe what he was seeing. The mop of black, shoulder length hair remained the same, as did the slight upturn of the man's mouth, set in a supercilious smile. Black's thick moustache remained, as ever, wickedly downturned at its ends, but it was the intensity of the spectre's electric blue eyes that told him that this was no illusion. The only noticeable difference was the deathly pallor of his skin, evident even in the flickering murkiness of the enclosed space. Barely daring to take his eyes off the man's face, Price turned his head to the right in response to a blur of movement as someone materialised out of nowhere, stepping forwards to join the group surrounding him. Price immediately recognised the woman who had mocked him and tugged at Lily's hair, but her earlier malevolent glee was gone. She looked fraught and dishevelled, and still a little breathless following her journey through the portal.

'Well met, Aurelia,' said the man on his left, whom Price immediately recognised as Liquid Lex from mugshots of the perennial crook.

Lex appeared unfazed by Price's scrutiny, picking nonchalantly at long, grubby fingernails, but his reaction was in stark contrast to the final man making up the quartet as he lurked hesitantly in the shadows. Price looked over his shoulder and flinched, instantly recognising the man, despite the glare of candlelight flickering unerringly in the thick lenses of his glasses. Abel Strange bowed his head, averting his eyes in, was it pity or fear, under Price's terrible gaze?

'Get up,' commanded Black, and as he spoke, Price felt the bonds holding him momentarily slacken.

He rose and looked around him. He was standing in the centre of a pentagram formed by the intersection of five lines running from the points of a star delineated by a candle positioned on each vertex and etched on the stone floor in bold, white, geometrically precise lines. At the apex of the shape stood Black with his confederates located on the other points apart from a single space that remained oddly unoccupied.

Just then, there was a loud pop before an amorphous figure emerged from nowhere, toppling forwards as if propelled by a redoubtable boot up the backside. The man fell in a heap from the momentum of his fall and slowly rolled to a halt in the vacant space adjacent to Strange.

Josef Frankl struggled inelegantly to his feet and looked sheepishly at the astonished faces staring directly at him.

'Bit of a dramatic entrance, Josef,' said Black, his words heavily laced with irony.

'I was, er, having some problems maintaining the link,' replied Frankl, looking flustered after his inauspicious arrival.

'That's odd,' replied Black suspiciously, 'there seemed to be no problems at this end. Still, at least you're here. And the girl?' he added expectantly.

'She's, er, been dealt with,' replied Frankl, failing to meet Black's quizzical stare.

Price looked over his shoulder to scrutinise the bloated features of Josef Frankl, surmising that this was the man lurking in the shadows at the summit of the tower. He had detected the hesitation in the man's voice, inferring that he was lying, and for a brief moment, his heart soared.

'Good,' replied Black noncommittally. 'At least now the pentagram is closed, and our guest is inescapably bound.'

With these words, Price fully understood the significance of the symbol engraved on the stone floor. The five-sided figure was a religious sign of mysticism and power with a practical significance for many alchemical sects, and here, maintained by the collective will of his captors, it was a means to incarcerate him in an invisible cell. To create and uphold such an obstacle was too great a burden for a single alchemist, even with the potency of Black, but with the support of his allies to aid him, Price knew that any attempt at escape was futile.

Price shook his head as if he could not quite believe what he was seeing. 'Well, Pearly, I must confess I didn't expect to find you at the root of such a convoluted trail, but here you are,' he began with as much composure as he could muster. He knew that Black meant to kill him, and if he was going to thwart him, he needed time to think. 'I always knew you coveted eternal life, Pearly, that much was obvious from your time at the Academy, but I never supposed you'd actually achieve it,' he continued, enunciating his words deliberately.

'The facts are irrefutable. I saw you tumble from the rooftop and witnessed you perish with my very own eyes. No one, even you, Pearly, could have survived such a fall. And yet, here you are. How can that be, I wonder?

'Let me see,' Price continued seamlessly, 'first of all a book goes missing from my library; a book I deemed to be of little consequence, yet the nature of its theft suggested otherwise. It transpires that this book was one of a pair written by Alfons Piotrowski, which when held in unison with its twin would reveal the darkest secret of the Esoteric Brotherhood. Yet I still had no idea of the exact nature of the secret, but with you standing here before me now, at last, I finally understand. I don't suppose I've ever congratulated you on your achievements before, Pearly, as so much of your work has been abhorrent to me, but at last, you've succeeded in something that has evaded some of our greatest predecessors. The control of exotic matter is one thing, but as for resurrection, well, who'd have thought it?' he said, shaking his head in mock bewilderment.

'Did you hear that?' Black announced to his allies, who were observing the exchanges with interest. 'The great Henry Price offering me his congratulations,' he continued, before returning his attention to his enemy. 'It should be music to my ears, but you don't fool me, Price. I hear the derision in your voice, yet you shouldn't mock me until you've learnt the truth. Only then will you realise how utterly you are defeated and know the depths of betrayal of those you consider your allies. Look no further than one of those amongst us,' he added, gesturing over Price's shoulder towards Strange.

Price smiled. 'It comes as no surprise to me, Pearly. Abel was always swayed by your easy charm and flattery, but have no doubt, he's been a rather useful ally all these years. I knew that by keeping him close, I'd be forewarned of a re-emergence of the Order, and on that count, I was right.'

Black's eyes flashed, but a calmness rapidly returned to his alabaster face. 'You'd be ill-advised to provoke me, Price. Perhaps you're yet to grasp the gravity of your predicament. Your assumptions regarding Piotrowski are not as precise as you may think, but before you die, you'll understand how utterly you're under my sway.

'Ironic, isn't it?' Black continued glibly. 'The manuscript behind our emotional reunion was right under your nose all along. How does that make you feel, Price?'

Price bowed his head, determined not to respond to Black's goading. He knew it would be impossible to overwhelm so many opponents, and if only to verify this, he flexed his hands speculatively against the invisible barrier and felt the insurmountable strength of the force that held him. No. There had to be another way. He had to keep Black talking.

'Go on then, Pearly, you're dying to tell me about Piotrowski and his terrible secret.'

'Ah, yes, this is a story that is both convoluted and strange.

'Piotrowski gleaned much of his information concerning the stone from Nicolas Flamel,' began Black in full oratorical flow. 'Flamel had previously learnt of the living stone in the fabled book of Abraham the Jew, but as my friends eventually discovered, that work was fatally flawed.

'Piotrowski's attempts at manufacturing the stone ended in disaster. After implanting the stone into an unsuspecting guinea pig, Piotrowski soon discovered that something was terribly wrong. When his victim escaped and embarked on a murderous spree, the Brotherhood were infuriated to learn of Piotrowski's duplicity, and conspired to cast him from their ranks. Piotrowski was never heard of again ... well, at least not by that name,' he added conspiratorially.

'Piotrowski escaped?' Frankl ejaculated.

'Exactly! When the Brotherhood forced Piotrowski to cease his work, they made him write everything down so that his knowledge would never be lost. Once he had completed the task, Piotrowski fled on the very eve assassins were sent to dispatch him.'

'So Piotrowski *wasn't* murdered,' said Frankl, shaking his head.

'Bravo!' Black replied sarcastically. 'Piotrowski knew the Brotherhood would never allow him to leave, and while he was enciphering his secret, he was also plotting his escape after forging an alliance with alchemists in England. He travelled incognito to

London and spent the rest of his years living in secrecy under the protection of the Cyllene Order, a clique of Rosicrucians who were happy to provide him with the resources to finish his work.'

'How are you so sure of this?' queried Price.

'Because I, too, became part of the same Rosicrucian Order over four hundred years after Piotrowski's death,' said Black triumphantly. 'When the Rosicrucians learnt of Piotrowski's predicament, they helped him escape, no doubt because of what they'd already gleaned of his work. The sect comprised of eight disciples, each sworn on pain of death to uphold the Order's traditions and to select their successor before their own death. Not long after Piotrowski arrived in London, a brother of the Cyllene Order was found in the gutters with his throat slit, seamlessly facilitating Piotrowski's transition into the sect.

'Piotrowski remained in London under the pseudonym of Edward Fludd until the time of his death. Little is recorded of him or his work, but after his exploits in Amsterdam, Fludd kept a low profile while pursuing his lifelong obsession with the stone.'

'And did he succeed?' queried Frankl. 'After our wild goose chase trying to unlock Piotrowski's secret, I always wondered how you managed to discover the secret for yourself.'

'Ah, at last we're reaching the crux of our discussion,' replied Black. 'Unfortunately, Piotrowski died as his work was coming to fruition. Having solved his earlier problems, he was preparing the final distillation of the Lunar Regulus when he was taken by the Black Death. One more week, and who knows? The stone may even have saved him, but alas, fate can be so cruel. But for Piotrowski's misfortune, I can only speculate what he'd have done with the stone, but as it was, his work lay hidden for many hundreds of years.'

'What happened?' said Frankl.

'The Cyllene Order were great believers in the Hermetic tradition and were committed to studying many of the great alchemical mysteries of the time. After Piotrowski's death, there was no one left to decipher his notes, written as they were in obscure hieroglyphics and littered with mysterious diagrams.

Nonetheless, the Order understood the value of his work, and kept it hidden until a time when a worthy successor could complete the task Piotrowski had fallen so agonisingly short of.'

'And that person was you, I presume?' Aurelia suggested.

'Not quite. It's true that by joining the Cyllene Order through the links I'd forged with the Golden Dawn, I gained access to Piotrowski's notes. Naturally, this aroused my interest, and with some astute historical research and a little luck, I slowly pieced together Piotrowski's life in Amsterdam and his association with the Brotherhood.'

'Just out of interest, Pearly, what became of the Brotherhood after Piotrowski left?' Frankl enquired.

'They were wiped out!' replied Black. 'The Brotherhood was a secret society of academics and alchemists, but to their opponents, they were considered dangerous subversives who threatened the delicate balance of power. Some years after Piotrowski's disappearance, the Netherlands became embroiled in a desperate struggle for autonomy against the Spanish during a period that culminated in the Eighty Years' War. The Spanish Holy Office condemned the entire Dutch nation to death as heretics, but in reality, they were far more interested in factions like the Brotherhood, whom they saw as the real heretics. The Inquisition learnt of the Brotherhood's blasphemous intentions and set out to destroy them. They infiltrated the Brotherhood and slowly acquired all knowledge of the group's activities and membership. When the time was right, the Inquisition acted with stunning efficiency. The Brotherhood was eradicated in a series of concerted strikes coinciding with the sack of Antwerp much the same as the destruction of the Knights Templar several hundred years before them. The act was quick and bloody, yet the atrocity that befell the Brotherhood went unnoticed amidst the Spanish Fury. Much of their work also disappeared, but somehow, the two copies of Piotrowski's manuscript survived the destruction wrought by the Inquisition, and years later, resurfaced in places where we were able to retrieve them,' said Black, throwing a condescending smirk in Price's direction.

'The survival of the manuscripts owed much to the Brotherhood's ingenuity in protecting their secret, despite the onslaught they suffered at the hands of the Spanish. A copy of Piotrowski's original manuscript eventually found its way to a lesser-known library in Amsterdam, a place to which I made several visits to determine how Piotrowski's thinking had evolved. Alas, even when holding Piotrowski's manuscript in tandem with the notes he'd made in London, it still wasn't enough to reveal the secret of the stone.'

'Which still doesn't tell us how you came to discover the secret for yourself. If not from Piotrowski, then how?' demanded Aurelia.

'You seem to be discounting one simple fact.'

'Such as?'

'My own natural brilliance, of course,' Black replied with a flashing smile. 'It's true that I gleaned much from the work Piotrowski had carried out during his latter years in London, but even that was incomplete and unworkable. No. There was still much to learn, and thankfully, with a little help, I completed the task for myself.'

'With a little help?' Frankl repeated.

Black beamed. 'Yes,' he said, his yellowish teeth radiating unnaturally in the guttering candlelight.

'Who helped you?' enquired Aurelia tentatively.

'Why don't you ask him?' Black said, pointing a finger at Price. 'I'd like to hear it from the horse's mouth.'

Price shook his head. 'I wouldn't want to give you the pleasure. No doubt you'll tell us anyway.'

'You bet!' Black replied gleefully. 'I'd never have completed the task but for the aid of my dear friend, Saskia.'

Aurelia glowered at Black while Price bowed his head.

'Yes, dear old Saskia,' Black continued, revelling in the pair's displeasure. 'The woman was a pure genius when it came to metals, but not so good at subterfuge. Despite her brilliance, she never came to understand my true aims in all the time we worked together. She thought she was helping to devise an instrument similar to that pitiful thing she worked on with you,' he said, looking at Price. 'I suppose she was right in a way,' he added with a chuckle. 'She just didn't realise the true purpose to which she was contributing.'

'What are you talking about?' said Price.

'You should know. You were as familiar with Saskia's unique metallurgical talent as I,' Black replied scornfully. 'It was evident from the moment we met that her ability to manipulate metals was unsurpassed. Her skill in the reconfiguration and reconstitution of metals, either by transubstantiation or in the crucible, was quite remarkable. It would've been a crime not to make the most of her extraordinary genius. The timing couldn't have been better. I'd already taken Piotrowski's work as far as I could, and I'd reached an impasse that even I was unable to resolve. I presented Saskia with a replica of Piotrowski's stone, manufactured in the way he'd described in the weeks leading up to his death. It took months of toil in the laboratory to reach that point, and even then, I still had grave reservations about how the stone would function. I dared not risk a repeat of the fiasco that befell Piotrowski, after all, but just by the look on Saskia's face when I presented her with the amalgam I'd fashioned, I knew she was entranced.

'She'd never seen anything like it and marvelled at the unique molecular lattice-like structure of that remarkable alloy. She immediately understood the metal's inherent mystery and was awed by its complexity. I told her that I aimed to produce a metal with the ability to store thoughts and memories—a concept she was already familiar with, of course. I knew of your puny attempts in creating such a substance while working with her at the Academy,' he said, addressing Price, 'and you'll no doubt recall my outrage,' he added with a chuckle, 'when I discovered that you'd been collaborating on some form of mystical research I knew nothing about ... which was ludicrous, of course. I had spies everywhere and knew exactly what you were up to. It was ironic that you both became interested in this area of research at a time when I'd first learnt of Piotrowski. The best you could come up with was that pathetic instrument of yours. What do you call it? The Hysteriscope or something ...' he said, laughing at his own ingenuity. 'An instrument, I might add that you intended to use against the Order, yet was used as a tool against you. Such bittersweet irony,' he extolled, his maniacal laughter rising to a crescendo and reverberating harshly around the vault.

'What do you mean?' said Price.

Black laughed again, this time a shorter, crueller sound before spitting his words out with contempt. 'You still have no idea just how thoroughly you've been betrayed, do you? How do you think Aurelia managed to lure your daughter away?' he demanded, enjoying the discomfort etched on Price's chiselled features.

Price shook his head.

'That stupid device of yours, you fool!' said Black disdainfully. 'It was hardly difficult to tamper with. When your daughter picked it up, it created the most perfect, yet entirely, fictitious images. How fitting that she should think that it was I, Pearly Black, who'd consorted with her poor, dead mother, to bring her into this world.'

'NO!' screamed Price, sensing the truth behind Black's words. He sank to his knees, pounding helplessly at the invisible bonds that held him. How could he have been such a fool? Black was right. Someone had betrayed him and he had not seen it. All he had done was embroil Lily in Black's deadly scheme.

'Yes, Price, I'm afraid so,' Black said softly. 'How do you think Josef found it so easy to walk into your house and take the manuscript? How galling to learn that someone was passing him information all along, and with a little prompting, was able to administer the appropriate tweaks to that pathetic contraption of yours that led to the flight of your beloved ex-daughter.'

Price shook his head but did not rise to Black's mocking, turning his mind elsewhere, preparing for the chance that must surely come.

'Ah, and so it was, all those years ago, that I tempted Saskia to come with me, lured by the beauty of the stone. And just how valuable she was in creating the final, perfect result; the genius that turned a dream into reality.'

'Reality. What reality?' said Price, straining to lift his head and return Black's gaze.

'Remember, Price, Saskia had already created a unique amalgam for the core of your instrument. Yes, that particular alloy is able to store memories, but it's still reliant on its own power source. It is, in effect, an electromagnetically driven system for storing information. Piotrowski's stone was fundamentally different, being able to act independently of any external power source, while Saskia's modifications enabled the stone to function as a material capable of integrating with an already functioning, self-powered system!'

Black waited patiently for the signs of enlightenment to register on the faces of his audience, but when none came, he smiled patronisingly. 'The human body can assimilate certain materials without ill effect,' he began with a sigh. 'Surgeons have implanted metals and ceramics into the body for years, but they've never produced anything that could flourish inside the brain.

'Saskia saw her work in perfecting the stone as an extension of the work she'd already conducted with you. But I knew better. Once she'd completed the task, I had no further need of her, and sent her packing ... back to you,' he said, pointing pitilessly at Price.

'Finally, with the stone in its final manifestation, I no longer feared the same fate as had befallen Piotrowski, and how my assurance was justified! With Saskia's aid, I created a stone that could be implanted without ill effect, to become a functioning, yet independent part of my mind that was always active, recording, duplicating and storing every thought, memory or emotion; a stone that became a mirror of my soul—my very own doppelgänger, if you will—and as my friends witnessed, a stone that could be retrieved, even in death, yet still able to retain all the information it had ever contained, ready to be reactivated when the time was right,' said Black, his maniacal eyes staring deliriously ahead.

Price sat with his shoulders hunched in a manner suggesting defeat. 'I must applaud you, Pearly,' he said monotonously. 'I find it hard to believe that you could create such a thing, but I still don't understand how your body could be preserved for all those years.'

'I appreciate your congratulations, Price, but I cannot accept all of the plaudits alone. I'd never have achieved any of this without the help of all of those here to witness your demise—'

'And one other I don't see,' Price cut in. 'What of Luca Nexus?'

'Well, well, well,' said Black incredulously. 'Perhaps you *do* know more than I supposed. What do you know of Nexus?' he snapped.

'Only that the man is a discredited charlatan.'

'Pah! You always were too eager to accept what those Council cronies of yours would have you believe. I've already warned you of your misplaced trust, Price. Without Luca to aid me, I'd never be standing here before you all tonight. The man's a genius.'

'So why's he not here now? You seem to be surrounded by all of your other sycophants. Why not Nexus?'

Black's eyes narrowed into slits as he appraised Price.

'Let me answer that for you,' continued Price seamlessly. 'Perhaps he doesn't wish to be at your beck and call like the rest of your lemmings or perhaps it's because you don't want him mixing with them. What is it, Pearly, or am I missing something?'

Black remained unusually silent, his eyes flitting back and forth, glancing nervously at his allies.

'I'm surprised that for one of your talents, you were so reliant on the abilities of others. First Saskia, then Frankl, and finally Nexus, not to mention all of your other lackeys. You must be losing your grip, Pearly. Tell me, how was Nexus so crucial to your scheme?'

'I'll answer your question purely for the sake of my friends. I wouldn't wish them to get the wrong impression following your pathetic attempts to undermine our bond.'

'I'm sure they're all dying to hear,' said Price, enjoying a fleeting sense of satisfaction stemming from his attempts to rile Black.

'I met Luca not long after I'd started working with Saskia,' said Black, casting an appeasing glance at his allies. 'I contrived to arrange a meeting once I'd identified him as having the necessary skills to implant the stone. Remarkably, he also had a great interest in cryonics, and we spent many long hours discussing its feasibility. It soon became clear that, with a little help, Luca had both the technical ability and the knowledge to overcome the seemingly insurmountable hurdles that had previously plagued the area. At last, I began to see a way round the problems Piotrowski had encountered.'

'Please continue,' Price said sarcastically.

Black glowered at Price. 'Piotrowski regarded the stone as a vessel for storing a person's soul that he could transfer from one person to another without consequence. What happened in his experiment proved him wrong. It is my belief that this occurred because of the stone's inherent ability to function independently.'

'How so, Pearly?' said Frankl.

'Imagine what would happen if the stone was implanted into the mind of a conscious, rational-minded man. It would be enough to send even a person with the strongest constitution insane, let alone some vagabond Piotrowski had dragged in off the streets. No. It was no surprise that this man's mind could not cope with the foreign thoughts and memories that came flooding into his head the moment the stone was implanted. It created a schism of such magnitude that it sent him insane. Remember how the man's madness lifted the moment the stone was removed? It was an instant cure for the battle that raged inside his skull.'

'Just as Bosch depicted,' added Price.

'Very good,' replied Black, failing to mask a further flicker of annoyance. 'It's always amused me how so-called experts continue to argue over the hidden meanings in Bosch's artwork. What those pretentious idiots never understood is the vital role Bosch played in the machinations of the Esoteric Brotherhood. Secrecy was paramount during Bosch's lifetime; what better way of circulating information than via cryptic images hidden in his art? The painting you refer to is but one of many, if you care to look hard enough. Bosch's painting was a message to the Brotherhood warning them of the inherent danger of Piotrowski's work. The painting was called *The Extraction of the Stone of Madness* for obvious reasons—it depicts the moment the stone was recovered, thus relieving the man of the madness the stone had invoked.

'But I digress, somewhat,' continued Black without stopping to draw breath. 'Piotrowski's mishap allowed me to fathom out the most obvious flaw in his work.'

'Go on,' Frankl prompted.

'It was obvious that the stone could never be implanted from one mind into another without sending the recipient spiralling into madness. No. The only solution was to reimplant the stone into the mind from which it had been harvested, or a mind that had been wiped clear.'

'And that's where Nexus came in,' said Frankl matter-of-factly.

'Exactly! Luca is undoubtedly one of the finest minds I've ever encountered, but, unfortunately, his peers were not so quick to appreciate his brilliance. He described many innovative surgical techniques, and his research was ingenious.'

'If you call unethical work on human guinea pigs ingenious, then perhaps you're right,' said Price.

'Typical. I'd expect no less from you, Price. You're no different from all of those moronic doctors who failed to see the true worth of Luca's work. I, on the other hand, was not so blind. What if he tested his work on patients? They went to him willingly in the knowledge that his research was for the benefit of mankind.'

'Ha! Don't you mean for the benefit of Pearly Black?' mocked Price.

Black waved a hand dismissively. 'Luca turned to me when he had no alternative. Just look at what he achieved!'

Price craned his neck theatrically. 'Beats me,' he said with a shrug of his shoulders.

'I know your game, Price, but you cannot provoke me. Perhaps the time for talk is over. Maybe we should just get on with what I brought you here for—'

'No, Pearly,' interjected Aurelia, looking oddly pensive. 'I think we ought to hear you out. It's the very least you owe us before we commit yet another atrocity in your name.'

'Aurelia's right,' agreed Lex.

Frankl remained uncharacteristically silent, his eyes flicking nervously between Black and the rest of the group, trying to gauge where all of this was leading. Strange, too, remained silent, keeping his head bowed.

'Congratulations, Price. It appears you've successfully unsettled my allies, but you'd be well advised to remain silent,' said Black, scowling. 'Still, a little more time before we finish you off won't do any harm. Very well, Aurelia, I shall acquiesce to your request. Where would you like me to begin?'

'Let's start with the night at the factory. With you gone, you left us all with a host of unanswered questions.'

'Such as?'

'Well, for a start, why you never told us about the stone and why you sent Josef on such a convoluted trail to work it out for himself. If you'd explained it from the outset, none of this would have been necessary.'

'Ah, Aurelia, so beautiful and so dangerous, yet somehow also so naive. It all boils down to a question of trust, you see. With something as critical as the stone, I had to be convinced of your loyalty. I was well aware of the cliques that had formed within the Order. I had to know who I could trust before revealing the truth. Unfortunately, I was not fully prepared on the night I went in search of the vital reagent for Luca.'

'Prepared for what?' asked Aurelia.

'Fox's waiting-party. We were surrounded the moment we broke in. They'd been expecting us, and that put me on my guard. Had the Council been watching us or had the Order been infiltrated? It was not the first time Internal Security had turned up when least expected. I began to suspect there was a mole amongst us, and that made me wary.

'At the time, I was still undecided about the stone, particularly as Luca had not completed his work. I resolved to keep what I'd learnt to myself until I could be sure of those around me.

Unfortunately, events overtook us … thanks to his interference,'
spat Black, pointing accusingly at Price. 'The moment I discovered
we were trapped, I knew Price would come, and that changed
everything.'

'But, Pearly, we still could have got away. Josef and I managed
it after you … after you …' Lex spluttered.

'Died?'

'Well, yes,' said Lex, sounding flustered. 'Although that hardly
seems the right word for it now. If there was so much at stake,
why did you wait for Price? Surely it would have been more
sensible to slip away as we'd done many times before.'

'Perhaps you're right, Lex, but I had my reasons.'

'If you really wish to know, it's because of his ego,' said Price.
'He couldn't bear the thought of skulking off and leaving me
behind. Surely you must realise that?'

Lex did not reply but gave a barely perceptible shrug.

'Your attempts to rile me are pitiful, Price, but it's of little
consequence. You're doomed to fail,' Black boomed. 'As it was,
I decided the time was right for our final showdown—'

'Or not as it transpired,' interjected Price, smiling
humourlessly.

'Indeed, but at the time, I saw it as an opportunity to rid the
Order of your meddling once and for all.'

'What actually happened, Pearly?' said Aurelia.

'I dispatched Lex to the rooftop on the pretext of finding out
what Price was up to. That gave me the opportunity to confide in
Josef about the stone, although I was purposefully evasive about
its true nature. I explained to him of the absolute need to recover
the stone in the event of my death and to take my body to Luca. I
also entrusted him with the vague whereabouts of some notes I'd
hidden at the Academy.'

'Why weren't you more explicit?' said Frankl. 'It would've
made life a lot simpler these past ten years.'

'As I've already said, I didn't wish to divulge what I'd learnt
until I was certain of who I could trust,' replied Black with a
dismissive flick of a hand. 'The key to eternal life is a rather

powerful tool, don't you think? A tool, I might add, that is capable of turning even the staunchest of allies. Even a simple grasp of the stone's power would've been too much for a single person to bear. I was worried that whoever learnt of it would use it for their own purpose; yes, even you, Josef,' said Black in response to the look of affront on Frankl's face.

'B-but ...' stammered Frankl.

'But what, Josef? The quest to recover Piotrowski's work was not one that could be accomplished alone. I knew you'd seek out the others, and that thought reassured me. Safety in numbers, you see.'

'And where does Nexus fit in?' demanded Aurelia. 'It appears you placed more trust in him than the rest of us put together.'

'All of you have your own diverse reasons for being here, yet your motives have always been clear to me. Power, greed, desire ... yes, and perhaps even loyalty,' he added, glancing at Strange. 'Luca's different. You have witnessed his taste for the finer things in life but his prime motivation is an unquenchable thirst for knowledge. With my unsurpassed mastery of alchemy, I provided him with the means to see his medical work afresh, opening up a world he'd only ever dreamt of. I gave him the resources to turn his ambition into reality, and for that, I am thankful, for otherwise, I would not be here standing before you now. Luca has no concern with petty motives but is driven by the power of understanding.'

'Did you let on to Nexus about the true nature of stone?' Aurelia said.

'Initially, no. He was always suspicious of my reasons for having the stone implanted and never believed it was to boost my alchemical abilities. With time, I came to trust his judgement, and eventually, I gave him a clearer insight into the real purpose of the stone. Even so, he remained sceptical. Luca's a man who understands science in only its purest sense. Nonetheless, I selected him to act as my vassal in the unlikely event of my death. I prepared him for the possibility that, one day, my body would be taken to him. He knew what he had to do, and while he did not necessarily share my conviction, he was sufficiently intrigued to follow it through. He knew of my intention to entrust the stone to Josef, but also of how little else I intended to divulge to him. I predicted what Josef would do with the snippets of information I'd left for him, and ever since, Luca has been watching to make sure everything proceeded as I'd anticipated.'

'What?' Frankl snapped.

'Come now, Josef, don't be so sensitive. I had to be sure my plan would work. Luca was my security. He was my ... shall we say ... guarantee of success.'

Frankl shook his head. 'I don't believe this. He's been watching us?' he said, affronted.

Black nodded. 'Luca was prepared for your return. He knew you'd resurface at the Academy, and ever since, he's been following your progress with interest. He was watching you on the night you stole the manuscript, and again when Lex was in Amsterdam. He was even there when you honoured me with a meeting in Wren's Cache. Luca was my insurance policy to make sure that everything came to pass just as I'd foreseen.'

'So what *really* happened on the night you died?' Lex said. 'We tried to find out, but everything that appeared in the papers was a blatant pack of lies.'

Price lifted his head laboriously as if his neck muscles could not cope. His eyes stared ahead into the dimly lit room like empty shells, barely meeting the gaze of his nemesis. 'Lex ... is ... right,' he said, articulating each word with great difficulty. 'You went ... to ... a lot of trouble to bring ... me here, why d-don't you tell him w-why ...' he added, his words trailing off as he gasped for air.

'If I must,' said Black. 'The reason, of course, is retribution, and while it's been ten years since that night, it's time for Price to pay for his actions.'

Price stared blankly ahead, his head lolling uncontrollably on his shoulders, yet all of this was lost on Black. 'You attacked me for no good reason,' he screamed hysterically, his voice rising into a frenzied crescendo, hurling accusations as if his words alone would strike Price down. 'Yours was no more than a cowardly act

452

of revenge. How did you feel when you found out who was responsible for Saskia's death? You should've known Fox couldn't be trusted. The shot came from nowhere. I threw up a shield to protect myself. How was I to know that the bullet would rebound and strike her? It was a chance in a million. No matter what, Price, it wasn't my fault.'

Price forced a look of astonishment to flash across his face as he teetered precariously back and forth.

'You ... you didn't know?' said Black incredulously, his voice falling to a whisper.

Price gave a barely perceptible shake of his head as he slumped forwards on the brink of unconsciousness, yet he still allowed himself a fleeting sense of satisfaction that he had managed to fool his nemesis.

'Now do you see how utterly you are betrayed? You never knew that Fox was responsible for Saskia's death!' Black said, shaking his head in disbelief. 'Is there no end to the man's deception? At least you'll die knowing that he, too, will meet with the same fate as your own. But this changes nothing. The time has come. I'll have my revenge!' said Black, oblivious to Price's predicament.

Black nodded to Strange and Frankl. 'Now!' he cried gleefully, giving vent to incipient madness.

Frankl raised his hands, but Strange hesitated, looking around him for support.

'Wait!' said Lex. 'We don't have to do this. We've committed many crimes in your name, Pearly, but never cold-blooded murder.'

'You all have blood on your hands,' whispered Black menacingly.

'Self-defence, yes, but never this. We don't have to do this.'

Strange looked at Frankl before turning to face Aurelia, tormented by indecision. Frankl nodded fervently, urging him to continue, but Aurelia shrugged her shoulders as if she did not really care.

'Do as I say ... or you, too, will be next,' Black commanded, staring fixedly at Strange.

Strange stood bolt upright, stung by Black's words. He launched into action and extended his arms. Frankl, too, was ready, and together, balls of fire materialised around their hands, engulfing the room in blinding orange light. The flames climbed high into the vault, illuminating crazed expressions on their faces, yet they held their power in check as white-hot flames fizzed expectantly about them.

'Now!' screamed Black.

The men unfurled their hands in unison, releasing the inferno to immerse Aurelia and Lex in coats of scorching flames, but no sooner than it seemed that they would be consumed, the flames made an improbable leap, arcing inexorably towards the pentagram's zenith and Pearly Black, who grimaced terrifyingly as he too was swallowed up by fire.

The energy flowed in graceful parabolic curves from Frankl and Strange, through the conduits of Aurelia and Lex, and finally into Black. The power hissed and crackled as it poured into Black's torso, engulfing him in a burgeoning corona of grey flames that reeked of corruption. His body appeared to swell amidst the raging fire, and slowly, ever so slowly, he raised a finger and took aim.

Price gave no sign that he knew what was happening, but Black neither cared nor noticed, entranced as he was with the sense of invincibility that arose from the exponential surge in power that built inside him.

The throng shielded their eyes, yet they dared not look away, mesmerised by the awesome spectacle of Black towering over his victim. Then, with an earth-shattering crack, a bolt of defiled light erupted from his finger, exploding like a supernova and tearing into its target with a certainty that was absolute.

31

THE STONE OF MADNESS

The Mysterious Zoë Tsing

L ILY RAN BLINDLY DOWN the stairs without any heed for her safety in her desperation to escape the tower. Her head was spinning like a merry-go-round from a combination of exhaustion and her descent of the spiral staircase. When she reached the ground-floor and spilled into the octagonal hall, she was on the verge of collapse. She skidded on the slick stone flags as she threw herself across the room towards the exit. To her surprise, the sturdy metal door flew open behind the force of her weight, and as her momentum carried her into a narrow corridor, she was enveloped by strong arms that pulled her back.

Lily flailed wildly at the unseen assailants, desperately punching and kicking in her attempt to escape 'NO!' she screamed. She had been taken before and would not let it happen again.

'Lily, Lily, it's us!'

The sound of familiar voices made her heart soar; it was her friends, Aedh and Seoc. Lily spun round, eager to see what she could not believe. 'It *is* you! I thought you were dead!' she cried, feeling foolish at how her words must sound. She smiled as she took in the pale, freckled appearance of the boys, who stood beaming back at her.

The boys hesitated, then threw their arms around her, this time in sheer joy. 'What's been going on?' they said in unison.

Lily shook her head. 'I could ask the same of you. C'mon let's get out of here. I'll explain later,' she said, straining for the exit.

Lily peered into the darkness that greeted her at the door and shivered involuntarily from the inrush of cold night air, but still she pressed on, desperate to leave the foreboding tower behind.

After putting some distance behind her, she paused on a gentle elevation and turned to stare forlornly at the stark monolith that was now shrouded in mist. She felt a sudden wave of fatigue wash over her, and as she set off once more, she prompted Aedh to lead the way.

Aedh overtook her in silence, gently sweeping the terrain with a torch to illuminate the way. Despite the uneven ground, they soon reached a steep escarpment, where they stopped to regain their breath while peering at the distant lights of the village nestled in the valley below.

'Come on. I'd rather not delay any longer than we have to,' said Aedh. 'There's a car waiting for us in the village,' he added for Lily's benefit.

'That's if the police haven't found it yet,' said Seoc.

'You mean it's ... it's stolen?' Lily said.

'I prefer the term "borrowed",' replied Seoc facetiously. 'I bet no one's noticed it's gone yet, rubbish old banger that it is.'

When they reached the village, Aedh led them to a small saloon parked in a narrow side street. By now, Lily was too tired to care, and she crawled into the back of the vehicle without a word of protest. She looked on with detachment as Seoc buried his head below the dashboard to hot-wire the vehicle, while Aedh sat behind the steering wheel impatiently drumming his fingertips, ready to speed off the instant the engine fired up.

After leaving the deserted streets of Up Wellow behind, Seoc turned round to speak. 'So, Lily ...' he began, but the sight of her lying spread-eagled across the back seat already fast asleep was enough to tell him that his curiosity would have to wait.

Aedh drove through the night, and when Lily awoke, she was amazed to discover that they were back at the boat, still moored at the same spot where she had been kidnapped ten days earlier.

Once safely inside the familiar craft, the time for explanations began. Lily went first, describing as best as she could how she had been bound and gagged, and taken to the tower. There, she had been drugged and used as bait to draw out the real prey, her father. The boys dared not interrupt as she recounted her tale, nodding supportively as if everything she said corroborated their own ordeal. She described in chilling detail the finale that saw, first her father, and then Aurelia Nightshade—or Mickey as the boys had known her—and finally the fat, evil man, vanish into thin air. The boys gently pressed her on the baffling disappearances, astutely aware of the uncertain fate of her father and how she must be feeling, but Lily admitted that she was just as mystified as they were. All she could say was that the trio had disappeared into a vortex, one after the other, and that it had dematerialised after the fat man's passing, scuppering any chance of pursuit. Although she had never encountered anything like it before, she speculated that the vortex was a bizarre and inexplicable form of transportation, although to where exactly it had taken her father, she dared not contemplate.

The boys listened transfixed and slowly came to see Lily in a new light, talking about things they could hardly comprehend. As she neared the end of her story, the boys exchanged nervous glances as it slowly dawned on them that there was a lot more to this girl than they had ever previously imagined.

When Lily portrayed how she had dispatched the man into the vortex using all of her cunning—but without mentioning her more abstruse abilities—Seoc could barely contain his delight, and whooped unashamedly at her victory.

Once Lily had finished her account, they continued the debate about why anyone would wish to abduct her father, but all they could agree on was that whoever had taken him had wanted him alive; or why else would Lily's captors have both so willingly followed him into the vortex?

Lily held onto this assertion and kept repeating it to herself as a way to stiffen her resolve. From time to time, she could sense herself faltering when she recalled the words the evil man had uttered moments before he had tumbled into the vortex.

'There's nothing you can do for him now; he prepares for his death as we speak.'

As she murmured the words, Lily realised how much she needed the boys, yet she was acutely aware of how she had already led them into danger. She even suggested that they went their separate ways, but despite her pleas, the boys remained resolute in their pledge to help her. When she reluctantly accepted that they were all in the same predicament, she opted to divulge everything she knew; after all, it was the very least the boys deserved.

Lily began by recounting her father's previous scrapes with the Order of Eternal Enlightenment followed by a detailed account of the thefts, firstly from her home, and more latterly, from the library in Amsterdam. She completed her story by airing her suspicions about how she had been manipulated into leading her father into a trap. They talked all day, barely stopping to draw breath, and following the inevitable questions the boys fired at her, it was finally their turn to relate the tale of when they had awoken to discover her gone.

Aedh began the narration, much to Seoc's disgust, but whenever anything interesting cropped up, the younger boy butted in excitedly, embellishing the story at every turn.

Not surprisingly, they had assumed that Lily's disappearance was linked to the man who had followed her and the Scotswoman who had drugged them. After awakening with thudding headaches trussed up inside their own boat, they had spent the next twenty-four hours aimlessly searching for the Largo Law. After drawing a blank, they had left the boat at Thames Lock and returned to the city to look for clues at Lily's house.

Two days after Lily's disappearance, the boys were watching the house from afar when a man they had never seen before crept up to the front door and deposited a note into the manservant's outstretched hand before turning tail. Minutes later, the manservant emerged from the house to ready the car. Henry Price appeared soon after and jumped in the vehicle without delay. Following a wheel spin that sent gravel spraying in all directions, Price left at great speed. The boys did not hesitate, and immediately set off after him, having earmarked a vehicle parked across the road to be ready at a moment's notice. It was a great testimony to the boys' tracking skills that neither Price nor Lily's abductors were aware of their pursuit, and Lily was overcome with pride when they described how they had successfully arrived at the tower hot on the heels of her father.

And that, of course, brought them up to date, leading naturally to a further debate about what they should do next. The chorus of yawns that rang out as their discussion went round in circles made them realise it would be wiser to sleep on it, and after a succession of goodnights, they sloped off to bed, vowing to be up early the next morning.

They were all as good as their word and awoke at first light. After a hasty breakfast, they cast off and got the boat underway. After all that had happened, they chose to return to the city instead of their earlier plans to head north, and after passing through the recently repaired Thames Lock, they reached the great river at long last.

Aedh set the engine to full throttle, wary that their enemies might still be on the lookout for anyone so obviously visible on the open river. After heading east, they picked up the Grand Union Canal at Brentford, away from the hubbub of the busy river traffic. From there, they followed the waterway's snaking route and travelled eastwards towards the relative safety of a backwater in Paddington known as Little Venice, where they moored the boat in a run-down basin that was reassuringly empty apart from a decrepit houseboat that was listing badly. After a light meal Seoc had miraculously conjured up from scraps and leftovers, they sat down to discuss their next move. They eventually decided it would be prudent to visit Lily's house to see if anything was happening there. Lily argued, convincingly she thought, that she should be the one to make the short journey across the river, but the boys vehemently disagreed. In the end, after being thoroughly overruled, she grudgingly accepted that Aedh should make the trip, and once the decision had been made, he set off without further ado just before nightfall.

Lily and Seoc awoke early the next morning. A fine drizzle had been falling since the early hours that had turned to a more persistent light rain, but even the quiet pitter-patter of rain striking the boat's canopy was insufficient to distract them while they sat waiting nervously for Aedh's return. He had promised to be back in time for breakfast, but as the rain continued to drum ceaselessly on the boat's awning, they became increasingly anxious at his failure to show. Once they finished eating, they sat staring vacantly at an untouched bowl of porridge they had left for Aedh.

'Do you think one of us should go and look for him?' asked Lily, jumping to her feet and banging her head on a lantern dangling from the galley's ceiling.

Seoc shook his head. 'No. We should wait. Aedh knows what he's doing. He'll be back soon,' he said, sounding more certain of himself than he looked.

Lily sighed. She was desperate to do something and waiting around for Aedh was only adding to her already frayed nerves.

'Come and sit down,' Seoc called to her as she paced nervously around the cabin.

'Lily. Why do you think Mickey didn't just do me and Aedh in?' Seoc asked. 'It wasn't like she didn't have the opportunity.'

Lily realised that this was a ploy meant to distract her, and while she was in no mood for conversation, anything was better than worrying about something she could not control. She sat down opposite Seoc and thought for a while before she responded.

'I'm not sure, Seoc. I thought I was pretty good at reading people, but evidently, I was wrong. I was sure Mickey … Aurelia … whatever you want to call her—'

'Let's just stick with bitch, shall we?' Seoc cut in, doing his best to lighten the mood.

Lily raised her eyebrows but then laughed and nodded. 'Very well, bitch it is. I was sure the bitch enjoyed the time we were with her. I genuinely felt it, Seoc.'

'Mm. Me too,' Seoc agreed.

'Maybe she was overcome by guilt or something. I don't know. She probably thought you were no threat to her, and in any case, she got what she wanted.'

Seoc shook his head. 'It still doesn't add up,' he concluded. 'After some of the things she's supposed to have done, her behaviour seems a bit out of character. She gave Cornelius half a chance to live and then she just dumps Aedh and me back on our boat. She doesn't sound like a callous murderer to me. Maybe what you've heard about her isn't true.'

'Maybe, Seoc, I don't know. You're just too forgiving, that's all. She behaved pretty maliciously towards me when I was trapped in the tower.'

'I don't suppose we'll ever find out, but I just wonder whether she's trying to impress someone or she's being manipulated.'

Lily vehemently shook her head. 'Oh, come on, Seoc. Do you really—?

Just then, Lily's words were cut short by the sound of footsteps splashing hurriedly through large puddles of water that had settled on the towpath.

Seoc jumped to his feet and poked his head through the galley's double doors. 'It's Aedh!' he called out gleefully to Lily, who was craning her neck over his shoulder to see for herself. They ushered the bedraggled looking figure into the galley and noted the grim expression set like granite on his face. Lily passed him a towel to dry his hair, which was dripping steadily onto the wooden floorboards.

'I'm afraid there's no sign of your father,' began Aedh, warming his hands in front of a small stove.

'I wasn't expecting anything else,' replied Lily glumly, yet still managing to force a smile to mask the sudden lurch in the pit of her stomach.

'What happened?' said Seoc, pushing a cup of steaming tea into his brother's grateful hands.

'It was difficult to get close enough to find anything out without being seen,' said Aedh. 'That's why I was so late getting back … I'm sorry,' he added, 'I knew you'd be worried.'

Lily and Seoc glanced uneasily at one another before simultaneously throwing Aedh reassuring smiles.

'There were two men keeping watch over the house. They weren't in uniform, so I don't think they were police. I guess they're something to do with this Fox you've told us about, Lily,' said Aedh.

'I'm sure you're right,' she replied, nodding her head. 'If Fox knows my father's missing, he'll be watching the place like a hawk.'

'I only managed to get close to the house once it was dark, although the men on duty were a surly old pair and barely said a word all night. It was only this morning when the shift changed that I managed to learn something, although the replacements didn't seem to know much either, I'm afraid. I did hear them say that no one's seen your father since he set off, though.'

'It's taken you all this time to find out what we already know,' said Seoc sarcastically. 'Well done, bruv!'

'I did find out a little more,' replied Aedh, casting his brother a withering look. 'Here, Lily, take a look at this,' he added, withdrawing a rolled-up newspaper from his coat.

'It's a few days old now, but look inside,' said Aedh, gesturing to her to turn the pages.

Lily unfurled a creased copy of the *Comet* and rapidly scanned the headlines until she found what Aedh was referring to. Seoc elbowed his brother out of the way so that he could read over Lily's shoulder, and their heads moved in unison as they followed the words in silence across the page, eager to read the contents of the article as fast as they could.

Price and Daughter in Double Abduction

The whereabouts of Professor Henry Price, alchemist and self-appointed leader of the Council for Home Affairs, are unclear following reports of his disappearance from the family residence in London two days ago. Early indications suggesting that Price had set out in search of his daughter, Lily, after she had absconded following a family rift have been discounted with the appearance of Nicolas Fox, Chief of Internal Security, and a posse of his operatives at the family home in the past twenty-four hours.

Following Lily's unforeseen departure, unconfirmed reports suggest that a ransom note was delivered to Price bearing details of his daughter's kidnap. Price's subsequent disappearance remains open to speculation, although it is possible that he has taken matters into his own hands and instituted negotiations with his daughter's abductors.

A spokesman for Internal Security would neither deny nor corroborate the story, but a source close to the organisation has confirmed that the investigation is now proceeding along the lines of a double abduction. Our undisclosed source has also intimated that the kidnappings are related to Pearly Black, a long-standing adversary of Price. Internal Security believes that the current predicament is related to Black's death following a botched robbery at a chemical plant in the East End over ten years ago. The role Price played in the death of his rival has been a perennial source of speculation, and in light of recent developments, concerns have been raised that Black's allies from the once respected Order of Eternal Enlightenment have regrouped and are behind the plot.

The Order was an ultra-secretive organisation that emerged under the auspices of Black, tacitly at least, to offer charitable aid to needy areas of society. After Black's death, the Order was exposed as a front for a secret society heavily involved in organised crime, although there has always been conjecture regarding the true nature of the Order's activities, and in particular, the role of their leader. The charitable work carried out in Black's name, however, is indisputable, throwing considerable doubt on whether Black's former allies would be capable of a heinous act of vengeance such as this. If we are to assume that the Order is not responsible for these unexplained disappearances, then the role of Internal Security in this sorry state of affairs must be seriously brought into question. After all, it would not be the first time for the shadowy organisation to promulgate an outrageous conspiracy theory as a means to further its own dubious motives.

One fact, however, is incontrovertible—the undoubted rivalry that existed between Henry Price and Pearly Black, originating from their time as students at the Academy of Arcane and Alchemical Arts, first as friends, but ultimately as bitter enemies. This doomed relationship was fuelled by intense academic feuding and their mutual love for Saskia Schalk, who herself died in mysterious circumstances from a single bullet wound to the chest minutes before Black's fatal plunge from the rooftops.

Following a coroner's inquest into Black's death, a verdict of death by misadventure was met with universal surprise bearing in mind the rumours regarding the true events of that night, and in particular, the role played by Price in the death of both parties.

Whether current circumstances are linked to earlier events in Price's life is, at present, unclear, but a greater in-depth exposé of this intriguing mystery will be considered in today's copy of The Evening Star.

'What do you make of it?' said Aedh tentatively.

Lily paused for a moment, clutching the newspaper tightly to her chest as if she was trying to digest the unpalatable contents of the article. 'I think some of what's written here may be based on fact, but there are just as many obvious inconsistencies,' she said finally.

'I thought as much,' Aedh conceded. 'Maybe we should just concentrate on what we know.'

'I agree,' said Lily pensively.

'What do you think, Lily?' Aedh prompted.

'Well, firstly, Aurelia Nightshade was undoubtedly involved in the plot to steal the manuscript from the library in Amsterdam by creating a diversion to delay my father. Secondly, she was also responsible for luring him into a trap. She was most definitely very close to Black and she was doubtlessly involved with the Order the paper refers to. I'm not sure where the information comes from, but whoever wrote the article seems to know an awful lot about what's been going on, both past and present.'

'What do you think we should we do?' Aedh asked.

'First, let's get a copy of the *Star,* and after that, we'll arrange a meeting with whoever's behind this article.'

'Any clue who that might be?' quizzed Seoc.

'Oh, yes,' replied Lily, handing him the newspaper. 'Take a look for yourself; it was written by Zoë Tsing.'

'Zoë Tsing?' repeated Aedh. 'Do you know her?'

'No ...' replied Lily, throwing the boys an enigmatic smile, 'but I soon will.'

32

THE STONE OF MADNESS

The Vault

P RICE WAS TUMBLING TO the ground even before he was struck by Black's bolt of defiled energy. The force of the blow sent him spinning round within the constraints of the pentagram, lifting him from his feet. In that freeze-frame of an instant, his limbs jerked spasmodically like a marionette on a puppeteer's strings, and his lips were drawn into a garish rictus under the sway of the tainted power.

Strange gasped at the unnatural smile that appeared on Price's face and felt sure it was directed at him. He turned away, unable to watch as Price slumped ingloriously to the ground once the macabre dance of his possessed body had waned. Price's arms and legs twitched fitfully before coming to rest at improbable angles about his torso.

The silence was absolute as smoke wafted up from the lifeless form strewn across the floor. The nauseating smell of charred flesh filled the air, testimony to the livid scorch mark, black as ebony, indelibly etched on Price's chest.

Dark rings had gathered like storm clouds around Black's eyes following the exertion of his effort, yet he looked on in fascination, daring not to believe what he had finally achieved. Aurelia stood nonchalantly inspecting her fingernails as if what she had just witnessed hardly mattered compared with the cracks that had appeared in her jet black nail varnish while Lex was silently retching and Frankl looked on with indifference.

'Perhaps you'd be kind enough to check the body?' said Black, addressing Strange in a voice that was hoarse and unyielding.

Strange straightened his spectacles despite the uncontrollable shaking of his hands. He jerked forwards then hesitated before kneeling beside the prostrate form. Gently, almost reverently, he straightened out the body and placed the flat of a palm on Price's chest before feeling for a pulse in his neck. Next, he reached for a candle, which he held aloft to inspect Price's ashen face.

Strange took a moment to compose himself before he looked at Black. He stepped back, startled by the expectant look burning brightly on Black's face. 'He's not breathing, and there's no pulse. His pupils are, er, fixed and miotic,' he said.

'What …?' said Black.

'He's dead,' responded Strange, and with great finality, he got up and turned his back on the body.

Black frowned before he allowed himself a smile, banishing the spiteful malevolence he had demonstrated while tormenting Price in his final moments. 'It's been a long and arduous path that has brought us to this point, my friends,' he announced, demonstrating his irrepressible charm of old. 'You've all made many sacrifices, but, at last, the greatest obstacle to our plans has been eliminated. Now is a new beginning. You've all done well and I thank you. You cannot imagine how amply you'll be rewarded,' he added enigmatically. 'There's no time for delay; we must begin our preparations … but first, we celebrate!'

So spoke Pearly Black, who turned promptly on his heels and disappeared from the shadowy depths of the vault with his ragtag medley of followers trailing up the stairs behind him.

Barely an hour later, Strange trudged disconsolately down the steep stone steps that returned him to the vault. He had always hated this place for the unpleasant memories it invoked, and that feeling had only intensified with the cold-blooded murder of a man he had known for almost as long as he could remember.

It was the second time in as many hours that Strange had made his way into the vault, only this time with the memory of Price's death still fresh in his mind. His head was spinning from a combination of chaotic thoughts he could not purge, and the mind-numbing effect of the vintage Moët Pearly had forced on him. It seemed perverse to be drinking champagne at a time like this, but he was thankful for the temporary release it afforded him from the memory of an event he dearly wished to expunge.

With each step, Strange reflected on how he had ended up on the opposite side to Price in a battle that had never been of his making. After Pearly's death, he had never anticipated that he would encounter a situation like this, but how wrong he had been. After Pearly's unexpected reappearance, it was as if a train of events had been set in motion that, no matter what, was destined to culminate in the same inevitable conclusion; circumstances, he reflected ruefully, over which he had no control.

Strange had always found it impossible to resist Pearly's irrepressible charm, and this, more than anything else, was the reason why he had always been drawn to him rather than the more level-headed and lugubrious Henry Price. Unsurprisingly, when circumstances dictated, he had always ended up siding with Pearly rather than the only other person to befriend him as a student all those years ago. Now Price was dead, and while it was easy to blame Pearly, he knew deep down that it was just as much his fault, despite knowing only too well what Pearly would have done had he not obeyed; but that was no excuse, there was always a choice.

In spite of everything he had done for Pearly, it was typical that he had chosen him, Abel Strange, to dispose of the body; why not Frankl or Aurelia? Neither of them would have given it a second thought, yet here he was performing a task that Pearly knew he would find utterly abhorrent. Maybe it was Pearly's way of showing displeasure at the hesitation he had shown moments before Price's death. Pearly was charismatic, yes, but also ruthless in a most terrible way.

Strange lifted a hand as he reached the final step, and following a quick, instinctive gesture, an eerie alchemical phosphorescence leached from the pores of his exposed skin, surrounding him in an ethereal halo that cast the windowless room in a sickly green light. Despite his glasses, he could barely see more than a few feet ahead, and he fumbled blindly across the vault's slick, stone flags with his arms outstretched.

As he approached the spot where Price had been slain, his stomach lurched; foreboding, he supposed. He slowed to a snail's pace and caught a glimpse of the intersecting lines deeply etched on the surface of the vault's floor. He squinted in the unearthly light at the star-shaped pentagram, and within it, the rumpled mass that lay there. He halted, unsure of whether he really could go through with the task Pearly had assigned to him, but then his body jerked spasmodically into life, inching forwards like an automaton, coerced by the knowledge of the fate that awaited him should he falter.

He reached out tentatively for the woollen fabric lying on the floor. The cloth felt surprisingly light as he picked it up, and he turned it vacuously through his hands. It was the coat Price had been wearing when he had arrived in the vault and was still wearing when he had collapsed under Pearly's fatal dominion. It was also the coat that had been draped around Price's lifeless body when Pearly had called on him to check for signs of life.

Now, weighing the garment in his hands, Strange's mind emptied like air rushing from a punctured balloon. He stared slack-mouthed at the empty space on the vault's stone slabs, unable to grasp the reality of what should have been glaringly obvious. He turned his head like a whirling dervish, first one way and then the other, half expecting and half fearing to find Henry Price standing there behind him. He paced agitatedly back and forth, searching every last vestige of the enclosed space until the unmistakable truth dawned on him—in the time since he and the rest of Pearly's followers had vacated the vault, Price's body had inexplicably disappeared.

The story continues in *The Quantum Engine*

Saving Faces

The Facial Surgery Research Foundation

As an Oral and Maxillofacial Surgeon, I will donate a proportion of the proceeds from the sale of this book to Saving Faces, the only charity in the United Kingdom (UK) dedicated to research aimed at reducing the incidence and improving the treatment of facial injuries, disorders and diseases.

Saving Faces works in partnership with the British Association of Oral and Maxillofacial Surgeons (BAOMS) in running and funding the world's only National Facial and Oral Research Centre (NFORC).

Over 300 surgeons around the UK collaborate to lead research for Saving Faces ensuring that studies are completed as quickly as possible while keeping research costs to a minimum due to surgeons giving their time free of charge.

The following are some examples of the work undertaken by Saving Faces:

- Supporting research into head, neck and mouth cancer, and the treatment of facial disfigurement, jaw joint problems and facial pain
- Managing the National Head and Neck Cancer Audit in the assessment of cancer patients throughout hospitals in England and Wales to determine best treatment and hospital performance
- Collecting data through two UK National Facial Injury Surveys to explore the causes and treatment of facial injuries
- Carrying out National Tobacco and Binge Drinking Prevention Projects within schools
- Funding for PhD students undertaking facial injury, stem cell, psychological effects and cancer genetics projects
- Running an Expert Patient Helpline to demystify treatment for new patients
- Providing a Diagnostic Advice Service for Medical and Dental Practitioners to speed up the referral of cancer patients to the appropriate surgeon
- Hosting public information events on topics such as face transplantation

Each year the work of Saving Faces costs £650,000. If you would like to learn more about Saving Faces or help financially, please go to **www.savingfaces.co.uk/support-us/ways-to-donate**